"Bloody and beguiling, with magic both enchanting and perilous, this story kept my heart in my throat and the pages turning at breakneck speed. With twists and turns, a forbidden romance, and a complex sisterly bond, this captivating tale swept me off my feet."
—ISABEL IBAÑEZ, #1 *New York Times* bestselling author

"One of my favorite romantasies of the year! With enchanting characters, dark and deceptive fae games, and a smoldering romance that delivers on all your fantasy romance cravings, *The Rose Bargain* is sure to be the next big thing. Without a doubt, my bargain with the fae queen would be for the sequel immediately."
—KERRI MANISCALCO, #1 *New York Times* bestselling author of the Kingdom of the Wicked series

"*The Rose Bargain* is an absolute confection for fans of historical fantasy— and anyone who delights in the competitive drama of *The Bachelor*. It will enthrall you with its cruel beauty and lush violence; I loved every minute of it."
—ALLISON SAFT, *New York Times* bestselling author of *A Fragile Enchantment*

"Sasha Peyton Smith has penned a novel that is gorgeously rendered and utterly enchanting from start to finish. *The Rose Bargain* is a story teeming with perilously high stakes, truly vicious bargains, and romance that left my heart thundering in my chest more than once. Readers who love classic fantasy done right will be charmed by Ivy's relentlessly fierce heart and Smith's whimsical prose."
—AVANA GRAY, *New York Times* bestselling author

"Prepare to meet your next obsession. *The Rose Bargain* is compulsively readable and deliciously fun, and I couldn't turn the pages fast enough. The ending will leave readers breathless, wanting to make bargains of their own for the next installment. I thoroughly enjoyed it."
—RACHEL GRIFFIN, *New York Times* bestselling author of *Bring Me Your Midnight*

SASHA
PEYTON SMITH

the
ROSE
BARGAIN

HARPER
An Imprint of HarperCollinsPublishers

Library of Congress Cataloging-in-Publication Data
Names: Smith, Sasha Peyton, author.
Title: The rose bargain / Sasha Peyton Smith.
Description: First edition. | New York : Harper, 2025. | Audience:
   Ages 13 up | Audience: Grades 10–12 | Summary: "Ivy Benton must
   enter into a marriage contest with a fae prince in order to free her sister
   from a bargain previously made with the vicious fae queen of England"—
   Provided by publisher.
Identifiers: LCCN 2024016120 | ISBN 9780063372528 (hardcover)
Subjects: CYAC: Fantasy. | Fairies—Fiction. | Courts and
   Courtiers—Fiction. | Sisters—Fiction. | London (England)—
   History—19th century—Fiction. | LCGFT: Fantasy fiction.
   | Alternative histories (Fiction) | Novels.
Classification: LCC PZ7.1.S6555 Ro 2025 | DDC [Fic]—dc23
LC record available at https://lccn.loc.gov/2024016120

Typography by Molly Fehr
25 26 27 28 29 LBC 8 7 6 5 4

First Edition

For Emilie, I couldn't do this without you
and I wouldn't want to anyway.

Come away, O human child!
To the waters and the wild
With a faery, hand in hand,
For the world's more full of weeping
than you can understand.
—WILLIAM BUTLER YEATS

Take pains. Be perfect.
—WILLIAM SHAKESPEARE,
A Midsummer Night's Dream

THEN

On the other side of the clearing, Henry VI dropped dead.

Britain had a new king, decisively. Edward IV.

The Lancasters went home, and the York camp torches burned all night as the victory celebration raged.

But the strange woman didn't watch them. She was already on the road in a carriage pulled by snow-white horses. With a coronation to plan, there was no time to waste.

Twenty-four hours and one minute later, Edward IV was dead as well. He closed his eyes and fell to the ground as if a string had been cut.

She had promised Edward he would be king, but she never specified for how long.

And so Queen Moryen of the Others took the throne at Eltham Palace, a serene smile on her face and a crown on her head.

All who raised a hand or sword against her found themselves suddenly unable to move, as if the act itself was forbidden.

The war was over, and Britain had a new queen. Immortal. Uncrossable. Inevitable.

NOW

CHAPTER ONE
London, February 1848

Lydia has been missing for eight days, and I'm beginning to fear that our parents are going to wake up in the morning and find my bed empty too.

A noise in the dark alley to my left makes me jump, but it's just a rat tearing through a pile of rubbish.

I've shivered my way through the city for miles, ignoring hecklers and stepping over half-dead beggars. Usually, my parents say to pay them no mind, that they've had the same opportunity to bargain with the queen as the rest of us, but they're harder to ignore tonight.

My freedom is usually limited to turns around the park arm in arm with Mama or safely ensconced within the velvet walls of our family's carriage. What I lack in experience I make up for in confidence. That confidence feels a lot flimsier now, lost, and cold down to my bones.

I thought it would be safer to stick to the main roads rather than risk traipsing through the ink dark of Hyde Park alone, but one wrong turn down a serpentine side street has me hopelessly turned around. Even the flicker of the gas lamps is weak. The biting February air is thick with coal dust, blotting out what little light the flames throw off. I pull back the hood of my cloak and tip my head to the sky in an attempt to get my bearings. Cassiopeia should be north, but the twinkle of the stars is too dim to be sure. An errant tear flows out of the corner of my eye and into the hollow of my ear.

I've been searching Lydia's room for days, praying fruitlessly for a clue about her sudden disappearance. It's as if she vanished into nothing, but I refuse to accept that.

Tonight, after Mama, Papa, and our skeleton crew of staff had gone to bed, I pulled on my cloak, wrapped myself in Papa's thickest scarf, and took off into the night.

Maybe I was being brave, like the knights in the stories Lydia and I read as little girls, noble and driven by love, or maybe I just wanted to feel something other than the maddening terror I've felt since my sister disappeared.

The police say she's either eloped or dead, but I don't believe them. She'd have told me if she planned to elope, and I'd be able to feel it if she were dead. There's no possible universe in which my sister's heart stops beating and I keep on living, unaltered.

My breath comes out in puffs of vapor as I cut down another alley. I sigh in relief as I finally recognize where I am.

The gates of Kensington Palace loom like a mouth in the near distance, the dark shadows of the Queen's Guard beside them.

I thumb over the cool surface of the necklace sitting deep in the pocket of my cloak like a talisman. I'll have to be clever, circle around Hyde Park again maybe, and sneak in the back way. I don't need to get too near the palace, only to the trees surrounding it. My feet are numb in my boots, but I must keep walking lest I look suspicious to the guards, now in sight.

When Lydia and I were small and our family still owned the

country house in Oakham, we spent our summers in the woods, catching frogs or making little houses out of leaves for the ducklings. Our legs scraped to ribbons, twigs in our wild hair, we'd only come inside once the moon rose and the bats emerged. We'd enter through the kitchen to avoid getting scolded by Mama, and there we'd be attended to by a particularly indulgent old cook named Mrs. Osbourne. Mrs. Osbourne was the oldest person I'd ever known, and as she bandaged our legs and snuck us lemon ices, she'd tell us stories. We loved the ones about the Others best of all.

She read to us from an old book that was wrapped in fraying sage-green fabric and dented at the corners. I was particularly taken by the concept of a faerie door. As the stories went, the Others could be compelled to open the door between our worlds, usually hidden in gnarled old trees, for clever humans who left objects of great significance at their thresholds.

I begged Lydia to try it with me. We found a squat ironwood tree, and in the divot of its roots we left our matching baby necklaces, one strung with a small pearl *L* charm and the other with a matching *I*. They were too short to fit around our big-girl necks, but they still hung on the posts of our beds. I was giddy with anticipation for the rest of the day, peeking through windows, desperate for a glimpse of one of Them.

The next morning, Lydia and I ran across the dew-damp lawn and dug our chubby little hands into the dirt at the base of the tree. The necklaces had vanished. I jumped and hollered with joy, so loud that my mother stomped out into the garden and demanded to know why I was giving her a headache. I told her everything. Without another word, she marched to the kitchens and made Mrs. Osbourne burn her faerie book. I was only six then, and I didn't understand that owning something like this was illegal. I wailed for days.

A year later, I found Lydia's necklace shoved in the back of her wardrobe. Two years older than me, she placed her hands on her hips and told me I had to leave babyish things like magic behind. It was the first of her three great betrayals.

She sauntered out of the room before I could ask her why we never did find the second of the matching necklaces—or if she also saw the silhouette of the man by the trees that night.

An icy wind whips down the street, sending a swirl of dead leaves scattering. My blond curls whip around my face, and I pull the cloak tighter around my neck.

The stories from Mrs. Osbourne's books were of an England where Others ran wild. Queen Mor would have us believe that she and her son are the only ones of their kind who live here now, but they came from somewhere, and even locked doors can be opened again. I can't get up north to our old home in Oakham, nor to the memorial battlefield from the Battle of Barnet, but if a door exists in London, wouldn't it be in the trees surrounding the queen's residence? I can't not try.

I double back toward the public entrance of the park, to where the bargain lines form on Sundays. The trees stand like specters in the dark, indistinguishable from one another. There's nothing remarkable about any of them, I'm just going to have to choose at random. I clutch the necklace in my pocket.

A shadow moves in the dark. "Who's there?" shouts one of the Queen's Guard.

I curse under my breath, drop my sister's necklace at the base of the nearest tree, and run.

I sprint down the path and across the wide lawns, then make a sharp left, turning back onto the street and off palace grounds.

From out of the silence comes the sudden clatter of wheels pitching over cobblestones.

I jump back, hoping to hide in the shadows, but I don't see the loose stone until it is too late.

My boot catches on the edge of it, and I trip and fall, my temple colliding with the curb. My body splays out like a rag doll in the dirt.

At first there is the blinding, sharp sting of pain, and then there is nothing but darkness.

I blink back to consciousness, unsure of how long I've been under, to find a shadowy figure sitting beside me in a carriage.

"I've got a knife," I whisper, terrified. I don't mention that it's a kitchen knife shoved in my boot, too dull to cut through anything and too difficult to reach now anyway.

"Are you going to stab me?"

"That depends."

"On what?"

My vision obscures as something warm pours over my left eye. I reach up to wipe it, and my hand comes away sticky with blood.

The figure swears and shrugs off his coat. "Take this. You can stab me later."

He presses his coat to my temple. It's still warm with his body heat, and I resist the urge to sigh in relief at even the smallest reprieve from the cold.

"Are you all right?" he asks.

"You hit me with your carriage," I reply weakly.

"I didn't hit you, you tripped."

"I tripped to avoid getting trampled by your—" I pause to look around. The carriage is massive, at least a six-seater, with thick velvet upholstery and polished brass fixtures. "Behemoth," I finish.

"I wasn't the one skulking around in the dark."

"I wasn't skulking. I was lost."

"Where were you headed? Maybe I can help you?" The stranger taps on the window to the driver's seat and it slides open.

"Where to, miss?" the driver asks gruffly.

Even I can admit when a mission has failed. "Belgrave Square," I answer, giving him my home address.

The horses whinny, and we're off with a lurch. As we make a wide right turn onto a main thoroughfare, a beam of yellow lamp-light streams in through the carriage window.

The boy brushes his unkempt hair from his forehead, and recognition hits me like a blow. I'm dizzy from the trauma to my head, but that's not why it feels as if the world has suddenly tilted.

Sitting opposite me, concern sketched across his fine features, is a face I've seen in portraits and across crowded concert halls my entire life. He looks younger tonight than any time I've seen him previously. He's usually in stiff cravats with well-coifed hair. Tonight it falls in dark waves over his forehead, partially obscuring his hazel eyes, but the high cheekbones, sharp jaw, and sullen mouth are the same. *Prince Emmett.*

"It's you." I blink.

A bemused smile crosses his face. "Who?"

"You're Prince Emmett."

"You must have hit your head rather hard," he replies. There's a crackle of fragility in the edge of his voice.

"I know who you are. There's no point in hiding it."

He narrows his eyes at me. "We've met." It isn't a question.

We haven't, not really, but I've seen him from a distance at enough events to be certain—and then there was that thing with Lydia.

"Lady Benton." I nod my head in some semblance of a bow, but he senses the sarcasm in the gesture and his mouth quirks up in a half smile. "Second daughter of the Marquess of Townshend."

"Aren't you supposed to be missing?" Emmett asks. "I've heard the rumors."

I shake my head. "No. I'm the other one. I was looking for my sister, that's why I was out." I feel the sharp stab of failure as the carriage carries us farther from Kensington Palace. I've just tossed Lydia's necklace into the dirt for nothing.

"Ahh, yes, the younger sister." He gestures vaguely to my face. "The resemblance is uncanny. You've got the same eyes."

"I'm surprised you remember her," I answer tensely.

"You think she's out there somewhere?" he asks, pointedly not addressing my remark.

"Yes. I can't explain it, but I'd be able to feel it if she were gone."

Emmett looks at me, unnervingly still. "Feel it?"

We jolt as the carriage rounds another corner.

"You wouldn't understand."

"I have a brother," he says. "I might understand better than you think."

I'm surprised to hear him refer to Prince Bram as his brother.

Emmett's status as prince is still a lightning rod for gossip, nearly two decades after his birth. He's the human son of Queen Moryen's husband, Prince Consort Edgar, and his first, human, wife, who died in childbirth. The queen legitimized Emmett on his eighth birthday, though whether it was a favor to his father, an act of love, or something else entirely, no one knows.

His name is whispered in drawing rooms across town. *A rake of a prince, why can't he be sweet like Bram?* There are always new rumors about who he is spotted with at whatever social events he deigns to attend. There was the scullery maid scandal in Lord Tremaine's rose garden last season. Only a month later, he was caught wrapped up in the curtains of Duke Cambere's study with the family's middle daughter. Just last week, I heard my mother mutter something about a ballerina. And my face still burns with anger when I think about how he was with Lydia during her first season. I wasn't there, but she told me all about it when she returned home in tears.

When he's not sullying someone else's reputation, he's causing an uproar over his refusal to begin his studies at Oxford—or his hunting trips with his friends, other lords, and second sons that sound more like bacchanalia.

Emmett turns to me, the full force of his gaze hitting me for the first time. I've never seen him about town without a surly frown on his face. But he doesn't look anything like that now. His eyes are a peculiar shade of hazel, lined with dark lashes and glinting with fire. This close, I can see the spray of soft freckles across his nose. I never recognized the refined, handsome face behind the pouting. But it *is* handsome. He's so handsome it nearly knocks the breath from me.

The carriage clatters through the night, down the still streets of a sleeping London. I tilt my head against the back of the seat and wonder how I'm going to get the blood out of this dress without Mama or the maids finding out.

"What are you thinking about?" Emmett asks.

"Stabbing you," I reply, eyes closed.

"That's not very polite."

"Running me over wasn't very polite."

"Again, you tripped."

There's a sudden flood of heat, and I open my eyes to find Emmett crowded into my space, peering up at me intently. I'm still holding his coat against my bleeding head, and gingerly, he raises his fingers and peels away the edges of the wool. It's gone sticky, half dried, and it pulls at my hair as he tugs it away.

"Ouch." I resist the urge to jab him with my elbow.

"Stop squirming. The bleeding has slowed," he declares. "But you should keep the pressure on it."

With the hand that isn't holding the coat, I salute.

He tilts his head slightly, still staring at me. "You know, you're really quite pretty."

An infuriating blush rises in my chest. "Are you trying to seduce me right now? I know your reputation, but I didn't expect the nerve."

"My reputation?"

"Being seen with you would ruin me."

His eyes narrow. "You don't seem like the kind of girl to worry about things like that." Men never do understand. The slow death of being cast out of society is a fate few are strong enough to bear.

"You don't know anything about the kind of girl I am."

"I know you snuck out in the middle of the night to search for your sister."

The carriage slows. I pull back the curtain to see my family's town house, the white limestone and soaring columns lit up with gas lamps.

I tap on the window and ask the driver to drop me around the back. I stand less of a chance of being caught if I go through the service entrance in the basement.

"Thank you for your assistance," I say as I take the driver's hand and hop down from the carriage.

Emmett leans out the door, a calling card clutched between his knuckles. He reaches out to me. "Please. Can I see you again?"

"Absolutely not," I reply.

"I beg of you, consider it."

I take the card out of habit and am a few steps away, nearly to the back staircase, when Emmett's voice calls from the darkness.

"You can keep the coat."

I turn back to him. He's enveloped in shadows, but his smirk is visible even from here. "No, thank you, I've got plenty of my own." I chuck the coat back in his direction, and it smacks him square in the chest. I've always been rather proud of my throwing arm.

He waits until I'm inside to pull away.

The fireplace is cold, nothing like Mrs. Osbourne's kitchen, where the bricks by the hearth were always warm. I'm not six years old anymore. There is no one waiting to tend to my wounds, no big sister's bed to crawl into.

I climb the limewashed back staircase up to my second-floor bedroom like I'm a ghost haunting this house.

I peel out of my bloodstained dress and am pulling my arms through the warm flannel of my dressing gown when I hear a commotion down in the foyer.

Someone is pounding on the door. For a minute, I freeze with terror, mortified at the thought that perhaps Prince Emmett has come back for me.

Then I hear footsteps. Someone shrieks.

I race out onto the landing just in time to see Lydia stumble into the marble hall, leaving a smear of muddy footprints in her wake.

CHAPTER TWO

Three Months Later

The doors to the atelier are thrown open to the street, bursting with so much activity it's impossible to keep it all inside. Girls and their mothers spill out onto the sidewalk in a crowd so thick we have to elbow our way in.

The seamstress has been slow to let out the hem of my sister's gown to fit me, and I know well enough it's because we haven't spent enough money in recent years to make us priority customers. My mother knows it too, but she just keeps on smiling in that pinched way of hers.

I wish I could have done this some other day, when there would be fewer people to hide from, but tomorrow is the first of May, and there is no time to waste.

All of London is whipped into an absolute tizzy. The start of the season—the moment for the debutantes to line up to make their bargains with the queen—is all anyone can talk about.

Most of the citizens of England will make their bargains on some other date. The queen's throne room is open every Sunday from noon until midnight, and anyone who wishes to bargain with her may do so at this time. Some make their bargain as soon as they come of age; some wait well into adulthood, until they find something they want desperately enough to make a deal.

Those from the Midlands say it's luckiest to make the bargain on the first Sunday of the month. Girls from Bristol always make their bargains sporting two left-footed shoes. People from Liverpool arrive at the palace wearing necklaces of their own braided hair. Counties and villages and families all have their own superstitions about the practice, entrenched now for over four hundred years.

Some never make a bargain at all.

But for girls like me, girls with titles or money enough to buy influence some other way, it is expected that we make our bargains on the same day we come out into society, officially available as merchandise on the marriage market.

Our clever bargains for shinier hair or prettier feet are just another line item on our wifely résumés, proving that we are *good girls*. Rose Bargains, they're called. Bargains to make us beautiful, fragile, sweet—perfect English roses.

The official debutante coming-out is always on the first of May. Such is the fanfare around the aristocratic girls in their finest lining up before the queen, it's been called *the Pact Parade*.

The bell to the shop chimes as we enter, barely audible over the chatter.

The Alton sisters drop their gazes as I approach. The little one turns away so quickly she trips over the edge of a rug. Our shame is contagious, and no one can afford to catch it, especially not now.

In the corner, with her sour-faced mother, is Greer Trummer, my former closest friend. I let out an anxious breath, turning my mother by the elbow so she doesn't spot them, but it's too late.

With a wide smile, my mother waves in a large arc over her head.

"Lady Trummer, Greer, how lovely to see you here." My face burns with shame as everyone turns toward us, disdain and pity all over their faces.

"Did you see the ribbons just here, Mama?" I say, trying to re-direct her to a display of silk and lace, but it's too late.

Greer's mother turns away, as if she hasn't heard us. Greer offers a sheepish smile, but doesn't so much as wave back.

My mother, undeterred, crosses the shop, pushing past a dozen people as she goes.

"Please, Mama, she's busy," I protest, but she pretends not to hear me.

"Greer, darling, Ivy told me you were nervous for tomorrow. You're going to do fabulously. I do hope the turn around the park you two girls took this morning did something to quiet your nerves."

For the first time in months, Greer looks at me. Something flick-ers behind her blue eyes as she catches me in my lie.

"The turn around the park?" She's confused. Of course she is. I've been lying for months, going to sit alone in the stables or skulking around the neighborhood with my cloak pulled tight, any excuse to escape the stifling misery of our house. I've been telling my mother I was with Greer, like she's any better than the rest of them. She dropped me at the first whiff of scandal, just like everyone else.

I brace myself, ready for Greer to give me up. She blinks a few times, then turns back to my mother. "Oh yes, the turn around the park. Thank you, Lady Benton," she says softly. "Ivy is *such* a good friend. Always so willing to offer an uplifting word." She turns back to me. We used to be able to communicate with nothing but a glance, but I don't know what she's feeling now. The tether between us is broken. "Now, if you'll excuse me, I hear Mama calling." Her mother definitely isn't calling, but neither of us say it.

I let out a sigh of relief as she walks away.

The seamstress waves me over, and I step onto the pedestal in front of the three-way mirror as the final adjustments are made to my gown. I pretend I don't hear the whispers of the other mothers and daughters in the shop: *"Surely she's not expecting any invitations this season."*

When the seamstress is finished, Mama muscles her way to the counter and pays with a stack of bills I feel guilty looking at.

We return home without discussing the whispers we both heard, as if by refusing to acknowledge our family's misfortune, we can make it not true.

Lydia made her debut in society—and her bargain with the queen—two springs ago.

She returned that day in her frothy white gown with a confused look on her face. She couldn't recall what happened in the throne room. She must have given up the memory in exchange for whatever the queen bestowed upon her, but in the two years since, we've never been able to discern what the gift was.

Her beauty remained the same, there has been no sudden talent or skill, only a Swiss cheese memory and a failure of a season that ended without a proposal.

Her lack of a match and her secret bargain were embarrassing, a blight on the family. My mother has spent the better part of two years saying I was the Benton family's only hope, though my slim chances of making a match went up in smoke when the scandal of Lydia's disappearance broke.

The news that she was missing reached the marble halls of London society before the sun was fully up. All the titled ladies in the neighborhood were at the door that very morning, with baskets of pastries and looks of concern on their faces. They could smell blood in the water.

And those same ladies passed the news of Lydia's shameful return around like petit fours at a tea party. The fun of grace is to watch someone fall from it.

Walking into the foyer of our house, I can't help but think of the night she returned. Sometimes it feels like I never really left that moment.

It was the constable who brought Lydia home, covered in grime. He shoved her by her elbow through the door with a sneer. "I thought this was a respectable family."

I was already at the top of the stairs when Mrs. Tuttle shouted to the whole of the house that Lydia had returned.

Mama cried as she burst out of her room wrapped in a dressing gown, and Father caught her as her knees gave out on the stairs.

I raced past them down to my sister. My beloved big sister, the one I'd wept for, feared for, snuck out of the house to search for.

I clasped her face between my hands and found her skin cold and clammy, as if covered with morning dew.

Lydia just stared, silent and still, like she wasn't there at all, like she was a ghost.

Then she collapsed in my arms.

Papa and Mrs. Tuttle carried her up to her room, but it was I who bathed her, wrapped her in a clean nightdress, and tucked her into bed.

It was I who first noticed that the soles of her feet were bloody, like she'd lost her shoes a long time ago.

And it was me to whom she spoke her first words since her return.

Floating in and out of consciousness, her lips pale, she snapped awake for one precious moment. Her eyes met mine, like she was finally back in her body.

"It wasn't worth it," she rasped.

"What wasn't?" I whispered in return.

The candle at her bedside flickered. "The bargain." Her eyes were wide, imploring me to listen. *"It wasn't worth it."*

She slept for three days, and I sat vigil at her bedside, relief at her return and terror at the state she was in intermingling to form an emotion I still can't name.

When she awoke after her long sleep, hope bloomed in me that she would be back to herself, armed with a plausible explanation for her disappearance. But all she had to offer was a paper-thin story about running away with a lover, some working-class printer. She said that they had arranged to elope but were accosted on the road and her bridegroom was murdered. Left lost and alone, she finally found her way back to the outskirts of London.

I brushed my sister's fringe from where it was stuck to her sweaty forehead. "Why are you lying to me?" We didn't lie. Not to each other.

She looked vacantly at the wall, and something inside of me died.

Mama and Papa grimly spread Lydia's explanation around town. None of us believed it, and it wasn't exactly an acceptable story, but it was less tawdry than *nothing.*

But the gossips of London have plenty of time on their hands, and it wasn't long before they discovered that no marriage records for one Lydia Benton were ever filed in Gretna Green.

I've only been invited to the Pact Parade as a courtesy, given my father's title as a marquess. But even if my mother is in denial, I know that no more invitations will come for the rest of the season. My debut in society will be over as soon as it has begun.

I dash upstairs to dress for dinner, hesitating as I pass my sister's door. I know better by now, but I can't help myself from turning the knob and stepping inside.

Lydia spends most days shut in the dark of her room—"convalescing," they call it. She wastes her time away, eating cut fruit brought up on silver trays by the ring of her bell. It's the only thing she wants. She devours whole oranges and cubes of hothouse pineapple and watermelon like she's starving and nothing else will sate her.

I heard our housekeeper, Mrs. Tuttle, complaining to our cook, Mr. Froburg, that our parents' coddling made us both soft. I couldn't even find it in myself to be upset about her gossip. She was right. I was too soft. Right up until the moment my sister disappeared, I really did believe the world was a kind place that wanted good things for me.

The curtains in Lydia's room are drawn, and she's nothing but a lump, her blond hair barely visible under her duvet.

I sit on the edge of her bed and lay a hand on her back. "Lydia, the Pact Parade is tomorrow." She doesn't roll around to face me, but I can tell by the rise and fall of her shoulders that she's awake.

She draws a breath. "Oh?"

"Will you dress my hair like you used to? Remember when you used Mama's necklace to—"

She finally rolls over and cuts me off. "I'm afraid I won't remember how. You'd best let Mrs. Tuttle do it."

She swipes a palm across her storm-cloud face. I don't know if she's only just finished crying or getting ready to start, but her eyes are rimmed in red. "Close the door on the way out, please."

I leave her in darkness.

I don't know why I keep giving her opportunities to break my heart.

She's ruined my chances of finding a husband. No family of any real status will let their son stoop so low as to marry a Benton. No real dowry to speak of, and now no honor either.

The truth is, I hate her more than anyone in the world. The rage rips hot and fierce through the walls of my chest, and I have to resist the urge to wrench her door back open and shake her until she can give me an explanation.

But by the time I reach my own bedroom door, I miss her. I just miss her.

I love Lydia more than anyone else in the world too.

She's easier to love when she's not in front of me. I like her so much more when she's not around.

My father goes to bed right after dinner, unable to bear the nervous tapping of my foot and my mother's forced cheerfulness.

It's just Mama and I in the drawing room. Outside, Belgrave Square is dark and quiet. Inside is a chorus of sounds I know well: the ticking of the grandfather clock, the crackling of the fire, and the incessant scratching of my mother's pen.

She's done this since well before I was born, dumping every single thought she's had all day into a journal. There are volumes of them scattered across the house, shoved into bookshelves and in teetering stacks next to threadbare armchairs.

I'm working on my own correspondence; I owe Ethel a letter. Now in her mid-eighties, she rarely leaves her home in Bradford, but I've been writing her for years about our shared interest in faeries.

I was twelve when Lydia and Greer told me that only babies were obsessed with magic, and that only the low-class worshipped the queen, so they didn't want to talk to me about the Others anymore.

They were right, at least partially. It's only the commoners, far outside the home counties, who wear fake pointed ears to celebrate Queen's Day, marking the day Queen Mor arrived in England. They're the ones who put her face up in the old chapels and built monuments in her name. It was far below a titled girl like me to find faeries interesting.

The London peerage like to think we're something close to her equals, though of course we're not. I think she let us keep the traditions of an England that was once ruled by humans, like our debutante parade, to give us some illusion that we still have any power left. An immortal queen letting English high society still have our little rituals is like an indulgent parent handing their crying child a toy.

These are the kinds of thoughts I write to Ethel about. When Lydia and Greer rejected me, all I was left with were secret letters to Papa's great-aunt's neighbor. We don't write as often anymore, but I like to know she's well. She was the only one I told about my theory of Lydia falling through a faerie door. I knew she was the only person on earth who wouldn't laugh at me.

"What do you think the other girls will ask for this year?" Mama asks casually, like she's only just thought of it, but she's been glancing at me anxiously over her page for the last hour. "The Itos' daughter has such a pretty face, and more money than she knows what to do with. Maybe she'll ask to play the pianoforte better. She didn't exactly impress at the summer solstice concert last year."

"Hmm." I nod noncommittally and continue sipping my tea.

"Greer will surely ask for a few inches of height, and that never costs much. You know the Duchess of Gloucester? She came out in my year. She asked for three inches, all in her legs. It cost her both big toes, but it landed her a duke, didn't it?"

My mother thumbs over the nub of her left pinkie, where it stops abruptly at the second joint. She gave it up for a better memory. She had such a fear of forgetting names and faces during the whirlwind balls of her season and getting a reputation for being rude. She remembers absolutely everything now. My father says that the way she recalled the tiny details of their past conversations is what made him fall in love with her. She made him feel seen.

My mother remembers everyone from her season, could recite their faces, their titles, and the addresses of their estates like an encyclopedia, but those people don't speak to her anymore. They've forgotten her in a way she can never forget them. It's why she writes in the journals. She hopes dumping everything from her too-full brain out onto the page will give her some semblance of peace. I'm unconvinced it helps.

She takes another small sip of port and tuts her tongue. I don't like the way her glance has fallen on me. Sometimes I'm afraid she'll look right through me, like I'm made of glass, and see everything I'm hiding from her. That's the thing about a mother who remembers absolutely everything; she's nearly impossible to lie to.

"And you know, as your mother, I think you're perfect, but have you decided yet the bargain you'll make?"

This is the dance we do. I've learned the steps as diligently as I practiced the quadrille in cotillion class, stepping around the topic of Lydia, her lack of a husband, the bargain she can't remember.

It never should have been me in this position. This was always

Lydia's job. My father used to joke about us being the heir and the spare. Lydia was the Benton family's great hope. Her advantageous match was a foregone conclusion. My only job was to stay out of her way and stop tearing my dresses when I skinned my knees.

"Not yet." I yawn dramatically, preparing to make my exit for bed.

But Mama just keeps staring at me. "I think you could do with sleeker hair, or a clever talent, like watercolor or the cello?"

"Hmm, perhaps." This little act we do makes me so sad, I have to blink back sudden tears. She must know as well as I do, I could be the greatest watercolorist on earth and it wouldn't help me receive any offers this season.

"Think on it, will you? You don't have long, and there's nothing worse than an impulsive decision."

I rise from the silk settee and cross the room to give her a kiss on the head. "Of course, Mama."

"Darling?" she asks.

I pause in the doorway.

"This family can't afford another failure. We're—" She swallows hard. "We're going to lose the house in the next twelve months unless something changes."

I freeze. I knew things were bad, but I didn't know our finances had become so dire.

I don't let the tears fall until I'm up in my room. The embers of the fire glow in the grate, casting my room in long, dark shadows.

I look to where the invitation to the Pact Parade sits on my bedside table, its gold lettering dancing in the firelight against the thick, robin's egg blue parchment.

I write down the words I plan to say to the queen one final time, ensuring that they're perfectly committed to memory, and then feed the paper to the fire.

Though I slept fitfully all night, I'm awoken by the chirping of birds. I roll over and gaze at the rinsed blue sky of a London spring morning. It's a certain kind of feeling, one that rests in the joints of my ankles, that today my life will change.

Lydia's words echo in my head. *It wasn't worth it. The bargain wasn't worth it.*

I am not my sister.

I'll make sure my bargain is.

When one makes a faerie bargain, one must be prepared to pay the price. There is one silver lining. I have nothing to lose.

CHAPTER THREE

Mama and Mrs. Tuttle dress me in my sister's Pact Parade gown, a confection of Swiss-dot chiffon and a bodice embroidered with English wildflowers, white thread on white fabric. It's been altered to fit me, but I still feel like I'm wearing a Lydia Benton costume.

I sit on the small stool in front of my vanity, and Mama's cool fingers wind my hair into a nest of braids at the back of my skull. Mrs. Tuttle helps her pin white roses, fresh from the garden, in my hair. The effect is beautiful, but no match for the diamond-encrusted tiaras and bandeaux the other girls will be wearing. Papa tells me not to concern myself with matters of finances, but how can I not when I overhear him and his business advisers arguing in the study all day long.

How could he have known that the land he bargained for the spring he turned eighteen had been so overfarmed it was barren? He was sure it grew plentiful produce when his father's tenants farmed the field right next door, but he gave up his childhood memories in exchange for the plot, so he can't be entirely sure. The tenant farmers have all packed up and left in search of literal greener pastures.

Others would have leaned on friends for advice, but Papa's lack of childhood memories made it difficult to bond with the other men of the peerage. He doesn't remember their boarding school stories or the tales of rugby victories in their youth. There's a hollowness to him that others seem to be able to sense.

He's tried to fill it in the years since with books and philosophy. We've spent our family dinners debating matters of politics and Plato, but it only helped serve to make us all a little odd.

"What will you ask for?" my mother asks one final time as she fastens her own mother's pearls around my neck.

I hate lying to her. "I'll ask for what you asked for, Mama, to have a better memory. I'll get to know someone so well he'll have no choice but to see I'd be the best wife for him."

My mother's hands go still, and she runs her thumb over the nub of her pinkie. She's no longer looking at me in the mirror; her eyes are far off, somewhere else. "That's a lovely thought, sweetheart."

"Then why do you still look so sad?" I smile as I say it, but my heart is aching too.

"Just be careful." She shakes her head and returns to fixing the flowers pinned to my head. "Remembering is heavy. It lasts so long."

My dress has a wide V-neck decorated with a ruffle that continues down sleeves that stop at my elbows. The bodice ends in a point at my waist, and the skirt is wide.

"You look perfect," Mama whispers.

I look like Lydia. Our curly honey-blond hair and brown eyes are the same, only Lydia has a face that's sharper somehow, as if my features are more settled on her face. My cheeks are rounder, my eyes a little softer around the edges.

She's been in her room all morning. I knocked on her door to ask her once more to dress my hair, and I had to pretend that I didn't care when she said no.

I poke my bare feet out from under the hem of the dress. "The matching slippers, Mama? I didn't see them in the atelier's box."

My mother looks down at the carpet awkwardly, her face turning the same splotchy, tomato shade of red I so often see on myself. "She must have forgotten them. You can borrow your sister's."

I can read between the lines well enough. We couldn't afford a new dress, and we couldn't afford new shoes either.

I've felt so much embarrassment over the past few months, the sting is taken out of this particular blow. I'm just annoyed.

Mrs. Tuttle walks through the door moments later, Lydia's white silk slippers dangling from her fingers. "Here you go, darling," she says pityingly. "Do you need my help putting them on?"

"No, thank you." I smile.

She closes the door behind her, and I grimace. Lydia's feet have been smaller than mine since we were children. On one particularly humiliating occasion when I was eleven, a cobbler told me I was shaped like the letter *L*.

I attempt to cram my toes into the delicate silk shoes, but they're pinching all over. I take two steps, and my left heel pops right out.

This day is going to be difficult enough without hobbling all over the palace.

I hide Lydia's slippers under a bonnet in my wardrobe and slip on my stockings and trusty, well-worn boots instead. Under the layers of my dress, they're hardly visible, and no one will be looking at me enough today to notice.

I'm tightening the final laces when my mother's voice calls from downstairs. "Ivy, we can't be late!"

"Coming!"

Praying she doesn't see my traitorous choice in shoes, I race down the stairs to join her.

The carriage pulls up at exactly eleven, and Mama and I make our way across town to Kensington Palace.

It's a perfect verdant spring day after a gray English winter. Yellow daffodils dot the roadside. The gardens of society's finest homes have only just sprung to life. Riots of pink explode in window boxes, and waterfalls of purple hyacinth drip from the eaves of the estates we pass.

We join a line of carriages at the entrance to the palace, and a veritable army of footmen stream out the doors, ready to greet us.

Today, all the debutantes wear white, as tradition for the Pact Parade demands: white to mirror the white gown Queen Mor wore when she first appeared on King Edward IV's burning battlefield.

I spot all my old friends among the crowd, as well as their mothers and chaperones. They shift slightly as we approach, putting their backs to us.

Lady Marion Thorne takes a small gasp as I walk by her, and she whispers to her mother, "I didn't think she'd be invited."

It's a fair enough remark. I didn't think I'd be invited either.

But next to me, my mother stiffens, and the familiar pangs of pity return. She belonged to this world long before I was even alive, and they've gone and thrown her out, like they weren't all girls together, once huddled and giggling in gowns on these very steps. "Ivy, fix your face," she hisses, and I realize I'm glowering.

We linger in an awkward semblance of a line outside, ready for the palace doors to open. It is tradition that each girl enters the queen's throne room alone. But instead, at the appointed time, the footmen open the double doors to the main hall of the palace and gesture with gloved hands for us all to step inside as a group.

Kensington Palace is the main residence of the royal family, but they keep larger palaces like Buckingham and Eltham for official events. It's intimate to be invited here, into the queen's home. I've never been inside, only to the gates a few times a year as a child to deliver my baby teeth. But everyone knows you leave those with the guards; she never comes outside to collect them herself.

My boots click over the polished black-and-white checkered marble floor as we enter the main hall. There are rumblings of confusion around me, but I'm too busy taking in the splendor of the palace to truly care. The ceiling soars four stories tall, and in the middle of the great entryway is an oak tree, hundreds of years old, its roots intertwined with the very foundation of this palace. Its branches soar above us, spring green leaves brushing against the honeycomb glass of the ceiling. The walls are covered in lush murals of emerald and gold, scenes of the Otherworld where Queen Mor grew up, a place where no human has ever set foot.

As if we are sheep being herded, we follow the lead footman up the stairs to the throne room. I trail my gloved fingers along the brass railing, which is fashioned to look like vines twisting their way up and up.

The footmen swing open the doors to the throne room and gesture for us all to enter as a pack. My mother throws me a questioning glance as another murmur of concern ripples through the crowd. We should be entering one by one, not all together like this.

The expansive throne room spans the length of a city block. My boots sink into the midnight-blue carpet threaded through with gold stitched into the shapes of constellations. The ceiling is painted in a mural of sunset pinks and blush lilacs. The walls are gilded in ornate gold molding, surrounded by yet more paintings of goddesses hunting in lush forests, their bare feet crushing flowers in their wake.

And at the end of the room is *her*. We've all learned the stories in school, how Queen Mor saved all of England, how she ushered in the longest period of peace for any nation in earth's history, how she's kept our little island safe and prosperous for over four centuries.

Seeing her in the flesh is profoundly surreal. No portrait could do her justice. She's lounging casually on her throne, which is a piece of art in and of itself: a massive bouquet of orchids shaped, impossibly, into a chair rendered in gold and a rainbow of gemstones.

Her dark hair is wound into a coronet of braids, and atop that sits a crown of diamonds and turquoise stones as big as chicken eggs.

Her gown is the same blue as the jewels, radiant silk that falls wide at her wrists. But it's her face I can't stop staring at.

It's said that she hasn't aged a day since she first appeared on King Edward's battlefield, that she exists outside the bounds of time itself. Her immortal skin is unmarked by freckles or lines. She could be a debutante herself, if not for her sharp, ancient eyes.

I think of my sister at home in her bed, of my father's misfortunes, of my mother's missing finger. White-hot hate pools in my belly at the sight of her.

"Welcome." She greets us. Her voice is cool, but easily fills the cavernous space. I can feel the nerves radiating from the girls who stand beside me as we all curtsy the way we've practiced our entire lives.

I cross my left leg behind my right and bend my knees nearly ninety degrees. I keep my eyes focused on a point a few feet in front of me, a golden star embroidered into the carpet, to keep from wobbling, just as Mama taught me to.

There's a commotion from the left side of the room. A gasp. A thud. Then Opal Fitzherbert rushes out of the room, limping slightly, her mother at her heels.

Poor thing must have stumbled during her curtsy. People thought she'd do well this season, snag a baron or better, but news of a public humiliation like this will spread quickly. Now she'll be lucky to get a second son.

The air is thick with tension. Queen Mor watches on, bored by all of us, I suspect. How could she not be after four hundred years?

"I'm sure you're all wondering why this break in protocol," she begins. "I assure you we will commence with the Pact Parade shortly, but first I must beg you to allow me this indulgence."

After an agonizing moment of silence, a hidden door, one painted to blend in with the lush murals, swings open next to the throne.

The entire room takes a small gasp as Prince Bram strides in and steps onto the podium to stand at his mother's side. He enters the room like he's straight from a brisk walk in the forest.

Like his mother, he is inhumanly beautiful. Broad shoulders, a wide smile, a mop of wavy brown hair run through with rays of gold bleached by sunlight. His gray eyes glint like steel, but there's something about him that feels more tangible than his mother, like he's of this world and not floating above it. Maybe it's the dip of the dimple under his left cheek, and the way he doesn't have a matching one on the right.

He greets us all with a welcoming smile. "Seems I'm right on time."

Beside me, Olive Lisonbee's mother catches her by the elbow as

Olive swoons at the sight of him and her knees give out.

I don't blame her. They're the most beautiful people I've ever seen.

People. My mind snags on the word like an errant piece of thread. Prince Bram and Queen Mor aren't people, not really, not like us.

Queen Mor clears her throat, and the room snaps to attention. "I don't intend to waste anyone's time. I've summoned you all here today for the joyous announcement of a mother who loves her son deeply." She straightens in her throne and casts a loving glance at Bram. "This will be the season my son, His Royal Highness Bram, Prince of Wales, will select a bride."

CHAPTER FOUR

The room erupts.

There is a chorus of gasping and shouting as everyone struggles to contain themselves.

Olive Lisonbee's mother doesn't manage to catch her when she falls this time, and her head bounces off the toe of my boot as she collapses to the floor, unconscious.

Bram is only eighteen, young for a prince to take a wife. No one saw this coming.

He shocked the whole of England when he arrived at court from the Otherworld four years ago, just fourteen years old. No one knew she had a son. One day he arrived wearing a beautiful green velvet coat and a smile so wide he had the entire court endeared to him in less than a week.

The details we know of the Otherworld are minimal, but we do know that time works differently for the immortals who live there. What was four hundred years here was only ten for Bram.

His presence at court over the past few years seems to have thawed some of his mother's ice. She sometimes lets a smile slip through; her bargains have become marginally less bloody.

Bram fits in at court so well, most people forget that he wasn't raised on palace grounds. The papers are filled with glowing reports of his studies, his heroics, his good looks. The whole of the country is half in love with him.

To marry him would be to make the greatest match of any girl in the history of England.

It would mean not only a title, influence, money, and security, but all of that *forever*. Bram and Mor are immortal. This isn't just about us, but about every generation that follows.

Queen Mor's cool voice rises above the cacophony. "Contain yourselves."

Olive blinks awake, and I haul her to her feet and pass her to her mother. Everyone hushes, but ragged breathing echoes through the cavernous room.

Bram coughs into his hand like he's trying to cover a laugh.

Queen Mor has had a human prince consort for as long as she's been queen, but it's been decades since the last royal wedding. Her kings age into old men while she stays young and beautiful, trapped in amber forever. Once they die, she waits a few months and then finds another young man to marry.

Some wonder if her original bargain with King Edward IV requires that she take a human spouse, some clever wording around the word *king*, but no one can be sure. I wonder if she might just be lonely. Castles are large and drafty, and eternity is an awfully long time to be alone.

Her current husband, Prince Consort Edgar, Prince Emmett's father, is in his late forties, with a reputation for being kind and sociable, but he doesn't accompany the queen on any official business. It is made clear that she is the ruler and he, her companion.

For one heartbeat, her eyes bore directly into mine. I glance away in shock, but by the time I look back, she's already moved on.

"I ask for decorum as I continue," Queen Mor declares, but her mouth is twitching like her son's, and I have a feeling they both find this whole circus entertaining.

"In order to ensure dedicated courtship and fair play through the season, any young lady who wishes to be considered as a potential bride must abide by the following rule: If you are not chosen, you will never take another spouse. You will live the rest of your days as a spinster. These are the terms."

There's an uproar from the crowd. Confused daughters, indignant mothers, shouts of "Why?" and "Surely you wouldn't do this to our girls?"

I can't hold back my laughter.

"What on earth has gotten into you?" my mother hisses.

I wipe my tears, but I can't manage to get any words out. It's all so absurd, standing here in this grand room, in this fancy dress, watching everyone panic about a future so terrible they'd shout at the queen, but it's a future they've already condemned me to.

When I turn back to face the dais, Bram is staring directly at me, his head cocked slightly to the side.

Queen Mor stands and the room falls into a hush. She's tall, but not inhumanly so. She just moves in a way that makes you look at her, like she's walking on water. "When I take a husband, my suitors abide by this same contract. This is protocol."

Of course, the men who don't find wives still have options and financial and social freedom; we poor girls will have nothing.

"Should you choose not to agree to these rules," she concludes, "you are welcome to join the season as usual."

The queen gestures lazily with her ring-encrusted left hand, and a footman steps forward with a scroll the size of his torso under his arm. Another footman comes from the right and sets up a delicate little table on which to unfurl it. A third places a quill, a silver dagger, and an empty crystal inkwell on the corner of the table.

"Any girl who wishes to be considered may sign the contract now. You have ten minutes to make up your minds, then we'll get back to the business at hand. You will all still get your bargains."

The queen sits down and casts a sidelong glance at Bram, whose face is unreadable, but his eyes—I swear they keep landing on me.

The room fills with voices, mothers and daughters discussing strategy. In this war we've been raised for, this is the ultimate battle.

I turn to my mother. She looks younger than her forty-nine years, clear blue eyes and blond hair barely run through with streaks of white. I want to give her a hug, tell her everything is going to be well. In so many ways, I feel like I'm the parent in our relationship, always reassuring her, playacting that everything is going to be all right. She opens her mouth to speak, but my mind is already made up.

I had a plan for today. I've played it out a million times over in my head. I wasn't prepared for this, but still, I know what I must do.

I take a step forward.

"Ivy!" my mother calls after me. "Darling, consider this, please!"

But I have. By presenting myself as a suitor, I will have to be invited to this season's events. I could get my family back in society's good graces, my mother could rejoin her friends, my father could meet again with business associates, save the house, and maybe Lydia would stop being so sad.

I think back to my six-year-old self, leaving her necklace at the base of the gnarled ironwood tree. I remember my face pressed to the glass and the shadow I swore I saw walking through the woods. I dreamed about that figure for years. In my head he was a prince, come to rescue me from the monotony of my life. That voice in the back of my head is the quietest as it whispers the wish I made that night—a child's wish: *Maybe if you're special enough, one of Them will love you.*

"It's going to be all right," I whisper to my mother. Maybe I'm lying. Maybe it won't be. But this is the first opportunity I've had to piece even the tiniest shards of our lives back together, and I'm not going to waste it.

A hush falls as I break from the crowd and approach the table.

The queen peers down at me from her throne. "You wish to be considered?"

I see myself as if through a spyglass, peering through time, struck with the knowledge that my future self will look back on this moment and see my life split into *before* and *after.*

I square my shoulders. "I present myself as a suitor for the prince."

"Very well." She gestures to a footman, who picks up the silver dagger in his white-gloved hand and passes it to me.

The handle is cold between my fingers.

"You'll sign the contract now." She pauses, sizing me up.

I look down at the empty inkwell and—*oh.*

Maybe it would be better to feign horror, to look weak and girl-ish in front of the prince. But I just want to get it over with.

I pull the crystal inkwell toward me.

Then I raise the dagger and slash through the center of my palm. I squeeze my eyes shut and wince as the blade pierces skin.

My heartbeat rushes into my ears. My nerves are so ragged I don't feel anything at first.

Beads of blood swell, but I haven't gone quite deep enough. I cut again, slower, with more pressure this time.

The sink of the knife into flesh is sickening, but I don't look down. I only stop when I feel the warm rush of liquid. I pull the inkwell to the base of my wrist and let the blood flow into it.

Once it's full enough to dip the pen into, I set it down. I should raise my hand to slow the blood flow, but I don't want to stain my dress, so I place my bleeding hand palm down on the shiny mahogany table instead.

Then I dip the quill into my own blood and lower it to the parchment. The room is silent. All I hear is the sound of the scratching of the quill and my own ragged breathing. In crimson red, I scrawl:

Ivy Elizabeth Benton

I look up at the queen.

She smiles, something horrible in the twist of her mouth. "I wish you the best of luck, Lady Ivy."

CHAPTER FIVE

The blood from my hand seeps into the edges of the scroll and dribbles down the spindly legs of the table.

I turn to walk back to my mother, but Bram bounds down the steps of the dais after me.

He reaches into his breast pocket and pulls out a midnight-blue silk handkerchief. Swiftly, he encircles my wrist with his cool fingers and tugs me closer to him. I let out a little gasp of surprise.

He wraps the fabric tightly around the wound and finishes with a knot. Then he presses his middle and pointer finger over the fabric right in the middle of my palm, where it throbs the worst. There's a sudden rush of heat, then the pain stops.

I gasp softly, confused and relieved all at once.

He looks down at me and quirks a smile, showing off his single dimple. "I look forward to getting better acquainted, Lady Ivy."

The shocked crowd parts, and I return to my mother's side. She doesn't scold like I'm expecting. Instead, she reaches down and squeezes my uninjured hand.

Hushed conversations fill the hall like a swarm of insects as the next few moments tick by.

I'm surprised when Olive Lisonbee takes a step forward. She's always been a shy little thing. I've never seen her look quite so determined.

The tips of her ears burn as red as her hair as she presents herself to the queen. She curtsies, then turns toward Bram. "I'd like to be your bride." Her voice shakes only a little.

Bram smiles and gestures toward the contract. "Go on, then."

One of the footmen places a fresh inkwell in front of her. It takes her four tries to cut deep enough to draw blood. She flinches each time the knife draws across her palm, but I respect her for not giving up.

When she's finished, she returns to her mother's side, but I don't miss the way she glances down at Bram's handkerchief tied around my hand with jealousy in her eyes.

After Olive, it's Emmy Ito who signs. Her black hair shines like onyx as the light from the stained glass catches it.

After Emmy there are three girls I don't recognize. Only one cries as the blade pierces her.

Next is Greer, my old friend, who is bodily pushed by her mother up to the now blood-soaked table. She drags her heels into the thick carpet, her face already streaked with tears. Her mother slices open her hand for her, and I'm close enough to hear her hiss, "He'll choose you if you stop sniveling."

A line has formed. Ten more girls in rapid succession. One signs her name, then stumbles and pretends to faint at Bram's feet. She waits for him to reach out to her, but a footman beats him to it, hauls her to her feet, and sends her on her way.

There's Lady Sara Middlebrook and her cousin Deidre Rutland next. They giggle audibly as they cut their hands and sign their names.

Queen Mor announces that there are only five minutes left, when Lady Marion Thorne comes forward. Her head is held high, her steps unhurried. She moves like she knows she's already won. She probably has.

Marion has always been the prettiest of the girls our age, the richest too. Her mother, the only child of the Duke of Sherwood, shocked her family when she married an untitled man who immigrated from Accra to London to make a bargain with the queen. He made a good deal. Enough to buy him a London mansion and more than a few country estates. The queen rewarded him with his own dukedom, the first awarded in nearly a century. The subject of Marion's match has been hotly debated. Whoever gets her and her sizable dowry will be lucky indeed.

She's either just thrown away her future or made herself a princess. If I were a gambler, I'd put all my money on the latter.

Marion's duchess-silk gown glows against her golden-brown skin, matching, perfectly, the color of the diamonds in the coronet set atop her dark curls.

Marion is so perfect, I used to wish I could hate her, but she's genuinely lovely and funny. We both got kicked out of a midwinter choral performance last fall because she kept drawing little figures on the program and making me laugh. Of course, that was before she abandoned me with the rest of them. She's easier to hate now.

I glance across the room to where Greer trembles next to her mother. She's still trying to stanch the bleeding of her hand with the silk garniture of her skirt.

Unlike the rest of us, Marion doesn't grimace as she cuts her hand. She stares the prince down, as if daring him to make it up to her.

"Less than two minutes remaining," Queen Mor announces.

Three more girls rush the stage, squabbling over the knife as they race to draw blood in time.

Then, with only seconds left, a girl I don't recognize pushes through the crowd from the back of the room.

She's exceptionally pretty, with parchment pale skin and masses of dark brown hair wound into an updo dotted with pearls.

In a single swift motion, she slashes her hand and scrawls her name.

She is the only other girl to get a reaction out of Bram. He presses his mouth into a thin line, as if he's trying to stop himself from saying something.

The dark-haired girl doesn't even look at him, as if he's the least important part of this for her.

The queen stands from her throne and looks over all of us once more.

The room, which had been so still and perfect before the queen's announcement, appears as if a storm has blown through it. Mothers are sweaty and sick with worry. Girls' hands and dresses are stained with red. There's a slow *drip, drip, drip* as blood runs in rivulets off the spindly table where the contract lies.

Twenty-four of us have signed up.

Twenty-three of us will leave this competition with nothing.

The queen cuts through the crowd, flanked by four stony-faced footmen in midnight-blue livery.

They swing open the double doors to the throne room as she peers over one shoulder and arches a brow. "Follow," she commands.

CHAPTER SIX

Kensington Park has been transformed into an enchanted garden. Dotting the lawn are floral displays as big as people, and baskets artfully arranged and overflowing with blooms. Gardeners have been hard at work on the eaves of the palace, giving the illusion that flowers are spilling from the roof and windows. Sparkling chandeliers hang from the branches of ancient trees, their crystals jingling in the gentle breeze.

Below the stone steps of the palace, in the middle of the festivities, is a maypole, a thin post about as tall as a streetlamp, topped with a rainbow of ribbons trailing down the side and fluttering in the wind.

Lords and ladies of London high society mingle in their tails and silks, draped in diamonds and wearing hats piled high with organza flowers. It's a Pact Parade tradition, this garden party. The ton gather to drink champagne and wait for the girls of the season to emerge and show off their new bargains. It marks the official start of the season, the gunshot that signifies the beginning of the marriage hunt.

The crowd goes still and silent as we step outside. We shouldn't all be appearing at once like this. There's a ripple of shocked gasps as people spot the two dozen girls with blood smeared across the skirts of their white Pact Parade gowns.

"Welcome, on this most joyous day." The queen's voice carries unnaturally through the crowd. "I'm pleased to announce that my son, Bram, Prince of Wales, intends to find a wife this season. Twenty-four girls have put themselves forward for consideration and, in their devotion, have vowed to never marry should they not be selected."

The crowd gasps. Bram stands still beside Queen Mor, his face unreadable.

"As a mother, it is my dearest wish that my son end up with his perfect match, and I'm sure we can all agree that twenty-four girls is simply too many to become properly acquainted with over twelve weeks. Therefore, we will be whittling down our accomplished group of twenty-four to six." She lets the announcement settle, as if relishing our fear. Panicked glances go through the girls. *Only six?*

"Determination and grit are two vital qualities that any girl who marries my son will need to possess, and so, as is tradition in my homeland, the debutantes will compete in a maypole dance to prove their mettle. The final six left standing will be invited to move onto palace grounds and compete for Prince Bram's hand. The rest will return home, your season ended."

"You didn't tell us that!" Sara Middlebrook exclaims, her face screwed up in panic and anger.

Queen Mor levels her with a glance. "Why would I need to?"

She turns back to the crowd, her serene smile back in place. "In the spirit of sportsmanship, the winning girl will be gifted the May Queen tiara I won on my very own betrothal day."

A footman steps forward holding an intricate floral tiara, set in a rainbow of gems, on a red velvet pillow.

"Shall we?" The queen gestures for us to join her as she steps down onto the lawn and over to the maypole.

The crowd gathers around us in a wide circle. There's a full bandstand off to one side, covered in white roses.

The queen turns to us with a final, sickly sweet smile. "Cheaters will be disqualified."

The band kicks up an overly cheery tune, and I take a violet ribbon in my hand, Lydia's favorite color. The pretty, dark-haired girl is directly in front of me, and Emmy Ito is at my heels.

We start skipping around the maypole, but the problem with the ground is evident almost immediately: a wet English winter has left the great lawn of Kensington Palace too soft.

The other girls' silk slippers sink right into the sodden grass, and after only one rotation the maypole field has been turned to slick, wet mud.

Deidre falls first, only four turns in. One of her shoes gets stuck in the muck, and she turns around to fetch it, falling right into Greer, who hops over her deftly.

Deidre screams and pounds her fists until the footmen haul her away.

All I can do is watch, horrified, as the weight of what we've all agreed to settles over me. By sunset, eighteen girls will have lost everything they ever planned for. I can't let myself be among them.

On and on we turn while the band plays. To keep from getting dizzy, I keep my eyes trained on the gables of the palace.

Onlookers gasp and cheer as we twirl, but I can't help but feel that they're just waiting to watch us fall like toy soldiers.

This is blood sport.

The rest of us last for the better part of an hour, but then one girl trips, and it's chaos before anyone can register what's happening. The debutante behind her topples, then another and another and another. The girl in front of me does a clever little spin out of the way, her arms out for flourish. The crowd explodes in applause.

But I'm coming up right behind her, Emmy at my heels, and she's not slowing down. The blonde who's just fallen can't get up off the ground fast enough, and she stumbles again in the muck, right at my feet.

I dig the sturdy heels of my boots into the mud and stop on a dime, able to sidestep, then skip over her. I sigh in relief.

Another half hour, and my back is wet with sweat, my lungs screaming for air. On my insistence Mrs. Tuttle tied my corset loosely this morning, but no matter how I try, I can't quite catch my breath.

With six girls down, there's still eighteen of us, and all the bodies circling around me are stifling. With few exceptions, everyone else looks as tired as I feel. Our hair, once perfectly dressed, hangs in sweaty tendrils down our faces and necks.

One of the white roses Mrs. Tuttle pinned to my chignon this morning falls and is trampled to a sticky mess of petals in the dirt.

One of the girls I don't know faints, and another falls on top of her.

Three more go not long after.

The crowd has regrouped around us; it's getting rowdier, with fewer girls and more champagne. They're shouting and passing money around. Most seem to be placing their bets on Sara Middlebrook and Marion Thorne.

I finally catch sight of my parents in the crowd. They're off to the side, alone, ignored as usual. The sight sends a stab of anger through me, and my resolve is renewed.

I offer them a smile, but in my moment of distraction, another girl falls, splattering mud all over my dress.

I only have to outlast six more.

From the other side of the maypole Sara Middlebrook shouts over the band, "He's never going to pick you, Ivy. A girl with your reputation, a princess? Spare us all the embarrassment and give up now."

I offer her a fake smile. "I'll take my chances."

"I'll let any girl who drops out right now be my lady-in-waiting when I win," she says to the group.

"Done." A redhead I don't know drops her ribbon and walks off. A cry goes up from the crowd, her parents I assume.

Bram stands at the front of the crowd, his face sketched with concern. Did he know this is what his mother was planning?

Two more girls fall, one right on top of the other. The world is spinning so terribly, my focus going in and out, and for a moment I'm terrified I might go down with them, but the footmen pick them up in the nick of time.

We're only nine now. I'm so close.

But my legs are shaking, my feet numb, even with the boots. There's a stitch in my side, and it's been ages since I fully caught my breath.

A tall brunette mutters something under her breath; I catch the word *whore* on the breeze. The girl behind her shoves her and they both go down screaming, the crowd screaming with them.

The party is a spinning blur, but in a single focused point is my mother, pale with worry. My father's hand is protectively laid on her shoulder. I resent her sometimes for coddling Lydia and me. She was the kind of parent who could never stand to see either of us in discomfort, and although it made for a golden, happy childhood, I worry that it hasn't prepared me for the world very well at all.

I only need to outlast one more girl, and I could save them from social alienation, from financial ruin, from all the pain I've borne witness to over the past three months.

I dig my heels deep into the mud as a shriek pierces through the crowd, and I look just in time to see Sara Middlebrook's delicate slipper get caught in one of the fresh divots from my boots. She falls forward, the mud splashing all over her face.

"No!" she screams. "No! It isn't fair!"

She rushes to Bram and falls at his feet. "Please, Your Highness, pick me, pick me. I'll do whatever you want."

Bram helps her stand. "Mother?" He looks over his shoulder to where the queen stands, her face expressionless. She nods her sharp chin at a footman, who carries Sara away, kicking and screaming.

I don't like Sara, but I do feel pity for her. I wouldn't wish her fate on anyone.

Despite it all, relief courses through my body. I've made it. I'm one of the final six. Marion Thorne falls next, though it happens a little too slowly and carefully to be an accident.

Olive gets tangled up in her ribbon and falls shortly after, immediately bursting into tears.

Emmy doesn't last much longer.

With only three of us left—me, the dark-haired girl, and Greer— the crowd is in an absolute frenzy.

Greer's face is wet with sweat, her eyes furious as they bore into mine.

Greer and I worked well as best friends because she always knew I was never going to be a threat to her. For years, it was always the same comments: *Ivy doesn't worry about being pretty, mustn't that be nice?* or *It's lovely that Ivy and I will come out the same season. She can help me manage my full dance card.*

She's staring at me now like I might actually give her a run for her money. For the first time in our lives, Greer Trummer is having to take me seriously.

"Thanks for lying for me at the atelier yesterday," I pant. "I'll let you be one of my ladies-in-waiting."

"Shut up," she hisses through gritted teeth. But in her distraction, her foot lands wrong and she falls, sputtering in the mud.

She curses, pounding her fist in the puddle before being dragged off.

I give myself only one turn around the pole to laugh.

The band slows as the musicians tire. We must have been dancing for over two hours.

The crowd is shouting, but I can hardly make it out over the pounding in my ears. "Ivy!" That's my father's voice. "Go, Ivy!"

There's another name being shouted. "Faith!" That must be the name of the girl in front of me.

Faith's cheeks are red with exertion, sweat dripping from her hairline down into the collar of her white dress.

But her face is stony, giving nothing away. I respect her for it.

I'm so tired. It would be easy to stop. But the sun catches the jewels in the May Queen tiara, and I picture giving it to my parents. They could sell it for more money than we've seen my entire life. It might save our house. It might even be enough for Lydia and me to live on without husbands.

I turn with renewed energy, my feet pounding into the mud.

Two little girls burst through to the front of crowd. "Faith!" they shout. "Go, Faith!"

She spots them and smiles, her perfect face finally cracking.

In her distraction, her left foot lands a little sideways in a crater of mud and she trips. She tries to hold on to her ribbon, but it rips. The crowd gasps, and Faith falls to the ground, splattered in mud.

There is stunned silence, and then comes a burst of riotous applause.

The crowd parts, and the queen and Bram walk toward us. Ever the gentleman, Bram helps Faith to her feet, but his eyes are on me.

The May Queen crown glints in the sun as the queen raises it high, so that everyone gathered can see it, then lowers it onto my head.

The crowd is cheering, there's a shower of flower petals raining down on me like snow, but my gaze lands on a single figure in the crowd.

His eyebrows are furrowed, his mouth screwed up in a scowl, his hands balled into white-knuckled fists. Standing completely still, staring at me like he absolutely loathes me, is Prince Emmett De Vere.

CHAPTER SEVEN

Bram approaches, and the sun comes out with his smile. His gray eyes are bright, and he's grinning wide enough to show his dimple.

"Congratulations, Lady Ivy," he says, just quiet enough for me to hear.

It's almost impossible to catch my breath, but the weight of the crown makes my victory feel real.

A footman stomps three times, and the crowd falls into a hush, but the queen is already walking back into the palace, the train of her gown trailing behind her. She waves an elegant hand dismissively. "We'll reconvene for the Pact Parade in one half hour. Let's have some clever bargains this year, girls. I'm getting bored."

With the garden party still in full swing, the debutantes are shepherded upstairs to the hall outside the throne room.

There are a little less than one hundred of us this year. Twenty-four girls are covered in mud, eighteen of them have tear-streaked faces, having lost their whole futures in the course of a few hours. All of them eye the crown on my head with barely disguised envy. My stomach churns with a strange guilt.

We're arranged alphabetically by family name, so I'm near the front.

Each girl will enter alone, present herself to the queen, and make her bargain.

It's like this that we are delivered to her, like flowers in a bouquet waiting to be pressed between the same pages. Beautiful at the cost of being fragile and stuck forever.

Though only six of us will be making bargains to attract the hand of a prince, all of us have marriage on the mind. What bargain will help one snag a baron under fifty, a duke with a full mouth of teeth, a lord with the prettiest summer estate? These are the calculations we have been trained in.

The same awkward glances pass between me, Greer, Faith, Emmy, Marion, and Olive.

We've all just become each other's competition, but the air is thick with mutual pity. We're only able to look at each other with sidelong glances. I don't doubt the same two questions play in all our heads: *What have we done to ourselves?* and *What will we do to each other?*

The other eighteen girls, the ones who didn't pass the maypole test, stand in various states of disarray. A few are openly weeping, while others try to keep their heads held high. Sara and Deidre seethe.

The clock strikes three, bells tolling out above the city. The doors to the throne room swing open, and Penelope Atkins enters first.

We take a collective breath as she walks in, but the hallway stays silent, save for the sound of breathing, while we wait. We're all too nervous to make a joke of the moment we've been raised for, the single opportunity we get to experience magic.

After a few minutes the doors to the throne room open once more and Penelope Atkins exits. The difference is obvious immediately.

Penelope's once dull strawberry blond hair is now falling around her shoulders in cascades of thick, glowing auburn.

The silk slipper on her left foot is soaked through with blood.

Her skin is clammy, her face pale, but her mouth is turned up in triumph. She hobbles out of the hall, leaving a smear of wet crimson footprints in her wake.

Wendla Avignon goes next. She exits less than five minutes later, her eyes damp with tears, but no other visible differences.

Then it is my turn.

I straighten my shoulders and take a deep breath as the doors swing open before me.

I think back to myself at eleven years old, sitting on the floor of my bedroom. My blond hair was tied up in ribbons, and I was safe and small.

I used to fantasize about this moment, scrawl in the margins of my school papers what I might ask for.

I imagined asking to talk to animals or fly. I pictured myself with the ability to make flowers bloom with the palm of my hand or to conjure rain clouds from nothing. If I only had a single opportunity to touch magic, I wasn't going to waste it. I couldn't fathom why people would ask for something as boring as a prettier face.

I close my eyes and give myself the space of a breath to mourn for my younger self. *I'm sorry*, I whisper through time, *for all the things you didn't get to be.*

The throne room looks so much bigger without anyone in it.

I cross the expanse to where the queen sits.

"Lady Ivy Benton." Her voice is low and syrupy.

I curtsy deeply and rise to meet her eyes. My hands are shaking, so I cross them behind my back and fiddle with the bow tied at the base of my spine. *Perfect*, I have to be perfect.

Queen Mor grins, revealing a row of perfect teeth, her canines sharper than any I've ever seen. "Tell me, Miss Benton, what have you come to ask for?"

CHAPTER EIGHT

I've pictured this moment for months. I've written down what I plan to ask for over and over, fed the paper to the fire until I was sure I would make no mistakes.

"Your Majesty." My voice is high and sweet, just like I practiced. I hunch my shoulders in an attempt to make myself as small as possible. So small, a nothing person, absolutely no one. "I wish to undo the bargain you made with my sister, Lady Lydia Benton, on Saturday, the first of May, eighteen forty-six. Whatever you gave her, let it be returned, and whatever she gave you, may it be given back to her, wholly and unaltered."

I take a breath as I finish, relieved to have gotten it right.

The queen presses her lips together as she watches me through narrowed eyes. "Are you finished?"

"Yes, ma'am." I bow my head reverently, desperate to impress her.

The queen laughs until it echoes off the walls of the throne room. "You cannot undo another's bargain."

"Your Majesty, I wish for nothing more than to undo the bargain of my most beloved sister. She can't remember what she bargained for, you see, and I want to end her distress. I'm sure you understand."

She peers down at me from the dais. "You may wish for whatever you please, but you will be disappointed."

"Will you tell me, at least, what her bargain was? Can you do me that one kindness?"

"The bargains are made in confidence."

"Are the bargains always undoable?" I ask, perhaps too boldly.

The throne room dims as a cloud passes over the sun outside. The queen's eyes flicker to a stained glass window and then back to me. "There is much about magic you will never understand."

"I cannot imagine you'd wish to see a subject as loyal and dedicated as Lydia so pained." I may have gone too far with that one. I need to be sweet, to be good, that's the only way any of this will work.

The queen arches a brow. "Your sister made the bargain of her own free will while sound of mind."

There's only one more question, the one that plagued me like the wind on that February night, and she's the only one who can answer it.

"Was she there? In the Otherworld?"

The queen lets out a long breath. "No. That door has been locked for four hundred years."

Something like sadness flashes in her dark eyes.

It's drafty in the throne room, but that's not why my heart feels like ice. Faeries can't lie. It's something I loved most about the stories when I was little, but I hate it now, hate it because I know she's telling the truth, and I don't want to accept it. If Lydia wasn't in the Otherworld, that means the police were right. She really was just another runaway who didn't care enough about me not to leave me behind.

"What about Prince Bram?" I ask somewhat desperately.

She shakes her head. "A special case. Doors are funny. Sometimes they only open one way."

It's more information than I thought she'd give, but it doesn't make it any easier to accept.

Queen Mor looks down at me from her throne, her back to its stony mask. "What are you most afraid of, Ivy Benton?"

I think for a moment, then answer truthfully. "Failing my family."

Queen Mor leans back and takes a breath. "I could help you."

But she can't. Not really. Not when what I want is revenge and she is the one to blame for Lydia's ruin.

"You could have more land for your father's failing estate, a particular mind for bookkeeping, the ability to play piano so beautifully it would calm the nerves of anyone listening. You need only pay the right price."

"No thank you."

She laughs again, no pity in it. "I give you one last opportunity, Ivy Benton, to take something for yourself."

I want my sister back. I bite my tongue before the words can escape.

When we were small and Lydia and I drove Mama and our governess up the wall by bickering and tattling on each other, Mama would grab us by our little faces and say, *You are not your sister's keeper.*

But who am I, if not a sister? And what does that mean if not this?

"There is nothing else I want, Your Majesty. I thank you, most sincerely, for your time."

The queen sighs against her throne. "Bring the next one in."

Mama talks the whole way home, babbling about my win and her friends, but the words run together, just a buzzing in my ears as I stare out the carriage window.

I fiddle with the edge of the handkerchief and peel it back to find the gash in the middle of my hand almost completely healed. I feel a sudden flood of warmth for Prince Bram. But even the memory of his perfect face and kind smile doesn't dull the sharp edges of my mood.

It's only as we pull up to our house that my mother pauses her frantic stream of consciousness chatting and pauses to look at me in earnest. "You know," she says, steadying herself as the carriage shudders to a halt, "you'd make a wonderful princess."

I wouldn't—not this new version of me who is so full of anger. But I smile softly and say, "Thank you."

"Your new memory will come in handy in the competition for his hand. What did she take in return?" she asks cautiously, as if afraid of the answer.

I see no reason to lie to her. "I didn't make a bargain."

"Oh, darling," she says under her breath, and it breaks my heart to hear her disappointment.

It's a kindness that she lets me race up to my room and sit there alone for the rest of the day. As the sun sets, Mrs. Tuttle brings up a tray for dinner, but even she has the good sense not to speak with me.

It's Lydia, back when she was herself, who would have made a good princess. Popular and beautiful, she had a reputation for her quick smile and quicker wit.

It's well past eleven when I pad across the hall to her room. I'm not shocked to find her awake. She never keeps normal hours anymore. She's propped up in bed, a gothic novel in her hands.

"Mama already told me," she says as I enter. "Will you make me curtsy to you when you win?"

I sink down next to her, like I used to when I was small and she let me sleep in her bed nearly every night.

"Who says I'm going to win?"

"You've never had enough faith in yourself," she whispers.

"You had plenty for the both of us." A family doesn't need two stars, and Lydia was already ours.

"No." She's staring at the ceiling, neither of us looking at each other. "You're misremembering." Maybe it's the dark, or maybe it's that I'll be moving to the palace tomorrow, but the wall between us feels less impenetrable tonight, like we're speaking honestly for the first time in months.

A beat of silence stretches between us. She closes her book and turns down the gas lamp at her bedside.

We're uncomfortably close to the subject we can't discuss. The second of Lydia's three great betrayals.

Lydia and I have had a deal since I was seven and she was nine.

We sliced our thumbs with a sharp garden rock and pressed them together until they became slippery with blood. She vowed she'd marry Lord Chapwick's son from down the street, and I could live with them forever. He was a nice boy with a freckled face and an obvious soft spot for Lydia. My life would be my own, and I'd get to be with my sister. I could think of no better future.

It might not have been a magical bargain with an immortal queen, but to me it felt just as sacred and unbreakable. Our deal was the bedrock upon which our relationship rested, a constant.

But then, after her bargain was made and her first season came and went, she didn't marry Lord Chapwick's son. Everyone in town thought their betrothal was a foregone conclusion, especially the Chapwicks, but she rebuffed him. I begged her to explain until I was blue in the face, but Lydia could offer nothing beyond "it didn't feel right." She pretended she couldn't hear me sobbing through our shared wall at night. I didn't understand. I still don't.

Lord Chapwick's son married Fiona Edgar instead. As for her two seasons out in society, Lydia barely tried at all, always standing at the edge of the ballroom, lying about a hurt ankle.

"We'll find someone better for you, Lydia," I'd say, but she'd just nod with that odd far-off look of hers. It was a betrayal I didn't know how to forgive her for.

Then she disappeared.

I blink back to the room. "Do you really not remember what happened?" This is the last time I'll ask her.

Her breathing stutters. "I swear it. It's awful, knowing that anything could have happened to me. Makes me feel like my body isn't my own anymore or something. I can't explain it."

"I'm not asking you to."

"I don't think I would have chosen to do this to you, but I'm sorry if I did. I'm sorry it happened at all. I should have protected you."

It's the first apology I've gotten, but now that it's out in the air, I don't think I ever needed it. I've always known this is how Lydia felt. We're too tied together that way.

"It's all right," I say, and I'm surprised to find I mean it. "We'll be old spinsters together."

Lydia laughs, but there's no real force behind it.

When Papa dies, his title will pass to a second cousin we've never met and the creditors will take the rest. I hope selling the May Queen tiara will help once I've lost the competition for Prince Bram.

"Mama told me you didn't make a bargain. That wasn't very smart," Lydia says.

I shrug. "Because it went so well for you?"

She frowns. "Mean."

I don't tell her what I asked the queen. Lydia would only feel guilt, and I see no need to punish her with it. "He's not going to pick me. I didn't see the point."

Lydia may have been meant for Lord Chapwick, but my poor prospects were an equally foregone, but much less appealing, conclusion. The awkward second daughter of an impoverished marquess—even at the best of times I could never have hoped for better than a widower decades my senior or one of the lesser members of the aristocracy with something so broken inside of him, he'd been rejected by everyone else: one of the cruel men, the liars, the cheats.

It's a relief to have saved myself from that fate, even if I've doomed us in a different kind of way.

"Can I tell you a secret?" I ask my sister.

"Always."

"I went out to look for you when you were gone. Snuck out in the middle of the night and everything."

She bolts upright, aghast. "Ivy! What were you thinking?"

"I was thinking that I'd be able to feel it if you were dead. You ought to give me credit; I was right."

I was hoping she'd laugh, but she just looks sad again. "What happened?"

"You're never going to believe me."

She holds out her pinkie. We only pinkie promise when Mama is not around, as she hates being left out. "I promise I will," she says.

"I got lost, and Prince Emmett ran me over in his stupid carriage."

"He did not!"

I nod. "He took mercy on me and escorted me home after that, but still."

Lydia frowns. "He was probably up to all sorts of lecherous things, out in the middle of the night like that."

"I pity any girl foolish enough to fall for his tricks."

"How are you going to stand him when Bram marries you?"

I roll my eyes. "I'll have you move in as my lady-in-waiting and we can torment him together. He'll never know a day of peace."

"He's awful," she sniffs.

"The absolute worst," I reply, a little thin. As proof, I run across the hall to my room and pull his calling card out from where I'd hidden it under my mattress. I don't know why I kept it. I was being stupid.

Lydia gasps in glee as I pass it to her, and she smiles wide when I tell her she can be the one to burn it.

She tosses it into the fire, laughing, and we both watch as it curls and turns to ash.

"Try not to miss me too much when I'm gone," I say with an elbow to her ribs.

"I always miss you," she says, and it's a little too honest. It's not something we can bear, so we say nothing at all.

CHAPTER NINE

Mama drags Lydia out of bed the next morning to say goodbye, and we share an awkward brief hug at the door. We're all elbows as we knock into each other. Her eyes are still swollen with sleep, but I don't know if that's the reason she can't really look at me. We can't bear how much we love each other. It's like an open wound we can't touch for all the stinging it causes.

"I'm going to miss you so much," I whisper, so quiet only she can hear.

"He'll fall in love with you if he has any taste at all," she whispers back.

Mrs. Tuttle kisses me twice on both cheeks and says, "When you're a princess, you'd better let your old Mrs. Tuttle visit you in that fancy palace of yours."

Papa hugs me last, his eyes wet with tears. "When did you grow up?" he asks into my hair.

He has to know as well as I do. But I just hug him back. At my feet is a bag of books he's given me, old volumes of Socrates and John Locke. I don't want to haul them across town with me, but as usual, I indulge him.

The carriage pulls away from Belgrave Square, and I watch my home disappear behind me in a cloud of dust.

When we reach Kensington Palace, there's a fearsome woman standing on the steps, waiting for us. "You're the last to arrive," she says curtly as the footmen haul my single trunk out of the back of the carriage.

Mama glances at the watch chain pinned to her waistband. "But we're right on time."

"Lady Marion Thorne has been here with her parents and lady's maid since first light," she replies. "The rest arrived after breakfast." I'm embarrassed that the other girls arrived early to get ready together. Did they talk about it without me?

Without waiting for a response, she marches with the posture of a military commander across the lawn as Mama and I skitter after her. England hasn't had a military since Queen Mor put an end to the War of the Roses, but I've read about it in books. Nothing described in the pages of novels was quite as fearsome as the lady before me. She's in her sixties, with white hair swept up into a bouffant and a serious gray spencer jacket buttoned over her gown.

"I'm Viscountess Bolingbroke, and I will be your chaperone for the season. I promise to guide you all, educate you to the best of my abilities, and ensure that your honor remains firmly intact. I'll reside with you and the five other girls here on palace grounds. I expect your behavior to be unimpeachable." She looks down at my embarrassingly small valise. "I'm glad to see you packed light. A trousseau of all required items will be provided to you by the Crown."

She leads us to Caledonia Cottage, a squat little building, crawling with ivy, perched on the wooded edge of the palace grounds.

We step through the threshold from the quiet garden to a storm of activity as the other girls and their staff prepare for the ball tonight. Viscountess Bolingbroke takes us up the carpeted staircase to what will be my room. It's fashionably decorated, but smaller than my room at home, with a slanting ceiling and a single window letting in streams of golden midmorning light.

Two beds with matching pale-blue silk damask canopies are placed against the far wall, the one closest to the window already rumpled and covered with discarded clothing.

"You'll be with Faith Fairchild," the viscountess says. "I will be staying down the hall for the remainder of the season, and you will be attended to by a full staff of palace professionals. Family visits can be arranged with me directly, but we discourage visiting too often lest it interfere with the girls' focus."

The viscountess swishes out the door, and I bid my mother a brief goodbye. She's never been one for tears; she just squeezes me and says, "Do your best."

A luncheon has been laid out in the dining room downstairs, a getting-to-know-you meal for me and the other girls. We don't have long to sit, though. As tradition demands, there will be a ball tonight at the home of the Twombleys, where everyone will show off their new faces and talents and whatever else people can think to bargain for. A few years back, there was a girl who bargained for a strange little clock that meowed like a cat on the hour. Still, no one knows why.

When I was eleven or twelve, at the height of my faerie obsession, I stole one of my mother's unused journals and listed every single bargain and cost I could find, desperate to identify some rhyme or reason to them. I came to the conclusion that they're random, completely reliant on the queen's whims, which terrified and thrilled me all at once.

The Benton household received our invitation from Count Twombley's footman at first light this morning. My mother pulled me into a tight hug, her eyes wet with tears upon tearing open the invitation's wax seal. It would never have arrived had I not been one of the prince's suitors.

Greer sits at the end of the table, the difference in her immediately obvious.

Her face, once ruddy and sweet, has been sharpened and thinned into something strikingly beautiful. I can't look at her, it's too uncanny and unsettling.

Olive, too, appears changed. She strides in and smiles widely, revealing two rows of perfect white teeth. She'd been missing an upper molar before, and the bottom row had been a mess of overlapping.

Emmy, Marion, and Faith remain outwardly unchanged.

"Greer, you look beautiful," Marion says, kindly. "You too, Olive." Olive, who hasn't stopped smiling since she entered, nods in acknowledgment.

Finger sandwiches are passed around and tea is poured. "So what did everyone else receive yesterday?" Marion asks, carrying the conversation as if she already knows she's the leader.

"More important, what did everyone give up?" Emmy says under her breath.

Olive tugs off her wrist-length white gloves. A fresh bandage is wrapped around the palm of her hand, identical to the one all six of us wear.

She extends her arms to the center of the table and wiggles ten perfectly smooth fingernail-less fingers.

Emmy gasps. Faith is stunned into silence. Greer shrieks. Marion just laughs.

"It was worth it, though, right?" Olive says. Her mouth cracks into an uneasy smile around her flawless teeth.

"Absolutely!" I exclaim, hopefully stopping Emmy from saying whatever negative remark looks to be on the tip of her tongue.

"What about you, Greer? What did it cost?" Olive asks.

Greer laughs, the same back-of-the-throat, snorting laugh she's had since we were children. She stands up, pushing her chair into the shiny mahogany table.

"Look at this," she says, but there's a hysterical edge to her voice, like she can't quite believe what is happening.

She closes her eyes in concentration but stays completely still. Then she relents with a sigh and walks in a wide circle around the table.

"I don't understand," Marion says.

"I can't turn left," Greer says.

"Ever?" I ask.

"Nope, never again."

Marion snorts back a laugh. "And you agreed to that?"

Greer shrugs. "It's what she offered, and it seemed less painful than losing toes, so . . ."

At that, all six of us dissolve into violent giggles, even quiet Faith, who slaps her hand down on the table so hard tea spills all over the scones.

"What about you, Marion?" Greer asks once she's seated again.

Marion takes a sip of her tea and waves her hand in dismissal. "I've been plagued with migraines all my life, so I asked to experience no more headaches."

Olive thumbs over the tips of her smooth fingers. "What'd she ask for in return?"

Marion shrugs, her diamond earrings swaying. "I can no longer smell flowers. No great loss."

We all mutter in agreement and turn to Emmy, awaiting her confession.

Emmy purses her lips. "I asked for painting talent. I'll never again be able to taste sweets. I never particularly liked sweets, but I didn't tell her that."

"And you, Faith?" Marion gestures to where Faith sits at her right. Faith has a cucumber sandwich pinched between her fingers, but she sits, completely frozen, staring oddly at Marion, something strangely charged between them.

"With all due respect, I don't see how telling this to any of you would help me," Faith says under her breath.

Everyone tenses. We know we're each other's competition. It's only Faith who seems honest, or brave, or cruel enough to say the truth aloud. "You're all just obstacles directly in the way of my happiness," she continues. "The sooner this is over, the better."

Faith pushes back from the table and stomps out of the room.

Olive sniffles, suddenly teary-eyed. "I was hoping we'd all be friends."

"We will be," Marion reassures her, but Emmy and Greer shift awkwardly.

Everyone turns to me, waiting.

"Sorry to disappoint." There's no benefit in lying to them. "I couldn't think of anything I wanted enough to bargain for it, so I didn't make one."

"You . . . didn't make one?" Greer asks.

"Nope."

Before anyone can question me further, Viscountess Bolingbroke appears in the doorway, her hands on her hips. "Up, girls, up! You must make haste!"

We abandon our plates and bound up the stairs to our bedrooms. At the foot of my bed I find a black leather trunk embossed with my initials, IEB, in gold, and overflowing with clothes. There's a rainbow of dresses: gowns made of silk so fine it nearly glows, smart cotton visiting dresses, even a velvet riding coat. Beneath that is a layer of new drawers, chemises lined with lace, and gloves made of kidskin and satin.

I peer over at Faith. Girls can debut in front of the queen and take part in the Pact Parade only if their own mothers had done it or if an older woman, usually a relative, sponsors their participation.

Last night, my mother was excited to tell me all the new gossip she learned at the garden party. Faith grew up in Brighton, and her alleged godmother, Lady Carrington, sponsored her coming-out. Mama recounted in perfect detail that Faith had been, up until recently, a ballerina in the Royal Ballet, hardly an acceptable position for a high society girl. Faith is rumored to be the bastard child of Lord Carrington. His mother, Lady Carrington, isn't Faith's godmother, but her grandmother. But that's not the only rumor about Faith Fairchild.

The silence between us is awkward. "You grew up in the country, right?" I ask her.

Faith levels me with a venomous glare. "Are you seriously stupid enough to think we're going to be friends?"

I have absolutely no idea how to respond.

"Stay out of my way, and I'll leave you be. Get in my way, and you'll regret it."

I salute. "Got it, boss."

She glares again.

If anything, I'm relieved to be sharing a room with someone who doesn't feel the need to pretend we're all going to be bosom friends at the end of this.

A flurry of lady's maids arrives soon after to ready us all for the ball. We're prepped and preened with curling tongs and perfume oils and rouge for our lips, like we're dressing for battle.

Shiny black carriages embossed with the queen's seal pull up after eight p.m., and we pile in, two to a carriage, our skirts too wide to allow for more.

My lady's maid must have tied at least six petticoats around my waist, and I know I'll be sore before midnight from carrying around the extra weight.

Faith stares out the window, her chin in her hand, as the mansions of Chelsea pass by in a blur. She's in a cornflower blue gown, exactly the same shade as her eyes, with matching topaz earrings and necklace, both from the royal vault.

My carnation-pink gown is an off-the-shoulder confection, with intricate pleating and floral embroidery up the skirt.

Settled on my collarbones is a weighty diamond necklace from the queen's private collection, brought to our room by a lady-in-waiting who said to consider it a token of the queen's best wishes as Prince Bram's suitors began their season. My May Queen crown glinted at my bedside, and my lady's maid had gestured to it in an offer to pin it to my curls. "No, no," I insisted, the idea of drawing any more attention to myself after yesterday's fanfare made me sick to my stomach.

Our carriage slows as we approach the Twombleys' manor, which is lit up with dozens of torches glowing against the night.

There's an orchestra on the open second-floor landing, and the dancing inside the palatial house is in full swing by the time we enter.

At the door, we're each handed dance cards, delicate little pamphlets with a tiny pencil attached with a ribbon.

Like a mother duck, Viscountess Bolingbroke corrals us, snatching the dance cards out of our hands one by one.

"Remember, ladies, you are not here to court. You will not accept any offers to dance, you should always be in the company of other ladies, and under no circumstances should you disappear from my view. Anything less than impeccable behavior could result in your removal from consideration for the prince's hand."

We all nod in understanding, but Olive is already swiveling her head, looking at the party, and Emmy has somehow procured herself a glass of champagne. I fear the viscountess may have her work cut out for her.

"The prince will be here tonight," she says. "This is your first opportunity to make a real impression on His Majesty. I suggest you don't waste it."

A hush falls over the crowd as the six of us enter, everyone craning their necks to get a look at us. Our names and faces were splashed over every paper in London this morning. From the dukes and duchesses in this room to the mud larks along the Thames, Queen Mor's announcement that this is the season her son will take a bride is all anyone can talk about. My May Queen victory was particularly noted. Whispers follow me as we cut across the room.

There goes Ivy Benton. Who knew she had it in her? He's still never going to pick her.

I spot my mother, surrounded by laughing women in the corner of the room, the widest smile on her face I've seen in months.

The chandelier reflects off the small tiara nestled in her curls. The stones are paste. We sold the real ones off a decade ago.

It seems my status as one of the prince's suitors has granted my mother immediate acceptance back into her old social group. The familiar rage at the fact that we could all be discarded, then reaccepted like it was all nothing, rises in me, but I brush it away. This is only a game, and the sooner I accept that, the easier the next few months will be.

At that moment, a trumpet sounds, the band lowers their strings, and the ballroom stills.

Prince Bram enters the room, flanked by Prince Emmett, both nearly a head above everyone else in the crowd. They wear matching black coats embellished with sky-blue sashes and badges of the eight-pointed star, the order of the royal family. Their high white cravats are flawless, their shoes perfectly shined. Emmett and Bram aren't biological brothers of course, but they do resemble each other. Prince Emmett's hair is a few shades darker, his cheekbones higher, his lips fuller. Their expressions are different, too—Bram's lips upturned in a wide, friendly smile, and Emmett's turned down in a bored frown. Together, they're a complete set, Bram the sun, Emmett the moon.

The attention of every girl in the room is divided between them. It's been a point of discussion among all of us for years, in hushed tones when our mothers weren't listening: *Are you a Bram girl or an Emmett girl?* Bram, sunny, kind, and safe, tends to appeal to girls who share similar qualities. It's Emmett, with his bitten lips and sad eyes, who plays in the fantasies of the risk-takers. I always thought the conversations were silly, but here, hit with the force of the princes' presence, I'm starting to understand.

Prince Emmett lingers at the edge of the crowd while Bram strides to the center of the now-empty dance floor.

"I'd like to thank our gracious hosts, the Count and Countess Twombley, for so generously facilitating tonight's festivities." He gestures to where they stand, and they bow humbly.

"And I'd like to take this opportunity to thank the six beautiful, accomplished young ladies whom I will have the pleasure of getting to know this season."

He gestures for us to join him in the center of the room.

Marion curtsies, and it seems the right thing, so the rest of us do it too, and suddenly the whole room is clapping and Prince Bram is smiling as he says, "I look forward to our time together, and to making one of you my wife."

Every person in this ballroom is staring at us, some with pity, some with jealousy, some with judgment, like there's already a betting pool for which of us will take the prize. At one of the seedier gentleman's clubs, there probably is. I wonder what my odds are. Yesterday's competition took so much out of me, I didn't have time to consider what this would feel like. But now, dressed up and on display, I feel desperately out of my depth.

The music strikes up again, and Bram extends his hand to Marion for a dance. She's the closest to him, so it could be nothing but convenience, but it smarts nonetheless. I watch as Olive's face crumbles into devastation, while Greer looks confused. Only Emmy's and Faith's faces remain as unreadable as ever.

A quadrille kicks up, and soon the ballroom is a swirling confection of silks and chiffon.

My mother has disappeared to gossip somewhere with her friends, and my father is off smoking cigars with the men. I feel a swell of pride that I gave them this acceptance. But the room is stifling with so many bodies, and I can hardly stand to watch Greer try to soothe Olive, who is now fully in tears. I don't miss it when Greer rotates their bodies just slightly so that Olive's tear-streaked face is in the eyeline of Prince Bram.

I scan the ballroom, looking for the other girls from yesterday, the ones who didn't make the top six, but they're nowhere to be found. I wonder if they were uninvited, or if the disappointment was too much to bear publicly.

Fiona Devon and Althea Jones sidle up to me. I would have called us friends once, before they ignored me pointedly for months. Neither presented themselves as Bram's suitors, so they'll have a typical season of husband hunting. "Hi, darling," Althea trills. "What did you bargain for?" She cuts right to the chase, no pretense of politeness or apology.

"You first." I smile sweetly. That is the point of tonight's ball, after all, to spread the news of every girl's new bargain. It always seemed unfair to me that the boys can make their bargains whenever they want, though plenty of them will this season, clever little business bargains that ensure their inheritance, shore up their estates, or expand their already impressive wealth.

Althea, like a lot of girls in this room, clearly bargained to become more beautiful. She blinks her now-thick eyelashes. "Oh, just a little tune-up here." She gestures at her flawless skin. "My hands and feet will be cold forever, but it's really not so bad. These grand houses are always so drafty anyway." She elbows Fiona, the quieter of the two, in the ribs. "Fiona's is hilarious. Tell her, Fee."

Fiona laughs shyly. "Her Majesty improved my singing voice, but now I'll forever vomit at the sight of frogs."

"After four hundred years, I think she must be running out of ideas," Fiona adds. "And what about you?"

"I didn't make one."

"Didn't make one?" Fiona repeats in confusion.

"I'm sorry . . . if you'll excuse me." I turn and skirt along the edge of the wall, wondering if I can sneak out to the garden for a moment of silence, to compose myself. My whole life, whenever I felt confused, I'd think to myself, *What would Lydia do?* Or whenever that failed, *What would Greer do?* But Lydia would be hiding, and Greer is in the corner with Emmy, laughing over a champagne tower, so I'm completely without a North Star.

I'm walking toward the open doors to the veranda when Viscountess Bolingbroke pops up in front of me like a banshee.

"Just where are you going?" she demands.

"Privy," I answer, and redirect my steps.

It'll be less welcome than the fresh air of the garden, but as a moment alone goes, it's better than nothing.

She nods and looks down at the watch pinned to her waistband. "You have five minutes. His Majesty will expect to dance with all his girls tonight."

The sounds of the ballroom are muffled in the carpeted hallway. I'm grateful for the silence, a moment to breathe.

I'm nearly to the end of the hall when a hand juts out of a room, snakes around my waist, and yanks me backward.

I fall into a body, tripping on my heavy skirts. Whoever has hold of me is strong enough to keep us both from falling.

The door slams, and I wheel around in terror to face my attacker, fists up.

It takes me a moment to get my bearings. The bedroom I've been pulled into is lit only by a small, flickering candle.

"Your Highness?" I gasp.

CHAPTER TEN

Prince Emmett loosens the cravat around his neck. "Sorry about that," he huffs.

Being caught in a bedroom with Bram's brother during a ball would ruin me all over again, and all my effort will have been for nothing.

He glances down to where my hands are balled into fists in front of my chest. "Are you going to punch me?" he asks.

He looked so casual in the carriage that night, but he's every inch the prince now. He's broad-shouldered, the planes of his cheeks and his straight nose are meant to be carved in marble, but there's a boyishness to him that the portraits never quite capture.

The muffled music of the quadrille is winding down. We don't have long before the viscountess will come looking for me.

I relax my hands. "Why won't you just leave me alone?"

He rakes an agonized hand through his hair. *"I can't."*

"Why not?"

Emmett hesitates.

I gather my skirts to leave. "I'm going."

He sidesteps to block the door.

I stare up at him, loathing his determination to ruin my reputation. He was so horrible to Lydia at a ball just like this one—maybe this is the only way he knows how to entertain himself.

"I'm not going to be one of your conquests." I shove him hard in the shoulder to move him, but he doesn't budge. "There's a party outside full of pretty girls who I am sure would be thrilled to be ruined by you. Go find one of them."

Undeterred, he doesn't move. He glares down at me, chewing on his bottom lip. "Did you cheat?"

"Cheat?" I ask, aghast.

"The May Queen competition yesterday, did you cheat? You have to tell me." He's panicked. It's an odd expression on someone who usually presents himself with the cool expression of elite detachment. He rakes his hand through his hair once more, and it falls in his face. Between that and the cravat, if anyone were to find us in this bedroom, they'd assume he'd been thoroughly debauched.

I push past him. "I'll be ruined if they find me with you."

He straightens up and lets out a low laugh. "You were a lot braver the first time I met you."

I roll my eyes. "I had a head injury."

"I remember. You ruined my favorite coat."

"It's your fault I was bleeding."

"All you need to do is say thank you."

"I'll send a lovely card along with the new coat I plan to buy you."

"No lasting damage, I presume? You look well."

I tilt my head so he can see the silvery line of the scar that runs along my temple. "It's had plenty of time to heal." I'd lied to my mother, told her I slipped in the bath and that's why I was black-and-blue for weeks. She was too preoccupied with Lydia to question me.

"I can't tell you how glad I am to hear it," he says.

I haven't any idea what's going on inside his head. All I know is that I need to get out of this room. I reach for the doorknob, but he stops me, placing his hand on the doorframe above my head, effectively caging me in.

"Give me the truth," he says, "and you can go back to the ball like nothing happened at all."

"Find me again, somewhere more private."

He shakes his head. "No. You'll tell me now."

"Nothing *has* happened, other than your failed attempt at seduction."

He crouches down so we're at eye level. His face is so close to mine I can see the constellation of faded freckles on the bridge of his nose, the tangled lashes that frame his sharp eyes.

"You think this is me trying to seduce you? If I were trying to seduce you, you'd know." He seems relieved that I'm finally standing still. It makes me want to kick him in the shins. "Once more, I beg of you, did you cheat?" he says.

"No. I didn't cheat. Now, if you'll excuse me, I'm off to dance with Bram."

I turn the doorknob, but Emmett juts his hand to stop it from opening.

"Wait—I hear voices." But he's not quick enough, and the door swings open, sending Emmett's entire body weight falling into me.

We tumble out of the bedroom through the open door and into the hallway. His legs tangle in my skirts, and I land hard on my back, with him on top of me.

I swear under my breath and try to roll out from under him, and he huffs and tries to pull me to my feet.

I have to hurry, if we're caught like this—

Suddenly, from the end of the hall, there's the sound of footsteps.

"Brother? Lady Ivy?" Bram stands stock-still, frozen in confusion at the sight of us.

My cheeks burn crimson with shame that is quickly evolving into panic. Emmett extends another hand to me, but I refuse it and push myself up off the ground.

"I can explain, I—"

Then, from behind Bram, comes someone else.

Tears well in Faith Fairchild's eyes at the sight of me and Prince Emmett, both out of breath, looking like we've been caught in a snare trap.

I expect her to turn to Bram, but instead her gaze stays fixed on a single point. Her voice breaks as she says his name, like she's said it a million times before. "Emmett?"

CHAPTER ELEVEN

Faith turns on her heel, and Emmett sprints after her, leaving me alone with Bram. For a moment we just stare at each other.

"I'm sorry—" I sputter at the exact same moment he says, "Are you all right?"

"I—what?" I expected scolding, outrage, anything other than the genuine concern on the prince's face.

"I can explain," I finally breathe out. "I went through the wrong door. His Highness was walking out at the same time I walked in. We collided is all."

"All right," he says again, looking at me with surprising kindness. There's a warmth to his features I didn't expect. "Would you like to dance?"

"It would certainly get Viscountess Bolingbroke off my back," I say.

Prince Bram laughs, and it lights up his whole face. I'm close enough to see the way his eyes crinkle at the edges. "She is a fearsome creature, is she not? I'd never leave you to her wrath. Shall we?" He extends a gloved hand, and I take it.

The ballroom is sparkling like a flute of champagne, completely drenched in golden candlelight.

Prince Bram takes me to the edge of the parquet floor as the orchestra kicks up a Viennese waltz. I've never danced with a boy—wasn't allowed to until I was officially "out" in society—but Bram is a steady lead even with my unsure feet.

Back when my parents still hosted dinner parties and Lydia and I were banished upstairs, we'd listen to the music drift up from the floors below. We'd grasp hands and twirl until gravity wrenched us apart and we landed on the floor, toppled over and laughing.

It's different like this, with a boy's broad shoulders under my palms. His back rises and falls under my hands, and it sends something kicking in my chest.

I'm an awkward partner. I don't quite know what to do with my limbs or where to move my head. It doesn't help that I'm still flustered from Emmett's infuriating confrontation. Twice, I step on Bram's toes. He doesn't say anything.

"You're a good dancer," I say, heart in my throat.

He grins as he turns us both in a wide circle around the floor. "I've had a lot of practice."

I scan the edge of the ballroom for Emmett and Faith, but they haven't returned.

In my distraction, I stumble, but Bram doesn't let me fall.

"Are your brother and Miss Fairchild acquainted?" I dare to ask.

"Their secrets aren't mine to tell."

I raise a brow. "Secrets—how scandalous."

He chuffs out a low laugh. "Scandal seems to be a favorite hobby of my dear brother."

The song ends, and Prince Bram bows to me. He begins to walk away.

"Wait!" I call. I'm not a romantic, I don't think it'll be me Bram chooses, but there's this . . . *tug* I feel toward him. I'm completely fascinated by this boy with an easy smile who healed my hand with magic like it was as simple as breathing.

He turns back to me, a question on his face.

"I didn't get the chance to thank you for the handkerchief."

His brows knit together in confusion. "What?"

"Yesterday, you tied your handkerchief around my hand to stop the bleeding. I wanted to say thank you."

A smile tugs at his lips. He looks so human, it would be easy to forget he's not.

He ducks his head shyly. "Thank you for believing I might be someone worth bleeding for, Lady Ivy."

Two songs later, Faith emerges to dance with Bram. She's a beautiful dancer, his equal in every way, but her eyes are rimmed with red.

Emmett has vanished completely.

Caledonia Cottage is a nightmare when all six of us and the viscountess are crammed inside like tinned fish. There's a kerfuffle before bed as Bolingbroke marches from room to room, counting us like chickens. But someone is always unaccounted for in the washroom, so we're one off, and she grows cross, convinced we're playing a prank on her.

When our tongue-lashing is over, Olive grows weepy over a missing doll, which Marion finds smushed at the bottom of her trunk.

Once everything has finally calmed down, Emmy wakes the whole house anew, clattering down the stairs in search of a midnight snack. ("I get hungry at night, and I miscounted the steps.") We light a candle, slice some bread, and wrap her ankle before going to sleep once more.

It's long past midnight when I jolt awake to see someone standing over me, a clammy hand clasped over my mouth. For a moment I think it's one of the other girls playing a prank, but the figure above me isn't laughing.

I kick wildly and raise my fists to swing, but in the time it takes for my eyes to adjust in the darkness, I see my lady's maid standing above me, her finger pressed over her mouth in a *shh* motion.

"Emmett sent me. Come quickly, now," she whispers.

I glance to where Faith is sleeping soundly.

"Tell him I didn't cheat and that I won't kiss him. I'm going back to sleep," I whisper.

She frowns. "I'm under instruction to report back. If you don't come with me, he's going to come here himself."

I groan and push myself up and out of bed, determined to end this business with him once and for all.

She leads me across the dark of Kensington Park, through the sunken garden, and into the orangery, a cavernous greenhouse of blooming citrus trees. The smell of orange blossoms hits me like a wall, and in the dark, the trees stretch toward the ceiling like spindly skeletons.

"What's your name?" I ask.

She turns back to me, the moonlight streaking across her face. She's got a tidy sort of face, her brown hair pulled back into a bun. I wonder if she's another of Emmett's girls.

"Charlotte Milbank, but everyone calls me Lottie."

Lottie's steps are quick and confident, like this is a route she knows well. She stops in front of the largest orange tree, one whose leaves brush the glass ceiling, and pushes it aside to reveal a nondescript door.

"I have no lantern. You must stay very close."

I reach my arms out and feel cool, rough stone around me on all sides.

We're in a tunnel.

My ragged breathing and the scraping of our shoes against the earth floor are the only sounds as we wind through the serpentine tunnels.

Before I can ask where we are, Lottie presses on a seam in the wall, and it swings open to reveal a room.

Suddenly there is a rush of fresh air and a strong hand in mine, helping me over the threshold. The room we've entered is warm, homey even, with teetering stacks of books and walls covered in tapestries. "Good evening," Emmett says with an infuriating smile, like he never doubted I'd come.

Against the wall opposite the fireplace is a four-poster bed covered in a forest green quilt. *We're in his bedroom.*

I'm too anxious to sit, and I don't want to give Emmett the impression that I intend to stay, so I position myself near the fireplace, next to the door.

Something rustles in the sheets, and I jump with a shriek. "What is *that*?"

Emmett shoves both hands into the quilt and scoops up a tiny, wriggling creature with scraggly wire hair and eyes bulging a little too far out of its skull.

"This *noble beast* is Pig."

Emmett tucks the little dog against his chest and gives it a kiss on top of its fuzzy head. "Bram has his hunting dogs. I have Pig. My dad gave him to me for my fifth birthday. As the story goes, I burst right into tears and asked why he'd given me a piglet, and the name stuck. He stays mostly in my room. Doesn't seem to like the smell of the queen."

His father, the queen's husband. "You must be close, you and your father," I say.

He turns suddenly to rearrange a nearby stack of books. "Something like that," he says tightly.

When he turns around again, the bravado is firmly back in place. "You told me to find you somewhere more private. Never let it be said that I do things by halves."

"I was speaking hypothetically. I didn't expect to be kidnapped by your henchman."

Lottie laughs. "This henchman is off to bed, good luck you two!"

"No, take me with you!" I protest.

Lottie doesn't listen; she shuts the hidden door behind her, leaving Emmett and me alone.

I stare him down, though I don't cut a very intimidating figure in my lace-trimmed nightdress.

Emmett furrows his brow as he sinks down onto the edge of his bed. "Why do you dislike me so much?"

"I—"

"And don't say it's because I ran you over. I absolutely did no such thing."

"You could have killed me!"

He huffs and leans back, now looking at the ceiling. "We're going to need to find some common ground."

"If I tell you why, will you let me leave?" I ask.

"You're not my prisoner. But I must admit I am curious."

My eyes sting at the memory. It was like a light within Lydia had been snuffed out by Emmett's hand. Some part of me has always blamed him for the way everything fell apart after.

It was two years ago. I was too young to attend events, but I was still awake, in the drawing room, reading with Papa, when Mama and Lydia clattered through the door, much too early to be home from a ball. It was Lydia's first season, soon after her bargain and debut at the Pact Parade, before things had gotten bad for her.

Lydia fell into Papa's arms, her body racked with big, heaving sobs. I rushed to kneel at her side.

"What happened?" I asked.

Mama was red-faced, talking too fast. "I can't be sure. One moment she was the belle of the ball, dancing with Prince Emmett himself; the next, she was stumbling, running from the party in this state. What happened, my darling?"

Lydia ran up the stairs, sobbing, screamed, "Leave me alone!" and slammed the door.

I called for a cup of tea and a few minutes later knocked softly on her door. I entered to find her crying, still in her rumpled gown.

"I'm off to murder him after delivering this tea, so you might as well tell me what he did," I said.

She looked up at me with her tear-streaked face. "We were dancing, and everything was fine. But then he—" Lydia hiccupped. "He asked me to meet him alone in the garden. When I told him no, he told me I didn't belong there, that I should go home."

"That's it. I'm killing him."

Lydia let out a watery laugh, "I'm sure you can find him in the garden with some other girl."

She told me later that it was particularly devastating because she suspected he was right. I could see how what he'd said haunted her.

I've hated him ever since.

I turn to Emmett now, his face unreadable in the low light of his room. "Two years ago, you attempted to seduce my sister at the Vaughns' ball, and when she rejected you, you told her she didn't belong there. She cried all night."

Emmett sits up, a disarmingly confused look on his face as he searches for the memory. "Lydia Benton? When did we?" His face falls. "Oh—"

"So you do remember?"

"Yes, but it wasn't what you think."

I reach for the hidden door. "I said why I don't like you. Now please let me leave. That was our deal—"

Emmett interrupts me. "She was hyperventilating."

"What?"

"Lydia. She was hyperventilating when I asked her to dance with me."

"That seems cruel, to pull a breathless girl into a dance."

"No, not like that. I could see her, sitting alone in the corner, panicking. I know how it feels at those awful parties. All those people watching you like you're something for sale, waiting for you to do something worth gossiping about. I was trying to give her an escape."

"That doesn't explain the rest of it."

Emmett sighs. "I asked her to come to the garden with me so she could catch her breath."

I shake my head. "You told her she didn't belong there."

Emmett throws his hands up in frustration. "It was a compliment! I hate nearly all those miserable people!"

"Oh." It finally sinks in that Emmett was trying to do the right thing. I don't like feeling stupid like this.

"Yeah. *Oh.*" Emmett rises from the bed and crosses the room to me. "Is it my turn now?"

I look down at my muddy bare feet. "I suppose that seems fair."

"Bram said you were a terrible dancer," he begins.

"That's what you pulled me out of bed in the middle of the night to say?"

"What if it was?"

"I'm more than my dancing!" I protest, annoyance back in full force.

"Sure, but it's going to come up time and time again this season. Do you want to look like a fool?"

"You're deflecting." But he isn't wrong.

"No. I'm proposing a solution. We talk while I teach you to waltz. Two birds, one stone, you'll be back in your bed within the hour."

"And if I refuse?"

"I'm your only hope of making it back through those tunnels. You can try the front door, but servants talk. Ivy Benton leaving Emmett De Vere's bedroom on the first night of the competition for his brother's hand? My, what a story that would be."

"I thought you were trying to prove to me that you're not horrible."

He arches a brow. "I didn't say I'm not horrible."

I huff out in frustration and extend my arms to him. "Fine."

He takes a step forward, wraps one arm around my waist, and takes my other hand in his.

My hair is loose around my shoulders, and the heat of him is stifling through my thin nightdress.

He starts counting out softly. "We start with the basics. One, two, three, one, two, three."

We're barely moving, but I can't quite get my balance. "Stop looking at your feet," he says. "Up here, at me."

There are those eyes again. Looking at me as if he's trying to undo a knot.

We settle into a rhythm. *Step, slide, step.* "Let's play a game. We each get a question. We each tell the truth. We go one by one."

Something straightforward for once. "Deal."

"Ladies first."

"Why won't you leave me alone?" I stumble, but his steady arms keep me upright.

"Because I need you to win. I intend to help you."

"Why—"

He shakes his head.

"My turn," he interjects. "Why were you wearing boots yesterday?"

"My family is too poor to afford new shoes." It feels like betraying them to admit it. "Why do you need me to win?"

Step, slide, step.

"My father's life's work depends on it. Is that what you bargained for? Something to help your family financially?"

I step on his toes.

He winces. "Try to keep your steps the same length every time."

"I didn't make a bargain," I say. "What was your bargain?" He's been eighteen for months, surely he's made one by now.

He shakes his head almost imperceptibly. "I'll never make a

bargain," he murmurs. "Why didn't *you* make one?"

I don't know how to explain succinctly. "I tried. I asked her to undo my sister's bargain, but she said it couldn't be done. There was nothing else I wanted."'

"Nothing?"

I shake my head. "It's not your turn."

"You didn't ask me anything, I figured I'd take my chances." There's a hint of a grin playing at the edge of his mouth.

"What is your father's work?" I ask. "Why does it depend on me winning?"

"Now it's time to attempt turning." He guides us in a wide circle. "Stop trying to lead."

"I'm not trying to lead! You're deflecting again."

"My father wishes to build a world better than this one. I share his wish."

I'm getting frustrated. "But what on earth does that have to do with me?" There's a storm raging behind Emmett's eyes. There's so much he's not telling me, so I decide to lay my own cards on the table.

"You want the truth? My sister's disappearance ruined not only her, but our whole family. We're sullied. Notorious. A laughingstock. I stood no chance of any invitations this season without this competition. My sister can't remember her bargain, nor anything from the weeks she disappeared, and I can't shake the feeling that they're linked. I thought if I could get the queen to reverse it, give my sister her memory back, she might begin to heal. But then the queen announced the competition for Bram's hand, and I saw, for the first time in months, an opportunity to help my family get back into society's good graces. We're going to lose our house. My father's tenant farms are failing. His business associates wouldn't speak to him before, but they might now. He could get a loan. I could make things right. My mother might stop crying so often."

Emmett's steps have slowed. We've stopped dancing, but he's still holding me in his arms.

"She wouldn't undo your sister's bargain?" Emmett whispers.

"She said the bargain cannot be undone, it doesn't work like that. And I hate her for it. I hate the things she's done to my family and to everyone else. I hate her. I'd be a terrible princess because of it. Bram won't pick me. He shouldn't."

Emmett's eye narrow. "You hate her?"

"As much as I've ever hated anything."

"And you want to undo your sister's bargain?"

"That's what I just said, isn't it?"

"We need each other, you and I."

My heart quickens. "What do you mean?"

"My father's bargain was this." He gestures vaguely to the palace walls around him. "My mother died in childbirth. For the first eight years of my life, it was just my father and me. He read books to me. We played in the garden, fought with little wooden swords. Sometimes I don't even know which memories are real and which ones I made up. It's all bathed in this hazy light. He was all I had. And then he married Queen Mor and bargained to legitimize me as a prince. The cost was that he could never speak to me again. Suddenly I was alone, in big, drafty palace rooms, with only toy soldiers and a governess to keep me company. I didn't understand. I still don't completely. I had a lonely childhood and then a lonely adolescence. It wasn't until Bram showed up that I remembered what it was like to have a family."

"You have my sympathy, but I'm not sure what that has to do with me," I say, confused.

Emmett rolls his eyes. "Are you always this impatient?"

"No." *Yes.*

"I was twelve when I first started finding the notes hidden in the books. My father, unable to speak to me any other way, started dog-earing passages and underlining words and phrases. He was communicating with me. It took me years to put it all together. He wants to unseat the queen."

My blood runs cold. Unseat the queen? If she found out about even a hint of rebellion, we would all be destroyed. She's hung people at Traitors' Gate for much less. "How?" It comes out in a whisper.

"I've spent the last six years researching. Books on the Others are forbidden, most were burned long ago, but from what I gather, a faerie bargain can be broken one of two ways. The first way is that the fae who made the bargain agrees to undo it. Obviously this is extremely unlikely."

My mind flashes to Mrs. Osbourne's storybook turning to ashes in the kitchen hearth. "But there is another way?"

"A faerie bargain is null and void if the fae who made it violates the terms of their own bargain. Queen Mor's first bargain was with King Edward on the battlefield. That bargain made her queen. All subsequent bargains have been made between a queen and her subjects."

I take a breath as understanding dawns on me. "Which means, if we can get her to violate the terms of the bargain she made with King Edward, every other bargain will be void. The whole system will crumble."

Emmett smiles in approval. "Exactly."

"But how do we get her to do that?"

"First, we have to figure out exactly what the wording of that bargain was. Which I believe my father has already done."

Emmett crosses the room to his desk and pulls out stacks of paper, pages ripped from books, torn scraps of fabric with ink scrawls all over them. I don't see how anyone could make sense of them. But Emmett begins to lay them on the floor in an arrangement clearly only he understands.

All of England, yours to reign over
The cities, valleys, and fields of clover
The one twice crowned, the ruler of all
As long as your heart beats, yours to call
These terms shall not bend
A sovereign twice crowned shall rule to the end.

"What do you think?" Emmett asks.

"That's some seriously bad poetry."

"Not the point I'm trying to make."

The words rattle around in my head. "Twice crowned? That's an odd phrase."

Emmett nods. "That was her trick. Edward thought she meant him, crowned once on the battlefield and once at Eltham Palace. But she meant herself, crowned once as queen of the Otherworld and once as queen here."

"How would we break it? King Edward is dead."

"But his bargain remains. She's already crowned you as May Queen." Emmett leans forward, his eyes flickering in the firelight. "If you win, you'll be crowned again as princess. 'The *one* twice crowned' will now be two. Her bargain will be void."

My head is spinning. "But why would she crown anyone as May Queen if it could threaten her rule like that?"

"It's been over four hundred years. Maybe she's gotten complacent and forgotten. Or maybe she's certain the one who won May Queen won't be selected as Bram's bride. We have to make sure Bram is so in love with you that even if his own mother says he cannot have you, he will elope. We have to make him love you. Love you for real."

An uncomfortable feeling curdles in my stomach. Sedition, trickery, risking my family, everything I've ever held dear for a shot in the dark.

Emmett must sense my hesitation, because he leans in. "It has to be you, Ivy. This is our only chance of unseating her, of creating an England free of her bargains and her cruelty. We could bring this country into the modern world."

"How does Bram feel about all this? Why not just tell him?"

"Bram loves his mother too much to betray her. And even if he wanted to, the Others can't lie. I can't confide this to him. It puts everyone at too much risk."

"I—" I stutter, but there's no way to verbalize the storm raging within me. It's all too much to take in.

"You're the only hope I have."

I cross the room in anxious pacing. "My family never thought I'd make a match, even at the best of times. I'm awkward and mouthy and not a beauty, not like my sister or the other girls in the competition. How am I supposed to make a prince fall in love with me?"

"You don't see yourself very clearly, do you?"

I stop, finally still, but he's been looking at me the whole time.

"You really were just trying to help Lydia that night?" I ask.

He blinks slowly, then nods. "She looked like she needed a friend."

"What about the night you ran me over—did I look like I needed a friend too?"

You know, you're really quite pretty.

He laughs like I've made a joke. "That was different."

An awkward silence stretches between us, and he crosses the room to me.

"I'm scared," I say. It feels worth telling him the truth.

Emmett places both hands on my shoulders, the warm weight of them steadying.

His voice is low and serious, but his eyes flicker like coals in the fire. "If you let me help you, Ivy Benton, you could be queen."

CHAPTER TWELVE

The other girls and I spend the next day at etiquette lessons, but I can barely focus, with Emmett's conversation from last night playing in my head.

That evening, we're summoned to the queen's private apartments for dinner.

She sits at the end of the table in a gown of green silk so dark it's almost black, a pearl tiara settled atop her dark hair. Behind her is a roaring fireplace, casting the room in oppressive warmth. There's a chandelier covered in live gardenias and white orchids. I spot an iridescent green beetle crawling for cover between the petals.

"Ladies, do come in." Her cool voice calls us as we skitter into the room like a flock of birds.

Faith and I haven't spoken since yesterday. She's avoided making all eye contact with me, but she's seated next to me now.

The queen pulls out this morning's newspaper and places it on the table.

"It seems you have already made quite the splash."

I peer around Faith's shoulder to get a better look. In bold black letters is the headline **THE SIX**.

The queen picks up the paper and begins to read. "'The lovely young ladies impressed at Count Twombley's ball, marking their first appearance in polite society as official suitors of the Prince of Wales.'"

The door to the dining room swings open, and Bram comes striding in, his muddy boots leaving footprints on the carpet.

"Mother." He leans down and gives Queen Mor a kiss on the cheek. Then he turns and gives us a short bow. "Ladies, I apologize for my tardiness."

"How was the shooting, darling?" Queen Mor asks, a warmth to her voice I've never heard.

Bram plops down in the empty chair next to her. "Terrible, but I must admit I am always a little relieved when the birds escape with their lives."

A parade of white-gloved footmen come into the dining room to serve us, but the queen sits alone at the head of the table, without a plate in front of her.

We eat in awkward silence for a few minutes, except Bram, who appears unfazed. He wears a gold ring on each finger, and they click against his wineglass as he takes a sip.

The queen looks over at us and twists her mouth into an unsettling smile. In the candlelight, her moonlight-pale skin appears almost luminescent. "As a mother, I prioritize my son's happiness above all else."

"Oh, that's embarrassing," Bram says good-naturedly. "I beg of you, please don't make me sound like a coddled mama's boy."

She faces him and crinkles her nose, an expression that's unnatural on her beautiful face. "I wouldn't dare."

She turns back to the rest of us. "It's my deepest desire to ensure that Bram ends the season with his best possible match. We have only twelve weeks, and during that time my son will be traveling between London and Oxford, as he's still finishing up his exams. Because of that, he has made a list of traits he seeks in a wife, and he's generously allowed me to advise him." She gestures to her son. "Tell them, darling."

Bram takes another sip of wine and pulls a paper from his breast pocket. "I hope for someone who is clever, dedicated, honest, and determined."

He puts the paper back in his pocket, and his mother goes on.

"During your stay, you'll take lessons with Viscountess Bolingbroke and lessons with me. I will evaluate you each in the traits my son has asked for and advise him on who will be the best bride—"

"Though the final choice is mine," Bram interrupts.

The queen pats his arm. "Of course it is, my darling."

I shift uncomfortably as I remember what Emmett said to me last night. We must make him love me so completely, he'll marry me no matter what his mother says.

The clock strikes ten as we push back our chairs and rise to leave. We're nearly to the door when the queen clears her throat, and we pause.

"Girls, wait a minute."

Bram pauses by the door.

"Not you, dear, we're discussing female things," the queen says.

We're left alone with the queen, who gestures for us to return to the table. "There's no need for Bram to know the details of our lessons. Men are such sensitive creatures. Not like us." The firelight reflects off her tiara, and I realize I was wrong. It's not inlaid with pearls, but with human teeth.

"Yes, ma'am," we all say.

Queen Mor takes her empty wineglass and pushes it toward Emmy, the closest girl to her right.

"A tear to ensure your silence."

We glance at each other uneasily, but the others know as well as I do, we have no real choice in this, not if we still want to be considered as Bram's bride.

"You want me to cry?" Emmy asks.

"Just one tear."

Emmy hesitates, then plucks out an eyelash hard enough to make her eyes water. One fat tear slides down the edge of the glass.

Marion wrenches her eyes open until they get dry enough to cry, and next to her, Olive and Faith follow suit.

Greer is trying to do the same but can't manage it. "Slap me," she begs.

I hesitate.

She swears under her breath at me, then slaps herself hard enough across the face that just watching it is enough to make me cry too.

She passes me the glass and I let one tear flow into it.

The queen looks us over and smiles. "What good girls you are."

As we rise to leave, the queen knocks the glass to the floor, shattering it. I don't think she needed our tears for the magic at all, she just wanted to watch us squirm. Disgust climbs up my throat.

A footman carrying a silver tray pushes past me as I'm nearly out the door. I turn back and make direct eye contact with Queen Mor as the cloche is lifted.

We leave the queen alone to take her evening meal, and it's only once the door shuts that I realize what it was: a bowl of milk and honey.

CHAPTER THIRTEEN

We wake the next morning to a flurry of activity in our little cottage. Our cook is in the kitchen below, with an army of maids setting out a lavish breakfast in our dining room. Three lady's maids, one per room, wake us all and get to work setting our hair in elaborate updos and lacing us into corsets and the fine silk gowns provided by the Crown for our season. Lottie's face betrays nothing of our secret rendezvous.

Once dressed and fed, we're shepherded by footmen across the dew-damp lawn to the main palace, where Viscountess Bolingbroke awaits us in a parlor.

"Welcome, girls, to your first etiquette lesson," she trills as we sit down in uncomfortable embroidered love seats, our skirts fanning out around us. "These lessons will work in tandem with Her Majesty's to ensure that whomever Bram picks is prepared for the royal duties that await her."

I expect to set a table or learn English history, but instead she leads us in a series of bizarre exercises, drilling us for hours in riddles, maths, and word puzzles.

We're given lap desks and sheets of paper. I've never been good at sitting down for school, and I keep getting distracted, gazing out the window at the green grass of Kensington Park. It's busy today, lots of governesses pushing perambulators and women twirling silk parasols. My mind keeps floating back to Emmett. How am I supposed to make Bram fall in love with me when we haven't been allowed any time together?

I wonder what my parents are doing right now. What about Lydia? Has she been told about losing the house?

Viscountess Bolingbroke raps her bony knuckle on the side of my desk. "Focus, Benton!"

Marion tips her page slightly toward me, and I copy her answers.

I suppose Bram did say he wanted a girl who was clever.

After tea, we gather on the south lawn. The queen is surrounded by a group of ladies-in-waiting, fanning themselves with feather fans, next to a champagne tower. Lingering on the edge of the crowd, I spot Bram and Emmett.

The party falls into a hush as we arrive. I hear whispers of "*The six.*"

It's Viscountess Bolingbroke who makes the announcement, but everyone still faces the queen, like she's the center of gravity and we're all in her orbit. "What better way to welcome you to Kensington Palace than with a bit of merriment," says the viscountess. "This afternoon, Her Majesty invited a few select friends to join us for a hedge maze. In the center, you'll find a small prize. Her Majesty loves a game."

It is said that games were often how the Others lured humans in order to make bargains with them. They'd ask them to play a round of marbles or jacks or billiards and then enchant the objects to ensure their victory.

There is some debate among underground faerie scholars regarding which games humans invented and which were introduced to us by our strange visitors.

Queen Mor's face twists into a smile as she picks up a full glass of champagne and smashes it on the ground. "Go!"

There's a flurry of laughter as everyone takes off into the maze. Olive drags me by the hand, giggling. "Let's find Bram."

We run into Emmy first, who is trying to climb the walls. "I see Marion!" Emmy shouts from halfway up the hedge. "Hi, Marion!"

From somewhere I hear Marion's distant "Hello!"

Greer smacks into my side as she does a full circle in an attempt to go left. I feel a little guilty for laughing. "Should we wait for her?" I ask Olive.

"No!" Olive squeals, and pulls me away by the hand.

Emmy points left. "The boys are that way, let's go!"

Greer shouts and kicks dirt at us as we sprint away.

We reach a fork, and Emmy and Olive take the one to the left. I veer right alone.

The hedge maze is darker here, and I soon hear the low sound of voices arguing.

I run into a dead end and find Faith and Emmett, standing too close. "Just tell me the truth—" It sounds like she's begging him.

I turn to go, but they freeze as they spot me. Faith walks away from Emmett, and as she passes me, she shoves me hard enough that I stumble backward into the hedge, the prickly branches cutting my arms.

"Faith!" Emmett exclaims in horror and then extends a hand to pull me from the hedge. "Are you all right?" he asks me.

I pull a clump of leaves from my hair. "I'll survive."

"Good," Emmett says. "Now go flirt with Bram."

"Flirt?" I reply in horror. I've never flirted with anyone.

"Yes, now's a perfect chance." Before I can say no, he yells, "Brother, this way!" and Bram rounds the corner, grinning.

Emmett raises his brows and nods toward his brother. "Uh, hi," I say.

"Hello," Bram replies good-naturedly.

"Lady Ivy, tell Bram that hilarious thing you were just telling me," Emmett says. I could kill him.

"Um—" I rack my brain for anything clever I've ever said. "Shrimps' hearts are in their heads," I stammer.

"What?" Bram says at the same time that Emmett says "What?" even louder.

"Uh, shrimps' hearts—"

"No, we heard you," Emmett says.

"Are you . . . fond of shrimp?" Bram asks.

"Not particularly."

"Oh," Bram says while Emmett stands behind him, looking at me wide-eyed and horrified.

"I'll go now." I turn to walk in the opposite direction.

"Wait, no, the *other* hilarious thing!" Emmett calls, and I run, not toward the center of the maze, but to hide from him.

I lose him and spend the next few minutes wandering aimlessly down corridor after corridor. Suddenly, completely by mistake, I find myself in the middle of the maze. Bram is already there, a golden trophy slung in his hand.

Emmett appears, seconds after me, out of breath, with a sheen of sweat on his forehead. He pushes his hair away from his face.

He tackles Bram good-naturedly. "Must you always win?"

Bram laughs along with him. "Yes."

OLIVE LISONBEE

I miss the kitchen at our country house in Hampshire. I miss our cook, Mrs. Varvel, and the way she used to wake up before sunrise to roll out pastry dough with me. I miss foraging for mushrooms with my baby sister on my hip. I've never felt quite comfortable in my skin, but this homesickness hurts in places I haven't felt before.

The kitchen in Caledonia Cottage is smaller, and I am here all alone. There's a rack of gleaming copper pots above my head and an unfamiliar brick floor beneath my bare feet.

But at least the fire is roaring and the lanterns are lit. I peer out the plate glass window and look hopefully to the horizon. The first blue streaks of dawn aren't here yet, I've got another few hours until their welcome arrival.

I don't remember a time I wasn't terrified of the dark. It was humiliating to ask Marion if I could keep the lantern lit all night and even more humiliating when she replied yes with that pitying expression she always has on her face when she looks at me.

She means well. They all mean well. Except maybe Faith, but I'm certain it's just because she doesn't know me yet.

Maybe if I win, they could all be my ladies-in-waiting. Then we'd all be friends forever. What fun that would be.

But I don't think I'm going to win. I should have asked the queen for something better than a pretty face with perfect teeth. I should have asked her to make me brave like Ivy or funny like Emmy or interesting like Faith.

But Mother said someone would fall in love with my smile, and I liked the sound of that.

I tap flour out on the butcher block and roll out the square of dough into a long, flat oval. This is my favorite part, the part where I get my hands dirty.

A log in the fireplace pops and I nearly jump out of my skin.

My governess used to say I was afraid of my own shadow. I think it was supposed to be a figure of speech, but it was true. It felt like it was chasing me.

The dark makes me feel like I'm being watched. I like that even less.

I long for my room at home, with its big window that faces east. There was a lantern on every table, and the shadows were familiar.

I begged my mother all winter to let me delay my coming-out at least a year. I felt so unprepared for the season and what was expected of me after it, but she refused, saying it would cause nothing but gossip.

When the queen announced the competition for Prince Bram's hand the day of the Pact Parade, I was relieved. Bram has such a sweet face and gentle demeanor. He seemed like the kind of boy from the books I read.

And being a princess seemed a more palatable prospect than being a *wife*.

Logically, of course, I knew I'd still be a wife, but it was different this way. Easier to stomach.

And I was right about Bram. He's a dream. He's been nothing but a perfect gentleman, the model of a prince right out of a storybook. He sent a footman with a handwritten thank-you note yesterday after I had a basket of iced buns delivered to him.

But I didn't expect to feel so foolish around the other girls. They seem so much more grown-up than me. Faith told me yesterday that she's kissed at least a dozen boys, and Marion already knows how to run a household and doesn't need any lights on to sleep.

Even poor, disgraced Ivy Benton seems to have a better chance than I do. Bram couldn't keep his eyes off her after they danced at the Twombleys' ball. He wiped the tears from my cheeks when he danced with me, but the sting of watching him with the others didn't fade.

Sometimes I feel like one day every other girl was given instructions on how to grow up, and I missed the lesson. It's why I love baking so much. There's no subtext or secrets in a recipe.

As I work the dough, I think of Bram. On nights like this I play out a little fantasy in my head, imagining that he visits the cottage late at night and finds me the only one awake. We talk for hours, and when dawn breaks, he takes me in his arms and kisses me as the first rays of sunlight dance across the grass.

In my dreams he tells me that he likes me just the way I am, that I'm the prettiest, most special girl he's ever met.

He'll fall in love with your smile. That's what my mother said. I just have to keep smiling. Stiff upper lip. *Don't let them see how scared you are.*

The day of the Pact Parade, I clasped my hands in front of me to keep them from shaking. The queen wasn't as scary as I thought she'd be. She smiled at me kindly and told me I was a very pretty girl. That was nice. She didn't have to say any of that.

When I told her I wanted a perfect smile, she said she thought it would suit me well. I made the deal in exchange for my fingernails easily. It doesn't bother me nearly as much as it seems to bother everyone else. It's honestly convenient. There's no more dough stuck down under them.

I take a spoonful of soft yellow butter and smear it across the rolled-out brioche.

The creak of a footstep in the hall makes me jump. "Who's there?" I whisper.

No answer comes. I'm always imagining things.

I return to my dough. But when I look up again, there's a figure darkening the doorway.

I shriek and drop my spoon with a clatter. The figure steps into the light. It's only a footman. I sigh in relief, but he crosses the kitchen with heavy footfalls and grabs me in his arms so tight my ribs are nearly crushed.

I open my mouth to scream, but a vial is tipped between my lips. The liquid slides down my throat, bitter and thick.

"I'm sorry, miss," the footman whispers.

He scoops me up into his arms, and before I can protest, I am unconscious.

I don't know how much time has passed when I come to with a gasp. The first thing I register is the pain of rocks digging directly into my spine. The second thing is how cold I am.

I'm shivering under my nightdress.

I blink my eyes open to an ink-black sky, a sliver of a moon, a smattering of stars.

I'm outdoors. *Why am I outdoors?*

There's a gasp to my left, a sniffle, someone cries out.

I push myself up and look over to find Marion, Emmy, Faith, Greer, and Ivy, all as dazed as I am, in their nightdresses as well.

There are footsteps in the trees. I grip Ivy's hand as someone approaches behind us.

Queen Mor's first lesson has begun.

CHAPTER FOURTEEN

Emmy springs to her feet first, then hauls Marion up after her.

"That bitch," Marion snaps. She hugs her arms tight around her middle to keep from shivering.

"Shh," Greer replies, gesturing across the clearing where the queen sits in an elevated chair like some kind of tennis referee. She's draped in furs to protect against the biting night air, and she has a pair of delicate gold opera glasses pressed to her face.

She's surrounded by her footmen, who are holding trays of steaming drinks and draping blankets across her lap.

"Where the hell are we? And how did we get here?" Emmy asks.

Olive pushes herself up onto her hands blearily. Her ginger hair is loose around her shoulders, and her eerie fingernail-less hands are covered in what looks like flour. "A sleeping tincture, I think," she says. "A footman accosted me in the kitchens and poured something vile down my throat."

That explains the bitter taste in my mouth. The idea of someone looming over my bed in the dark to knock me out makes me want to vomit.

The lights of Kensington Palace flicker in the distance. We're still on palace grounds, but the darkness around us is complete. In front of us is a solid wall of trees, their leaves rustling like phantoms in the dark.

We all jump at the sound of snapping twigs.

A footman appears, holding a lantern. In his other hand is a silver tray and a folded square of parchment. He stares at us, unnervingly still, until Emmy takes the paper from him.

She unfolds it gingerly and reads out, "'The prize is in the middle. Good luck.'"

"A prize in the—" Greer questions, but she's cut off by the groan of *something*.

I stretch my hand out in front of me and feel a wall of small, waxy leaves. I wheel around and feel the same on the other side.

"It's the hedge maze." Marion puts it together at the same time I do.

Relief courses through me. We've already done the maze in the light of day. I remember the way well enough.

We can no longer see the queen, but I am certain she's watching us through her opera glasses.

Greer takes off running, disappearing into the depths of the maze, her white nightdress trailing behind her like a ghost.

Olive bursts into tears.

Seeing her in such distress stokes the fires of my hatred for the queen. "It'll be all right," I tell her. "Please don't cry."

I take a step toward her, but then the ground shakes again and more hedges spring from the ground, growing *up, up, up,* until I've been cut off from the others completely. My blood runs cold as I realize that this isn't going to be anything like this afternoon's maze.

"Ivy?" Olive shrieks.

"Olive? Emmy? Ivy?" Marion calls back. The hedges have separated us all.

"Who's there?" Emmy shouts.

Then Olive starts screaming.

That's when I run.

I whip around. In front of me is a fork, the hedges at least ten feet tall.

I cut to the left, another fork, left again.

Olive's frantic screaming is getting fainter.

I look up to the sky and try to get my bearings. What was it the footman's note said? *The prize is in the middle.*

I take the right fork this time, distracted by the rough soil biting into the soft soles of my bare feet, when a body slams into mine.

Just like earlier today, Greer is stuck, spinning in a circle in an attempt to go left.

"Good luck, Greer!" I take the path to the left and leave her alone, cursing in frustration.

I'm sprinting toward what I hope is the center of the maze when a hedge springs up from the ground, throwing me flat on my back.

The wind is knocked from my lungs. I push myself up to find my nightdress ripped and the palms of my hands shredded and bloody.

I slowly rise to my feet, faltering as blinding pain shoots through my body. It's like pure fire is running up the column of my spine and down my limbs. In the space of a heartbeat it is gone, but it leaves me shaking in the aftermath.

I take off again, more careful this time. Something white flashes in my peripheral vision, and I pause, thinking it's another girl in her nightdress, but it's charging at me in a flash.

Not a girl—a . . . goose? I nearly laugh, but then it expands its massive wings and flaps at me until my back is flush against the sharp edges of the maze.

No, not a goose—*a swan*. The biggest swan I've ever seen. It lunges at me and bites my ankle hard enough to draw blood. I cry out.

It lunges again, its sharp beak connecting with the soft skin below my knee. I swear and kick at it, but that only makes it angrier.

There's a clatter of metal next to me, and I look down to see a sword, a full-blown sword with a ruby-encrusted handle, spit out by the maze.

I scoop it up off the ground, and the wretched swan takes the opportunity to bite onto a lock of my hair and yank me to the dirt. I kick and kick, but it just keeps pulling, so I lift the sword and behead the creature in one fell swoop.

It dies with a honk, a splatter of blood, and a storm of white feathers. Then its body crumbles to dust, like it was never real at all, but its blood remains splashed across my face.

I'm panting desperately. It's getting darker by the moment, as if the moon is being dimmed.

Every minute or two I hear screams from other sections of the maze. I think I hear a low laugh too, but that could be my imagination.

I round a corner and find nothing but a solid hedge in front of me. I turn back to see the passage I came from knit together, trapping me in a box.

Do I climb like Emmy did earlier today?

I slash at one wall with my sword, but it doesn't make so much as a dent. I cry out in frustration.

Suddenly, glowing script appears on one wall, as if an invisible hand is writing it in front of me.

I'm always running but have no feet; I have a bed but do not sleep.

A riddle? Somewhere to my right someone is screaming. They sound close.

"Who's there?" I call.

The walls of the hedge inch closer, closing me in. I try to steady my breathing. It's no good if I panic. I wish I'd paid attention during lessons today instead of copying Marion's answers.

I read the riddle once more: *I'm always running but have no feet; I have a bed but do not sleep.*

"A river!" I shout, and a hole opens up in the hedge in front of me, barely large enough to step through.

The hedge closes behind me the moment I'm on the other side, and I'm faced with yet another blocked path, boxed in between hedges in a space so small I can't extend my arms.

What breaks but never falls, what falls but never breaks.

More screaming. "Olive?" I call. "Emmy?" I shouldn't have left Greer alone, spinning in circles.

From over the hedge comes the sound of footsteps getting closer, steady and persistent. Or is that a heartbeat? The ticking of a clock? I cover my ears to find that the sound is coming from inside my own head.

Tick, tick, tick.

I need to focus. I squeeze my eyes shut and do my best to tune it out.

"Day and night!" I answer the riddle, and the hedge splits open, revealing yet another closed chamber.

The incessant pounding in my ears is tearing me apart from the inside out, thrumming through my bones with a force strong enough to splinter them.

What three numbers, none of which is zero, give the same result whether they're added or multiplied?

Shit. I've always been rotten at maths.

"Anyone there?" I call. No answer.

The walls inch inward. "Help!" Still nothing.

If I don't move, I'll soon be crushed. I do the only thing I can think of and begin to climb.

The hedges are covered in razor-sharp thorns, and it is nearly impossible to get a firm hold on them. My hands and feet are slick with blood; it drips all over the leaves and into the dirt below.

I'm halfway up the hedge when a vine lashes out and snakes around my ankle like the loop of a lasso. It yanks me hard, and I fall to the ground, sputtering, wheezing as I crawl my way back upright.

The riddle has disappeared and in its place are the words *Tell me a secret.*

I think of all the secrets I am keeping, so many they may burst out of me at any moment. Emmett's face pops into my mind, but not the night alone in his room, the particular way he chewed on his bottom lip at the ball.

I think of my sister and all the stinging, awful ways I still resent her.

I think of the queen and how I hate her.

I think of Emmett's rebel father.

I look down at my blood-soaked nightdress and say the truest words I can think of, the words I wouldn't say to anyone.

"I am afraid."

The hedge opens, and I sprint down the corridor. A snake slithers in front of me with a hiss, and I drive my sword into the top of its head and try to not vomit at the crunch.

I turn and find another dead end. The hedge behind me knits together, and I'm trapped once more.

In front of me sits a table with seven glass jars atop it. Six of the jars are marked with our names, *Ivy, Olive, Greer, Emmy, Marion, Faith.* The seventh is full of sea glass marbles.

There are a few scattered marbles already in the other jars. One in mine. Two in Faith's. One in Marion's.

I don't know what it means, but I have a vague notion of what I'm meant to do. I pick a marble from the jar and run my fingers over the smooth glass surface. I plink it into Olive's jar at random, and as soon as it hits the bottom, there is a shrieking scream of pure pain from somewhere in the maze.

My blood turns to ice, and I think of the blinding pain I experienced minutes ago, seemingly from nowhere.

Steeling myself, too curious to resist, I pick up another marble and drop it into my own jar.

The pain is so complete I can't hold myself upright. It runs down each of my limbs like I'm being stabbed in a thousand places at once. My knees hit the ground as I collapse in on myself like a dying star.

Then, as soon as it started, it is over, and I can breathe again.

I look at the jars in horror, then pick up the jar of marbles and shatter it on the ground. They roll everywhere, and I step over them and the broken glass and continue on my way.

The blood, both mine and the swan's, has dried in big, sticky patches, and I'm shivering under the thin fabric of my ruined night-dress. My knuckles are white around the hilt of the sword.

Then, like a miracle, I round another corner and see a perfectly square crossroad and, in the middle, a golden goblet on a mirror-glass table.

I sprint for it, more desperate for this to be over than to win. My feet, having gone numb ages ago, slide in the spring-damp earth.

From the corner of my eye comes a flash of white. Emmy emerges, running, from the opposite hedge. She's faster than I am, closer too.

Greer is there too, but she's come out on the wrong side and has to turn in a full circle to face the direction of the goblet.

I'm so focused on her, I don't even see Faith until I collide with her. Both of us topple to the ground in a tangle of limbs. Our skulls crash together, making my head spin.

"Yes!" Emmy exclaims in victory. She snatches the goblet from its perch and reaches inside, producing a small roll of parchment and reading out in confusion: "'You win.'"

"What?" Faith half moans from where we're both splayed out on the dirt.

"That's what it says. *You win*."

"Damn you, Ivy!" Faith shoves me hard in the shoulder, rolling me off of her.

"You ran into me!" I shout back.

Our bickering is stopped by a deep rumble. The three of us freeze as the hedge maze sinks back down into the earth, swallowed by the soil as if it were never here at all.

What was once the maze is now a large dirt field. The only evidence it ever existed are the cuts and scrapes all over our bodies.

Marion is a few yards away, but it takes me a minute to locate Olive. She's nothing but a lump, curled on the ground in the fetal position at the place we all started.

"Olive, honey!" Marion shouts, and runs for her. "Are you all right?"

Olive doesn't move. We all run for her.

Faith's dark hair is in knots around her shoulders. The silk scarf tied around Marion's curls has been torn, and clutched in her hand is a pearl-handled switchblade. A cut across Greer's eyebrow drips blood down her cheek. The hems of our nightdresses are caked in mud up to our knees. Emmy holds a kitchen knife in one hand and the golden goblet in another.

As if on cue, the weapons turn to dust, dissolving in our hands in a shower of ash, just like the swan.

Across the lawn, the queen is still high up on her referee's chair, the opera glasses pressed to her face and trained on us.

The other girls seem to have forgotten she's even there, but I can feel her watching us. I can't help myself. I paste a big, fake smile on my face and wave.

Marion makes it to Olive first and turns her on her back gingerly.

Her eyes are squeezed tight, and she's crying softly.

Marion has to unwind her arms from around her middle to haul her to her feet. "Darling, shh, it's all right," she soothes. It takes Olive a few moments to come back to herself. She blinks her wide eyes and wipes away her tears with one of her smooth fingers.

She sniffles. "I hate the dark."

"It's all over now." Marion comforts her, but there's an edge to her voice that makes me wonder if she believes that's true. We've still got twelve weeks of this.

We all startle at the sound of footsteps in the dark. Queen Mor has come down from her chair, still wrapped in furs, a tiara on her head. No mud stains her shoes; she's as pristine as always, her expression like ice.

"Well done, ladies," she says as she approaches us. "I do love a game."

We stare at her, our breathing ragged.

"Congratulations, Lady Emmy. You've won a favor: time with Bram. He's all yours for dinner, evening after next. The rest of you will see him at the Grosvenor Cup Regatta tomorrow. Carriages at eight a.m. Get yourselves cleaned up."

She walks away, but turns back and adds, as if it's an afterthought, "And remember, let's keep our little games between us, yes?"

CHAPTER FIFTEEN

We hobble back to Caledonia Cottage, Marion and I supporting the weight of Olive, who is in such a state of shock she can barely walk. Emmy's ankle is twisted. Greer's face is still bleeding, and Faith gingerly touches the spot where our heads collided.

The cottage is dark and still when we return, no baths have been drawn for us, and no staff wait at the ready to help us get cleaned up.

On each of our pillows rests a small scroll of parchment. Faith and I unroll ours at the same time. In black ink on mine is the number 3.

Faith wordlessly turns hers to me, her brows knit together in confusion. On hers is the number 2.

I follow her out into the hall, where we find Marion holding her paper, emblazoned with the number 4. "Any idea what this means?" she asks.

Greer and Emmy emerge from their room. Greer's paper says 5 and Emmy's says 1.

Olive comes into the hall last, a blanket wrapped tightly around her. Her eyes are still red, her face gaunt, but at least the weeping has stopped. "I got six. That means I lose, right?"

And all at once it clicks. We've been ranked.

Back in my room, I throw my number 3 into the fire, then peel myself out of my ruined nightdress and throw that in alongside it.

When I awake, it's to someone screaming.

My eyes snap open and I tumble to the floor with fright as I find Lottie standing directly over me, screeching as if she's just witnessed a murder.

"Sorry, miss!" she exclaims, her face sheet white. "You're covered in blood."

I look across the room to where Faith is groggily pushing herself out of bed. She doesn't look much better than I feel. The skin under her eyes is dark, with bruiselike circles, and her nightdress is ripped at the knees, where she fell.

"I'm a sleepwalker," I say. "I must have tripped." I stumble to my feet.

Lottie reaches out and plucks a white feather from my matted hair. "Into a goose pond?"

"Looks that way."

She turns to Faith. "Are you a sleepwalker too?"

"Ask the queen," Faith deadpans.

Downstairs, a breakfast of iced pastries and oatmeal is laid out for us on silver trays. "We have to tell him," Marion declares. Olive shifts in her seat uncomfortably. We all know that by *him* she means Bram.

I agree with Marion, but I'm already in a precarious position. I can't risk making myself a target.

"You do it, then," Greer mutters under her breath, staring down at her thumb. She must be thinking the same thing I am. *What will the cost be?*

Faith stares her down. "Fine. I'll do it."

"What do we expect him to do? Go against his mother?" Olive asks.

"Yes," Faith snaps. "That's exactly what he owes us. If he can't protect us, what good is he?"

"But what about the vow we made?" Olive demands.

"Screw the vow," Faith says. We finish our meals in silence and then head back to our rooms to prepare for another day of courting.

I'm bruised all over, but my hands have it the worst. They're bloody and raw, completely ripped apart from when I tripped. Tenderly, Lottie wraps them in bandages thin enough that they won't show under my elbow-length white gloves. She dresses me in a sporting dress of blue-and-white pinstripes, with a little boating hat pinned to my curls.

All the lady's maids have done an impressive job with us. Greer has a smart straw hat pulled low over her face, covering her forehead wound. Faith's hair has been braided to cover the bump on her head where we collided, and Emmy's twisted ankle has been set by a brace hidden under her skirts. Olive looks the worst of us, her eyes still red from where the blood vessels burst with the force of her sobbing.

We're driven in glossy palace carriages to the Thames Rowing Club, a glorious boathouse right on the edge of the river, near the finish line of the regatta. The green lawn of the boathouse has been transformed by a white marquee tent decorated with cheery red and blue bunting. Beneath the tent are tables piled with champagne and caviar and oysters.

Viscountess Bolingbroke emerges from the crowd to lecture us on propriety and sportsmanship.

As she drones on, Emmy leans over and whispers in my ear. "She should just say, 'Remember, absolutely no fun,' and save us all some time." Then she ducks behind my back to drain a flute of champagne I have absolutely no memory of seeing her grab.

We're sequestered from the rest of the party, instructed to sit on a shaded bench near the water and clap politely for the boats.

We're as on display as the boats are. We sit straight-backed in our corsets and watch for hours as the junior club rows by, then the university boys in their uniforms. Gossips surround us, along with the newspaper reporters who scribble away on their little notepads as they study us like a zoo attraction. I find it all a little mind-numbing, and end up playing rock, paper, scissors with Olive to pass the time.

The queen doesn't deign to come to things like this, but she's still everywhere: her face on the money passing between hands for bets, in the statue by the water, her profile in the royal seal that marks the side of every boat.

Finally, the clock strikes two and the main event begins. It's a lively scene now as the party guests crowd around us, and on the opposite bank of the Thames, citizens have gathered for their own festivities. The air is thick with tobacco, river water, coal, and the slightly burnt aroma of spun sugar. Children laugh, perched on their father's shoulders in their smartest little sailor outfits.

From far off, a gunshot rings out, and then there is the distant cheering of "Hurrah!" from both banks of the river as the boats pass by.

We all look to London Bridge, lit brilliantly by blue sky, and anxiously await their appearance.

"Here they are!" A cry goes through the crowd as the boats come into view. Each shell is marked by a flag, and everyone in the crowd cheers for their favorite color. "Let's go, Pink!" or "Bravo, Yellow!"

But the loudest shouts go up for Blue, the boat clearly in the front of the pack, careering down the Thames.

It passes by us, nearly to the finish line. It's an eight-seater, and just behind the coxswain, in the starboard seat, pulling as if his life depended on it, is Prince Emmett. Beside him, in the portside seat, working just as hard, is Prince Bram. Unlike the rest of the crew, he's not sweating or gasping for breath, he's just got that wide grin on his face, like he's having the most fun of anyone here.

At the sight of him, we all spring up from the bench and cheer.

The crowd explodes as the Blue team crosses the finish line. Confetti rains down from somewhere, and the band kicks up a cheery tune.

The princes step out onto the shore and brush their hair off their foreheads. Together, they accept the sterling silver cup and hoist it above their heads in triumphant victory.

Viscountess Bolingbroke herds us over to them, and one by one we curtsy and congratulate Bram on his win.

I'm rising from my curtsy when a gust of wind whips up from the river and something sharp flies directly into my eye. I blink against the tears and reach up to wipe it away, but realize I can't take off my gloves without revealing last night's injuries.

The boys from the boat are clapping each other on the back, and the other girls are lingering in an attempt to steal time with Bram. I take advantage of the chaos to disappear into the boat storage shed a few yards away from where the celebration is raging.

I yank off my gloves and rub aggressively at my offending eye.

I'm not making much progress when a noise behind me makes me jump.

From behind a pile of boats that are stacked all the way to the ceiling, Emmett emerges from the shadows.

"You scared me!" I breathe out.

"I thought you wanted me to follow you." He's glossy with sweat, wearing a blue-and-white-striped sweater. He reaches up to push his hair off his forehead, and his sweater rises, revealing a sliver of his toned abdomen.

"No, I was trying to get this clod of dirt out of my eyeball without making a complete fool of myself."

"Let me see." Before I have the chance to lurch back, he grasps the edge of my face with one hand, the pads of his fingers gentle on my jawbone. To see better, he tips my head toward the beams of sunlight streaming through the dusty glass ceiling.

"Ahh, there it is," he whispers. With his other hand he reaches up. "Stop blinking."

"Hard not to when there's a hand in my eye."

"I will physically restrain you."

"I'd like to see you try," I shoot back.

"You just saw me sail. I'm good with knots."

"I'll bite through them. Very strong teeth."

He swipes a finger along the lower rim of my eye. "Ahh, got it," he whispers in victory.

Holding my gloves in one hand, I reach up to wipe my errant tears with the other. I realize my mistake the moment I do it. Emmett's eyes flash, and he grabs my wrist.

The wounds are only hours old and haven't had time yet to

scab over. There are red splotches where they've bled through the bandages.

I yank my wrist back, but Emmett keeps his hold strong.

"What happened to you?"

"I tripped," I reply, averting my eyes.

I retreat a few steps until my back hits another stack of boats.

"Why are you lying to me?" he asks.

The door to the shed squeaks open. Emmett shoves me by my shoulders, and I stumble back into a narrow hiding place, behind a rack of oars.

"Who's there?" he calls, his voice pointedly friendly.

"Just me," a soft female voice replies.

Faith Fairchild's footsteps are near silent as she makes her way through the storage shed to him, delicate like everything else about her.

"You shouldn't be here," Emmett whispers.

"I had to see you," Faith half sobs. "Why won't you respond to my letters? I waited for you at our statue for ages—"

"Faith—" Emmett interrupts her.

"You can't keep ignoring me! Not after everything. This isn't anything like what you said it would be, last night—"

There's an odd choking sound as Faith sputters. I peek out from around the oars to see her red-faced and hunched, like she suddenly can't breathe.

"Faith?" Emmett thumps her on the back a few times, until she takes a large gasp.

"I'm trying to tell you that—" Again, she heaves, choking on something, before taking a breath.

"Are you quite well?" Emmett crouches and peers up at her face, worried. "Let me call one of the maids and have you taken home."

"That goddamn witch," Faith hisses under her breath.

We should have known that she meant we *literally* wouldn't be able to speak of her lessons.

"What's changed? Is there someone else?" Faith asks. She doesn't sound sad. She sounds absolutely furious.

Emmett squares his shoulders. "I've decided it shouldn't be you. I'm sorry if that's disappointing. I don't think you're right for him. All I want is for him to be happy."

"Bullshit." She punches him square in the shoulder. "You lied to me."

"I didn't lie. I changed my mind."

"Why would you do this to me? I know we've had our disagreements, but at the very least, I thought you respected me."

"I'm sorry." Emmett's voice is tense.

"I'll tell him," Faith snarls. "I'll tell him everything about us, all the ways you were willing to manipulate him."

"No you won't."

"Why not?"

"Because then he'd never pick you."

Faith punches him in the shoulder once more. He takes it gallantly. And then she storms out.

I poke my head out from my hiding place. Emmett swipes a hand over his exhausted face and sighs. "I'm sorry you had to witness that."

"It was supposed to be Faith—" I was stupid not to have put it together before now. Emmett was never going to leave the May Queen up to chance. My stomach turns as the realization dawns on me. "No wonder she hates me."

"I'm sorry."

"You should be. You should have told me."

Emmett looks down at his hands. It's the first time I've seen him look truly unsure of himself. "She was a ballerina. I thought it would give her an advantage at the maypole. We've known each other for years."

"So the rumors about you two were false? She's not your lover, but your pawn?"

He opens his mouth. Closes it. Opens it again. "Not exactly."

I push past him, disgusted. "You were willing to let your brother take one of your castoffs?"

He chases me through the boathouse. "Please, let me explain."

"I'm interested in only one thing. How much does she know?" If Faith knows about Emmett's plan to unseat the queen, she could easily blow this plot up. I could be executed for sedition.

"She doesn't know my true goal. I promised only that I'd help her marry Bram. I told her to win May Queen, but not why."

"Oh, perfect," I snarl sarcastically.

He worries his bottom lip between his teeth. I have to look away to keep from staring. "I'm going to help *you* win. This changes nothing. He'll fall in love with you. I know he will."

The idea of anyone falling in love with me is so ridiculous it makes me nauseous.

"Did you love *her*?" I ask.

"Ivy—" He says my name like I'm a horse he's trying to settle. Outside, a harpist begins playing, a sign that the latter part of the party has begun and I've been missing from the group for far too long.

I turn for the door, but Emmett captures my wrist in his hand once more, his hold gentler this time, an apology in it. "Meet me in the sunken garden tonight at midnight and I'll show you every last one of my cards." He has the audacity to look wounded as I walk away.

I march out of the boathouse, the anger in me so hot and blinding I don't see Bram until I've smacked directly into him.

"I'm sorry!" I exclaim.

He just chuckles. "We have to stop meeting like this, Lady Ivy." He has the regatta trophy slung casually in one hand and a bottle of champagne in the other. Like his brother, he's wearing a blue-and-white-striped sweater, his hair tousled from the wind and water. Unlike the rest of the rowers, he looks distinctly unwinded. His gray eyes don't squint against the sun either. His posture is perfect, everything about him at ease.

I panic, afraid that Emmett will follow me and we'll be caught once more. Bram may be good-natured, but I doubt he's stupid.

"Will you show me the boat?" I ask, not giving him a chance to answer. I'm already bounding down the dock, leading him far enough away from the boathouse that Emmett should be able to escape undetected.

The door to the shed squeaks open, and Emmett peeks out. I widen my eyes at him in an attempt to tell him to stay put. He nods in understanding and pulls the door shut. It squeaks again. I grit my teeth in frustration.

Bram glances back. I have to act fast.

"How many of you fit in this thing?" It's the first question I can think to ask.

"Uh, nine. Eight rowers, one coxswain."

Great, now he thinks I'm dull. Or dim. Or the worst possible combination, dull and dim.

From behind his shoulder, I see Viscountess Bolingbroke eyeing us judgmentally from the lawn.

I distract Bram, gesturing to the small space in the stern of the shell. "Does the coxswain really fit in here?"

"Johnny is the smallest on our team. We fold him up like an elegant napkin, and he barks orders at us like a stern governess."

"Sounds terrifying."

"It is."

Emmett steps out of the boathouse just as a gust of wind swings the door wide, slamming it against the frame.

Bram's eyes flicker, and he half turns around.

I have to do something quick. "Like this?" I jump into the boat.

The shell starts to flip the moment my foot hits it.

Bram shouts and lunges for me, but he's not quick enough.

By the time I register what is happening, I'm fully underwater.

CHAPTER SIXTEEN

I open my mouth and inhale a lungful of the Thames. My legs kick on instinct, but I don't know which way is up, so I might be swimming deeper. The thought makes me panic. I whip my head around, but the darkness is so complete, I only disorient myself further.

My body coughs reflexively, and I suck in more sludge.

Then a beam of light breaks through the darkness. A strong pair of arms grabs me around the middle and hauls me to the surface.

Bram kicks at the boat with his strong legs, and I realize now that I was trapped under it.

I blink against the sudden light. My lungs are screaming. I roll to my side and vomit river water all over the dock. My eyes sting with the force of it. I suck in grateful breaths and try to slow the frantic beating of my heart.

Bram stands over me, looking concerned. He's soaked to the bone. His hair is plastered to his forehead and his sweater clings to every curve of his torso. "Lady Ivy, are you all right?"

I try to respond, but only manage to wheeze in a shaky breath. Another wave of brown water comes pouring out of my mouth. I cough and cough, unable to catch my breath. Bram pounds me hard on the back a few times until my lungs expand enough to manage a gasp.

From the lawn, the music has stopped, and dozens of London's high society players are staring at me, frozen with shock. The other girls and Viscountess Bolingbroke run down the dock to us.

"Give her space," Bram commands, and their footsteps stop immediately.

He leans down closer, so near I can feel the heat of his breath against the shell of my ear. "Let's get you out of here."

I wipe my eyes, acutely aware of how pathetic I must look, and nod in silent agreement.

Bram hauls me to my feet, and Greer rushes toward me to hold me steady on the other side.

My dress is sticking to every part of me, made unbearably heavy by the water. My hair, so artfully styled this morning, half hangs sodden down my neck. My straw hat is gone completely, bobbing sadly down the river.

I want nothing more than to rip off my soaked gloves, but I can't risk revealing my bandages.

"I'll help," Greer says over me to Bram. "Ivy and I are the best of friends, you know."

I sputter again, and Bram claps me on the back. "Easy now, get it all out."

I look up through a curtain of my wet hair at Greer, who has a smug look on her face. She knows as well as I do that ratting her out will only make me look bad. Throwing myself back in the river and floating to the nearest home county is tempting.

Together, Bram and Greer assist me into a carriage, Viscountess Bolingbroke nipping at their heels.

"I think it'd be best if I accompany her," Bram says. The viscountess purses her lips but knows she cannot deny a prince.

"Lady Greer will go too, for propriety," the viscountess replies.

Bram bows his head. "I insist upon it."

He sighs and leans back against the walls of the carriage. "Thank you for giving me an excuse to get out of there. If I had to listen to one more person give their thoughts on which of you I should wed, I may have jumped into the Thames myself."

Greer's eyes meet mine. We're both shocked at his sudden casualness. It's as if a curtain has fallen and the real Bram is in front of us. He looks younger, his shoulders more relaxed.

"Thank you for coming to my rescue," I say.

Bram flashes a half smile, showing off his single dimple. "Trust me when I say, anytime. Any body of water too—the sea, a lake, a particularly deep bathtub."

The carriage rattles down a few more blocks. I'm shivering in my waterlogged dress but desperate not to show it. Bram's clothes are wet too, but he doesn't seem to mind.

"So, who are they saying?" I ask after a moment.

Bram looks from the window to me. "Excuse me?"

"Who are they saying you should choose?" I ask it with the lilt of a joke, but my curiosity really is killing me.

"I feel fairly sure that everyone is advocating for who they've put money on at the clubs. Lady Marion Thorne has the highest odds, but you, Ivy Benton, will bring the biggest payout."

"That's a kind way of saying everyone thinks I'm going to lose." I laugh, and Bram laughs along with me. I'm surprised to find that I love the sound of it, love this version of him, so unencumbered by the constant surveillance of the ton.

"Tell me, how did you two meet?" Bram asks us.

Greer and I look to each other. "Ivy smashed my fifth birthday cake, and then her sister tried to smush it back together with her bare hands," Greer says. "She was . . . unsuccessful."

And even with all the things I feel about Greer, I can't help but smile at the memory: Lydia, Greer, and I all covered in pink icing on the floor. Greer smiles too, and it looks odd on this new face of hers, but I can still feel the echo of the girls we used to be, and for a heartbeat, I miss them.

"You have a sister?" Bram asks.

"I do," I reply. "Lydia is a remarkably sparkly sort of person. Even at seven, she commanded the spotlight."

Greer nods in enthusiastic agreement that I'm surprised to find genuine. "She was the star of every party she ever walked into. Ivy wasn't quite as elegant and polkaed right into the French butter-cream our cook had spent all week on. I sat down on the floor and wailed until Ivy scooped me up and placated me with a water ice. In Ivy's defense, she felt terrible—still does. It's been over a decade, and she still shows up on my step with a cake every year."

Every year except for this year. She doesn't say that part.

There's a lot she doesn't say, like how she and Lydia grew tired of my obsession with faeries when we were twelve. Lydia gave me a dressing-down about needing to stop acting like a baby, but Greer didn't say a word, she just stopped showing up to play with me. All I knew was that one day I was making faerie court dresses out of flower petals with my sister and best friend and the next I was alone. They left me alone in the garden.

It felt so unlike her, I thought for the better part of a year that maybe she was a changeling. That would explain why we'd grown apart. I wrote my theories in a notebook I stole from Mama's stash, like I was a detective.

Eventually I moved on. It was either play alone or play with Lydia and Greer: I chose the latter.

"You said *was.*" Bram's brows knit together in a question.

"What do you mean?" Greer asks.

"You said Lydia *was* the star of every party."

Greer glances at me nervously.

"She's taken ill these past few months," I say quickly. "Her nerves have been poorly, and she's been convalescing. I'm hopeful the season will prove an excuse for her to reenter society."

Bram smiles warmly. "Lydia." He says her name slowly, like he's committing it to memory. "I'd love to meet her, though I appreciate the warning to keep the Benton sisters away from any cakes."

When we reach Caledonia Cottage, Bram shoos away the footman and helps me down from the carriage himself. I linger awkwardly as he looks down at me. I wish I could ask him to heal my hands again, the way he did the first day we met, but that would require an explanation of how the injuries came about, and I can't do that.

He delivers me to the door, and I horrify poor Lottie for the second time today. She blushes deeply as she curtsies to him and rushes me upstairs. "What on earth happened?"

"I fell into the river."

"Was it so he'd jump in and catch you?" She cranes her neck to get a look at Bram through the window as his carriage pulls away. "That might be the handsomest boy I've ever seen."

"It wasn't like that," I grumble.

Once in dry clothes, I meet Greer downstairs for a late luncheon, both of us having missed the rest of the regatta party.

I know she didn't hop into that carriage for my sake, but I still thank her, only to break the silence.

She plucks a sugar cube out of a porcelain bowl with delicate silver tongs, and an expression that might be shame comes over her. But I can't be sure. I don't know this new face of hers. I'm struck with the feeling that I haven't known Greer in a very long time.

"Remember when we used to hide in the wardrobe during cotillion class?" she asks softly.

We'd tuck ourselves behind piles of fabric and whisper about a made-up land where girls didn't have to learn to sew and we could explore glaciers and volcanoes and forests on horseback. Her horse was snow-white, and she told me that mine was smaller, with brown spots, but in my head it was always golden. They had names, but I can't remember them now.

If it was her governess who found us, we'd be scolded. If it was her mother, we'd be slapped.

"I do remember," I whisper back.

I remember everything. I remember everything so much I am being crushed under the weight of it all. If I weren't so horribly defined by everything I've ever loved and lost, maybe I could be the kind of person who moved through life easily. I'm only eighteen, but I'm beginning to understand what my mother meant when she said, *Remembering is heavy. It lasts so long.*

I think, now, of Greer's mother dragging her up to the dais and taking the knife to her hand the day of the Pact Parade.

I look at Greer and feel all that ugly resentment and love tangling together into a mess I can't unknot.

I hate myself for how much I hate her. Why is it always like that with me? Why is it I can only hate people if I love them first?

"Do you want to win?" I ask her.

"He seems kind."

"He does," I agree. "But do you want to win?"

Her teeth worry her full bottom lip. She winces when she bites too hard and draws blood. "I have to win."

It's such a Greer answer. "You could say that's true for any of us."

She shakes her head sadly. "If you lose, at least your mother will look you in the eye again. Mine has promised I will be disowned."

Knowing Greer's mother, I doubt it's a figure of speech.

We eat the rest of the meal in the silence of two people who no longer know how to talk to each other.

I'm dipping a dessert spoon into a carafe of cold pudding when she clears her throat.

"Do you remember Joseph?" she asks.

I dig through my memories. "The cook's son? The one we used to chase around the walled garden?"

She's got a far-off look in her eyes, one I can't read. "He was kind."

"I suppose so. Do you still see him?"

"He works in the stables now."

"Greer," I say more forcefully, and she blinks a few times, coming back to herself. "Greer, do you still see him?" We both know I'm asking more than that.

She takes another sip of tea, and her eyes go remote. "Of course I don't."

Sneaking out is easier than I thought it would be. Faith snores the moment her head hits the pillow, and Viscountess Bolingbroke takes to bed promptly at ten p.m.

Starlight is reflected in the long, rectangular pond running down the length of the garden, and I'm shivering as I wait. It's been an unseasonably cool spring, and even my thickest cloak isn't helping much.

I jump at every long shadow, every rustle of leaves in the dark, terrified I'll find a snake, or a swan with razor teeth, or Queen Mor herself.

My hair is unbound around my shoulders, and beneath my cloak I'm wearing nothing but a nightdress. Faith is a heavy sleeper, but I didn't want to press my luck.

A twig snaps as someone approaches. "Emmett?" I whisper.

He steps out from the cover of rosebushes. "It's Lottie's night off. I'm sorry to make you meet me like this—I didn't want you lost in the tunnels alone."

I follow the dark silhouette of his shoulders through the orangery tunnels and up to his room.

He crosses the room to pull a quilt off his bed and wraps it around himself. A disgruntled Pig, who had been napping in said quilt, scrambles to get onto Emmett's lap.

"Why is it so bloody cold in here?" I ask.

"Couldn't risk having the servants discover us. I told them to stay out this evening, so no one has made the fire."

"Why not make your own fire?" I kneel at the hearth and pull away the grate.

Emmett hesitates.

"Oh my god." I laugh. "You don't know how."

"It's not my fault!"

"Of course it is. Come here." I wave him over.

He relents with a groan and kneels next to me.

There's a neat stack of firewood and a box of matches on the hearth. I point to them. "Give me three logs and those matches there."

"No. See, I tried that already. The logs don't light."

I turn to him so he can see the full force of my eye roll. "You need kindling. Did your fancy tutors teach you nothing?"

"If you need an Old English text dissected, I am the boy for you."

I pull a tangle of grease-soaked rags from the silver tinderbox on the mantel and arrange the logs over them. "Like this. You have to light something smaller first."

He leans closer, the heat of him suddenly overwhelming despite the cold room.

Snick.

The rags go up in flames quickly, bathing his face in the glow of orange firelight.

He turns to me. "Do all the other daughters of marquesses know how to build fires?" His voice has gone softer. I know what he's really asking.

I look back toward the hearth. "Only the ones whose household staff had to be let go."

At first it wasn't that noticeable. The butler served us at dinner instead of the footmen. Then my mother's lady's maid got married and wasn't replaced. Then the carriage was sold. Then the housemaids went, and things really started to fall apart.

Lydia and I learned to build our own fires, iron our own clothes, and darn our own socks while other girls were sewing lace with their governesses. My mother was very clear that we must keep the state of our household a secret. I hated lying. I never developed a stomach for it, so I let Lydia do it for me.

I straighten my back. "Back to the matter at hand. You and Faith. All your cards. I'd like to see them on the table now."

He leans back on his hands and stares at the fire. "From the moment I heard this was the season the queen planned to marry Bram off, I knew I couldn't leave it up to chance. I spent the better part of a year trying to find the perfect candidate. It's actually what I was doing, that night we met. I was going to meet Christine Cambere, but she was all wrong."

Everything that happened that night comes rushing back to me, the way he leaned his face in close to mine. *You know, you're really quite pretty.*

No one had ever called me pretty. When they wanted to pay me a compliment, they'd say, *You look like Lydia.*

I don't understand why I suddenly feel like crying. I smack him in the shoulder instead. "Is that why you asked to call on me?" Is his rakish reputation just a clever misdirection, hiding his much riskier true motives?

"Yes."

"You were never actually interested in me."

"I'll remind you, you rebuffed me. My ego never recovered."

"Your ego seems just fine."

I look away from him back to the fire, which is properly roaring now. The heat seeps into my bones.

"I knew Faith," he says. "I liked Faith. Faith's father said she must marry this season, though the whole of that story is hers to tell. She asked me to be the one to do it, and I refused. Once I dodged the crystal goblet she threw at my head, I agreed to help her marry Bram instead."

"Why didn't you want to marry her?"

Emmett considers his words carefully. "Because I did not love her. Not like that."

"So you agreed to help her marry your brother instead."

"You make it sound so ugly."

"Isn't it? Manipulating your ex-lover and your brother like that?"

Emmett's mouth is turned down in a frown as he feeds another log to the fire, which goes up in a shower of sparks.

"I never claimed to be good. It's why Bram should be king. He's so much better than me."

"So you promised you'd help Faith win."

"I did."

"And now it has to be me."

"It does."

You could be queen. "All right, then. Help me."

Emmett nods, all business now. "Bram loves strawberries, all fruit really, says it's different from what grows in the Otherworld. His favorite color is green. He loves his horse, Mab, adores any type of competition. I think his ideal match will be someone who challenges him."

"Did you tell Faith what bargain to make?"

Emmett shakes his head. "Even I have my moral limits. I couldn't ask her to do that, not when I don't believe in the system myself. And besides, what could she have asked for? She's already the most beautiful girl in London."

He's right, but it stings to hear him say it.

"Did she make a bargain?" he asks.

"I'm not sure. She refused to tell us."

Emmett laughs. "That sounds like Faith."

"One more question."

Emmett looks at me expectantly.

"Why are you and Bram so close? I imagine you'd have every reason to hate him. You hate his mother."

Emmett's eyes narrow, still looking at the fire. "I did hate him, at first. I was an absolute terror when he first arrived. We were both fourteen. I refused to acknowledge his existence, even as he tried to speak with me or join me for horseback rides or lessons. I know now how lonely he was back then, how scared, but at the time I could see him only as an extension of his mother. She doted on him, which only made my hatred stronger. Then one day, about a month after he arrived, a few of the other sons of noblemen and I were taking shooting lessons on the grounds. Some of the bigger boys liked to push me around, call me a bastard, nothing terribly creative. I'd never been much of a fighter, but I'd grown three inches that year and thought maybe it was time I stood up for myself. I ended up with three broken ribs and a black eye. They pummeled me. A footman had to carry me kicking and screaming back to my rooms before I let them knock me unconscious. Bram walked in a few minutes later, with torn clothes, a bloody knee, and a matching shiner. 'I got the ones you missed'—that's what he said to me. We were the same age, but he was so much bigger than me back then. I looked like a scrawny kid still, but Bram was nearly a man. I asked him why, and he said, 'I won't let them call my brother a bastard.' I just laughed, even with the broken ribs. I couldn't help it. And from that day on, we were inseparable."

I can imagine it so clearly. "He's a good person, then? As good as you say?"

"He's better than good. He's the best."

"I need time with him," I say. "I'm never going to win if we don't spend time together."

"Then you have to learn how to flirt. I'm not leaving the future of the country in the hands of someone who thinks shrimp heads are romantic."

"That's not fair! You sprang that on me out of nowhere!"

Emmett levels me with a glance. "All right then, give it another go."

"What?"

"Flirt with me."

"Yuck."

"For practice." He gives me a big grin. "Pretend I'm Bram."

I look down at my feet, hesitating. I picture Bram, his kind eyes, perfect jawline, that single dimple. It makes me nervous just to think of him. "Um . . . how was your day?"

Emmett tips my chin up with a flick of his thumb. "Eye contact helps. You sound like you're talking to your grandmother. Try again."

"Have you read any good books lately?"

"Are you quizzing him?"

I throw my hands up in frustration. "You show me how to do it, then!"

He bends so we're eye level, cocks his head slightly. His eyes flit down to my lips, then back to my eyes. "I never noticed your eyes before. They're so beautiful."

My stomach gives a sickening swoop. "Thank you. I grew them myself."

He rolls his eyes and huffs in frustration. "We're doomed."

"I know you're lying," I say. "No one ever compliments brown eyes."

"People have no taste. Try again."

"I want to get to know you better."

Emmett puts his hands out in a so-so motion. "Touch my arm while you say it."

I reach out and brush the inside of his wrist. "I want to get to know you better."

He clutches his heart. "Oh, Ivy, I'm flattered."

"Shut up."

"People like honesty," he says. "It helps them feel closer to someone. There's no quicker way to bond than with a secret. Tell me something."

"You want a secret?" It's just like the maze all over again.

Emmett nods.

"I'm terrified. You said it yourself. The future of the whole country depends on me making him fall in love with me. What if I can't do it? How will I live with myself if I doom everyone to her cruelty forever because I wasn't charming or pretty enough?" There's a part I don't say, that Emmett scares me too.

Emmett looks at me for a minute, really listens. "I'm not worried."

"That makes one of us."

He glances at the ticking clock on the mantel. "We should get you back. You need your rest."

The door to the cottage is unlocked, and I climb the stairs on my tippy-toes so I don't make any noise.

There's a shadow moving in the darkness. Faith is sitting upright in bed.

"You little snake," she snarls. "I wonder how Bram will react when I tell him you were out all night."

"Faith, please," I beg. "It's not what you think."

"Emmett can't save you."

"What do you want from me?" I croak.

"I want Emmett back."

"He's all yours. That's not what this is." I don't have the energy to fight her. I feel suddenly weak at the knees. The room tilts.

"Then what is it?"

It would be easier to be angry with her if she didn't sound so broken. "I wish I could say," I reply.

"Then we have nothing else to talk about," she snaps.

Her tone chills me. I crawl into bed, unable to stop shivering, and let an uneasy sleep pull me under.

CHAPTER SEVENTEEN

I awake at dawn to the sound of the bedroom door swinging open with a clatter. Standing there in her nightdress and sleeping cap is Viscountess Bolingbroke, Faith by her side.

"She was out in the middle of the night," Faith declares, like she's proposing to burn me at the stake. "It was all so terribly improper. I had to let you know as soon as possible."

I open my mouth to protest, but my throat is on fire. I'm shivering and sweaty all at once. My body aches from the inside out, as if something is bruising and breaking endlessly. I blink away the sleep from my eyes and find my vision blurry at the edges.

Viscountess Bolingbroke rushes to my side and places her cool hand on my forehead. "She's sick with fever, Miss Fairchild. Fetch the doctor and your lady's maid. I'm not sure what sort of prank you're playing, accusing your visibly ill competition of impropriety, but the next time you lie, I may have to tell Her Majesty."

Faith sputters, her face bright red with anger, then storms out of the room.

When I awake, it's to Lottie dabbing a cool cloth on my forehead.

"Shh, miss, you're all right." She soothes me like I'm a child, and I let my eyes flutter shut.

"What happened?" I rasp. Light streams in from the windows, and I suspect I've been asleep for a very long time.

"You're running a fever, darling. Just relax."

My hands hurt the worst. They're swollen and ugly, my knuckles too stiff to move.

When I awake again, it's Greer who is standing over me. "They told me to make you drink," she says, and tips a glass of cool water into my mouth. Every swallow is agony.

The darkness is freezing as it swallows me whole.

EMMY ITO

Marion and Faith are in the garden, Greer is holding vigil by Ivy's bedside, Olive is in the kitchen, and my hair has never looked worse.

I swear my lady's maid must hate me. Tonight I'm having dinner with Prince Bram, my reward for winning that blasted hedge maze—a meal, alone, with him, and I look like a poodle.

My maid used a curling rod on my front pieces and they're dangling in front of my eyes like little springs. I swipe them away, frustrated, fold my fashion periodical, and pad across the cottage to see what Olive is doing in the kitchen.

"You've got flour in your hair," I say.

She wipes it away, leaving a streak of white across her face.

I gesture at the rising dough by the hearth. "You're going to bury us in brioche."

"Poor Bram, then he'd have to die alone."

The reminder of his immortality always makes me feel sick, but I laugh anyway because it's Olive, and she smiles so big when I do.

I lean my elbow on the counter. "Be honest, do I look ridiculous?"

Olive taps flour out over the butcher-block counter as she considers. "You look like a very fancy dog."

"Rude!"

"I said a fancy one!" She wipes her hands on her apron. "Come here." She cranks the spout and wets a towel to run over the front pieces of my hair, smoothing out the horrible curls. She then rearranges the pins. "Much better."

There's a knock on the front door, and together we run to get it. Bram has come alone, wearing a burgundy waistcoat, his cravat in a ruffle, his face as perfect as always. He bows his head at us. "Lady Ito, you look lovely."

"I did her hair!" Olive exclaims, but I've already slammed the door behind us.

He leads me up a path, along the gentle hill that winds around the palace. "I hope you don't mind I've arranged for dinner in the orangery tonight."

I'm startled by the sound of footsteps behind us and turn to see an old woman in a horribly out-of-fashion dress following us.

"Our chaperone for the evening," Bram explains. "I am committed to propriety, but thought you might like to be rid of Bolingbroke for the evening. The Countess of Tribley is one of my school chum's great-aunts. She's really good fun, a hell of a cardplayer, but half-deaf, so I figured she'd do perfectly well."

I laugh and wave to the old woman, who waves back.

The orangery is covered in one thousand votive candles that flicker against the glass walls in the dark.

There's a table set with candlesticks, silver, and a white tablecloth under one of the orange trees. I'm not one for grand gestures, but it really is lovely, even I have to admit.

Countess Tribley takes an armchair in the corner and pulls out her knitting.

Bram is an attentive listener. He asks all the right questions. How many siblings (four brothers, I'm right in the middle). My interests (reading, the pianoforte, painting). What my hopes for the future are (travel).

"Travel?" He looks taken aback. "Like, to the sea?"

"Across it," I answer too boldly.

I never wanted to marry, not like the other girls. It's ironic, I suppose, that my great-grandparents risked everything crossing an ocean to come to this country and I've spent my whole life longing to leave it. I was never going to be able to do that with a husband by my side and an estate to run.

I didn't plan on being a wife. I planned on being a painter, or a pirate, or a poet.

That's the thing about girls like Marion and me, who were raised on stories about lands ruled by humans and not by a faerie queen. We know just how wide the rest of the world is.

I should have ducked out of the May Queen competition early, but as usual, my pride got the best of me. I spotted my father in the audience and remembered the lecture he'd given me over and over again in my youth. *Whatever you do, try your best.* It would have broken his heart to see me fail on purpose, and he would have been able to tell. I know he would have.

Bram's face lights up. "I've seen so little of the human world. I dream of seeing more."

I'm surprised to hear him say something in direct contradiction to his mother's strict isolationist policies.

I tell him what my grandparents said about Kyoto, the winding streets and damp, hot summers. He's alarmingly pretty as he listens, his perfect jawline cradled in his hand.

When I'm finished, he gestures at the beaded handbag I placed on the table.

"What's in there?" he asks.

I pretend to be offended. "It's rather rude to ask a lady what's in her handbag."

"But you're not a typical lady. Is it money for passage? Are you leaving me so soon?" he jokes.

I take the bag and pull out the worn deck of tarot cards my governess gave me for my thirteenth birthday. I was worried we might have nothing to talk about, and the cards are good for conversation. It's easier than talking about myself.

"Will you read for me?" he asks. "We have oracles in my homeland, but they live mostly in trees and caves. I much prefer your company."

I pass him the deck and have him shuffle, then pull a card. The devil smiles up at us from the table. Bram tuts his tongue. "Oh, I don't like the look of him."

My heart stutters in my chest, the affection I feel for Bram catching me off my guard. "It means someone is going to betray you."

A look of worry flashes across his face, but he replaces it just as fast with that kind smile. "You now."

I don't need to bother, it'll be the same card it's been for months now. No matter how many times I shuffle, it's always the same. The world.

"What does that mean?" he asks after I draw the card.

It means I'm going to leave. "That I can have everything I want, if only I'm brave enough to take it." Looking at Bram in the flickering candlelight, I'm struck with the feeling that for the first time, I may have something I want to stay for.

Countess Tribley is napping in her armchair, so Bram walks me back to the cottage alone.

He leaves me at the front door with a gentle kiss to my hand. I suddenly understand what people mean when they say something has given them butterflies. There's a riot of them in my stomach. "It's been a pleasure, Lady Ito."

"For me as well," I say, and I'm surprised to find I mean it.

He turns just in time to miss the flash of movement from the side door, but I see it: his brother, sneaking out of the cottage and fleeing into the night.

CHAPTER EIGHTEEN

I have a vague recollection of Marion reading at my bedside by candlelight. Then, of Greer rebandaging my hands. "This is what you get for jumping into the Thames with open wounds," she lectures, but her voice is gentle, her face etched with concern.

Will the Crown pay my family if I die like this, or will I become just another Benton girl sacrificed to the gossip mill? It is a little funny, I suppose, to attempt a coup against the queen and die of an infection instead.

The dreams set in, places where the colors bend all wrong. I'm at a coronation, a crown on my head. I'm at a tea party, and the walls are melting like chocolate left out in the sun. I'm cantering on the back of a horse through a land that looks nothing like this one.

There's a strong, calloused hand against my forehead, soothing, like he could brush away the fever.

Brown hair. Sharp eyes.

That one feels the most real.

When I wake again, it's Olive who is keeping watch. She gasps from where she sits on the chair placed next to my bed and drops her book to the floor.

"You're up!" she exclaims.

I'm more lucid than I've been in days, though still too weak to lift my head.

"We thought you were going to die for certain!" she continues, and I wonder if Olive has ever had a thought she didn't immediately voice aloud.

Emmy appears in the doorway, leaning casually against the door-jamb. "Don't say that." She turns to call down the staircase. "Ivy is awake!"

There's a flurry of footsteps, then a pile of girls tripping into my room. They're wearing silk gowns, diamonds in their hair, dressed for a ball. Greer drops her fan of albatross feathers as she rushes to me. "I thought you were dead."

"I'm sorry to disappoint," I croak. The other girls laugh, but something brittle and sorrowful crosses Greer's beautiful face.

Lottie pushes past where everyone is congregated in the door-way. "Give her space!" she calls as she wipes away the hair plastered to my forehead and props me up with pillows. My bones feel one hundred years old, but the burning of the fever has receded. I test the joints of my fingers and find them less swollen. I'm past the worst of it.

"How long have I been out?" I ask.

"Three days," Olive chirps.

I've missed Wednesday's string quartet concert, and now I'm missing the Harrowfields' ball. I assume there have been no more trials in my absence, given that no one is sporting visible wounds, but I've wasted so much potential time with Bram.

Lottie disappears to find broth for my dinner, and each girl bids me her best before filing out the door for the carriages.

It's another day before I'm out of bed and allowed to continue activities with the others. Everyone but Faith babies me, even Greer, who seems to have softened.

I remember what Olive said the first day in Caledonia Cottage: *I was hoping we'd all be friends.* I never shared her hope, but perhaps a near-death experience was all it took. Faith hasn't brought up my late-night escapade again.

The next day, I'm finally strong enough to be out of bed, and I'm eager to be outside. Lottie is dressing me for my first full outing since my sickness, a turn around the park, when she slips a note into my hand. She continues to button my dress as if nothing has happened, but I tuck the square of parchment away in my palm. I can't read it now, with Faith watching.

The larger green of the palace grounds is open to the public, and today's walk feels as if we are on display. People whisper behind fans as we pass, judgments on our beauty, our charms, which of us will make the best princess.

I've got a lace parasol in one hand and the other looped through the crook of Olive's arm. Olive is a perfect companion for these sorts of things, as she never stops talking, so I don't need to say a word.

"The thing about croissants is you have to fold the dough into layers—" She's been droning on about dough lamination and filling technique for ages.

I tune Olive out and take in the gardens, vibrantly green from a damp English winter. There's a patch of purple crocuses along the gentle hill and a tangle of rosebushes beyond that.

There's a gentle breeze today, but the shawl tied in a knot around my ribs keeps me from shivering. My bonnet hangs loose down my back; it's not exactly proper, but the sun on my skin after so many days indoors feels like heaven.

Faith and Marion stroll arm in arm ahead of us, Emmy and Greer at our heels.

Our group stills as two horses round the path. The riders slow to a walk and take off their top hats as they approach.

"Lady Ivy, you're up!" Bram hops down from his horse, a wide smile on his face. Emmett stays mounted, looking down at me with an expression I can't decipher.

There's a flurry of skirts as the other girls crowd around us, all talking over each other at Bram. Greer is asking if he likes her new hat. Olive is asking if he got the basket of scones she sent over. Faith trips over the toe of her shoe artfully and ends up in Bram's arms.

He rights her quickly with a grin. Emmy sidesteps in front of her, saying, "I've always been praised for my balance."

High up on his horse, Emmett jerks his chin at me. *Do something*, he mouths. The other girls are too distracted by Bram to see.

What? I mouth back.

Emmett raises a gloved hand to his forehead and mimics swooning.

That sounds humiliating. *No.*

Emmett clears his throat loudly. "My, Lady Ivy, you look rather wan."

"I'm feeling quite well, thank you for your concern, Your Highness."

"No. No. Brother, doesn't she look poorly? You'd best get her inside." If Emmett weren't so out of reach, I'd kick him in the shins.

Bram looks down at me with concern. "Yes, you've been so ill."

I swallow my annoyance at Emmett and remind myself that I've got a role to play. I have to make Bram love me. Emmett is right, even if he is annoying about it.

"I'll ask the other girls to take me back to the cottage," I say weakly. "I wouldn't dream of ruining your nice afternoon." I dab a handkerchief at my brow and flutter my eyes, really selling it.

"You're not ruining anything. I insist on seeing you home safely." He's as chivalrous as I expected he'd be.

I catch Emmett's eye just as I go to turn down the path. "Your horse is a beauty," I say to Bram, remembering Emmett's advice.

Emmett canters off, leaving in a cloud of dust.

His eyes crinkle as he grins. "Her name is Mab, and I promise she's more polite than my brother."

"Do you have any others?" I ask.

"A few, though none I like as much as her."

"I'm feeling better, now that I'm out of the direct sun. Perhaps we could take a detour to the stables? I'd like to see them."

Bram considers for a moment. "You sure you're feeling well enough?"

"Very sure."

We cut across the lawn to the mews on the other side of the palace, shaded by trees and far from the watchful eyes of the viscountess and the other girls. It's improper, but unlikely anyone will see us.

As we walk, I remember something else Emmett said, about Bram liking the fruit here, since it's different from what grows in the Otherworld.

I produce a green apple and a pocketknife from the tie-on pocket hanging down the hip of my walking dress.

I always thought the ability to cut slices of fruit while walking was one of the more stupid etiquette lessons we were given, but I liked that it gave me an excuse to carry a knife, and it's certainly coming in handy now.

I pierce the skin and carve out a neat little wedge. "Would you like some?" I offer it to Bram on the tip of my knife.

He grins and takes it. "You know," he says, still chewing, "we have different fruits in the Otherworld."

I could laugh. Emmett clearly knows his brother well.

"Really?" I ask.

"Oh yes. Something like a pomegranate but as big as a dinner plate, with seeds as sweet as sugar, and berries blacker than night that taste of smoke and salt." I wish I had a notepad. I can't wait to write Ethel about all of this.

"Which do you like better, the food here or back—" I nearly say *home*, but I don't know if Bram considers the Otherworld home anymore. It's an unsettling concept, a world near to ours but somewhere just out of reach, maybe that's why I was so obsessed with the idea of it as a child.

Bram must glean my meaning because he takes a moment to consider, then answers. "The food here, but the drinks there. Fizzy cordials that taste of lemon and roses, wine brewed from night-blooming flowers . . ." He's got a far-off look in his eyes as he imagines a place I can't see.

"You must miss it." I think of my own golden childhood, how it pains me that I can never go back.

He thinks for a moment, and our boots crunch along the gravel path. I take the opportunity to look up at him, haloed by green leaves. He's got a freckle on his angular jawline I hadn't noticed before. He's so beautiful it hurts to see him straight-on like this, like looking directly into the sun. I wonder if I will ever get used to it if I marry him, or if I'll spend the rest of my life feeling this starstruck.

He runs a hand through his wavy hair, streaked with sun-bleached gold.

Brown hair. A strong hand on my forehead soothing away a fever.

The stable boys scatter as we enter the sun-dappled barn. We walk slowly along the stalls, petting the velvety noses of the horses.

"I want to thank you for visiting me while I was ill."

He furrows his brows in confusion. "I've been away."

"Oh, it must have been something I dreamed." That's humiliating.

He stops in his tracks and gestures to a stack of hay bales. He lays out his coat for me, and I lower myself beside him.

There's a deep furrow between his brows, and he twirls the thick gold ring on his pinkie. "I actually wanted to apologize for that. I sent flowers but you deserve more than that. I wish I could have helped."

"Healed me like you did the day of the Pact Parade, you mean?"

A crease appears between his brows. "No. I would've if I could've, though. My magic isn't as developed as my mother's—more parlor tricks than anything. I can manage small cuts and bruises, but not much more."

Emmett's face flashes into my mind. I reach out and brush the sleeve of Bram's shirt. "I want to get to know you better."

His mouth pulls into a half smile. "Is that so?"

I nod. "Tell me more about magic." Emmett did say that people valued authenticity. I spent most of my life longing for information about faeries. If only ten-year-old Ivy could see me now.

"No one ever asks me these things." He smiles. "Small magic, the kind I can do, is innate." There's a dandelion patch growing along the edge of the barn. Bram waves his hand, and it bursts into a cluster of pink tulips. I gasp.

Bram just laughs. "It's really not all that useful." The tulips crumble to ash as he says it.

He closes his fist and opens it, revealing a shiny gold coin. He hands it to me, and I'm surprised to find it ice cold.

"Wait," he says softly. And the coin melts into a small puddle of water in my palm.

I laugh in awe.

"Big magic, the kind my mother has, is the product of years of study in palace schools. I never had the patience for it, and I came here when I was so young. There's no one to teach me but her, and she doesn't have the time or the interest."

My breath catches at the mention of the Otherworld. There are a million other questions on the tip of my tongue. *What does it look like, what does it smell like, does it rain all the time like it does here, is everyone there as beautiful as you, how does the magic work?*

"I have a confession," I say.

He raises his brows. "Is that so?"

Color rises in my face, and I suddenly regret saying it, but there's no turning back now. "I spent half my life completely obsessed with faeries. I collected every bit of information I could, drew pictures of the Otherworld, made my sister and Greer play faeries with me." I don't say that I never quite grew out of it. "We had this book that our old cook would read to us, *Faeries of the British Isles*. I must have traced the artwork inside at least a hundred times."

I clamp my hand over my mouth. I shouldn't have admitted to owning illegal information about faeries to the son of the queen.

"I'm sorry!" I exclaim. "The book was burned the moment my mother realized what it was."

Bram studies my face. "I'm not going to tell. In fact, I'm a little relieved. No one ever talks to me about this. It's like they're uncomfortable with the idea of me being different."

"I like that you're different." I mean it. "And never doubt that I'll always want to hear more."

He presses his lips together. "Home can be difficult to talk about. Things didn't end well between my parents. I felt stuck in the middle."

"Is that why you decided to come here?"

He shrugs. "It wasn't much of a decision. My mother and father once ruled together as king and queen of the Otherworld, but they disagreed on a few things, particularly on how humans should be treated. My mother, like many in her court, was fond of using humans as playthings, but my father had a soft heart and no stomach for it. When my mother tried to oust him in a coup soon after I was born, he had no choice but to close the door permanently between our worlds."

"That's how she ended up on the battlefield that day?" I marvel. "How did you father defeat her?"

He looks so sad I regret asking. "Iron." The word is only vaguely familiar. I must have read it in Mrs. Osbourne's faerie book.

"I don't know what that is."

Bram shrugs. "I suppose you wouldn't. It's a natural element, a type of metal you can melt down to make things like weapons, tools, chains. She had all mention of it scrubbed from history."

"And your father used it against her?"

"He was afraid of her. He had good reason to be."

"So she came here instead."

Bram nods. "She couldn't go home, but she still needed to be queen of something."

"If the door was locked, how did you get in?"

Bram looks down at the ground solemnly. "My father may have been softhearted, but he was still a king, and the closer I came to being of age, the bigger threat I was to him. Court in the Otherworld is vicious and competitive. Everyone lives forever, so the only way to succeed to the throne is by killing its previous occupant. My father feared that I was still loyal to my mother, or maybe just plain old ambitious, and he became paranoid that I was trying to kill him. The enchantments he put on the door allowed only our bloodline to travel through. He threw me out in the middle of the night and locked it permanently behind me."

Grief roars through me, grief for Bram at being cast out of his homeland, for his father's betrayal, and grief for myself at this final blow to my theory that Lydia could have fallen through to another world. She was right, I am childish. Lydia isn't a girl from a faerie tale, she's just a girl.

But Bram has shown me that magic does exist, even if it's small.

"I'm so sorry, Bram."

He reaches up and wipes a tear from my cheek. I hadn't even realized I was crying. It's on the tip of his finger, and he turns it into a snowflake before it melts into a bead of liquid once more.

"It's all right," he says. "I'm here, aren't I?"

"It's so stupid. When my sister went missing, I thought that maybe she was . . . there."

Bram looks at me, not with pity but with shared sadness. "I'm so sorry, Ivy."

He fidgets with the ring on his right pinkie finger. He has a band of gold on all ten of his fingers, but this is the most delicate band, inlaid with a tiny pearl.

I gesture to the rings. "Do they mean anything?"

Bram shrugs. "Tokens from home."

He slips the pearl ring onto my pointer finger.

"You don't have to do that."

"I want to."

"Why?"

"When I look across ballrooms and see it on your finger, it will feel like I am touching you, even when I'm not."

I blush, and he reaches out and tips my chin up to look at him. "I want to know you too, Ivy Benton."

I'm suddenly terrified he's going to kiss me, and I want to kiss him too, in an abstract sort of way, but I don't feel ready. I take the apple and knife out of my pocket just to have something to do with my hands. Bram watches intently as I carve out another wedge. I offer it to him on the tip of my knife once more.

His eyes bore directly into mine as he leans down, as if to kiss me, then wraps his full lips around the slice and eats it directly off the knife.

I exhale shakily, but he just grins as he chews.

I place the apple and the knife back in my pocket, but my knuckles bump the folded-up note Lottie handed me earlier in the day.

Later, in the privacy of my room, I unfold it. In unfamiliar, boyish handwriting are the words *I believe in you. EDV.* And below that, a tiny sketch of a shrimp with a heart right in the middle of its head.

MARION THORNE

Faith Fairchild might really be the death of me.

"Psst, Marion," she whispers on our turn around the palace grounds. Before I can protest, she's pulling me by the crook of my arm into the glass walls of the orangery. Ivy Benton's little stunt with Prince Bram might have been insufferable, but at least it got Viscountess Bolingbroke off our backs for a little while.

Faith is panting, her cheeks flush with exertion. Her chestnut hair is braided in a crown up on her head, but it's humid today, and little wisps are curling around her ears.

She runs a tongue over her full bottom lip and—

"*Marion*," she says more harshly, and I blink back to myself. Get a grip.

"There was something I wanted to speak about with you," she says.

Anything, I nearly say, but that would be silly, so I just nod.

"Would you mind if I swapped rooms with Olive?"

I blink a few times. "Swapped rooms?"

"Yes, so you and I can share." Faith exhales. "I can hardly stand to look at Ivy. I know she's been sneaking off with Emmett, and after that stunt with Bram, I'm even more tempted to smother her in her sleep. It's really for everyone's safety. I don't think Olive would mind moving across the hall, and then I could take her spot with you."

I laugh at her joke, but it comes out hollow. It's about Emmett, of course. I should have seen this coming. I was so stupid to assume anything else.

Faith confessed her history with Emmett to me our second night in the cottage. I was outside watching the sunset in the rose garden when she stomped out and said something under her breath about longing for some air.

I stole two flutes and a dusty bottle of something from the kitchen and settled down with her on an old stone bench that was crawling with moss. "You look like you need someone to spill your guts to," I said. And she did. I wasn't lying, but I also wasn't about to pass up the chance to be close to her. Since the moment I first spotted her in profile the morning of the Pact Parade, I was . . . enamored. Yes, that's a word. Let's go with enamored. She felt so familiar to me, like there was a string tied directly to my heart, and every time I saw her face, an invisible force tugged at it.

"I thought I could love him," she explained that night in the garden. "That feels silly now."

"I don't think love is ever silly," I replied.

"Is that why you're here?" she asked. "Because you think you could love Bram?"

"Oh no," I answered honestly. It was quite the opposite, though I didn't tell her then.

"Is that why *you're* here," I asked her in turn. "For revenge?"

She sighed, like the weight of the world was pressing down on her narrow shoulders, and shook her head. "No, Emmett doesn't love me like that. I couldn't get that kind of reaction out of him if I tried."

"You could have fooled me."

"What Emmett and I had . . . it's hard to explain. We needed each other."

That I understood, at least a little. "If you're not here for Emmett, then why?"

Faith worried her lip again, I was afraid she'd draw blood and I'd be forced to do something chivalrous, like produce a clean hanky and dab at the wound.

"My father told me I had to enter the season, and I didn't want to leave anything to chance. My father would have made me accept the first offer that came my way just to make me not his problem anymore. I figured Bram was my best option. What a cliché, right?"

"I think you're more than a cliché," I said, too honest.

Faith smiled. I wanted to keep making her smile. "You might be the only one who does."

I thought I was so clever when I signed up for the competition for the prince's hand. The subject of my match has been a conversation at the Thorne family dinner table for as long as I've been alive.

Queen Mor's England is deeply isolated from the rest of the world. Other than tightly regulated, necessary economic trade, there is functionally no contact with the outside world. It's said that on a sunny day in Dover, you can see all the way to France. The light is supposed to be beautiful as it reflects off the remnants of the wall they built four hundred years ago to keep Mor out.

Every country seems to have its own explanation for Queen Mor and her eternal rule. Angel or demon, depending on who you ask. To my father's people, she was a monster. There was no other reasonable explanation for a woman who lived forever. You don't go into the forest on Thursdays, and you certainly don't leave your home to sail to England. But as my father tells it, drought had dried up his family's land in Ghana, and he was out of options. So he boarded a boat with others who believed that demons were the stuff of myth, and he crossed an unfriendly ocean.

Per the Royal Decree of 1597, all who are brave enough to make a bargain with Queen Mor are made citizens.

He was just eighteen when he knelt in front of her and bargained for one hundred bolts of fabric and a sewing machine.

Within the year, he'd become the most sought-after tailor on Savile Row. A year after that, he used his profits to open a department store. He now controls half of London's shopping district in the West End. He changed his last name from Agyapong to Thorne, like slipping on a new coat that he didn't like half as well as the last one.

Queen Mor took from him the ability to dream. He once told me that if he could dream, he'd dream of home.

An incredible storyteller and ruthless businessman, he quickly became a favorite at court, and the queen granted him a dukedom in less time than it took to buy his first two-story storefront.

The summer he turned twenty-three, he met my mother, a prim and proper English girl who grew up on an estate near Cornwall, and they were wed two months later. I came along the following winter, and the scheming began immediately. He might have been a duke, but he hadn't been one for long, and he knew he needed to secure his family's legacy. That meant marriage. That meant me.

My future always felt like a pit filling with sand. There was nothing I could do to stop it. I stitched samplers that said nice things about being a nice girl. I learned to play the pianoforte, became a wizard at whist, and could identify all the plants growing on the edge of the forest that bordered our family's estate.

My little sister, Este, was my shadow, my partner. Our governess and tutors drilled us like little soldiers, and by ten and twelve we could plan a banquet, balance a household's budget, and dance a perfect quadrille.

We were good girls, so we could become perfect wives.

After our lessons, I had to go for long walks to cool myself off, until I stopped feeling like I needed to claw my way out of my own skin.

When I was fifteen, I kissed a girl for the first time at Lady Richfield's spring equinox tea party, and then I threw up in a hydrangea bush. Penny Richfield was two years older than me, and she blushed when our hands brushed over the clotted cream. She married the second son of a viscount last fall and now pretends not to know who I am.

My future became a grave filling up with dirt.

I made everyone laugh at every event of the social season. I dreamed about hopping on a boat to Accra, finding my father's family, and building a life different from this one.

But I couldn't break my parents' or Este's hearts like that, so I shoved everything real about me deep down to a place that was hard to reach.

I put on my Pact Parade gown like I was dressing for my own funeral.

But then Queen Mor announced that this was the season Bram would take a wife.

The plan popped into my head with the weight of inevitability. I would enter. I would lose. And then I would be free.

Signing that contract in blood was the easiest thing I've ever done.

No husband. *Oh boo-hoo.* I'll find some way to carry on.

I've only lost sleep at night over the reaction of my parents. They've fought so hard for the life they've given to my sister and me, the last thing I want to do is let them down. I can't bear it. But I'll find some way to spin the tragic tale of my failure when it comes to telling my family. We could all still come out of this winning.

It's why I still worked so hard at the May Queen competition. I had to make it look like I was trying.

There's absolutely no way Bram is going to pick me. I'm not trying at all now, but they don't need to know that.

They also don't need to know about my bargain. The story I made up for the other girls about the headaches are real. I've been plagued with them for as long as I can remember, but that's not the bargain I made.

When Queen Mor asked me what my greatest fear was, I looked her right in the eye and said, "Living a life as small as this forever. If I have to embroider one more cushion, I'm going to throw myself into the Thames."

She laughed, and it made me strangely proud.

When I asked her to make me a great writer, her face turned serious. "I can do that. For a price."

"I understand." I could picture it so clearly, the life I would have when all this was over.

What she took from me in return was so strange, I didn't completely understand it in the moment. In fact, I only barely understand it now. But I fill my notebooks with sonnets and novels that flow out of me like water, and I don't think about what I lost at all.

The only thing that causes me to ache now is looking at Faith Fairchild.

"Marion?" Faith prompts, and I come back to myself, back to the orangery, where she's standing in front of me with *that face*.

"So, room swap?" she asks.

"Anything," I reply, again too honest.

"Fabulous. I'll move my things into your room tonight. You're sure Olive won't mind?"

"She's an angel. Ivy will have to tolerate sleeping with a lamp on, but it's really not so bad."

"Done." Faith extends her hand and I take it in mine.

"Done," I agree.

CHAPTER NINETEEN

It's been an awkward morning. I was awoken by Olive huffing and dragging her trunk over the threshold of my room.

"Faith said we're swapping," she explained, and went back to arranging a family of stuffed dogs on her pillow.

"Did she now?"

I marched across the hall to where Faith and Marion were unpacking Faith's things. "No one thought to consult me about this?" The truth is, I pity Faith. But I doubt she'd take kindly to me expressing that to her.

They looked up. At least Marion had the manners to look sheepish.

"Didn't think it necessary," Faith answered for both of them.

She scares me too. She has all the same knowledge about Bram that I do, but with an angelic face and actual experience with boys. I bet Emmett didn't have to teach her how to flirt.

Now we're all crossing the wide green lawn over to the main palace residence in tense silence, heading to tea in the queen's private drawing room.

A dozen of those strange, silent footmen are waiting for us in a parlor tucked away in the queen's private apartments.

Viscountess Bolingbroke places her hands on her hips. "I hope you're ready for another of Her Majesty's lessons. I heard you all had such fun at the last one." I knew this was coming, but it still sends a chill down my spine.

"A good wife possesses many talents," Bolingbroke says. "She must be a perfect hostess, a dedicated bookkeeper, the very heart and soul of her household. She must provide her husband with comfort and understanding."

"Is that what Queen Mor does for her husbands?" Marion asks. She's standing behind Faith, but her voice carries across the whole room, which settles into tense silence.

Viscountess Bolingbroke cocks her head, her face as stony as ever. "She is not a wife. She is a queen."

Dread beads in cold sweat at the nape of my neck.

The viscountess stands and gestures to the footmen lined up along the wall.

They open a set of double doors at the end of the room, revealing another sitting room, this one even larger.

Emmy, perhaps emboldened by her status as the current leader, takes a step into the adjacent room. Greer, unable to turn left, has to make a full circle to follow us in.

Three large windows look out onto the park, where visitors and members of court stroll idly in the spring sunshine.

The sitting room is ordinary, save for its size. The wallpaper in hues of sage green and lavender matches the elaborately patterned carpet. There are a few distinct sitting areas, collections of chairs and sofas, a pianoforte, a whist table, a basket of embroidery supplies, and a roaring fire.

Silently, like she's floating on air, the queen strides into the room and settles on a silk fainting couch. As if to discourage us from acknowledging her presence, she flicks open a peacock feather fan.

"What now?" Greer asks.

A footman clears his throat, and we turn to him. "Per Her Majesty's design, you will find six different stations." He gestures around the room to the golden pendant flags placed throughout. "You will complete the work of a station for ten minutes, then a bell will ring, and you will rotate. This will go on until there is only one young lady left, and she will be declared the winner and the recipient of the queen's favor."

It's an endurance exercise, like the May Queen competition.

"Ready?" the footman asks, and because we have no other choice, we say yes.

I sit first on the sofa by the basket of sewing supplies, figuring it's a simple enough place to start. I've been sewing since before I could read.

Arranged in a row are six embroidery hoops, each tied with a silk ribbon that's been embroidered with our names. I pick up the one that says *Ivy*.

Someone has already sketched the design in tracing pencil. I hold it up to the light to make out the letters. *Brash and unrefined. A less pretty version of her mad, ruined sister.*

My eyes well with tears as fury pulses through me.

At random, I choose another embroidery hoop, Greer's. Traced on the fabric I find *Destined to age as poorly as her mother, with half her social graces.*

Emmy's next. *Untalented, unreliable, a blight on her family name.*

"What is this?" I ask in horror.

"Any bride of Bram's will have to have thick skin. Don't let the needle prick you, dear." The viscountess strolls casually into the other room, and I know this conversation is over. I swallow my anger and thread my needle.

Greer sits down at the pianoforte by the window.

Olive takes her place at a larger table covered with slips of paper.

Faith, Emmy, and Greer walk into an adjacent room.

It's so ordinary, which makes it all the more sinister.

The footman rings a bell, and our ten minutes begin. The room is silent and uneventful for a few minutes, but then Marion misses a note and gasps, pulling her hand back from the keys as if she's been burned.

In my distraction, I miss a stitch. There's a sudden prick to my middle finger, like I've just been stabbed by an invisible needle. Blood beads on the tip and drips down the silver thread pinched between my fingers.

I glance at Olive, who is sitting with gritted teeth, bouncing her leg up and down uncontrollably.

From the other room comes the sound of voices, music, and then, suddenly, the smashing of porcelain. I keep my eyes down, terrified to miss another stitch.

I sew for another ten minutes, letting my eyes glaze over the horrible words I'm stitching, and then rotate to the next station, the pianoforte.

It doesn't take long to realize why Marion gasped. I hit an incorrect A minor, and a sudden burn rips down my finger, right to the bone.

I jerk my hands back, and from across the room Olive cries out as the sewing needle pricks her.

The bell chimes after another ten minutes. A bead of sweat trickles down my spine. I'm stiff with terror, afraid of the pain that awaits me if I make a mistake.

My third station is the larger table. Scattered are lists of names—lords, ladies, other members of the peerage—and a diagram of a ballroom. She wants us to plan a seating chart.

I begin by arranging the names by seniority, bracing myself for whatever pain I'll face if I get this wrong. I set down a name, and a shooting pain goes up my foot, through the joints of my ankle, then my knee, then my hip. I nearly buckle, but I'm too afraid to fall.

The bell rings. I rotate into the next room. The first task is to sit in a chair across from a footman who is playacting as a party guest telling an extraordinarily boring story about gardening. If you slouch or avert your eyes for even a second, an agonizing zip of pain goes down your spine.

The next rotation involves placing a porcelain plate on your head and walking the length of the room with perfect posture. Once you make one full lap, a footman places a second plate on your head, and then a third, and so on.

If you drop a plate, you must hold the shards in your hands as you make the next circuit.

The weight on top of my skull is heavier than I expected. I'm making my first circuit when the queen glides by, watching us. I don't understand which part of this she enjoys. Is it our suffering? The power she has over us? Or is she just so bored after all this time, she can't think of anything else to do?

She kicks up the corner of the rug with the tip of her silk slipper. My heel catches on it and I fall to my knees.

"That will never do, Lady Ivy. A princess must have perfect balance."

I gather the shards in my hands and seethe. I make another turn, so angry I stumble again, and a second plate shatters at my feet.

The pieces leave tiny, stinging cuts along the edges of my fingers.

My final rotation is a solo country dance. The torture of this exercise is quickly revealed. If you miss a step, your knees buckle, sending you to the ground. I fall four times, each one harder than the last. Silent tears of pain stream down my face.

We must be halfway through the ten minutes when a shout startles me. I immediately fall to my knees as if cut like a marionette. The carpet bites into my skin through my thin stockings.

"Enough!" Marion Thorne is standing in the other corner of the room at the porcelain plate exercise. A stack of plates lie shattered at her feet. The footman rushes to the shards and picks them up to place in her hands, but Marion doesn't allow it. She sidesteps and, with one full swipe of her arm, topples the white porcelain plates stacked in the corner of the room. There must be hundreds of them, and they fall with a mighty crash that shakes the floor.

The music stops. The other girls rush in from the adjacent room. Our hands are bleeding. We're sweaty with an hour's worth of effort, all of us panting.

"Enough!" Marion says once more. "If Bram wants me as his wife, he knows where to find me."

She storms out of the room, leaving nothing but a swinging door and stunned silence in her wake.

CHAPTER TWENTY

For a moment we just look at each other. Olive slips her pointer finger into her mouth to suck at where it's bleeding. My whole body is so shaky with effort, I collapse onto a love seat, and Emmy joins me with a heavy sigh.

As if nothing out of the ordinary has happened, the footman rings his golden bell signaling the start of the next rotation.

There's a glance of recognition that goes around the room, as if the thought crosses all our minds simultaneously. If we all refuse to do this, a loser and a winner cannot be chosen.

"Let's call it a tie?" Greer proposes.

"It's like you read my mind," Emmy says.

"Agreed," I add.

"Obviously," Faith says.

Olive just nods, her finger firmly in her mouth.

We're halfway down the stairs when Olive stops suddenly. "My bracelet!" she exclaims. "It must have come unclasped. Just one moment, I'll be back." As we wait, I stare up at the tree that reaches the ceiling, its green leaves quaking slightly, the very tops brushing the honeycomb glass.

I felt such determination the first time I saw this tree on the day of the Pact Parade. Now I just feel wrung out.

Olive comes bounding down the stairs a few moments later.

I'm half expecting the footmen or royal guards or the queen herself to stop us, but the six of us stride right out the door and across the lawn to our cottage, with no fanfare at all.

Marion is waiting for us, sitting at the dining table, where the cook has laid out an impressive lunch.

She pops up, her eyes wide with surprise. "What happened?"

Emmy plops down at the table and grabs a scone. "We decided you were right."

Marion's eyes get misty with tears, but she doesn't say another word. Faith sits down next to her and lays a comforting hand on her shoulder.

Lunch passes with the tense silence of children expecting a scolding. We all flinch at the slightest creak in the floor, expecting some consequence for walking out of the queen's second trial.

At teatime, there's a sharp rap at the front door. We startle. "I'll get it," I say. Standing there is a footman with a package wrapped in brown paper. He hands it to me. I peel back the paper to take a peek and find an achingly familiar shade of green.

I run up the stairs to my room. "Who was it?" Olive calls.

"Just a letter from my mother!"

I toss the book on my bed and tear the paper open to reveal the cover. In gilded lettering it reads *Faeries of the British Isles*.

I flip open the cover to find a note from Bram. *A book about magic, for a girl who already has plenty. —B.*

It's the same edition as the one I had as a child. There's an annotation inside the front cover. *From the Library of EJB, 4 Waters Lane, Alton, England. 1702.*

I clutch it to my chest, savoring the smell of it, then tuck it under my mattress.

Tonight we're expected at the Welbys' masquerade ball. Count and Countess Welby are some of the younger members of the peerage, with reputations for throwing full-on bacchanalia. Tonight's party doesn't even begin until after ten and is anticipated to rage until sunrise.

The cottage turns into a tornado of silks and jewels and feathers. Olive runs back and forth from our room to Marion's in nothing but her chemise and a pair of butterfly wings. Greer's enormous peacock feather backpiece is too large, and she is momentarily lodged in the stairwell. Emmy has to push her through, both of them laughing so hard they're on the verge of tears.

All the while, Lottie holds me still in front of the mirror, painstakingly placing crystals in my upswept hair. She even uses little bits of paste to stick a few to my cheekbones and at the corners of my eyes.

My dress tonight is midnight-blue silk, with sleeves that fall wide at my wrists and a daringly low neckline. It's embroidered all over with a golden spray of constellations.

Lottie gestures for me to stand and then ties a cape around my neck that shimmers with hundreds of falling stars.

The final piece is a tiara made of stars, with one crescent moon in the middle.

Even I can't help but gasp upon seeing myself in the mirror. "Oh, Lottie, you've outdone yourself."

She smiles proudly. "He's going to faint when he sees you."

I bite back a smile, picturing Emmett's stunned face across a crowded ballroom. Then I immediately wipe the thought away, angry that it was there in the first place.

The party is roaring by the time we arrive. The grand front steps of the house are aglow with torches, everyone in their fancy dress spilling out into the night.

We help each other tie on our masks when we are out of the carriages. Mine is fashioned from a delicate silver mesh. Olive's is made of monarch wings, matching perfectly her orange and black butterfly dress, nearly the exact same shade as her ginger hair.

The crowd parts as the six of us enter the room. We make quite a sight in our costumes. Emmy to my right is in ink black, dressed as a bat, with wings tied around her middle fingers that extend when she stretches her arms.

Marion shimmers in her mermaid costume, complete with a tiara made of shells and pearls.

But it's Faith I'm jealous of. She's dressed as Romeo's Juliet. Her dress is the simplest of all, a warm cream silk that laces up the front. There's a golden circlet on her head, and her brown curls are pulled off her face and cascade down her back.

She glares as she catches me staring.

As usual, we're not handed dance cards like the rest of the eligible girls our age. Instead, we mingle by the champagne tower and gossip about the other attendees.

There's a sudden pull on my arm, and I jump, completely unladylike, into Lydia's arms.

"What are you doing here?" I gasp.

She looks better than she did the last time I saw her. There's more pink in her cheeks, and her hair is markedly less dull. Her costume, however, is uncharacteristically lazy. She's wearing a lavender silk dress Mama had made for her first season, two years ago, with fresh flowers woven through her blond curls.

"Mama thought it would be good for me."

My mother appears behind her, my father in tow.

I give them all tight hugs, surprised at how my body relaxes, a bone-deep longing for home I didn't even realize I had.

My mother grips both my hands conspiratorially. "How have things been?"

I'm sad I can't give her the juicy gossip she wants, and I refuse to trouble her with my fears. That's the thing about having a mother who remembers everything. I have to be careful about what I give her to worry about.

"It's been lovely. The other girls are so nice, and Prince Bram is such a gentleman."

She grins, and again I remind myself that every moment of pain is worth the joy on her face.

Trumpets sound, and the doors swing open as Prince Emmett and Prince Bram come striding in.

At the sight of Emmett's face, I feel the fault line crack down the center of my chest, the two sides of me at war. There's the side that wants only to be a good girl, a good daughter, and to help my family be integrated into society once more, and then there is the side that is allied with Emmett, the side that's willing to risk burning this all to the ground to build a world better than this one.

Anxiously, I twist Bram's pearl ring around my index finger.

With my parents in front of me, I feel very much like a child again, with a child's heart that only wants them to be safe and whole and proud of me.

Emmett's voice echoes in my head. *You could be queen.*

Viscountess Bolingbroke waves me over to rejoin the rest of the group now that Bram has arrived at the party.

Bram walks right over to us, taking in our costumes. He's dressed as something of a pirate, in a black velvet coat and a billowing white shirt open wide around his throat.

He turns to my parents and politely introduces himself. My mother giggles like a schoolgirl, and my father looks up at him like he's the son he's always craved.

Bram pulls Olive into a waltz first and then proceeds to dance with us one by one. "You're getting better," he says as he twirls me across the ballroom.

I look into his eyes, the way Emmett taught me. "I've been practicing."

The clock strikes midnight, and Bram disappears with the men to the upstairs drawing room to smoke cigars and discuss topics too worldly for our delicate ears.

It's been hours, and I haven't seen Lydia again. I wonder bitterly if she's snuck home without saying goodbye.

The party shows no sign of dying down, but Viscountess Bolingbroke is snoring softly in the corner, slumped in a chair after one too many glasses of champagne.

I slip out into the garden, where torches cast long shadows over hedges and twisting oak trees, to look for my sister.

There's a raucous game of croquet happening off to my left, but that's not where Lydia would be, so I go right, where it's darker and quieter. "Lydia?" I call. There is no answer but the rustle of wind through the fruit trees and the hedges trimmed to look like zoo animals.

"Lydia?"

"Lady Ivy, is that you?" a male voice answers.

"Emmett?"

I see him now, moving toward me in the shadows, haloed in moonlight.

"I was looking for my sister," I say.

"And I was looking for you."

"Oh?"

"Come quick." He reaches down as if to grab my hand, but thinks better of it and shoves his hand in his pocket.

He's wearing an open doublet, with a costume crown slightly askew on his dark waves. Both our masks were discarded hours ago.

I gesture to his outfit. "What are you supposed to be?"

"A prince." He looks over his shoulder and flashes me an infuriating half smile.

"That doesn't count—you're already a prince."

"I'm one from"—he gestures his hands vaguely—"the days of yore, or something."

"This is the laziest costume I've ever seen."

He clutches his heart in mock distress. "You wound me, Lady Ivy. We can't all be lucky to have costumes as impressive as yours."

"Are you impressed?"

His eyes rake down my body, then back up again to my face. I shiver, as if he's just touched me. "You look like a fallen star." There is no hint of laughter in his words now.

We come to a garden gate at the back of the house, where the noise from the party is dampened. It's partially hidden by overgrown rosebushes and shadowed by a willow tree.

He reaches around me to pull the gate open, then gestures for me to go on without him. "Bram is waiting for you."

I told him I needed more time alone with his brother. "I'm glad to hear you can take direction," I reply, but it comes out strangely choked.

"You know me," he replies, face stony. "So obedient."

I do want to win. I want to help Emmett and the rebellion and my family. Time with Bram will help me win. So why does it feel like I'm losing?

I step through the gate, and Emmett disappears into the darkness. I don't have it in me to watch him as he goes.

Bram is waiting for me in the center of the hidden garden under the weatherworn statue of a trumpeting angel.

"Lady Ivy." His face lights up as I approach. "A sight for sore eyes."

"Were you expecting someone else?"

"I wasn't sure what to expect. My brother led me here and told me to wait for a surprise. I must admit I was a little nervous, given the venue, but you're better than anything I could have hoped for."

I'm confused, but then he gestures to the patch of earth closest to us, and I see the fine mist net over the plant and the little stake in the ground that reads *foxglove*, next to it, *monkshood*, and behind it, *laburnum*.

"He left you in a poison garden?" I ask.

Bram just laughs that easy laugh of his. "My brother does have a sense of humor."

"Or maybe he just thought no one would come looking for us here. I hear he's clever, your brother." Emmett's face pops into my head again, the infuriating smile, the hair he can't seem to tame, those goddamn eyes.

"Ahh." Bram nods sagely. "Very clever indeed."

Brown hair. A strong hand on my forehead soothing away a fever. Emmett is just something I need to sweat out. I'm nothing to him but a means to an end.

"I don't want to talk about my brother," he says, his gray eyes sparkling like starlight. They're not a color I've ever seen on a person.

"What do you want to talk about?" I ask.

"I don't think I want to talk at all." He picks up my hand and traces along my pointer finger. His hands are warm. "You're wearing my ring."

"Haven't taken it off."

My heart leaps into my throat, but the space between us goes quiet and still. It's not desire I feel, but the burn of inevitability.

I swam in the sea once as a child and got knocked over by a wave. I tumbled in the surf, scraped my knees against the sand, and snorted water up my nose.

It was the first time I felt truly small, the first time I knew what it felt like to be carried away by a force I couldn't control.

I taste salt water in the back of my throat now.

"Ivy." He whispers my name under his breath like he's been longing for his mouth to taste it.

Then he takes one more confident step toward me and presses his lips to mine.

I've never been kissed before. It's warmer than I expected, a little wetter, too.

For one panicked second, I just freeze, but Bram takes over, confident and sure. It's obvious he's kissed others, but in this moment I'm not sure if I care.

I move my lips against his and thread my hands through his curls reflexively.

He pulls me closer, his hands strong on the small of my back.

I keep waiting to feel *something*. I thought I'd feel sparks or church bells or licking flames. But all I can think is *Am I doing it right?* I have to get this right. I have to make him want to marry me, or I'll let Emmett down. I could be letting the whole country down.

Bram wrenches back as if it pains him and looks down at me. He really is extraordinarily handsome, his face just this side of other-worldly. I reach up and trace the pointed shell of his ear, just because I can. He shudders against my touch.

He smiles softly, and finally I feel something, a hollow wrenching in my heart.

I have to fake it, so I smile back, then duck my head. I don't think I have it in me right now to play lovestruck, but shy, I can do.

"I have to go find my sister," I whisper.

"I'll help you," he whispers in return, and I have the feeling that there is little I could ask Bram that he wouldn't do for me.

We're rounding the corner back to the house when I see a small figure in the dark, hunched over on a bench.

"Lydia?" I call.

She raises her head, and I can see her better now. The flowers in her hair have wilted.

Bram follows me to where she's sitting. She's got that dazed look on her face, the one I loathe so much because it makes me worry that's she's lost again, and I cannot survive her being gone for good.

I bend down and peer up at her face. "Lydia, let's get you back to Mama."

She blinks back to herself, like she's been wandering somewhere I can't see. "Oh . . ." She trails off. "Yes."

Bram walks to the other side of her to help her to her feet.

"You must be the famous Lydia," he says kindly, with a voice one might use to speak to a small child.

She looks up at him, as if only just now realizing he was there. There's a moment of pause, and I'm racking my brain for something charming to say to defuse the situation, when Lydia clutches her stomach and retches all over Bram's fancy shoes.

"Lydia!" I exclaim. Bram steps back in shock. Vomit splashes all over the gravel and onto the stars embroidered on the hem of my dress.

"Lady Benton, are you all right?" I don't know which of us he's asking. He pulls a handkerchief from his breast pocket and passes it to Lydia.

She doesn't take it. Instead, she mutters, "I'm sorry. I'll find Mama," and runs off into the big house before either of us can stop her.

"I'm sorry about my sister—oh, and thank you for the book!" I call over my shoulder, but I'm so busy chasing her, I'm not sure if Bram hears me.

I race inside, near frantic with a sickening combination of humiliation and worry. The golden candlelight stings after the darkness from outside. My eyes burn with tears of embarrassment, and my mouth still aches, as if bruised by the kiss.

Bram doesn't follow us, and I hardly blame him.

Back in the ballroom, the music swells like nothing has changed.

Viscountess Bolingbroke still dozes in her wing chair, and the other five girls lean on the wall nearby in various states of boredom.

Marion looks on the verge of falling asleep herself; Olive swivels her head around the ballroom, giving her an air of quiet desperation; Emmy, Faith, and Greer have stolen a bottle of champagne and are giggling, barely disguising the sips they are taking behind their feather fans.

For a horrifying second it looks like Lydia is about to run directly through the center of the dance floor, where couples are spinning like tops. I've done so much work to rehabilitate my family, and this would undo it all.

But blessedly, she cuts left, to where my mother is lounging in a half circle of love seats with her friends. Lydia collapses into our shocked mother's shoulder. I make it to them seconds later. Lydia is inconsolable, incoherent.

"Darling, what happened?" My mother isn't asking Lydia, but me. Sweet Lydia, always given every benefit of the doubt by our parents. Of course my mother assumes it must have been my fault.

"I haven't the faintest idea," I say. "She humiliated me in front of Prince Bram, though." I loathe the rage that rips through me, the concern I felt just seconds ago transforming into a familiar anger.

Lydia and I, always two sides of the same coin. Her hurt is spilled out onto the floor, messy in a way that demands it be witnessed. Mine, shoved so deep down, my steps are heavier with the weight of it.

Why can't she suffer in a more palatable way? Why can't she find a way to make her agony lovable, her pain marriageable, when I'm trying so hard?

Be prettier when you cry, the part of me I hate most wants to say to her.

Maybe this is the crux of my anger with Lydia. I am ready to marry a man I do not love to save our family. I am relieved that Lydia, the person I love most in the world, will be spared the same fate, yet I resent her for letting me do it all alone.

My mother hauls Lydia to her feet. "I'll send a note tomorrow with news of your sister's health. I'm sorry, sweet girl, she didn't mean to do this."

How could my mother know anything Lydia means to do, when I don't think Lydia knows herself?

Lydia raises her tear-streaked, snotty face and meets my eye. "I didn't mean to."

She never means to. That's the problem.

I love her too much to bear looking at her like this.

So exhausted by the turn in the night's events, I walk out the door and to the carriages without an escort. If I get scolded by Viscountess Bolingbroke in the morning, so be it.

The carriage delivers me to the front of the palace, and I cut through the grounds to the cottage.

A parade of storm clouds has blown in, nearly blocking out the light of the moon and stars. I drag my heavy, beaded dress through the grass, trying to outrun the rain. The air smells of it; it won't be long now.

I expect the cottage to be dark and quiet with the other girls still at the ball, but I startle at the sound of fabric moving through the grass.

From the corner of my vision a flash of movement makes me jump. For a split second I think it's the other girls returning from the ball, but it's not.

Queen Mor walks toward me, only a few dozen feet away, her

steps completely silent. Her pale skin is a near-ghostly pale blue in the moonlight, her dark hair loose around her shoulders.

She's in an ornate gown of cerulean silk the color of the night sky. She's carrying something, a basket, perfectly still in her right hand.

Shit.

Like a prey animal, something primal pings in me at the sight of her, a long-forgotten instinct to run.

Her black eyes stare me down.

I unlatch the door to the cottage. "Please, won't you come in," I say, because politeness is the only armor I have.

"This is my house," she replies with a serene smile.

Nonetheless, she follows me in to the sitting room, where the staff have stoked a roaring fire.

We step inside just in time for the rain to arrive, beating on the roof and windows.

"May I ask the reason for your visit?" My voice wobbles.

"No."

I call for tea because it seems the right thing to do, but I don't drink a drop as we wait. I have to hold the cup steady against my leg so it doesn't clink against the saucer as my hands shake. The clock on the mantel ticks and ticks, each second slower than the last.

The agonizing silence doesn't seem to bother Queen Mor in the slightest. She sips her tea, and I wonder if an eternal lifetime feels a lot like waiting. We must be nothing but a blip to her. I wonder if she'll even remember the first crop of silly girls she tortured to find a bride for her son. I'm struck with the deeply unsettling feeling that we may be the first class of many.

Perhaps I am delirious from lack of sleep, or perhaps it is because I fear I will never get another chance, but I set my teacup down on the table and open my mouth to ask a question. "Will you tell me what my sister's bargain was?"

Her gaze snaps to mine, and she shakes her head like a mother, ever patient but exasperated. "I will not."

There's another question on the tip of my tongue. I can't stop it from spilling out. "But do you know where she was those weeks she disappeared?"

This time she answers more slowly, like she's chewing on my question and can't quite decide how she wants to react.

"Of course I do."

The words land like a punch to the stomach. She wasn't in the Otherworld, I know that for certain now. *Where the hell were you, Lydia?*

The front door swings open and Viscountess Bolingbroke and the rest of the girls come piling in, finally home from the ball.

There is giggling, the swishing of silks, wet shoes plopping onto the stone floor.

And then the hush of terrified silence as they enter the sitting room to find Queen Mor and me in front of the fire.

"Sit," she commands. The drawing room is small, and with this many bodies, it's crowded.

Olive perches on the edge of my armchair, her butterfly wings wilting behind her. Faith and Marion tangle together on the chair across from us, Marion's seashell tiara now askew on Faith's head. Greer and Emmy sit on the ground right in front of the fire, and I'm terrified that Greer's peacock feathers are going to catch some embers, but I'm too afraid to break the tense silence to warn her.

"It seems you didn't enjoy our game today," Queen Mor says, frowning. "There are few things I hate worse than poor sports."

My stomach curdles with fear. Olive's knuckles go white as she grips the edge of the armchair.

"These lessons are important, they help me get to know you. Bram needs my help in selecting his bride," she continues. "One of you will one day become a most-beloved daughter-in-law, and we can't leave something like that up to chance, can we?"

None of us answer, too scared or angry or frozen to manage it. But she stares us down with those uncanny black eyes until Emmy breaks.

"No, ma'am." We echo her in a shaky chorus.

"I realize now, the fault was mine," Queen Mor says. "I should have given you more instruction. How can one play a game when the rules are so poorly defined?"

She lets her words hang in the air, then closes her eyes and takes a big inhale, her body visibly relaxing, as if luxuriating in our fear. "Let's add a few more terms, shall we? The girl with the lowest score at the end of all this will have her family stripped of their titles and their land. Any more acts of insubordination will be your last. Understood?"

My blood turns to ice. She'll kill us all if we don't play along.

CHAPTER TWENTY-ONE

Marion jumps to her feet in protest. Greer's face turns bright red with rage. Olive bursts into tears. Emmy just laughs, hysterical on the edge of a scream. Only Faith appears unaffected, perfectly still, her mind somewhere far from her body.

The queen bends to dig into the basket at her side. One by one she pulls out our samplers from today's trial and passes them to us.

In various states of completion, they're speckled with blood from our pricked fingers. In the middle of each is a number stitched neatly in crimson thread.

There's a 6 on mine. I glance at Marion's, a 6 as well. We've all tied for last place.

The queen gives Olive hers last, and I'm shocked to see it emblazoned with a bloodred 1.

I think back to earlier this afternoon when she ran back up the stairs claiming to have lost a bracelet. That little snake. I didn't know Olive had it in her. Honestly, I'm a little proud.

"You'll join Bram for a ball at Count Doncaster's the day after tomorrow, before we all leave for Hampshire. There will be a hunt this weekend." She claps her hands together and grins until each and every one of her teeth is showing. "What fun we'll have."

Olive—with her sweet face and red hair and croissants. How foolish we were to discount her.

The door slams behind the queen as she leaves us alone in tense silence. The cottage is small and stifling. Olive looks as if she'd like to sink into the floor.

Chaos erupts as Greer launches herself across the room. Olive screeches as Greer snatches at her hair, pulling hard enough to wrench her head back.

Olive flails and screams, "Get her off of me!"

It takes both Faith and Emmy to restrain Greer, who is shaking, her fists full of ginger hair.

Olive gathers her skirts to make a break for the stairs, but I grab her butterfly wings and yank her back. "Don't you dare," I snap.

Olive bursts into crocodile tears, blubbering in the way we've all given her sympathy for.

"There wasn't a bracelet, was there?" Emmy asks, more betrayed than angry.

"You don't understand." Olive sniffs.

"What don't we understand?" I ask.

Olive looks to each of us, one by one, then blurts, "I love him!"

Faith bursts out laughing. "How could you possibly love him?"

Olive juts out her bottom lip. "I just do. It was love at first sight. You're all so jaded, like it makes you clever, but it just makes you bitter."

"So you what, lied to us about a bracelet and completed more tasks upstairs?" Greer asks.

"I only played one more song on the pianoforte," Olive whines.

"But it was enough to put you ahead of the rest of us," Greer shoots back.

Olive rips off her butterfly wings and stomps up the stairs. "Blame the queen, not me."

"Get back here!" Marion shouts.

Olive pauses on the stairs, then turns around and plops down on the ground in the sitting room, a scowl on her face.

"So what do we do now?" Marion asks. "We all signed up with the knowledge that we'd never take a husband if Bram didn't choose us, but I would never have agreed to this if I knew my family would be doomed to poverty, or worse, if I lost."

"Agreed," Greer says. "My mother won't survive it."

Emmy nods emphatically. "My parents, my siblings . . . I can't fail them like this."

"So what do we do?" Marion prompts again.

"We could stab her in her horrible little back," Faith grumbles, now fully horizontal, staring up at the ceiling.

"If anyone figures out how to make that possible, I'm all ears," Marion jokes. I nearly choke.

"What if we all make an agreement," Olive offers, her voice small. "Whoever wins will be a princess, right? She can petition the queen to rethink the punishment of the other girls' families."

There's a beat of silence as we think on it.

"We could be sure to ask her while she's in a good mood," Emmy says.

"In front of Bram!" Greer adds excitedly.

You could be queen.

A familiar feeling curdles in my stomach. I have to win, not just to protect my family, whose titles are all the protection they have, but to protect everyone. If Emmett and the others get this right, we could unseat the queen, end her centuries of torture, and I could ensure everyone in this room and their families are safe from her.

This is the first time she's directly threatened our lives. If her patience with us is wearing thin enough to consider being rid of us completely, there is no room for error.

I have to find a way to tell Emmett.

"Deal." I stick out my hand to shake.

"Deal." Emmy agrees.

"Wait, how do the boys do it?" Marion asks. Then she spits into the palm of her hand.

The rest of us follow suit and clap our sticky hands, one on top of another. Even Olive and Greer. The dying embers of the fireplace flicker, and the comradery feels crystallized, but I know it will fracture tomorrow once Bram is in front of us and reality sets in.

"May the best girl win," Marion says gravely.

"May the best girl win," the rest of us agree.

The Doncasters' ball is a decidedly dull affair. The count is pushing ninety, and his stifling manor doesn't exactly encourage merrymaking.

Viscountess Bolingbroke is in the drawing room playing whist with some elderly friends, so I wander off to go find Emmett. This isn't the kind of thing he'd usually deign to attend, but I caught a glimpse of him earlier, sneaking in through a side door in a navy-blue waistcoat.

I'm wandering down a corridor of closed doors, far from the noise of the ballroom, when I hear his voice.

"Emmett?" I hiss.

I get no reply, but hear the low rumble again. I swing open a door just in time to see him lean in to kiss Faith Fairchild.

I jump back as if I've been burned, then close the door silently. Neither Emmett nor Faith even realized I was there.

My heart is pounding as I exit the long hall and, in a daze, go to the garden to catch my breath. My skin is too hot. I need to be outside.

I lean both hands against the cool stone balcony and wipe at my stinging eyes. The sound of blood rushing in my head is so loud, I don't hear Bram approach.

"Are you quite well?"

I must not look it, because when I turn to him, his perfect face crumples in concern.

It's like I can't catch my breath. I can't remember the last time I didn't feel panicked, not since the Pact Parade, at least. That's what this season has been: a perpetual drowning.

"Just breathe," Bram whispers. "I've got you."

I've got to get it together. I don't need Emmett. I can do this all by myself. "I'm afraid I've rolled my ankle," I lie. "Can you take a look?"

"Of course," he answers.

The others glare as he walks me inside and lowers me to a chair. He kneels at my feet and reaches under the lilac purple layers of my skirts to rotate the joint a few times. "Does that hurt?" he asks.

"I think I'll survive," I answer. "This party is awfully dull. Is there somewhere else we can go?"

He glances around. "A few of the men were talking about leaving for the club."

Every gentleman in London belongs to a private club where they gather to dine, drink, and gamble.

I hop up and walk toward the line of carriages in the drive. "Then let's go."

Bram smiles. "Lead the way." I grin. I didn't actually expect him to say yes. He holds my hand as we hop into the carriage out front, no sense of hesitation in him.

Once inside, Bram sighs against the plush seats and pulls my ankle into his lap. "It's good to keep it elevated," he explains.

"Do your healing powers extend to twisted ankles?"

He smirks. "But that's so much less fun than this." He trails a finger around the hollow of my ankle. Warmth pools in my belly and my cheeks flush.

"I never got the chance to properly thank you for the book." I change the topic, so nervous suddenly, it's difficult to look him in the eye.

The corners of his mouth tug into a smile. "I'm just pleased to have the opportunity to do something for you."

"Where did you get it?" I'm too curious not to ask.

"An old friend."

The carriage slows as we approach his club. Like the other members of the royal family, Bram belongs to Kendall's, which on the outside looks like any number of the luxurious town houses in Mayfair, but covers the whole city block.

I heard a rumor that the owner, Lord Bexham, used his bargain for better house odds and gave up his hair. He denies it, but I've seen him without a hat, and I'm inclined to believe it.

I crane my head as I follow Bram, taking it all in. The box beam ceilings are dotted with crystal chandeliers, the walls are covered in art depicting hunting dogs and elegant horses. Women generally aren't allowed in places like this, but no one is going to say that to the Prince of Wales. Tomorrow the gossip mill will be set alight by news of my being here, and for once I can't wait. Let the whole town know I'm his favorite.

"Should I call for dinner?" he asks. "We can use one of the private rooms."

I muster every bit of false confidence I have. This needs to be as public as possible. "No. I want you to teach me to play poker." Bram looks down at me and grins.

The cardroom goes silent as I walk in on his arm.

I smile sweetly and blink away the cigar smoke burning my eyes. Bram knows everyone. He circles the room, clapping men on their shoulders.

"How's your wife?" he asks a younger-looking man in a top hat.

"Better, thank you, Your Majesty."

I look up at Bram. "What did you do?"

"I sent a private physician to check on his wife. It was nothing, just a friendly favor."

Another man approaches. "My mother-in-law loved the azalea bush you had planted. Positively cannot stop talking about it."

Bram waves his hands like it's nothing. "Give her my best."

"His mother-in-law?" I whisper under my breath.

"The Duchess of Marlborough. A mostly bedbound widow but an absolute genius at puzzles. I stop by from time to time. Thought I'd give her something nice to look at from her window."

We sit down at one of the green-felt tables. This room is paneled in dark wood and covered from end to end in plush maroon carpet.

There are a dozen or so tables, all surrounded by men in crisp cravats and impeccably tailored coats. I recognize a few of my father's old chums and business associates.

Bram greets the other men at our table warmly. "Ah, Perkins!" He looks to the man next to us, then waves over a waiter. He knows everyone's drinks, goes around the table ordering them, then gets to me. "Champagne, right?"

The waiter hurries off, but Bram snaps his finger, and dark red port magically appears in Perkins's water glass.

Perkins takes a sip, then grimaces. "Why is it sour?" he asks. Everyone dissolves into uproarious laughter.

Bram shrugs good-naturedly. "I'm afraid my gifts are limited, Perkins!"

From somewhere in the far corner a cry goes out. Someone shouts.

"What's that?" I gesture in the direction of the game that seems to be going wrong.

"Don't worry about it," Bram says tightly.

The dealer flicks us our cards.

There's a flash of movement. The man who was shouting at the other table throws himself at Bram's feet. His hands are clasped in prayer, his head on Bram's lap. "Please, please, Your Highness. Speak to your mother for me. I'll do anything!"

Bram stands up. "This is neither the time nor the place. My mother's business is her own."

A guard wraps his arms around the man and pulls him away from Bram. "Please!" he yells as he's dragged out of the room. "I made the bargain on the twenty-third of July, 1826. It's ruined me! I've already lost my family. My estate is all I have left. She tricked me! Ask her for mercy!"

The activity in the gambling hall starts right back up, as if nothing is out of the ordinary.

"I'm sorry you had to witness that," Bram says grimly.

I place my hands on the smooth edge of the table to keep them from shaking. "Does that happen often?"

There's a sadness in his eyes. "I don't agree with all the things my mother does, but they make the bargains of their own accord. I cannot help them."

"Are you ready, milords?" the dealer asks. "And . . . milady," he adds awkwardly.

"Please, continue," Bram replies smoothly.

I place my hand on Bram's knee under the table, more desperate than ever to win his affection. I can hardly stand to think about Emmett right now, but if he's right and I'm the only hope of putting an end to this, I cannot fail.

"Which one is this?" asks Lord something-or-other as the cards are redealt.

"Lord Hambleton, may I present Lady Ivy Benton," Bram answers curtly.

I nod my head, but Lord Hambleton goes back to his cards. "I thought the other one was prettier. Trummer's daughter, isn't it? Or your brother's ballerina?"

Bram glares. "That's not any way to speak in front of a lady."

"Well, she's not supposed to be here, is she?" the lord grumbles.

My chest burns hot with embarrassment, but I keep on smiling sweetly. The dealer flips over the first card. "Remind me what a full house is," I whisper to Bram as an excuse to get close to him.

"Three of a kind and two of another," Bram whispers back. "We can go if you want."

I lay a hand on his upper arm. "No, no, I'd like to stay."

We circle the table, giving bets. My hand is rubbish, but I can bluff. "I call."

"On whose money?" Lord Hambleton scoffs. "Your father's line of credit was cut off years ago."

"That's enough," Bram says coldly.

"You don't need to stand up for me," I reply. "He is right."

"She's playing on my account, and you'll treat her with the respect she deserves," Bram says loud enough that heads turn around the room. "I call."

The dealer pulls another card. The queen of hearts. We go around the table again in tense silence. I raise. Lord Hambleton scoffs audibly.

"She's welcome to spend every last shilling I have," Bram says. "Which, if I recall correctly, is several million more than you."

I fold on the next go-round. My hand is bad, and I don't need Bram to defend me over nothing.

Bram and Hambleton go back and forth for a while, but Hambleton takes it in the end. He extends both arms to pull the pot of chips toward him, and I catch a glimpse of something in his sleeve.

Without thinking, I lean over and yank an ace out of the silk lining of his jacket. The table goes still. "You were cheating," I say.

"You bitch," Hambleton snarls.

There's a mighty crash behind me as a chair is toppled and Bram launches himself at Hambleton, throwing his body against the table and sending chips flying. Bram punches him once in the face, then again. The lord's nose cracks, sending a spray of blood across the cards.

CHAPTER TWENTY-TWO

"Bram!" I shout, then throw myself onto his back in an attempt to pull him off.

"Ivy!" I turn to see Emmett sprinting across the room.

He pushes through the gathering crowd and lifts me off of Bram, then sets me down safely before pulling Bram off of Lord Hambleton.

"What is going on?" he pants, wild-eyed, in the middle of Bram and Lord Hambleton with his arms extended.

Lord Hambleton landed only one punch, but it split Bram's lower lip open. He licks away the blood. "He called Ivy a bitch."

Emmett's eyes flash, and he punches Lord Hambleton squarely across the face. The man stumbles back, collapsing against the table.

A whistle blows, and the club manager, a portly man in his fifties, barrels into the room. "That's enough!" he bellows. "I think you'd best be going, Your Highnesses."

Bram pulls his coat from the back of his chair and wipes the blood from his knuckles. "Gladly."

The three of us pile into a carriage. "You didn't have to do that," I say to both of them. "I'm perfectly capable of throwing my own punches." I don't add that the only person I've ever punched is Lydia, and not since I was ten, but I do feel confident I could do it.

"Hardly the first brawl we've gotten into," Emmett says.

"Not even the first brawl in that room," Bram adds. He licks his split bottom lip and it knits itself together, healing right before my eyes.

He notices my shocked expression and laughs. "One of my better party tricks." He glances down at my dress. "Oh no, we've gotten blood on you."

There's a small splatter above my heart, probably from when I flung myself onto Bram's back.

"Don't trouble yourself," I say. "I have so many now."

Bram brushes my skirt with his index finger, and the stain disappears, my dress turning from a pale lilac to a deep burgundy. "This brings out your eyes more." He smiles.

Gas lamps flicker at the doors to the palace. Emmett walks directly inside, giving Bram and me a stolen moment alone.

"Thank you," I say. "You didn't have to defend my honor tonight. I was being a bit of a bitch."

Bram laughs. "He deserved it, and I've been looking for an excuse to deck him for a while. You did me a favor."

He takes a step closer, his face so perfect it still knocks me off my axis. It's like I'm always caught on the wrong foot with him. He looks at me, gaze flickering down to my lips. My eyes drop closed as he leans in, but his lips just barely brush the top of my cheekbone.

"Sleep well, Lady Ivy."

I cross the lawn, my face burning with embarrassment.

I'm nearly to the cottage when I hear the sound of footsteps through damp grass behind me.

I turn, hopeful I'll see Bram, ready to kiss me for real this time, but I deflate as Emmett comes into view. He's probably just coming to Caledonia Cottage to wait for Faith, to finish what they started earlier.

I walk quickly, hoping he'll give up, but he speeds into a jog behind me.

"Slow down."

"Were you watching us?"

He slows as he catches up, falling into step beside me. "So what if I was?"

"You shouldn't have done that tonight," I say.

Emmett laughs awkwardly. "Unfortunately, it's always been punch first, think later with me." But I'm not sure if I believe him. He thinks so much about everything, it's like I can see him constantly tying himself in knots.

I turn for the door, but Emmett reaches for my sleeve, brushing but not quite touching me. "You seem upset with me."

"I'm not upset." I'm not. I have absolutely no reason to be upset with Emmett for kissing Faith tonight.

Emmett's knuckles are bruising like violets. "Does that hurt?" I gesture to them, desperate to change the subject.

He runs a thumb over the mottled skin. "I can have Bram fix them later." His eyes narrow, as if he hopes to see right through me. "You're sure you're not upset?"

I swing open the door to the cottage. I'd rather face the wrath of the other girls—who, no doubt, are annoyed with me for stealing

Bram away—than spend another second looking at Emmett De Vere's face.

"Never, ever been better."

He stops the door with his foot.

"Good. Because everything is going according to plan. Up until now, the only person he'd ever thrown a punch for was me."

The next two days are absolute chaos. We're rushed to the modiste for last-minute alterations to our hunting wardrobes, Viscountess Bolingboke calls an emergency etiquette class on how to conduct ourselves while on the road, and all the while the queen's new terms loom like storm clouds over our heads.

That night, the memory of Emmett at the ball comes back to me. I sleep fitfully, imagining the way Emmett held Faith's waist as he kissed her.

I think of my parents, who married for love and doomed us to a life of instability; of Olive, who moons after Bram so openly I'm humiliated on her behalf; of Faith and the crystal goblet she threw at Emmett's head. Love can't exist for me. I refuse to be made so foolish.

My mother sends a note, as promised, with news of Lydia. It reads only *Your sister's health is much improved. She misses you and we all wish you the very best of luck. Most sincerely, your devoted mother.*

She also sends a newspaper cutting, an article titled **PRINCES BRAWL AT KENDALL'S CLUB**. It's a sensationalized account of events, but it does mention my presence and speculates whether this means that Prince Bram has already introduced his favorite suitor to his friends at the club. In the margins she's written *Well done!*

It's perfect, just enough intrigue to make me interesting, but it falls short of a full-fledged scandal.

I tuck the letter and the article away in the back of *Faeries of the British Isles* alongside the maps I stole from the books in the sitting room. I tore them out of atlases when everyone else was asleep.

I pore over them by moonlight, planning the best routes. I learned my lesson the night I went out to search for Lydia, and I don't plan on making the same mistake twice.

I read the book too, rediscovering the magic I felt as a child within its pages. It transports me back to Mrs. Osbourne's warm hearth. The book was printed over two hundred years into Queen Mor's reign, long after information of her kind was banned. She's not mentioned at all, as if the author was hoping that by not acknowledging her, its contents would be less incriminating. Every piece of information is hidden in children's stories. I'm reading a passage I must have heard one hundred times as a child—about a fae revel on the summer solstice and the human girl lured there—when a line catches my eye: *Though faerie wine was sweet, there was none so sweet as the love of a mortal.*

Emmett would likely be furious with me if he knew what I was plotting, but if all goes according to plan, he'll never find out.

On Tuesday night Olive returns from her private meal with Bram like she's walking on air. She floats into the sitting room, where we're all engaged in a half-hearted game of whist, and flops down onto the love seat.

"He kissed me!" She giggles and kicks her feet. "I can't believe he actually kissed me."

We fall silent. Greer's cards crumple as she grips them too hard. I burn with something akin to embarrassment. Was I naive enough to believe that the moment with Bram in the garden meant that I was special? Bram may be a prince, but he is also just a boy.

"I'll let you be my ladies-in-waiting when I win," Olive says.

"Screw you, Olive," Faith says.

Marion nods in agreement. Greer puts her cards down and marches up the stairs, the rest of us following.

The road to Hampshire is long and muddy. We're piled into post chaises pulled by teams of four horses for a day's journey southeast of London, and I'm jittery with nerves the whole way.

We play I-spy games out the window but see little other than trees and thatched-roof villages. Emmy falls asleep against the window, and Marion and I pull out sketchbooks and little nubs of charcoal to pass the time.

I find myself drawing Pig and his ridiculous little face.

"What is that?" Marion peers at my paper from across the carriage.

"A dog," I answer.

"It's hideous," Marion replies. I crumple it up and throw it at her, both of us laughing.

The sun sinks golden behind the trees by the time we arrive at the hunting camp.

Palace staff have transformed the Hampshire wilderness into a small city overnight. Elegant canvas tents have been built on wooden risers. There is cheery red and white bunting hung all over the camp, an impressive firepit, stables for the horses and the dogs.

The footmen take us to our tent, comfortably set up with seven beds.

Viscountess Bolingbroke is already there when we arrive, laying a baby pink duvet, five different-size pillows, and a lacy doily on top of her bed.

"How do they expect us to live in these conditions?" she huffs. The hem of her traveling dress is caked with dust, and her normally pristine white bouffant is looking deflated.

Palace staff carry in our trunks, complete with everything we'll need for a weekend hunting party. We've all been outfitted with sporting dresses. Mine has a smart overcoat made of spring-green tweed, with gold buttons that pin in my waist. Greer chooses the bed next to mine. She's been particularly quiet since the queen's visit. I look over and give her a small smile. She gives me one in return, and it feels like ice thawing. It takes so much energy to be mad at her, I don't know if I have it in me anymore.

A bugle horn blows, and we poke our heads outside the tent to see the hunting party arrive. Bram and Emmett cut through the center of camp atop their horses. I recognize some of the sons of dukes and barons among their group of friends, familiar faces from this season's parties and their rowing teammates.

I catch both Emmett's and Bram's gazes as they pass our tent. Bram has a wide smile on his face, infectious and warm. Emmett's expression is predictably unreadable, his mouth in a tight line.

We dress in gowns and meet for dinner at long tables that wind through the trees. As the young, unmarried girls of the party, we're set at the very end, under Viscountess Bolingbroke's ever-watchful eye.

This whole trip is in celebration of Bram's nineteenth birthday, coming in just a few days.

He stands up halfway through dinner, a crystal glass raised in his hand. "If you would all indulge me in a toast. Each and every one of you has welcomed me and embraced me as one of your own, but tonight we revel the way we do back home. Cheers!"

He raises his hands, and a few dozen globes of light, each a pale shade of shimmering gold, float into the air, casting the forest in sparkles. A cheery tune floats in on a breeze, and someone pulls out a fiddle to play along.

Everyone cheers, their drinks sloshing over the table. "To Bram!"

After dessert is served, Bram walks along the table, greeting his guests with a ready smile and clapping his friends on their shoulders. Emmett stays close to his side, silent and sullen, his brother's foil, as usual.

"Thank you all for attending my birthday celebration. How lucky I am to count you among my blessings this year," Bram says once he reaches us.

Olive looks up to him, grinning, like he's hung the moon single-handedly. I catch a subtle eye roll passing between Faith and Marion. Something has shifted since the queen's rule change, the veneer slowly chipping away from us all.

I lean over to Bram. "Happy birthday. Any good gifts this year?"

He smiles at me. "This."

"The party?"

He shakes his head. "You. Here." I smack his shoulder, taking it as a joke, but it still sends a riot of butterflies through me.

The party rages until dawn, but we turn in for bed long before that, when Viscountess Bolingbroke declares it unladylike to stay up past midnight. Really, I think she just wants to go to sleep, but no one protests, exhausted after our long journey.

We can hear Bram's friends outside our tent, talking and dancing for hours.

I sleep fitfully, going over my plan for tomorrow. Again and again, I walk the route in my mind.

The next morning, a lady's maid dresses me in my green velvet hunting dress. As the others get ready, I swoon back onto my cot and declare myself too weak for the day's festivities. It isn't proper for the girls to join the stag hunt, but they will follow the party on horseback for a field lunch and then a celebratory dinner back at camp.

Viscountess Bolingbroke places a bony hand on my forehead and tuts her tongue. "You do feel warm."

"Please don't miss the fun on my behalf," I reply weakly. "There are plenty of staff at camp to look after me."

The viscountess looks at me and then at the other girls waiting impatiently by the mouth of our tent. She does the calculation; it is preferable to leave one girl on her own than five.

"Please call for them if you need anything," she replies hesitantly. "We'll be back by sunset."

I salute her in reply, which she doesn't find funny at all.

From outside the tent come the sounds of jingling horse reins and barking dogs eager for a hunt. Then the camp goes quiet and still, and everyone but me and a skeleton crew of staff are left.

I jump out of bed, hastily lace my boots, and grab the book and the maps from where I've hidden them at the bottom of my trunk. I need to be quick if I'm to be back before sunset.

The back entrance is closer to the horses, so I sneak out the rear of my tent and creep quietly to the paddock.

Most of the horses have been taken on the hunt, but there's an old cart horse that will do just fine. I take his reins in my hand. "Hi there," I whisper.

A twig snaps behind me, and I whirl around.

"Going somewhere?" Emmett stands there with a half smile, wearing hunting breeches, his wavy hair a mess. He's got a basket in one hand, like we've arranged to go on a picnic.

"Don't do that!" I hiss. "You scared me half to death."

"What are you doing?" he asks.

"I'm sick."

He reaches out, touches my forehead. I recoil from his touch. "I'm happy to inform you of a miracle. You seem to be completely healed."

"What are *you* doing? Shouldn't you be leading the charge?"

"Never had much of a stomach for hunting. We must have come down with the same thing because I was feeling ill this morning, but I appear to be cured."

"Please leave me alone."

"So you *are* cross with me."

I'm not cross with him. I'm cross with myself. "I'm not cross! I'm late."

Emmett takes the horse's reins and begins to hook him up to a cart. "I'm not letting you travel alone, so you might as well tell me while we ride."

"I can't convince you to let this go?"

"It's go with me or not at all, I'm afraid. Chivalry and all that."

I sigh, annoyed. "What's in the basket?"

"I'm not skipping lunch no matter what mad adventure you have planned."

I hop in beside him, and we're off, out of the camp, rambling down a dusty country road.

I pass him the map, and he takes a long look. "What is this?"

I hand him the book next. He traces his finger over the cover. "'*Faeries of the British Isles*,'" he reads. "Where did this come from?"

"Bram." I explain everything about our cook, about Bram gifting me the book, and then, about the idea it gave me. "Your theory about the May Queen is good, but completely uncorroborated. If we're going to stake everything on it, I need to talk to a second source," I say.

What I don't say is the part that keeps me up at night. If I'm going to manipulate someone as kind as Bram into running away with me, it needs to be for a good reason.

I've thought about writing to Ethel about it, but I'm pretty sure the footmen are reading the letters we send out, and I couldn't risk it.

When Bram gave me the book and said it was from "a friend," the idea took hold. The original owner is surely long dead, but there's a chance that this friend of Bram's still lives at the address inked on the inside of the front cover, or perhaps more books remain.

"When were you going to tell me?" Emmett asks.

"I was going to tell you the other night, but you seemed rather tied up with Faith." It's too petty, I shouldn't have said it. It does me no good, and he doesn't deserve my vitriol. He's allowed to kiss whomever he pleases.

Emmett presses his lips together as he thinks, then understanding dawns on him. "At Count Doncaster's horrible excuse for a party? When did you—"

"I went searching for you and found you . . . otherwise occupied." There's that horrible feeling again, the one where my skin is hot all over and I can't quite catch my breath.

"Oh," Emmett breathes. "It's not what you think."

"I don't think anything. It's none of my business."

"Faith loves someone else." Emmett sighs.

"Oh, of course. Let me guess. She tripped, and her mouth fell into yours."

Emmett casts a sidelong glance at me. "Faith kissed me to make sure it felt different. You don't have to believe me, but I promise you, it meant nothing."

"All right." I hate how petulant I sound.

"I've never lied to you. I'm not starting now."

The old cart horse clomps along.

We reach the outskirts of the market town well before lunch and stop along the roadside to water the horse and eat half a loaf of the bread Emmett smuggled from breakfast.

The paths become increasingly narrow as we journey farther into the woods, where the trees grow so thick they block out the light, and the world turns a few shades darker.

On and on we go, deep into the depths of the old-growth forest. There's something eerie about these woods, off in a way that makes my skin crawl. "No birdsong," Emmett says, realizing it at the same moment I do.

It's gone completely quiet save for the trudging of our old horse down the road.

"Not a great sign," I say.

"I don't believe in signs," Emmett replies, but his knuckles are white where they grip the horse's reins.

We come to a sharp hook turn in the road, and the horse whinnies and digs his hooves into the soft ground, grinding to a halt. Emmett hops out of the carriage and lays a comforting hand on his neck. "Shh, what's wrong?"

He tugs on the reins, offers an apple, tugs again. But the horse will go no farther.

He doesn't use a whip. My heart feels strangely warm.

"I think we're on our own from here," he declares.

I hike up my skirts and hop down from the cart, refusing the hand he extends. "Believe in signs yet?" I ask.

We walk in nervous silence for about ten minutes before we come to a stone house deep in the darkest part of the wood. *House* is a generous term. It was probably once a grand dwelling, but the forest is doing its best to reclaim it. It's covered all over with a green-gray moss so damp it appears to be dripping off the stones. What once was the garden is now an angry tangle of thorns and half-dead holly crawling like a desperate animal upon what used to be an intricate mosaic of flower beds.

Cautiously we approach the rotting fence, flecks of paint barely visible along the weathered wood. Emmett reaches for the gate and the whole thing comes apart under his hand, collapsing to the ground like it was held together with dust.

He turns around, and I offer him nothing but an arched brow.

"Good afternoon," Emmett calls. In the crook of his elbow he carries a basket of fresh jams left over from our field lunch. *It would be rude to show up without a gift*, he said.

No answer comes from the house, but up on the rotting thatched roof a chimney is puffing black smoke into the sky. A shadow flits by the dust-caked window. Someone is home.

CHAPTER TWENTY-THREE

Emmett approaches the door confidently, like we've been invited for tea. I trail behind him, his willing shadow.

With one large hand he reaches up and knocks on the ancient door. The sound reverberates through the silent forest. No answer. He knocks again.

The shadow in the window stills, watching us. From behind the door comes the sound of five locks being undone, agonizingly slow.

Click

Click

Click

Click

Click.

The door creaks open wide enough to reveal a single eye. "Who are you?" a male voice asks.

"We've come to call," Emmett says pleasantly. "I believe you know my brother."

The single visible eye narrows.

Emmett holds the basket up with a hopeful grin. "We've brought jam."

He slams the door in our faces, the sound reverberating through the forest.

Then, one final lock slides, and the door swings open.

"Might as well come in," the man says.

He's not what I expected. I'd pictured some sort of grizzled, ancient creature from a children's story. What stands in front of me is just a man. He looks to be in his late thirties, with a close crop of dark blond hair. He has a forgettable face, nice enough, but unremarkable in every way.

The house is musty and dark, every curtain drawn or window so covered with filth it lets in little light. There are stacks and stacks of books piled on every available surface, some covered in dust, some brand-new. Over every doorway hangs an upside-down horseshoe.

I follow Emmett through the door, but as soon as I step onto the flagstone floor, I'm hit with a stomach-curdling revulsion. A disgust so strong I suddenly feel the need to run out the door and go anywhere that isn't here.

I look to our host, who is standing still in the hallway, watching us like he expected this. His face is neutral, pleasant even, but when I look at him, I feel nothing but bone-deep disgust. It crawls up my throat until I'm choking on it. I hate this man. I hate him urgently, without reason.

Emmett's fist tightens around the basket of jam, and there's no longer anything funny about our gift.

"Come in, come in," the man says. "The sooner you get your answers, the sooner you can leave." He's got an odd, stilted sort of accent.

We follow him into the sitting room, as gray and overcrowded as the rest of the house. He gestures for us to sit on a pair of wooden chairs by the fire, and Emmett and I acquiesce, despite every bone in my body resisting.

He blows dust off of two teacups. "I don't receive many guests."

He pulls a black kettle from the cavernous fireplace in the middle of the room and fills our cups.

I slip the book out from where it was tucked under my arm beneath my cloak. "Do you know anything of the original owner of this book?"

The man gives it only a cursory glance. "I am the original owner of that book."

"That's not possible?" Unless—

"I'm sure you've put it together by now," the man says casually.

Emmett just holds his tea, and I do the same, terrified to take a sip. "Put what together?"

"The cost."

It hits me all at once, this sensation of loathing I'm feeling is the queen's doing. "You bargained for eternal life, but no one can stand to be near you," I guess.

He winces, clutching an invisible wound. "That's a tad harsh. I believe the exact conditions were eternal life, but a life without love."

"You agreed to that?"

"I was young, what did I know?" the man replies. "I was fresh out of the war. My parents and siblings were long gone. I took a girl every now and then but considered myself a bachelor. What did I need love for? I was a fool. I paid her price."

Emmett shifts in his seat uncomfortably. "What is your name?"

He takes a sip of his tea, then lets out a slow breath. "It's been a long time since anyone has asked me that. I was called Eduart Burnhamme."

Emmett leans forward, his elbows on his knees. "Will you tell us your story?"

Eduart considers us, and even though I know this sick feeling congealing in my chest is the queen's magic, I still feel nothing but revulsion.

"I fought for the Yorks." His gaze lands on the fire. "I was there that day on the battlefield when she first appeared. We thought she was an angel. We saw what she did for old Edward, how she cut down the Lancaster army like they were wheat ready for the harvest. She placed the crown on his head like it was nothing. But we all know how that particular story ends. When she took the throne at Eltham, she made an announcement—anyone who wished to make a bargain with her should come and kneel before her throne. I was certain no one would; you'd have to be an absolute fool to trust the old witch after what she'd done. But people lined up by the thousands. Day and night, she made bargain after bargain. I saw paupers become lords, farmers pull gold straight out of the ground like turnips, daft fools marry the most beautiful girls in the village. Fingers and toes and memories went missing, but everyone agreed the price was fair.

"There came a time I could no longer resist. I waited three years to make my bargain. I thought I was very clever back then. I didn't want land or a wife, I wanted adventure.

"I was greedy for the world, but I was afraid of it too. I'd seen the way the Black Death had taken my mother, father, and sisters, snuffed them out like candles. When I kneeled before her, I asked for eternal life, and she laughed in my face."

Emmett stares at Eduart, completely enraptured, but I can't look at him. I dig the sharp corner of my thumbnail into the cuticles of my other fingers until my nails are rimmed with blood.

Eduart continues. "'What is so great about living forever?' she asked, but I knew she was mocking me. I said, 'You tell me.' She smiled that awful smile of hers and said, 'It's knowing that nothing truly matters. You'll outlive the consequences; you'll outlive meaning itself. All that's left is entertainment.' I didn't know then what I know now. After an eternity, there is only boredom or the lack of it. She asked what I would do with an everlasting life. I said I'd travel the world, see all there was to see, and then see it all again. But I was lying, to her and to myself. I'd seen so much death on the battlefields and at the cruel hand of disease. Every time I closed my eyes, I saw my friends' guts strewn out over the grass, heard their screams anew. I told the queen I wanted adventure, but the truth is, I was afraid of death. I wanted to live without being afraid.

"She told me she would grant me eternal life, but it would be a life without love. I was a young man, *what did I need love for?* At the time, I thought it meant I would never take a wife. That sounded all right to me, a wife would only slow me down. I didn't know the depth of it then, what it would feel like to live so long alone."

"What did you do?" I whisper, horrified, disgusted.

"At first I did exactly what I told her I'd do. I sailed around the world. France first, then the rest of Europe. I sailed down the coast of Africa, spent a few years in China, then to the Americas. But everywhere I went, it was the same. Inns shut their doors to me, barmaids refused to pour me ale. I would walk into a room and everyone else would walk out. Eventually I came back here, to this house I grew up in, the same house where the last people on earth who ever loved me died."

"What do you do now?" Emmett asks.

"I sit and I read and I wait for the end of the world," Eduart answers gravely.

"We can help you. We have a plan," Emmett says.

At this, Eduart laughs, an upsetting, full-body chuckle that sends tea spilling over his pants. He gestures behind him to a plaster wall caked in decades of dust and dirt. "Sign the wall before you leave," he says, and though it's difficult to make out in the low light, I see now that there are dozens, if not hundreds, of names scrawled on it.

"What?" Emmett looks properly angry now.

"That's the problem with living forever. You have to witness each new generation act like they invented everything. It gets so tedious." He sighs heavily, like the weight of our cluelessness is pressing on his lungs. "Visitors just like you call once every fifteen years or so, like you're the very first people who ever thought about unseating her."

"What do you mean?" I ask uneasily.

"The first group came about a decade into her rule. I was abroad then, but she made examples of them, hung their bodies at the Tower in low tide and invited the town to watch them drown as the river rose. The next ones came about fifty years later. One of the stupider attempts to blow up Apethorpe Palace. They too died at Traitors' Gate. I actually joined the one in the 1660s for a bit, just to have something to do. There was an attempt to locate the door from which she came. The idea was, if she could not be killed, perhaps she could be returned to her own land. It was a fool's errand. Every member of the search party died of old age before any evidence was found. Then there was the uprising of 1724. That one got ugly. A bargainer from Penzance locked himself in the throne room with her and meant to starve them both out, his compatriots guarding the door. If a hand could not be raised against her, he would let natural causes take her. The queen just laughed, strolled out of the throne room completely unharmed, and left him to starve to death within."

"There is no record of any of this," Emmett says, his whole body tense.

"Of course not. Why would a despot provide a record of her people's hatred toward her? It's the same reason there are no books on the Others in any library across this great, wide country. She rules in fear and shadows."

I glance around at his stacks of books. "How did Bram end up with this book?"

Eduart takes a sip of his tea. "Now that is an interesting story. I met the Prince of Wales last fall. It takes a lot to shock me in this never-ending life of mine, but it was a great surprise to find him at my threshold. Bram has a bit of a morbid fascination with those his mother has made immortal."

"There's more of you?" I ask, horrified.

"Oh, of course. Where do you think her footmen came from?"

A chill crawls down my spine. I recognize it now, the same sallow look in Eduart that permeates the skin of the queen's strange, silent, ever-loyal footmen.

"She learned her lesson after me. Everyone else who wishes to live forever must give up their freedom to serve her. She is clever, you've got to give her credit."

"And Bram knows this?" Emmett asks.

"He found out about a year ago. It's when he came to see me. I didn't have much information to give the poor boy, but it's never easy to acknowledge that your only parent is a monster. I hadn't heard from him since, until I received his letter asking if I had a particular book in my collection. The book, it seems, was for you." He gestures to me. "There's nothing in there that would lead to her demise—trust me, I've looked. Their only weakness is iron, and she had all our weapons melted down after the war."

Iron. "Bram told me that's how his father defeated her," says Emmett. "Can we find more?"

Eduart shakes his head. "I gave up in 1789, but you're welcome to keep trying."

"We don't need iron or tricks or anything else. We're not like the others," Emmett interjects. "We plan to undo the bargains themselves."

"I'm sure you believe that," Eduart says, not insulting, but world-weary.

"Do you know anything about the bargains?" Emmett presses, undeterred.

Eduart sighs, like he's humoring him. "Only that they've gotten more creative over the years. She likes to play with her food, but I think she's getting bored with the whole spectacle. To my knowledge, no bargains have ever been undone, though many have regretted theirs and tried. Your own father darkened my door a decade or so ago, begging for information."

Emmett's brows knit together in an expression of shock. "My father?"

"I know exactly who you are, Emmett Alexander De Vere. Your father is a good man, and he is sorry."

It's as if I can hear Emmett's heart crack right down the middle. He blinks away his welling tears. "He regrets his bargain?"

Eduart nods. "He does, says he should have run away with you in the night rather than subject you both to a life without each other."

"Then why'd he do it?" Emmett asks, his voice thick with tears he's too stubborn to let fall.

Eduart shrugs casually. "The queen ruined your grandfather's life. He bargained for an exceptional mind for numbers in exchange for never finding anything funny again. It made him hardened and cruel, to the point where he abandoned his family when your father was just a boy. Your father joined a group of like-minded rebels in his adolescence and dedicated his life to the queen's downfall."

Emmett stares at his teacup, his grip so tight around it, I'm afraid it might shatter. "Why did he marry her?"

"He thought his best bet was taking her down from the inside. He made himself the perfect suitor, but once they wed, the queen grew suspicious of him. He spent too long in the library, asked too many questions, cavorted with people she didn't trust. He believes that's why she separated the two of you. The queen is afraid of her husband and didn't want to give him the opportunity to raise you as his protégé. Your father overestimated himself, thinking it would only take him a year or two to solve the problem of the bargains and everything would be right in the world. But he was wrong."

"His abandonment was hubris? I was left alone with nothing but a governess for company because of his misplaced confidence?" Emmett sounds furious now.

"He loved you, and he thought that legitimacy as a prince would protect you in the meantime. His ego was his downfall, as it is for so many."

"Well, he must have figured it out. He left me clues that spell out

Moryen's original bargain. If we break that, everything else falls to pieces."

"It works only if you're right."

"We're right," Emmett says through gritted teeth.

"It is a fool's errand, and you will die in the pursual of it."

"I refuse to accept that," Emmett says.

"That's another thing I've learned in this exceptionally long life of mine. It doesn't matter if you accept things or not. They happen anyway."

"I didn't come here to be lectured," Emmett snaps.

Eduart takes another slow sip of his tea. "Of course you did."

Emmett stands to leave. "If you will not help us, we have no more business with you."

Eduart turns his attention on me. "You're one of Bram's girls, aren't you? I read about you in the paper. Does he know about the two of you?"

"No," I spit venomously. "Bram doesn't know about the plans to unseat his mother. Do you take us for idiots?"

Eduart shakes his head. "No, I meant does poor, sweet Prince Bram know you're in love with his brother?"

"I'm not—" I stand to leave, my face scarlet red. It takes all the self-control I have not to dump my full teacup directly onto his horrible head.

"Let's go, Ivy." Emmett stomps through the hallway but pauses at the door. "Thank you for your hospitality, sir. I hope you enjoy the jam."

Eduart calls after us as we stomp out the door. "You didn't sign the wall!"

We step out of the house into the tangled garden where the air feels thinner, and we both sigh in relief. The tension between my shoulders and the nausea pooled in my throat dissipates.

"Horrible man," Emmett says.

"The absolute worst," I agree.

"You, in love with me? You barely tolerate me." He laughs but it comes out strained.

"Exactly," I reply thinly.

We walk from the house into the forest. Birdsong starts up again, and I am relieved for one blissful minute, until it all comes crashing down. Where the horse and cart used to be is now only a kicked-up patch of dirt and wheel tracks.

"Dammit," Emmett hisses.

On foot, getting back to camp will take hours. We'll be lucky to return before the hunting party, and we have no reasonable way to explain our absence, let alone why we're together.

"I'm ruined." I panic, pacing. I'm tempted to pick up my skirts and start running, but we're so far from camp, it wouldn't be of any use.

Emmett looks at me, a steely set to his jaw. "I'm not going to let that happen."

We follow the path out of the forest to a larger dirt road that leads back to Alton. "We'll pay for a hackney in the village." Emmett is walking so quickly it's nearly a jog. He must know as well as I do, the timing will still be tight. We'll have to get extraordinarily lucky.

Storm clouds gather on the horizon as the sun sinks dangerously low. Emmett and I both refuse to acknowledge it, as if ignoring time will make it pass more slowly.

We walk onto the Alton high street right as the storm breaks wide open. Lightning cracks across the sky and we are drenched in seconds.

We sprint down the road to a thatched roof coaching inn. The sign hanging above the door sways in the howling wind. It's got a faded crest under the words *The Swan*.

Emmett and I burst through the doors to a ground floor pub teeming with people desperate to get away from the weather.

The proprietor, a steely-eyed old woman, marches over to us. "You're dripping on the floor."

Emmett looks like a drowned puppy, his hair plastered to his forehead, his coat hanging heavy off his shoulders. I'm sure I don't look much better.

"We'll be on our way soon, ma'am," Emmett apologizes. "We need a hackney."

The old woman tuts her tongue. "In this weather? Not a chance." As if to prove her point, another crack of thunder echoes outside.

"We're part of the prince's hunting party. Please, we need to get back to the celebration," Emmett insists.

"I don't care if you're the prince himself. No driver is going out in this weather. Half of them are drunk in the pub and the other half are in for the night. Weather like this spooks the horses."

"Please—" Emmett tries once more, but she cuts him off.

"You're in luck, though." The foundation of the inn creaks as it sways in the force of the storm. "I have one room left. It's all yours if you want it, milord."

I choke back a laugh, though exactly none of this is funny.

Emmett turns for the door. "No thank you. We'll walk."

He wrenches the door open, and we walk back into the storm.

Immediately I'm thrown back with the gale force of the wind. The rain pierces my face, and my already sodden hem becomes so heavy it's hard to move.

I take two steps before the toe of my boot catches against a pit in the road and I trip directly into a puddle. I land on my knees with a *splat*, and Emmett rushes to my side.

"You may walk home," I shout over the thunder as I push myself to my feet, ignoring his outstretched hand, "but I am taking that room." Better ruined than frozen to death.

I march back into the inn, muddier than before, with an exasperated Emmett at my heels.

I slap my wet hands down on the counter. "We'll take the room."

The innkeeper looks at me smugly. "I assume you're married?" she asks, like she knows we're not.

Emmett makes an unintelligible noise of protest behind me, but I just smile sweetly and say, "Blissful newlyweds."

The innkeeper's quill is poised over her register. "Names?"

Emmett shoots me a glare, then says, "Fern and Edward Bennett. From Nottingham."

"Eight shillings."

Emmett fishes out some money. Eight little portraits of Queen Moryen on the coins stare up at us judgmentally from the counter.

The innkeeper turns and pulls the last remaining key off of a pegboard behind the desk. "Come with me."

The inn is overly warm with so many bodies packed inside. We pass through the raucous pub and follow the owner up a rickety flight of threadbare stairs.

My wet dress must weigh at least ten pounds, and even with the heat of the inn, I'm shivering against its cold weight.

We're led up to the third floor, and though I don't look, I can feel Emmett glowering behind me.

The woman unlocks the door with a *click* and waves us inside.

The door shuts behind her with a *thunk*, and we are alone.

CHAPTER TWENTY-FOUR

I smack Emmett on the shoulder, his jacket so wet it squishes under the force of my palm. "Fern?"

"It was the closest I could think to Ivy."

"Isolde, Isabelle, Imogen?"

"You make a more believable Fern."

I huff and go to throw another log on the weak fire.

Will I be kicked out of the competition immediately? I wonder. Publicly shamed like my sister, destined to spend the rest of my life crying into a pillow, alone in a dark room? Strung up at Traitors' Gate like the rebels Eduart described? Or maybe the queen will keep me around. She does love to play with her food.

Emmett is silent as he takes a seat by the fire, soaked clothes and all. He drops his head into his hands and goes completely still.

He can't so much as look at me.

The fire hisses and pops as I stoke it. "Since we're here, we might as well not freeze to death," I say.

I strip off my green velvet coatdress, my ruined shoes, my crinoline, my soggy stockings, then pause. I won't be able to manage the corset on my own.

I glance over to where Emmett is standing in front of the fire. As if he can feel the weight of my gaze, he lifts his head and his eyes meet mine.

He pauses. "What?"

"I—" I can't very well ask him to undress me. "It's nothing."

He rises and crosses the room toward me. I curse the way my cheeks turn scarlet red. Maybe I should have let the storm drown me.

"I know my way around a corset, Ivy."

A million petty comebacks are on my tongue, but I bite it. With careful fingers, he undoes the knot at the small of my back.

His hands creep up my spine, tugging at the laces with deft skill. "You're shivering," he says after a tense second.

His fingers still, but the warm weight of them hovers over my spine. "So hurry up," I say.

Emmett sighs heavily and returns to his work on the corset. "There," he says, with one final tug, and the corset falls to my feet. I step out of it, now in nothing but my soaked chemise and drawers made transparent by the water.

"Better?" His voice is quiet, tense.

"Yes," I answer reluctantly.

Emmett is gentlemanly enough to avert his eyes. He picks up my soaked clothing and arranges it carefully by the fire to dry.

With his back to me, I slip out of my undergarments and wrap myself in the quilt at the foot of the bed.

I settle into the wingback chair in front of the fireplace, and the warmth sends prickles up my body, every joint beginning to thaw.

"Are you trying to ruin me?" I say with a small smile. Emmett is now slumped low in the chair next to me, still soaked to the bone in his wet clothes. I hope the joke will get a smile out of him, but it only deepens the crease between his eyebrows. I've never seen him look so upset.

The fire crackles, and I wiggle my toes out from under the quilt to move them even closer to it. "You're no use to the cause if you die of hypothermia," I say to him.

He doesn't answer, just keeps staring at the flames, his breathing ragged. The storm outside howls like a banshee.

"Emmett—" I say more forcefully, and he blinks back to himself. "I don't understand why you're angry with me right now."

This gets his attention fully. "Angry? I'm not angry with you. I'm angry with myself."

"You can't control the weather."

"No, not that. I should have left you alone, let you be. The most selfish thing I've ever done is let you get involved in this."

"It was my idea to sneak off today."

"But you wouldn't have had to if it weren't for me."

"Stop acting like you're the only one with ideas! I hate her too. I want to unseat her too!"

"I didn't mean to suggest you didn't have ideas of your own."

"You don't own the market on being a person with radical ambitions. The only reason I've received any of Bram's attention is because of your help. I agreed to this, remember?"

"I manipulated you. I manipulated Faith. I manipulated my brother. I'm horrible. Your sister was correct in her judgment of me. I'm a horrible person."

"I don't believe that's true."

"I'm trying—" His voice cracks like he's swallowing tears. "I'm trying so hard to do the right thing, but I can't seem to manage it."

"I know," I say softly. The devastation on his beautiful face is obvious.

"I'll protect you the best I can," Emmett says, and I know he means money. I hate that he knows I need it. I can picture it now, being swept away to a far-off country house, not kept like a mistress, but kept like a secret. Queen Mor will continue ruling, and all will be as it has been. Only Emmett and I will know the truth of what could have been.

I can't bear to talk about it anymore. "Please change out of those wet clothes. It hurts to look at you like this." And it does. It *hurts* in an aching sort of way I can't ignore anymore.

Emmett tears his gaze from mine and finally slides out of his wet boots. I turn away to stare at the fire but hear his clothes fall to the floor in succession.

Wrapped in another blanket, he joins me again by the fire. The color is already returning to his lips, and I am relieved to see it.

He arranges his clothes next to mine to dry, and now all we can do is wait. The storm outside shows no signs of slowing down, and judging by the band that has now struck up downstairs, neither does the party below us.

"I'm sorry about your father," I say to him. What Eduart said has been weighing on me all day, and I have a desperate need to talk about something other than the two of us.

"It would be easier if I was mad at him, I think," Emmett says. "But I'm just sad. It's strange, loving someone you don't know. It's even stranger knowing that they live just down the hall. I have these . . . memories of him. I remember reading books on his lap and him teaching me to skip stones on the pond behind our house."

"Did he ever try to contact you beyond the hidden messages in the library?"

Emmett shakes his head. "The terms of her bargain seem to forbid it. No letters. He can't even pass messages using someone else; their voice goes suddenly mute. Nearly gave my old governess a heart attack the first time it happened. It's one of my earliest memories."

"Are you still close to your governess?"

Emmett shifts uncomfortably. "I was. She died just over a year ago. I think she would have liked you. You're tough like she was."

I shake my head. I'm stubborn, which is different and not nearly as admirable. "I don't think I'm tough."

Emmett just chuckles. "Well, she would have seen what I see."

"I would have liked to meet her," I say. I have a feeling that the list of people Emmett loves is small. He keeps them tucked away, close to his chest.

"She was a walking contradiction. Tougher on me than anyone, but the closest I ever got to parental love. I was a lonely child, spent all my time on the floor, making up stories with my toy soldiers. She loved the ballet, so I loved the ballet; we went every chance we got. It was the only time I ever left the palace grounds."

This room feels removed from reality, a bubble of only two.

"That's actually where I met Faith," Emmett continues. "It was last summer, after my governess died, and I was sitting in the audience alone. Faith took pity on me."

The warmth in my chest dissipates into something cold and petty. "That sounds just like Faith, so beatific. A saint, really," I say sarcastically.

"Are you jealous?" Emmett raises a brow, and I think of his earlier confession, the tenderness in it. I don't feel tender at all, I feel scared of this well of emotion I can't control.

I paste a smile on my face. "That's hilarious. You should try comedy more often."

Eventually our clothes dry enough that I'm able to slip back into my chemise and drawers. The thin cotton doesn't offer much in the way of modesty, so I keep the blanket draped over my shoulders. Emmett pulls on his half-damp breeches and goes downstairs to get us some dinner. The sun has long since gone down, but the storm is still raging.

He comes back up with a tray of cold cuts, crusty bread, hothouse peaches, and watered-down ale. "I turned down the mysterious stew," he says, laying the tray on the small card table by the window.

"What if mysterious stew is my favorite food?"

"Then we'll have to refine your tastes before you become a princess."

We eat in ravenous silence, and Emmett places our now-empty tray out in the hallway. The party downstairs has quieted some, though the storm has not done the same.

"We ought to try to get some sleep," Emmett says. "I want to be off at first light. We can think of our excuse on the way back to camp."

"Agreed." The panic-induced nausea has mostly retreated. My life may very well be ruined, but today has been so long, I'm too exhausted to truly consider it. I'll save the worry for tomorrow.

We both stand awkwardly, not knowing what to do. Our glances flit to the bed, impossible to ignore in the middle of the room.

"You should take the bed," Emmett says. "I'll sleep on the floor."

"You paid for the room, that hardly seems fair," I protest.

"I'm a gentleman," Emmett argues back.

"Is that what you tell all the girls you seduce?"

"Are you feeling seduced?"

"I wasn't talking about me!"

I cross to the far side of the bed in a huff and slide under the covers. The linen sheets have been washed nearly to death, but it smells clean, and the mattress is soft enough to sink into.

I toss the other pillow to Emmett, and he lies down on the floor on the other side of the bed. I blow out the lantern, and the room is drenched in darkness, the only light coming from the flickering embers in the fireplace.

I can't get settled. I'm too acutely aware of Emmett's warm body on the floor, just feet away from me. From the sound of blankets rustling, he can't get comfortable either.

I lie still and listen to Emmett and the tapping of the rain on the windows until my whole body feels electric. After a few minutes, I can stand it no longer. "Oh, for goodness' sake, just come up to the bed. It's big enough for two."

The mattress creaks as Emmett climbs up and settles in next to me. He lays his head on the pillow and then turns to face me, both of us on our sides. He's so close I can feel the heat of his breath, see the fringe of his dark lashes and the way his hazel eyes glint in the low firelight.

"I bet you wish I was seducing you right now," he whispers, a ghost of a smile on his mouth.

"What would you do if I were one of those girls you take out into the garden during balls?"

"I took you to the garden during a ball."

"You know what I mean."

Emmett looks at me for a breath and then slowly extends a hand, laying it, featherlight, on the side of my face, his thumb at my jaw-bone.

A shiver goes through me. "Your hands are cold," I whisper.

"The girls I seduce aren't usually this critical of me."

"Am I not one of those girls?"

If I were, this is the part where they'd kiss, right? I bet he'd cradle their jaws in his hands, really gentle, and tip their heads to taste them better.

If we were anything but friends, we'd probably be kissing by now.

"You belong to my brother."

"I don't belong to anyone."

He sighs heavily. "You know what I mean."

"What would you do, Emmett?" I ask, even though I know I shouldn't. I have a perverse need to push him to reject me outright so I can extinguish this stupid, insufferable fire in my rib cage that ignites in his presence.

"You're being mean, Ivy."

The rain on the windows mirrors my own frantic heartbeat. Just the heat of his body next to mine sets me on fire.

I roll over on my back, terrified I'll lean in and kiss him if he keeps looking at me like that.

"Have you ever kissed someone?" His voice is so quiet I can hardly hear it over the sound of the storm.

The image of him and Faith, their lips touching, the way his hand fell to the swell of her hip, flashes through my mind.

"Yes. Bram," I answer, deliberately petulant.

"You know what I'm asking."

I hesitate.

"No one is going to want to kiss you if you can't look at them," Emmett says.

"I'm not looking at you, and you want to kiss me." I want him to deny it, *tell me I'm wrong*.

"I want to kiss everyone," he says, and that stings more.

"And everyone wants to kiss you, how lucky." I try to make it sound like a joke, but I can't manage it, my voice comes out brittle.

"But not you," he says quietly.

"No, not me."

"Did you kiss him back?"

"Yes." *Did I? I tried to.*

"You looked beautiful that night," Emmett adds almost guiltily. "I'm not surprised he kissed you. You're doing your job well."

"There's no need for flattery," I reply.

"It's not flattery if it's the truth."

"I'm not so sure about that. I'm pretty sure I froze up. He didn't try to kiss me after that fight at the club. Maybe he didn't want to."

"You asked what I would do if you were one of those girls I take to the garden at parties. You want the truth?" Emmett asks. "I wouldn't do anything, not if you don't even know how to kiss."

"Now you're the one being mean."

He's silent for a moment, and it's as if I can hear the wheels turning in his head. There's an unceasing heat where his eyes bore into the side of my face.

"I could teach you," he says.

The excuse is gossamer thin. He knows as well as I do, I'll be kicked out of the competition, or worse, upon our return to camp tomorrow. I'm never going to kiss Bram again.

I should say no. But it's Emmett.

It's Emmett, as in, I have no control over it.

I turn to look at him, our faces only a breath apart. And his eyes, *his eyes*. The peculiar hazel color dances gold in the moonlight.

His gaze pins me like a shadowboxed butterfly.

"All right," I whisper. I'm flushed all over, like the knowledge that he's about to touch me is as good as the touching itself.

I push myself up so I'm sitting cross-legged on the bed. Emmett rises and places a warm hand on my knee.

He leans in, but just as I expect his lips to brush mine, he pulls back and makes me chase it.

For a moment, there is just warmth, and pressure.

I press my lips to his, harder, but don't know what to do next. Emmett stills against me. I pull back and huff out a sigh of frustration.

Emmett chuckles, and I slap his chest.

"You're too stiff," he says.

"I *know*. So teach me how to do it better."

His gaze flicks down.

He presses his thumb to my bottom lip. Automatically, my jaw unhinges and my lips drop open. "Relax," he whispers against my mouth.

It's softer this time. He weaves one hand through the tendrils of unbound hair on my neck and another around the small of my waist. The heat and the weight of him is everywhere, as if my body is covered with a cascade of sparks.

My hands scramble for purchase. I wind them through his hair and tug just a little too hard. "Easy," he murmurs.

His tongue darts between my lips, and I freeze.

"Let me in," he breathes. "Take it."

I open to the velvet pressure of his tongue, his mouth soft but unrelenting.

He tugs hard at the hair at the nape of my neck, tipping me back onto the bed. He hovers over me, caging me in with his tall frame.

I move, desperate for some relief, and he pulls me against him until I can feel every hard plane of his body. I gasp, desperate for air, and he trails his tongue along the jackrabbit beat of my pulse until he reaches my earlobe. His teeth close around the tender skin, not hard enough to hurt but enough to make me arch against him.

He kisses the exact opposite of his brother. He's not polite at all, it's like he's starving for it.

His hands wander even lower down, ghosting over my breasts, then grasping the soft part of my waist hard enough to bruise. I want him impossibly closer. He's unlocked something in me. I didn't know kissing could feel like this. I didn't know *anything* could feel like this.

Suddenly he pushes me away. I raise my hand to my kiss-swollen lips. "Did I do something wrong?"

"No."

"Then why—"

"Ivy," he says in that peculiar, exhausted way of his.

"What?" I whisper.

He stands suddenly, backing away from the bed. "You've done perfectly well. I think the kissing lesson is over."

I'm feverish with jealousy of the girls who got to have him before me, for real, without the veil of pretense and denial.

"Perfectly well?" I try to keep my voice light. It's taking all my strength not to reach out to him and beg for more. "Top marks in His Royal Highness Prince Emmett De Vere's school of kissing? Will I be valedictorian?"

He laughs humorlessly. "Don't get ahead of yourself."

I'm just another in a long list of girls. I would be foolish to let myself think I was special. "I wouldn't dare."

I wrap my arms around my middle and hug myself tight. I try to think of Bram and his easy smile. He's such a lovely boy. Emmett isn't lovely at all. He's reckless and mercurial, and he will never be mine.

I felt his body against mine. I'm not foolish enough to think I'm alone in my want. Emmett would give me more, I know he would. All I'd have to do is push a little harder, and he would have me pinned to this mattress in seconds.

But I am alone with this stupid, throbbing ache in my rib cage that longs for something like love. Emmett can't give it to me, and it wouldn't be mine to take anyway.

He disappears into the attached washroom and is in there for so long, I begin to fear he's sleeping in the bathtub, but finally I hear the squeak of the door and the soft padding of his footsteps. The bed sinks as he lies down next to me.

Emmett's ragged breathing slows after a long time, and I think he must be asleep. It gives me the bravery to ask a question that's been weighing on me.

"Were you always on the lookout for the perfect May Queen?"

I roll over again to face him, but he stays on his back. I stare at his profile, silhouetted in the moonlight streaming in from the window.

"I hoped you were asleep," he replies.

"You have quite the reputation. Was it all subterfuge?"

"A lot of it," he admits. "But not all."

I hate that it stings to hear him say it.

"Would you like to know the truth?" he asks.

"Always."

"The Tremaines' youngest daughter was meeting up with the scullery maid. I was simply providing lookout, and then a cover story when the two young lovers were almost caught."

"And Christine Cambere?"

"Got her shoe caught in a trellis trying to climb the garden wall to return to her bedroom unseen. I was only helping to get her unstuck. Parties bore her."

"So none of the rumors are true?" I ask.

"None of the more popular ones. I'm not a saint, I'm just not clumsy enough to get caught. The tryst I had was actually with Christine's sister Georgia, though we were quite good at keeping that one under wraps. I've had my fair share of lady's maids, barmaids, milkmaids."

I can't tell if he's joking. "And Faith," I add.

Emmett goes quiet. "And Faith."

"You said you didn't love her."

He wrings his hands in the sheets before he answers. "Faith and I hurt each other because we weren't what the other wanted. I was too self-obsessed to give Faith the respect she deserved, and she didn't love me in the way I was hungry for. We were clumsy, and things got broken, but it doesn't mean some great love story was ruined. Faith and I have talked, we're friends now. I can assure you she does not love me, nor I her."

I expect to feel jealous, but instead I just feel sad for him.

"I was only eight when my father gave me up," he says. "I so desperately wanted love that I searched for it everywhere. They had to switch out the maids who built my fires daily, after I started growing too attached to them and asking them to stay with me. At night, when I was supposed to be sleeping, I'd sneak out to the stables and read stories to the horses, like they were my friends, even though the grooms told me they weren't. I spent the first few years after my father's separation writing him letters at night, detailing every single thing I did that day. I thought one day we'd be reunited and he'd want to know all I had done in his absence. But I stopped believing that some time ago."

I want to reach out and touch him, offer some comfort, but I can't.

"My confession is this," Emmett continues. "I grew up without a family, in drafty palace rooms with nothing but a governess, a tutor, and a battalion of toy soldiers for company. I've spent my whole life on my hands and knees, clamoring for crumbs of love. I don't know if there will ever come a time I am not hungry for it."

Emmett's sullen nature, his recklessness with his heart, it's all coming into focus now.

I offer him a confession in return. "Sometimes I'm afraid that I was too coddled. I think my parents and sister loved me so much, I'm not prepared for a world that doesn't love me the same way."

"The only person on earth I'm certain who loves me is Bram," he replies.

Like a girl possessed, I reach out across the expanse of our shared bed and grasp his cold hand in mine. He squeezes, and I squeeze back. *I could love you. Let me love you*, but I can't, and he knows it as well as I do.

I will be Bram's or I will be no one's.

And now the only thing I can do is live with it.

CHAPTER TWENTY-FIVE

If my favorite story in *Faeries of the British Isles* was about faerie doors, Lydia's was about the faerie king. We made Mrs. Osbourne tell it over and over again until it was as well-worn as the grooves on her butcher block. As the story goes, long before Queen Mor, when England was a wild place, the portal between worlds was open. The Others passed through freely, looking to make bargains and use fragile humans as their playthings. Milkmaids would wander off into the night and return at sunrise, strangely hollowed out. Fields would turn to ash in a single afternoon, others would sprout wheat of pure gold that melted in the rain. Babies were snatched out of their cradles, strange copies left in their stead.

Clever humans knew to stay away from the edge of the forest, not to let a stranger inside after dark, and never to respond to someone calling your name if you did not recognize the voice doing the calling. There was one such girl who thought she was very clever indeed.

Her parents, terrified by their daughter's remarkable beauty, kept her locked up on a country estate much like ours, tucked away from the world outside and the dangers that lurked there.

The girl was content to live a quiet life with her garden and her brothers and sisters and her books. But on the evening of her eighteenth birthday she heard music so beautiful she couldn't help but weep. With big, fat tears rolling down her cheeks, she followed the music beyond the safe walls of her estate and into the bordering woods. It was there, under a willow tree, that she found a man strumming a lute. Except it wasn't a man. As she got closer, she noticed something just the slightest bit off about him, his too-long fingers, his pointed ears, his face so beautiful it made her weep harder, and she knew she had stumbled upon one of the Others she'd been warned about.

She turned to run before he saw her, but she wasn't quick enough. Immediately stricken by her beauty, the man grabbed her by the hand, fell to his knees, and begged her to be his wife.

Thinking herself very clever, she promised to be his wife for a year and a day and then she would be free to live as she pleased. The man agreed to her terms and took her back through the portal to his land to wed. It wasn't until a crown was placed upon her head at their wedding that she found out her new husband was the king of the Otherworld and she had been tricked. Time doesn't pass for the Others like it does for humans, and a year and a day in the Otherworld could be as long as a human lifespan on earth.

In some versions of the story she eventually fell in love with her husband and they reigned side by side for many years; in others, she escaped him and he spent the rest of his eternal life searching for revenge upon her and her offspring. I always liked the version where they fell in love best. Lydia and I would make tiaras of dandelions and pretend to be the faerie king's human bride.

In my dream, I am wedded to the faerie king, attempting to

escape the prison of our shared bedchamber. He runs his hand softly over the front of my body, cupping me from behind. "Come to bed, wife." His tongue flicks against the shell of my ear and I shiver all over. He moves his mouth lower, trailing his tongue over my pulse, down to where my collarbones ache. "Come to bed," he says once more, and this time I follow him.

His hands are hot as they press against the planes of my back. He cradles my face gently and tucks a loose curl behind my ear. I writhe against his body until I'm aching for him all over. I don't understand why he's making me wait. He rolls so he is on top of me and cages me in with his arms. His knee nudges between my legs, and I drop them open for him. "Kiss me," I whisper against his mouth. "Take me. I was only ever yours." The faerie king comes into focus. He has Emmett's face.

"Ivy," the faerie king says.

"Ivy." It's louder this time.

"Ivy!" I blink awake, confused and clammy, the wanting all over me like a fever. The room I'm in is shabby and unfamiliar. I blink again, and my eyes adjust to the low light of dawn.

Oh, right. The storm. The coaching inn. *Emmett.*

I tilt my face up and see Emmett staring down at me, a bemused smile on his face. His hair is wild with sleep, his eyes slightly puffy. "You're difficult to wake up," he says.

My head is tucked against his warm chest, his heartbeat hammering in my ears. He's got an arm tucked against my back, his hand falling right on the small of my waist.

The tips of my ears are freezing, but the rest of me is warm with the heat of Emmett's body.

"I'm sorry." I scramble across the bed, hot with embarrassment.

"The fire went out in the night. You were cold," Emmett replies.

"Yes. Cold."

Emmett swipes a hand across his face, like he can wipe away the blush of color along his cheeks. "I'll get it going again."

"Aren't you lucky you had such a good teacher," I say as he bends to open the tinderbox.

He's ditched his shirt sometime in the night, and he wraps himself in a blanket to get to work on the hearth.

I understand what Emmett meant when he said he would always be love-hungry. I feel a stab of desperate hunger when I look at him.

The storm has finally quieted, and dawn arrives with a wash of pale blue pressing against the windows.

I notice for the first time that Emmett's left collarbone juts out unnaturally under the skin. Usually hidden by his high cravats, it's poking out from under the blanket now.

"What happened there?" I gesture to it.

Emmett touches the bone gingerly. "I broke it jumping horses when I was twelve. I was afraid my governess would scold me, and I had no one else looking after me, so I hid it, and it healed all wrong. Hurt like the devil."

At twelve, I was still playing dolls with Greer. Emmett was so alone, he didn't have a single person he trusted enough to tell about a broken bone.

His back is to me as he stokes the fire. "You talk in your sleep."

I shuffle down under the quilt until I am completely covered. "Please leave me here to die," I call out.

Emmett laughs. "Don't you want to know what you said?"

"No. I want to be drowned in one of the puddles outside."

"It wasn't all that bad. Something about a king."

I poke my head out from under the covers and hope he doesn't see me blush. I pray I said nothing about what the king was doing. "That's not so terrible."

Emmett turns and flashes me a devilish grin. "And my name."

"Ugh," I shout, and dive back under.

"It's not as bad as when you were sick. You said all sorts of things."

Brown hair. A strong hand on my forehead soothing away a fever.

I poke my head out of the covers again. "That was you? I thought maybe I'd dreamed it."

He stills. "I felt so responsible. It was my fault you had to jump in that blasted river in the first place. I made Lottie sneak me in to sit by your bedside in the night."

Picturing the scene makes my heart ache. Emmett in the dark, sitting in that hard, wooden chair while I tossed and turned. "It wasn't your fault."

He won't look at me. "Of course it was."

I can see it all in the slump his shoulders, like the weight of the world is resting on them. "Emmett, you're not responsible for keeping me safe."

"That's a stupid thing to say."

I don't understand why he sounds angry with me.

Downstairs in the pub, Emmett shakes awake a mostly sober driver, and at dawn we climb into a gig, a two-wheeled cart pulled by a single horse. Emmett hopes the lighter vehicle will do a better job at navigating the sodden Hampshire landscape. He pays the driver double to pull us as fast as he can, which proves to be not very fast at all.

The bogs have flooded, and the hard-packed dirt roads from yesterday have turned into rivers of mud.

Something strange happens on the drive. I can see Emmett retreat inside of himself again. The softness behind his eyes hardens and the cool mask of disinterest falls over his face once more. It's suddenly like last night didn't happen and I'm just another girl he's ignoring at a ball he didn't want to be at in the first place.

"Emmett?" I nudge him with my elbow. "Are you quite well?"

"Perfectly fine." He still won't look at me.

"What will we tell them?" I ask.

"I'll tell them that I went to go get drunk in Alton, and you, with your kind heart, came to see if I was all right. We were trapped in the inn by the storm, but slept separately. I've already bribed the driver to corroborate."

"It's not a good story," I say. It still involves me sneaking off, spending time with Emmett without a chaperone, outside of polite society. I'll still be kicked out of the competition, but it might just keep me alive.

"It's the best I can do."

The poor cart horse trudges along for over an hour until we finally reach the outskirts of the hunting camp. The cheerful bunting has been blown down by the storm and it droops sadly, tangled in tree branches.

Emmett and I hop down from the cart, and he pays the driver at least triple what he's owed.

And here it is. The moment I've been so afraid of. Time for my reputation to go up in flames. Will the queen strip my family of their lands and titles as she's promised? Will I be killed? Surely

Emmett and Bram wouldn't let that happen, but perhaps even they will be powerless against her.

My knees are weak, my hands clammy. All I ever wanted to do was fix things, and instead I've broken them beyond repair. Last night felt like a dream, but the cold light of reality is here now, and it stings my eyes.

Emmett marches in first, like I'm not even here. I trail after him like a shadow.

I expect a flurry of activity, of scandalized shouting and heavy glares. Instead, we find . . . nothing.

The tents are still secured to their platforms, though bedraggled after the storm. The ground is little more than a mud pit, the tables and chairs from the first night half toppled and covered in filth.

"Did they leave?" I ask.

Emmett looks just as confused as I am.

Just then a footman comes from out of the larger staff tent, caked in mud up to his knees. He bows to Emmett, startled by our presence. "Your Highness, has the party returned?"

"I—" Emmett scrambles for an answer.

Suddenly from behind us comes the jingling of reins and the barking of dogs. We turn to see a parade of horse-drawn carts and carriages trooping through the entrance to the camp. Leading them on horseback is Bram, who looks as perfectly unmussed as usual. The same cannot be said for the rest of the party, who look as if they've been trudging through mud for hours.

Bram comes down from his horse and gives me a quick bow and Emmett a warm hug. "One of my more memorable birthdays. How did you fare here at camp?"

"Oh—" Emmett stumbles as we both process what's just happened. Bram's hunting party must have been delayed by the storm as well. We've beaten them by mere moments. Emmett blinks and squares his shoulders. "A little damp, but no worse for the wear."

In our muddy clothes from last night, we look no better than the hunting party. We both make up half-hearted excuses of not wanting to call the staff from their tents during the storm to prepare us for bed.

Emmy, Marion, Greer, Olive, and Faith hop down from their carriage looking as if they've just been through war. Even Viscountess Bolingbroke is disheveled, which feels outside the bounds of reality, like watching a dog walk on its hind legs.

"Goodness, what happened?" I ask.

"It was horrible," Emmy says. "A deluge stranded us in the woods."

"You were out there all night?"

"The cooks had set up tents for our luncheon, so we weren't entirely exposed to the elements, but one of the tents ripped halfway through the night and dumped water all over Greer," Marion explains. I look to Greer, whose hair still hangs in damp strands down her back.

"Bram's magic kept a fire going, but I honestly thought I was going to drown," Faith says.

Bram smiles apologetically. "I'm regretting I never tried harder to study magic."

I follow the others into our tent. They all dress in dry clothes and wrap knit shawls around their shoulders. We take turns braiding each other's hair while they ask me questions about my night.

"Our tent held up fine," I lie. "It was a little cold, but it sounds as if we fared much better than you all."

"Was it just you and the staff?" Greer asks.

"Horrible Emmett was here too," Olive reminds her.

"He's not horrible," Faith snaps.

"Oh god, did he try to seduce you?" Greer says. "I bet he'd say something about needing body heat to survive. The absolute cad." She laughs, and it takes all I have to laugh along with her. Faith's hands are still in my hair, and she tugs slightly harder as she finishes my braid.

"Don't let Bram hear you say that," Faith warns.

Camp is packed up quickly, everyone eager to be out of the forest and back to the warmth and comfort of the palace.

It takes over ten hours to return to Kensington Palace, a miserable, bone-rattling day on mud-choked roads. It's a relief to arrive back at Caledonia Cottage and its copper tubs full of steaming water and perfumed oils. I scrub my skin until it's red and stinging, like I can wash away the weight of Emmett, but I only end up raw.

The next few days pass with each of us on edge, waiting for the queen's next lesson. Instead, we're met with nothing but more of Viscountess Bolingbroke's etiquette lessons during the day and countless games of whist at night. We don't even see Bram, who seems preoccupied with his own social calendar.

I can't stop thinking about what Eduart said about Emmett's father. Hastily, I write a note addressed to Emmett, saying simply, *We need to speak*, and pass it to Lottie, folded in with the rest of today's post.

Friday is the Hinchingbrooks' annual garden party, and we're all itching to get off palace grounds.

The palace tailors have made us all custom day dresses, each adorned with our birth flowers. As an October baby, mine is embroidered along the neckline, hem, and sleeves with marigolds, bright pops of orange yellow rendered with such expert care I gasp upon seeing it. The rest of the dress is constructed of pale green moire silk. Lottie produces a matching headband, with two sweet yellow bows, one resting just above each ear.

Olive's pale blue dress is crawling with larkspurs, Marion's with daisies, Faith's with paperwhites that look vaguely bridal.

The party is hosted at the Hinchingbrooks' sprawling gardens. They've hung crystal chandeliers from the trees, set out delicate tables with pastel petit fours, and tied rainbows of ribbons from eaves and balconies and hedges.

We mingle for hours as the orchestra plays cheery melodies that float through the gardens.

I've got a mouth full of cake, and I'm standing in the rose garden when a tug at my sleeve startles me. I turn to see Emmett, standing in the brilliant sun in a cobalt-blue coat with gold piping. He looks every inch the prince today, his hair finally tamed and no longer falling across his forehead. It's the first time I've seen him since the disastrous hunting party, and relief floods through me at the sight of his face. But then comes that familiar ache, right in the center of my chest. It would be better if I could forget the sharp line of his jaw, the tiny wrinkle at the corners of his eyes, his dark lashes, his full mouth. His face is stony, like he doesn't feel anything looking at me.

"Downstairs drawing room, five minutes," he whispers, and then he is strolling across the garden again, like we never spoke at all.

I weave my way through the party and, five minutes later, find the door to the Hinchingbrooks' drawing room down a quiet side hallway.

Inside, the curtains are drawn and the furniture is covered in white sheets. I pace around for a minute or two until the knob turns and Emmett strides in.

"Good afternoon, Lady Ivy," he says.

"Are we back to formalities after we—" *We shared a bed, touched in the dark.* I can't bring myself to say it aloud. Emmett seems to be thinking the same thing, and a charged look passes between us.

We pause as we hear footsteps in the hall. Then the door swings open with a *bang* and Bram comes crashing in. I dive behind the sofa, hidden from his view. He closes the door behind him and clicks the lock. Emmett goes still, shocked and silent.

Bram's jaw clenches. "I'm not a fool. It's time we finally spoke about what's going on."

CHAPTER TWENTY-SIX

"Brother." Emmett extends his hands toward Bram, and the familiar mask of cool detachment drops over his face.

"I beg of you, stop treating me like I'm a child," Bram snaps. I've never seen him look like this. His hair is disheveled, his burgundy velvet coat hanging half-off one shoulder, and his face, usually open and kind, is shattered, as if he might be on the verge of tears.

"I'm certain I don't know what you're referring to," Emmett says.

"Lady Ivy Benton," Bram snarls. "I just saw you two together in the garden. You looked rather close."

"There was a bee I was shooing away—you know how ladies are," Emmett answers.

Bram throws his hands up. "Do you expect me to believe these weak excuses? Please do me the honor of not insulting my intelligence. I saw you in the boathouse too."

The color drains from Emmett's face.

"I'm not naive," Bram continues. "I knew not every girl who entered to be my bride would fall in love with me, but I did not expect to be betrayed by my own brother." His voice cracks. It would be easier if he were angry with us, but he just looks so sad.

"It's not what you think," Emmett insists.

"Do you love her?" Bram asks.

"No, of course not," Emmett says emphatically. It stings more than it should.

"At least if you loved her, I could understand," Bram says. "But if you're just sneaking around to—" Ever the gentleman, he stops short of saying it aloud. The implications make my face burn.

"We're not sneaking around. I barely know her. I tried to seduce her mad sister once, and it went so poorly I'd be a fool to try another Benton girl. Give me some credit, at least." Emmett lays a hand on his brother's shoulder, but Bram shakes it off and crosses the room, pacing like a caged animal.

"Bram, please just listen," Emmett begs.

"Listen to what, more lies?"

"Please don't shout. Making a scene at a party is my specialty, not yours."

"I know you weren't at camp that night," Bram says, and Emmett goes deadly still. Dread pools in my stomach, and the sickly sweet tea cake goes sour in the back of my throat.

"Of course we were—" Emmett tries, but Bram raises a hand to silence him.

"Stop lying to me," he shouts. Then he sinks down onto the love seat that I'm hiding behind. I can only see the backs of his shoes. "Please don't lie to me," he says once more, his voice a whisper. I remember what Emmett said about the fae, that Bram is incapable of lying. A hairline crack traces the center of my heart as it breaks for him.

Emmett's eyes well with tears at the sight of Bram so upset. I feel helpless and overwhelmed, my heart beating in my throat like

I might throw up my guts all over the Duke of Hinchingbrook's expensive carpets.

Emmett sighs deeply. "Lady Ivy asked for my help in getting to know you. She's inexperienced. I pitied her. I hoped if I helped her, you'd pick her, not Faith Fairchild."

"You could have just told me you didn't want me to pick Faith."

"I should have, I know that now. I was being stupid. I didn't want you playing with my toys."

"Where were you that night?" Bram asks. He doesn't sound angry, just sad.

"I took a horse and cart and went to the coaching inn in Alton to drown myself in ale. I'm a horrible shot, and I didn't wish to embarrass myself on your birthday. I'm sorry for my pride."

"You're not *that* bad a shot."

"You're being too kind, as always."

"What about Lady Ivy Benton?" Bram asks.

"I haven't the slightest idea. Probably sick in her tent like she said. If any of the servants said she was with me, they were only generating pointless gossip. That would be scandalous, wouldn't it?"

Bram sighs heavily. "You swear it?"

"I swear it," Emmett offers immediately. "She's not my type at all, so overly coddled by that embarrassing family of hers." Anger rises like bile in my throat. I can't believe he's using what I told him in confidence as a weapon.

"She's a lovely girl," Bram says in my defense.

"Oh, without a doubt, and she'll make a perfect bride for you, but I could never be content with a girl like that . . ." He trails off.

"Like what?"

"That inelegant."

I think of beautiful Faith Fairchild and the way she walks, like she's floating. Anger rises in my throat. I know Emmett can't tell Bram anything other than *of course I don't want her*, but this rejection feels personal.

"I happen to like her the way she is," Bram replies.

"All the better. Come, brother, let's steal a bottle of champagne and leave this horrible party. I'm not having any fun. There's only one pretty girl here, and I've already had her. I'm bored." Faith, again. Always Faith.

Bram stands and Emmett approaches the couch. There's a rustle of fabric as he slings his arm around Bram's shoulder. The door closes behind them, leaving me alone in the room, my heart beating like I've just run a mile.

I swipe away my tears with the heels of my hands and enough pressure to bruise.

Emmett is right. We aren't a match.

As soon as the door slams behind them, I spring from my hiding spot, press my ear against the door until I'm sure the coast is clear, and then run down the hallway, back into the thick of the party.

That night, once everyone else is asleep, I sneak out of the cottage and through the palace tunnels to Emmett's room, for what I hope will be the last time.

Pig greets me at the hidden door, wagging his tail so hard his whole body shakes. Emmett is at his desk, reading by candlelight. He jumps as I enter.

"Ivy?" There's no time for him to put on his cold mask of detachment. He's staring at me, like he's looking for something. His words from earlier play in my head. *Coddled. Inelegant. A girl like that.*

"Just one question, and then I'll go. I'll never ask again."

He just nods, something dark flickering behind his eyes.

"Did you mean what you said to Bram? That I'm not the kind of girl you could ever want?"

"Don't make me answer that," Emmett replies tightly.

"Please, I just need to hear you say it." *Give me closure,* I want to beg, *then maybe I will stop remembering how your hands felt in the dark.*

Emmett looks out the dark window. There are no stars tonight. "You're making a fool of yourself, Ivy. Bram is going to be a wonderful husband. But you and I?" He sighs, his voice remote. "There was never going to be a you and I. I'm sorry if I ever made you think differently."

I get the impression that this is a well-worn rejection speech, one he's given to dozens of lovesick girls just as foolish as me.

GREER TRUMMER

When my mother first told me that I couldn't speak to Ivy anymore, I cried for a week. Then she sold my second favorite horse and told me she'd sell the other if I let my blubbering get in the way of preparing for the season, so the tears dried up quick. There was no winning with Mama. After eighteen years, I knew it well enough. She'd mostly stopped hitting me when I turned sixteen, but sometimes I wish she'd start again. Her psychological games are worse because they're so much harder to predict.

Mama never liked the Benton sisters. They were so completely themselves, and I think that scared her, because Mama didn't want me to be anything but her perfect little soldier. I didn't know what a family looked like until I sat at the Bentons' dining table and watched them gossip and debate things like art and philosophy. No one was told to lower their voice—that surprised me most.

Ivy would sometimes make biting comments about how she lived permanently in my shadow, but I was jealous of her too. Our jealousy fed on itself until it tangled into the very fabric of our relationship.

I wasn't entirely surprised when Lydia ruined her family. She'd lived with the recklessness of someone who'd been told her whole life she was perfect. She didn't fear missteps, because every step she'd ever taken had been met with applause. She was good at this life of ours. She loved being on display, living as if she were on a stage and this was all some big game. When I was small, I thought I hated her; now I have enough self-awareness to know what I was feeling had another name: envy. It doesn't matter much now, there's no use in dwelling on it.

But something changed the year of Lydia's debut. Ivy would turn up at my house with a worried look on her face and stories of whatever had happened the night before. Lydia wasn't getting any callers, let alone any offers.

Between that and Lydia's lack of a public bargain, it was an embarrassment, a blight on the family, and I pitied Ivy because she didn't seem to realize it yet. She was too busy being worried about her sister to be worried for herself.

Everyone always thought Lydia would marry Percival Chapwick. The day she refused his proposal, Ivy came over and wept in my bed all evening. "She promised," she wailed. I've never been good with people crying.

I wasn't like the Benton sisters. I've always known exactly what my bargain would be. Mama and I decided it together when I was ten and it became clear I wasn't going to grow into my nose. I'd spend hours looking at myself in the mirror, Mama just over my shoulder. She'd stroke her pinkie over the bridge and say "just there." It felt something like love. It was the only way she knew how to take care of me.

The Benton girls had none of our practicality.

It's why Ivy made a good best friend. She always had stories about faerie kings, or she wanted to make little houses out of leaves for the ducklings. I loved living in her world with her. I relished evenings at the Benton home, where no one was screaming. Her parents seemed to really like each other; I didn't even know that was possible until I met them.

Friends are tricky in this business of ours.

It hurt to leave her behind, but I knew why I had to do it. I snipped the threads that bound me to her like I was finishing an embroidery. I loved Ivy, but not enough to let her ruin me.

I learned at my mother's knee how to shove feelings deep down until I couldn't reach them anymore. Ivy fit well in that dark place.

Her absence in my life left a hole in more ways than one. I'd lost not only a confidante and a friend, but also a way to fill my time. The hours I'd usually spend with Ivy were suddenly freed up. I took to going to the stables early in the morning, before fittings or etiquette lessons or promenades around the park. I was mostly avoiding my mother, but it was nice to stroke my horse's neck and braid her mane.

It was there that I first started talking to Joseph again.

We'd been friends when we were young, and he used to let Ivy and me torment him. We'd chase him down and tie ribbons in his hair until he squirmed away from us. But he'd grown into nearly a man. I didn't even realize he still worked for our family, thought maybe he'd gone away to school or something.

But there he was, in the dappled morning light of the stables, an apron on and a farrier's file in his hand.

"Milady." His voice was so deep it made me jump. "I didn't realize you were here."

I startled, which startled the horse, who whinnied and bucked. I stumbled backward and tripped over the hem of my dress. I would have gone flying into the stone floor of the mews if Joseph hadn't caught me.

I remember looking up at him and realizing I'd never really seen him at all. "I've got you" was all he said, and I fell in love right then and there.

I went to the stables every morning after that. We'd sip tea together on bales of hay, and he taught me how to polish the tack. He was the first person who had truly listened to me since Ivy.

I scrubbed my hands raw so Mama wouldn't see the black smudge of polish under my fingernails. We all laughed at Olive's bargain, which left her with no nails, but honestly, she may have been smarter than the rest of us.

Joseph was too polite to kiss me, even though I'd hinted at it for weeks. In the end, I'm the one who had to lean in. It was a gray morning, misty with rain, and I raised up on my toes and pressed my lips to his in the doorway of the barn. He was so startled he didn't move, and I thought I'd misread everything. I pulled back, and he looked at me with his big blue eyes, then lifted me off my feet and confessed he'd loved me all his life. It was everything I'd ever wanted.

We met in secret for months. Joseph begged me to run away with him, said he'd use his bargain for a carriage fast enough to carry us to the Scottish border, or to have both our families forget we ever existed, so we could live in peace, but I wasn't brave like him. I looked at my nose in the mirror and stuck to my mother's plan.

Mama caught us on the morning of the Pact Parade. It was reckless, I knew that, but I needed to say goodbye. He'd made me promise to show him my old face one last time. I didn't tell him then, but I had it all worked out. I'd marry some stodgy old widower and hire Joseph to work in our stables. We could live a life together, even if it was only in the shadows.

Mama barreled into the stables and caught us just as the sun rose. The fury on her face screwed up her features so intensely, for a moment I didn't recognize her. She dragged me by my hair back up to my room, and Joseph knew well enough not to stop her. She hit me on my stomach so the bruises wouldn't show through my Pact Parade gown, used the heels of her hands so the blows landed sharp and precise. My father watched, his arms folded across his broad chest, and told me it was all my fault, that I should have known better.

I think maybe my mother dragged me to the dais to compete for Bram's hand because she wanted an excuse to take a knife to me, to watch me bleed. But the joke was on her. I didn't feel a thing when she cut me.

When I entered the queen's throne room to make my bargain, I was so numb I couldn't think, so I asked for what Mama and I had always planned. I regret that now.

I was surprised when Queen Mor looked down at me with a quirked head and asked, "What is it you are most afraid of, Lady Trummer?"

No one had ever asked me that, not even Joseph.

I settled on "having to tell the truth." It was the truest answer I could think of, and one day, maybe, I'd be able to laugh at the irony in that. I'd built a life based on lies; I was honest enough with myself to know that. I told my mother I loved her. I told Joseph I'd be his forever. I acted like I didn't miss Ivy at all.

I planned a life in which I'd keep lying—to my eventual husband, to my mother, to myself.

The queen just laughed as I told her, and she said, "I've always admired skilled liars."

I walked out of that room with a new face and turned right at the door, the queen's laughter still echoing behind me.

Joseph gasped when he saw me for the first time.

I snuck to his closet-size room in the staff quarters the night of the Pact Parade. I was surprised to find him there. I thought for certain my mother would have fired him, but she knew keeping him around would hurt me more. The flickering of his lantern lit up my new face. "Aren't I prettier now?"

He hesitated, and it made me angry enough that I was sick to my stomach. "Tell me I'm prettier now, Joseph."

"I thought you were perfect before." He was still polishing the saddle he was working on, like he couldn't bear to look at me.

An errant tear rolled down my cheek. "You're wrong. You're a stable boy, what would you know about refined taste?"

I pushed and pushed until he said it, even though I could see in his face that he didn't believe it. "You're prettier now," he said, but he wasn't as good a liar as I was. In fact, he was rotten at it.

"I know," I replied.

"You'll be a princess," he said later, as he traced my bare shoulder when we were in his bed together.

I could tell he believed it. I shook my head. "Probably not. He'll pick Marion." My hand stung where Mama had cut me.

"How could anyone not want you?" But he didn't look at my face as he said it, like he couldn't anymore.

It's been easy enough to sneak away to see him. Viscountess Bolingbroke sleeps like a log, and my parents' residence is walking distance from the palace. I sometimes see Ivy's shadowy figure crossing the lawn at the same time. I hope it's to see Bram. I'd be happy for her.

I sneak through the streets at dawn and meet Joseph in the barn, just as the first rays of light stream through the dust of the tack room. He closes his eyes as he kisses me, and it's like nothing has changed at all.

When Bram chooses some other girl and I'm a confirmed spinster, I'll move back home and we'll continue as we were. No one ever needs to know the truth.

CHAPTER TWENTY-SEVEN

"Why are you so sullen, Ivy?" Greer asks me over breakfast the next day.

"I'm not sullen."

Greer shrugs, unconcerned. "You've had a sour look on your face since yesterday. Did something happen? Is Lydia poorly again?"

"No, no, nothing like that."

I take a bite of currant scone and blink a few times. Focus up, Ivy. No time for self-pity now. "It's kind of you to ask, though."

"I love you, Ivy. I'm sorry if I ever made you doubt it."

Doubt it? All she did was make me doubt it. From the very first moment she left me alone in the garden, I've doubted it. I've spent half my life chasing her approval. It's the entire reason we made a good pair of best friends.

But then she pours me a cup of tea, two sugars, the smallest splash of milk, just how I've always taken it, and something in me softens.

"I love you too, Greer."

A footman strolls into the cottage, straight-backed in his midnight-blue livery. He's carrying a scroll of paper on a silver tray.

Emmy is the one brave enough to take it. She unrolls it and reads, "'Lady Ivy Benton, Lady Greer Trummer, Lady Emmy Ito, Miss Faith Fairchild, Lady Marion Thorne, and Lady Olive Lisonbee are cordially invited to an audience with Her Majesty, Queen Moryen. Immediately.'"

Our lady's maids flood into the cottage with well-practiced choreography. Within minutes, hats are pinned and dresses are buttoned and we are off across the damp lawn to Kensington Palace.

We follow one of the queen's unsettling footmen up the main staircase, just like we did on the Pact Parade. I can't believe I missed it before, how strange and mottled the veins of their hands are, the hollowness around their eyes. A human body wasn't built to last forever. I wonder how old this one is, who he was before this, if he even remembers.

A steady stream of rain falls on the glass roof, and the tree in the middle of the atrium sways slightly.

"Any guesses?" Emmy whispers to me.

"Not a one," I reply honestly.

We veer left at the top of the stairs into an expansive ballroom. My heels slip against the carpet as I stop short. All six of us take identical gasps.

The ballroom has been transformed with rosebushes, dark ivy crawling up to the ceiling, ferns shoved into every corner.

There's an orchestra playing a strange, off-kilter tune and tables covered in mismatched iridescent china.

There's a crowd of women here already, and I spot my mother and sister surrounded by a gaggle of my mother's old friends, including Greer's mother.

The queen approaches us.

She's dressed in a gown of silver silk, so bright it looks like molten metal has been poured over her lithe body. The sleeves are covered in glass beads that trail along the floor behind her. There's a smear of kohl around her black eyes and a bloodred salve on her lips. But what is most remarkable is the half a deer skull she's wearing as a crown.

It's as if she wants us to remember that she's not one of us.

"What is this?" Marion asks.

"A tea party," Queen Mor answers with a sick smile.

My heart is in my throat as I make my way toward my mother and Lydia, terrified that they've been caught up in this. I haven't seen Lydia since the disastrous night at the masquerade ball, nor have I heard anything since Mama's letter.

"I miss you. I miss you," I say fiercely when I reach her.

"I know." Everything passes between us in that wordless way only sisters understand. The guilt and resentment and love all tangled up into something too difficult to put into words, so for a moment all we can do is sit there and feel it, take the force of it as it washes over us.

I hug my mother around her shoulders and she turns around with a gasp. "Darling! The house has been so dull without you."

Lydia nods. "It's true. She doesn't like me much at all anymore."

They've both got a strange, glassy look in their eyes. Their pupils are too blown out, their skin waxy.

"Are you feeling quite well?" I ask.

My mother takes a sip from her porcelain teacup. "Grand. From what I hear, you're going to win. Honestly, I didn't think you had it in you."

"Mama?" I ask, confused, but Greer's mother interrupts me.

"Oh, Ivy won't win. Both your daughters are failures. It rubbed off on Greer, I fear. It's the only explanation I can come up with for her disappointing performance. She'll be victorious in the end, though. We Trummers always are."

Before I can respond, a butler dings a bell.

"Shall we?" says the queen. Flanked by footmen, she sits down and gestures for us to join her. The table, which stretches the length of the room, is covered with more food than necessary for a tea party. Green grapes are piled high next to split pomegranates and spiral-cut hams. In front of me is a three-tier dark chocolate cake, its icing half melted by the flickering taper candles.

Someone clutches my hand, and when I look up, I'm expecting to see anyone but Greer. Her blue eyes are wide with fear as she looks straight ahead.

I glance around the table. We are surrounded by our family and friends. Greer is on one side of me, Lydia and my mother on the other. Across from me are Faith, her sharp-faced grandmother, and a man with eyes the same shade of blue as hers.

Marion sits to the left of Faith with her mother and younger sister. Down a ways are Emmy and Olive and their mothers, as well as a few of the other debutantes from the season, Deidre Rutland, Sara Middlebrook, Fiona Devon, Althea Jones, and their chaperones.

The queen sits at the head of the table, the candlelight reflecting in the empty eye sockets of her deer-skull crown.

The whine of the violins seems to itch right under my skin, and I'm suddenly ravenous.

"Welcome, honored guests." The queen extends her arms over the feast. "How lovely it is to have you all here today."

"You terrify me," Althea Jones pipes up. "I'd really rather not be here."

The queen shoots her a deadly glare. "Well, you are here, and you will be here as long as I am amused."

I tense up, terrified for Althea. She's usually such a shy girl.

"Well, I'm honored to be here," chimes in the man I suspect is Faith's father. "I never thought we'd be invited again after my little secret was revealed." He gestures to Faith.

Faith spits out her tea. "Secret? I'm a person."

"Don't take that tone," her grandmother snaps. "He's done you a favor by acknowledging you now. He could have left you to rot with that whore mother of yours forever."

"That's enough!" Marion bellows.

"Marion—" Faith whispers, like she doesn't want the rest of us to hear her.

"They don't get to speak to you like that," Marion says.

"I'll speak to my daughter however I please."

Soon everyone around the table is in a frenzy. "What is happening?" I ask.

The queen claps her hands with glee. "I'm so glad you asked, Lady Ivy." The crowd goes still. "Welcome to my next lesson. Any wife of Bram's will need to learn to tolerate gossip and rumor. What better way to test that than to have your friends and family tell you exactly what it is they think of you. Your loved ones have been enchanted to speak the truth, without the filter of civility or concern for your feelings. When they leave this room, they will forget this day ever happened."

But we'll remember. That goes unsaid. We'll be left to live with whatever we learn today.

The deer skull, the awful music, the piles of food all make more sense now. The queen isn't throwing us a normal party. This is like the faerie revels I used to imagine. If everyone but us is going to forget, she might as well throw exactly the kind of party she wants.

She wants to be entertained, that's all. I remember what Eduart said. *After an eternity, there is only boredom or the lack of it.*

The chatter starts back up. Emmy bursts into tears at something her mother has said and runs for the door. She pulls and pulls, but it's locked.

"You must last an hour," the queen declares, watching with a glint in her eye.

I turn to my family.

"I was the one who spilled that bottle of ink on your favorite shawl two years ago," Lydia says. "I'm sorry I blamed it on the cook's cat."

"I know. Your hands were smeared with black, and you're a terrible liar," I reply.

The worst part of me thinks about asking them both for things I know I don't actually want the answer to, like which one of us is my mother's favorite or if Lydia loves me as much as I love her.

But there's only one thing I truly want to know.

"You might as well tell me—" I say to Lydia. She doesn't need me to complete the rest of the sentence. *You might as well tell me where you actually were those two weeks you went missing.*

Lydia sighs, exasperated. "Ivy, I don't remember where I was. It's all one big blank spot."

She has to be telling the truth. Nausea pools in my stomach. "You don't remember anything?"

"Not one single thing. But I have these dreams." Her voice trails off, soft and distant.

"What does that mean?"

"I don't know. I can't explain it any better than that."

My mother watches us, that uncanny glazed look in her eyes.

"I think it's your turn to tell the truth," Lydia says to me.

I've tried so hard to be the perfect sister, to save our family from ruination by any means possible, tamping down my anger, my own wants, in the process. I've done it all because I love my parents, and I love Lydia more than I will ever be able to explain. But the anger in me is rising again, that awful tide of hurt I feel powerless to stop. *She's so much easier to love when she's not in front of me.* "We had a plan, Lydia, and I can't understand why you abandoned it."

"Ivy—" She says my name like a warning. This is the one topic still too sensitive to touch—not her disappearance, but her third and final betrayal.

"We made a pact," I say. "We had it all figured out. You were going to marry Percival Chapwick, I was going to live with you forever, and we would have been *happy.* I was never going to be any good at any of this." I gesture at my gown and swept-up hair and the palace. "You were the one who was meant for society. You were always perfect and sweet and good."

"I couldn't stand it!" Lydia stands up at the table, knocking her chair over behind her. "I was perfect and sweet and good, and then I realized one day I was never going to get to be anything *but* that. You, Mother, and Father all put me on this pedestal I never asked for. I couldn't live up there forever."

"We were going to be together!"

"Are you mad that we're not together, or are you mad that you finally had to grow up and take some responsibility?"

It stings as badly as if she'd just hit me. "I've taken all of the responsibility! You've left everything on me. I'm not strong enough to bear it—this wasn't the role I was supposed to play."

"It was a child's fantasy, Ivy. I was never going to marry Percival Chapwick. I thought we were just playing a game when I promised you. It was never real."

"It was real to me!" It was the bedrock upon which my life was built, and it crumbled underneath me. I'm not under the queen's enchantment, but I can't stop myself from telling the truth. What does it matter anyway? She's never going to remember.

We're both crying now, big, ugly tears we're powerless to stop.

"I don't want you to hate me," Lydia says. "I'm sorry I don't remember the bargain I made. All I know is that I went into that throne room and I panicked. I thought of a life as small as our mother's, and I couldn't bear it. I don't know what came over me."

I feel so unbearably guilty. What's the point in doing everything I can to save my family if I can't save my sister—the person I love most in this world—from my own vitriol.

"I don't *want* to hate you!" My voice cracks, echoing through the marble hall. "You were always the most beautiful, the most refined, the most beloved of us. You don't understand what it was like to live in your shadow."

She takes a step toward me, and I step back, swiping a hand roughly down my tear-streaked face. "You were *perfect*."

She throws her hands up in frustration. "I was perfect so that *you* got to be everything else. You think I didn't want to talk back to my tutors, or fall asleep during etiquette lessons, or run in the woods instead of needlepointing with Mama? I might have been perfect, but you were the bravest, the most daring, the most fun. You were everything I never got to be, because I was protecting you."

None of it matters anymore. "And now you've abandoned me."

Tears stream down her cheeks. "That's not my fault."

"But our future rests on me, all the same," I say. "I had no other choice. Mama and Papa aren't strong enough to survive exile from society. I never would have stood a chance at getting an offer of marriage otherwise."

My mother is too deep in conversation with Faith's grandmother to overhear us. I don't even know if she'd be offended to hear me say it.

"You don't know that for certain. Sometimes I think you enjoy your martyrdom," Lydia replies.

I thought I could carry the responsibility of this family on my shoulders, but it's crushing me. It's like I can't breathe anymore.

"It's not your responsibility to save us," Lydia says.

"Of course it is! No one else is stepping up! This would all be so much easier if you weren't so willfully naive. The world isn't a fairy tale, Lydia. Things don't always magically work out for the best. There's no handsome prince coming to save you."

She rolls her eyes and throws her head back, laughing. "That's rich, coming from you, who, at this very moment, is hoping for a handsome prince to save her!"

"Screw you, Lydia."

I look over the table, which is now in full carnage. Faith is huddling with Marion in the corner while her father and grandmother scream at each other.

Emmy's mother is listing her physical flaws one by one on her fingers.

Marion's sister is writing down every last article of Marion's clothing she's stolen in her absence.

Olive's mother is giving a detailed account of an affair she had with her husband's brother, while Olive watches, horrified.

But eeriest of all is Greer's mother, sitting perfectly silent. She's never missed an opportunity to say something biting to her daughter.

The queen circles the table. The antlers of her crown keep snagging in the vines and rainbow of ribbons hanging from the ceiling.

She lays a pale, bony hand on Greer's mother's shoulder. "Anything to share, Lady Trummer?"

Her mother clears her throat. "As a matter of fact, there is something that has been on my mind."

"Please share," Queen Mor urges.

"Mama," Greer whispers, as white as a sheet.

Her mother turns to her. "Does sweet Prince Bram know about your filthy stable boy?"

Tears roll down Greer's cheeks. "Mama, please don't do this."

"Because he really should know that your father and I caught you tangled up in a rather compromising position the morning of this year's Pact Parade."

She turns to the queen. "All the finest governesses and tutors in the world, but what a disappointment she turned out to be. Greer's virtue can never be recovered."

Greer sobs. "Please, no."

I'm frozen in horror.

"Greer—" Lydia says, reaching for her, and it pulls me out of my trance.

Greer springs from the table with a clatter and sprints for the door. The queen waves her hand lazily, and it opens for her. "Let her go," she says coldly, and Greer races across the room.

"Greer!" I shout as I give chase, but she doesn't slow down. She doesn't even look back. I've nearly reached her, my hand outstretched, but the moment she passes through the door, the queen waves her hand, sending it slamming in my face.

I fall back, landing hard on the parquet floor.

Lydia helps me up. "She's gone. It's not your fault," she says. But it feels like it is. *I love you, Ivy.* That's what she said to me earlier. I love her too. I love her too much to stand to watch her suffer like this. Emmett says if his plan works, I'll save everyone from the queen's cruelty, but I feel so helpless, unable to save them now.

"Oh, that's nothing. Faith—" Faith's father starts to say, but I don't let him finish. I climb up on the table, sending teacups shattering, my foot squishing in a frosted coconut cake.

"I kissed Bram at the Welbys' masquerade ball!" I shout. The table goes still. I might not have been able to help Greer, but I can still help Faith.

Everyone is staring at me, scandalized into silence, but my eyes land on the queen. She's standing perfectly still. Her gorgeous face doesn't reveal a single emotion.

"What?" Olive's mother gasps.

"Well done, you," Lydia says, but she's not smiling, not like my mother, who looks like the cat who has gotten the cream.

I hop down from the table, leaving a foot-shaped smear of cake on the carpet.

Throwing myself on my sword seems to have distracted the party well enough that Faith's father doesn't return to the topic of her love affair with Emmett. Instead, the conversation turns to which of us will win.

"Marion is so much prettier than you," my mother clucks. "But I'll still be proud, even when you lose."

A bell chimes when the hour is up, and the queen is out the door without another word.

I'm not sure exactly when the enchantment will wear off, but I want time alone with my sister to clear the air. I hate fighting with her. We know exactly how to hurt each other.

I tell our mother that I'm taking Lydia to the cottage to lend her a dress, that she'll meet her at the front entrance shortly.

I take the long way around, toward the back entrance of the palace, to avoid the other guests. The sound of footsteps echo through the marble hall. Emmett enters the room, startled at the sight of us. "Lady Benton and . . . Lady Benton."

Emmett looks at our tear-streaked faces. He shifts awkwardly from foot to foot. "I didn't mean to interrupt."

"Hello," I say awkwardly, unable to tear my gaze from him. He's dressed in a cream linen double-breasted jacket, his face as infuriatingly perfect as ever. Our last conversation rings in my ears. *You're making a fool of yourself, Ivy.*

He drags a hand through his hair. "Hello," he returns awkwardly.

"We really ought to be going." I grab Lydia by the elbow and pull her toward the door.

At that moment Bram strides into the statue hall and slings an arm around Emmett's shoulders. He's got a tennis racquet in his other hand, identical to the one I now see hanging at Emmett's side.

"Ready, brother?" Bram stills at the sight of us, then gives a bow. "Ah, the Benton sisters. Always a pleasure. Fancy doubles tennis?"

"No, thank you," Lydia answers sharply, pulling me down the stairs.

We're halfway across the lawn to Caledonia Cottage when she finally speaks again. "You like him." She elbows me in the ribs.

I return the jab. "Bram? Of course I do. He's very difficult not to like."

"Not him," Lydia says in a singsongy voice. "What happened to our plans to torment horrible Prince Emmett together?"

"They still stand."

"You're such a rotten liar."

"It doesn't matter. It's silly. I'll get over it."

She raises an eyebrow. "Silly?"

"It's nothing."

Lydia shakes her head. "Like I said, rotten liar."

We reach the door of the cottage, and Lydia pulls me into an awkward hug. "I won't pretend to know what's going on here, but I have confidence you'll handle whatever it is. When I said you'd make a wonderful princess, I meant it. Just . . . take care of yourself. You don't need to do everything on your own."

"I know, I know."

We turn to see Bram running across the lawn, the tennis racket still in his hand. He approaches us, panting.

"I'm sorry for my rudeness back there." He brushes a sun-kissed lock of hair off his forehead. "I should have asked how you were getting home, Lady Lydia. Please allow me to accompany you."

"Oh—" Lydia looks at the ground and blushes. "That's hardly necessary. My mother will be waiting."

"No, I insist. I'll accompany you both. If not for your sake, then for Ivy's."

A part of me warms, seeing Bram wanting to take care of the person I love most in the world. Her eyes flit to the ground. "Oh, all right, then." He takes her hand in the crook of his arm.

"When you're back, will you ask after Greer?" I prod Bram. "She seemed unwell earlier."

Bram bows. "Of course." I watch them disappear across the great lawn together.

I'm sitting in bed that night, reading a novel, and Olive is downstairs baking, when Faith Fairchild appears in my doorway. "Can we talk?"

I nod, surprised, and fold my book. She sits down on Olive's bed, what used to be her bed, and exhales. "I'm sorry." The words sound unnatural coming from her, like she's not used to saying them. "Thank you for what you did this afternoon, for protecting me. You didn't have to do that."

It's been a tense evening. Greer still hasn't returned, and I'm sick with worry. The tea party this afternoon has left me feeling like a raw nerve, and Faith's unexpected apology makes me want to cry.

"Of course I did," I say.

"I've been unfair to you," Faith says. "I'm sorry. It's just . . . I'm so angry all the time about everyone and everything."

"I understand. More than you may know. I'm sorry you had to go through that today."

"It's fine," she says, like she knows it's not. She rises and then leans in the doorway, like there's more she wants to say.

Marion pokes her head in and rests her chin on top of Faith's head. "Is she saying thank you for both of us?"

"Both of you?" I ask.

"Very subtle, darling." Faith rolls her eyes and closes the door behind her.

We awake the next morning to a fresh newspaper laid out at the foot of each of our beds. In big block letters is the headline **LORD TRUMMER'S ONLY DAUGHTER, DEAD AT EIGHTEEN. BODY PULLED FROM THE THAMES THIS MORNING AT DAWN**.

CHAPTER TWENTY-EIGHT

"No," I whisper. I turn to Olive, who looks stricken, her face parchment white as she stares down at the paper. On each newspaper is a number written in the corner. Mine is emblazoned with a bold 1, though what I did to win, I don't understand.

Someone is weeping across the hall. I race to Marion and Faith's room to find Emmy in tears and Marion holding Faith in her arms.

"She killed her?" Emmy asks.

"All because of a stable boy?" Faith adds.

Greer wouldn't have done this, so it must have been the queen, punishing us for disrespect just like she promised she would.

"We can't let this go on—" I manage through my tight throat.

Without another word I race across the dew-damp lawn on my bare feet and in my nightdress.

My lungs scream as I climb the stairs to Emmett's room two at a time. But the physical pain is nothing compared to my breaking heart.

I burst through the painting on the wall and find him tying his cravat in the mirror.

He jumps as I barrel in. "Ivy?"

For a moment I say nothing. I just stand there, trying to catch my breath, and end up sobbing instead. Big, hiccupping, body-racking sobs. Emmett races across the room and catches me in his arms before my knees hit the carpet.

"She killed her—" I gasp. My tears leave splotches all over his freshly pressed shirt. "She killed her."

"What? What are you talking about? Breathe, please." He lowers me to the edge of his bed. "Put your head between your legs, it will help." He gently guides me into the position, but Pig keeps trying to climb on my lap, making it near impossible. Emmett scoops the tiny dog under one arm and with his free hand, he brushes the tears from my cheeks.

"That's it." He takes a deep breath. "Just breathe."

"The—" I mean to say the queen's lesson, but it's as if my tongue has suddenly inflated and I'm choking on it. In my panic, I've forgotten I cannot tell him outright. I'm going to have to be clever about this.

Wait. "Get Faith," I demand.

"What?"

"Just do it."

Fifteen minutes later, Emmett comes back through the tunnels, Faith beside him. She's still wrapped in her dressing gown, her eyes made an electric blue by the ring of red around them.

I stare pointedly at her. "She said we couldn't talk to anyone else about her lessons, but she said nothing about speaking to each other." I'm angry that it took me this long to put it together.

"What?" Emmett mutters, confused.

"Faith," I begin. "I desperately want to tell Emmett about the private lessons the queen has been giving us."

Her eyes light up as realization dawns on her. "Yes, of course. We've been so stupid."

I tell Faith everything I want to tell Emmett, while he listens silently behind us. I go through lesson by lesson, the maze, the etiquette class, the tea party, the way we've been ranked and wounded. Emmett looks as if he might be sick as I recall the way she showed up at the cottage and threated to kill us if we stopped cooperating. Faith chimes in occasionally with her own details. Finally, we reach the subject of Greer. Faith was clever enough to bring the newspaper along with her. She drops it on Emmett's lap.

The blood drains from his face as he reads the headline. "She killed her for this?"

"It has to be her. I promise you it wasn't Greer," I answer. There's so much regret weighing heavily in my stomach, I fear I might be sick with it all over the floor. I should have been kinder, more forgiving. I should have asked her more questions when she brought up Joseph. I could have done more for her yesterday.

Emmett pulls on his coat. "Then I have to tell Bram. He won't let this continue."

On the way back across the lawn, Faith reaches over and squeezes my hand. "I might owe you my life."

I feel dead inside, like all my sorrow has burned through me, leaving nothing but a husk. "Don't mention it," I say flatly.

Viscountess Bolingbroke and Queen Mor leave us alone in our cottage for the rest of the day. If I had to guess, she's letting us stew in our fear and agony over the loss of Greer.

It's long dark when a footman arrives with a summons for dinner. No lady's maids come to get us. We dress each other in sorrowful silence and cross the lawn hand in hand, all five of us in a line.

The candlelit dining room goes deadly silent as Queen Mor strides in and takes her place at the head of the table. She's wearing a gown of forest-green silk, her hair in an intricate pattern of braids. She doesn't sit down.

I hate her, violently. I ball my hands into fists under the table to keep from launching myself across the table and hitting her.

All my hope now lies in Emmett's plan, and the thought that soon I will have the power to punish her as thoroughly as she deserves.

"I thought we'd all agreed to keep our time together between us." Her voice booms across the space, vibrating at a frequency I feel in my rib cage. "Today my son came to me and insisted I put an end to our lessons. He's got such a soft heart, that boy. He doesn't share my revulsion with having a group of snotty little aristocrats make demands. While we may disagree on this, it simply isn't worth the trouble. I'll do it better with the next batch. Fifty years passes by so quickly." We shift uncomfortably at the reminder of how disposable we are to her. "Your season is coming to an end early. Without any more lessons, I see no reason to prolong it. Bram will propose at the Kendalls' ball Saturday evening."

That's the day after tomorrow. I thought I had twelve weeks to make Bram fall in love with me. We've had only five. Panic rises in me. I thought I had more time.

Emmy's grip on her knife tightens. Faith and Marion share a tense glance.

"I hope you're pleased with yourselves. I won't forget this," Queen Mor says.

She sweeps out the door. "Have a pleasant dinner."

I can't stand it anymore. I wait a minute or two, just long enough to be sure she's gone, then push back from the table and walk out the door, down the stairs, and into the twilight.

I'm waiting for the guards to stop me, but no one says a word as I stride out of the gates and onto the street. I'm not naive enough to imagine it won't get back to her, I simply no longer have it in me to care.

There's a patter of footsteps behind me. I turn to find an out-of-breath Faith. "Ivy, slow down!" She pauses to hike up the heavy silk skirts of her evening gown, and then falls into pace by my side "Damn, you're a fast walker. Where are you going?"

"To see if Greer is really dead."

"All right, then," Faith says.

We walk a minute or two, until we hear more running, quick on our heels. "Wait!" Olive calls, her ginger hair flying behind her. "Wait for us!"

A noise somewhere between a laugh and a sob escapes my mouth as I see Olive, Marion, and Emmy jogging up the street.

"What are we doing?" Emmy asks.

"I'm following Ivy to make sure she doesn't get herself killed," Faith replies.

"I'm following Faith," Marion says.

"I'm not letting you go on an adventure without me," Olive says.

Emmy gestures to herself. "Typical middle child, can't bear to be left out. She can't kill all of us, there has to be someone left for him to marry."

I'm properly crying now, both in sadness for Greer and over-whelmed with the rush of love I feel for these girls.

I keep walking, feeling braver and less hollow than before. "Let's go, then."

It takes about a half hour to reach Belgravia, and though we keep anxiously glancing behind us, no one follows. It's a quiet night in London, with just a few carriages trotting past us into the blue spring evening.

We don't bother knocking on the door of the Trummers' grand limestone mansion. No one we're looking for would be inside.

The girls follow me around back, to the mews where the horses are kept. I knock on the side of the stable, but the door is already open. "Hello?" I whisper. "Anyone in here?"

A stable boy no older than fifteen jumps in surprise out of one of the stalls.

He wipes his dirty hands on his apron. "Miladies." He offers us a startled little bow.

"We're looking for Joseph," I say.

The boy takes off his cap and fidgets with it. "I'm sorry I can't be of help. He didn't show up for work this morning. Is he in trouble?"

"Did he leave anything?" I ask.

The boy looks confused. "Just a few of his tools."

"But not all of them?"

He shakes his head. "I don't think so, no."

"Thank you. That'll be all."

"I thought you were going to speak to her parents," Faith says as we walk back to the palace.

I shake my head. There's nothing the Trummers could say to me. If I know anything about them, they're probably inside, mourning not Greer, but the loss of their social standing.

A weak smile spreads across my face. "What if they got out? What if they're together?"

"Or what if she killed him too?" Marion replies. Faith elbows her.

It's a possibility as well, one I've considered. "But now we have hope. We didn't have that before."

I tip my face up to the stars and send a wish to my friend, wherever she may be, that she is safe and whole, in the arms of a boy who loves her. I picture her halfway to Gretna Green by now, in the back of a carriage, in love and free. That is how I'll choose to remember her.

The guards offer no hint of displeasure as they open the gates to welcome us back to the palace grounds. The rest of the girls go back to the cottage, but I wave them on, too restless to sit inside in front of the fire.

The gravel path is lit with torches that offer only flickering views of the expansive green lawn.

"Ivy?" a voice whispers in the dark.

"Bram?"

He comes striding up the path, smiling that heartrending Bram smile, the one that makes him look lit from within.

"Terrible day," he says.

"The absolute worst."

He opens his arms, and I fall into them, burying my head against his chest. For a long while he just holds me. For once, I'm not thinking about making him fall in love with me, I'm just letting myself be held when I need it so badly.

He pulls back and picks up a loose curl that has fallen over my shoulder. "I'd do anything for you, Ivy."

I can't help the blush that rises in my cheeks.

We crunch down the gravel path to a copse of trees by the edge of a pond, far enough from the torches that the light doesn't reach us.

He leans in, and in that split second, all I can think of is Emmett. I've been trying desperately not to think about that night at the inn, but I can't help it. It comes back to me in flashes. His hands in my hair, the hungry pressure of his lips, the solid planes of his body against mine.

Bram's lips brush mine, and I banish all thoughts of Emmett. Bram is good and kind and *wants* me.

I pull Bram closer to me, gripping the width of his shoulders. The kiss grows more urgent, and he slips his tongue behind my teeth.

He's kissing me like he means it. My veins thrum with the knowledge of his want. Bram may be a prince, he may not even be human, but I have all the power here.

I pull back and look at him. We're both panting, and he's nearly unbearably pretty in the moonlight. I reach up and trace the line of his perfect eyebrows, his sharp jaw, the hollows of his cheekbones. I tuck a lock of hair behind his ear to get a look up close at the slightly pointed tip.

"That's a start," I say.

He smiles, and I can't help but poke his dimple. He presses his face into my hand. "Good. Because I do not intend for it to be the end."

"Where is Emmett? I didn't see him tonight," I ask Lottie later as she takes down my hair.

Her fingers hesitate. "He's left. Gone on a hunting trip or something."

He said he never had the stomach for hunting. *Gone.* Why didn't he say goodbye?

"When will he be back?"

"Not for a while, I presume. He took enough clothes for a month or two. His valet was complaining about it all afternoon."

"When his brother is about to get engaged? That seems odd."

Lottie just shrugs. "Classic Emmett. Never found an important event he couldn't weasel his way out of. I'm surprised he didn't tell you," Lottie says. "He wrote a note to Faith. I delivered it this morning. Perhaps she has more details."

I frown at myself in the mirror. "Perhaps."

"Oh!" Lottie exclaims. "Speaking of De Veres." She pulls my note, the one addressed to Emmett's father, out from the front pocket of her apron.

"Prince Consort Edgar is also away, has been for weeks apparently."

"Why?"

Lottie's brows furrow. "You know, it's the strangest thing, absolutely no one knows. No word has come from him at all."

A cool breeze comes from the cracked window, but that's not why I feel suddenly cold. I'm hit with the realization that the season is nearly over and I have been left completely on my own.

FAITH FAIRCHILD

The first time I realized my mother was lying to me, I was four years old. She tucked me into bed, kissed my forehead, and whispered to me what she always whispered.

"Good night, my sweet girl. Say your prayers, and may your papa in heaven watch over you."

I had been aware for some time that my family was different from other children's families. My mother and I lived on the top floor of a boardinghouse, just the two of us. Other children had siblings and fathers and big green lawns to run around on, but I had only my mother and the little world we created.

But that day was different. The first thing I noticed was that there was a man in our flat. I don't think a man had ever been there before. There were always boarders in the house. They taught me to play chess in the shared parlor downstairs or let me help them hang their laundry in the garden outside, but inside our attic, it was always just my mother and me.

The man was tall and broad, with a sneering sort of face and big, blocky eyebrows.

The second thing I noticed was that the man was making my mother cry.

The memory is fuzzy now, fourteen years later. I think I must have just woken up from a nap. But I do remember what the man said when I climbed onto my mother's lap to wipe away her tears. "I just wanted to see my daughter."

"You can see her whenever you like," my mother replied.

He paced the room, too large for it. I worried that he was going to knock over the wooden cradle where my doll slept. "You know that's not true," he said.

I realized at once that this strange man was my father—that my mother had been lying to me my whole life. She had told me my father was a sailor who died at sea. Every night I prayed for him, but my father was right here in front of me.

I learned a valuable lesson that day: no one is to be trusted, anyone could be lying at any time, even the people you love most.

I wasn't brave enough to confront my mother about it until I was ten. She crumpled like a house of cards and told me everything, explaining that my father was a lord of a nearby estate. When my mother was in his employ as a maid, they had an affair. *Affair* wasn't the word she used, but I was old enough to glean her meaning. He was unwilling to claim me, and he sacked my mother unceremoniously the moment she told him she was with child.

Still heartbroken after all these years, my mother cried as she spoke about him. I feel guilty about the disdain I felt for her in that moment. I vowed I would never be that pathetic over something as trivial as a man. My next thought was about burning his estate to the ground. We weren't very much alike, my mother and I.

I left home a few years later, moving to London all by myself at fourteen to study full-time at the Royal Ballet School.

Dancing calmed my racing thoughts. I couldn't control much about my life, but I could control my body. I loved the rules of ballet, how concrete they were. The ballet mistress hit the backs of my ankles with rulers until I could do the perfect tendu or frappé or plié, and I never could explain to anyone else how I relished every moment.

I worked for hours in front of the mirror, until my muscles were burning and I was soaked through with sweat, but it was all worth it for those few moments onstage, when it truly felt like I was flying.

The days were long and lonely. I missed my mother, we were too dependent on each other, and even though I knew it was unhealthy, I longed for her.

She got sick when I was sixteen. I took six months off from school to return to Brighton and care for her in that attic room of ours. But no amount of love or warm broth could fix her lungs. I soothed her as she coughed so hard her ribs broke, hacking up clot after clot. I held her as she took her final, rattling breaths, and then I returned to London and danced until my feet were bloody and I couldn't feel anything.

I met Emmett the next summer. He was sitting in the front row, watching me with those big, wounded deer eyes of his.

I found him waiting in my dressing room backstage with an armful of two dozen red roses. I kissed him before I even told him my name. Kept kissing him until the roses were dropped on the ground, forgotten.

Emmett continued attending shows and meeting me in my dressing room afterward. He begged me to let him take me to the theater or buy me extravagant gifts, but I didn't want things like that from him. More than anything, I think we both needed someone to talk to about our unyielding grief. He held my hand as I cried about how much I missed my mother, and I pushed his hair out of his teary eyes as he told me about his governess and the father he couldn't speak to.

It wasn't love—neither of us held any illusions about that—but it was a life raft when we both desperately needed something to cling to.

Sometimes we'd kiss until our lips bruised and we felt nothing at all. But more often than not, we didn't touch each other at all. We sat on opposite ends of the room and listened while the other spoke. Emmett had walls a thousand feet high, and I wasn't much of a climber, but we were there for each other.

I'm still not sure how my father found out about my dancing career, but I suspect it had something to do with the rumors that started flying about me and Emmett.

It had been six months since we'd met, and my name was now regularly whispered in clubs and drawing rooms around town. Prince Emmett and *that ballerina*, they'd sneer.

Men sent flowers to my dressing room, hoping to steal me away from the prince as a point of pride, but I never answered the door for any of them.

Then one night my father turned the knob without knocking. I hadn't seen him in fourteen years, hadn't thought about him in nearly as many.

It took me a moment to recognize him, but that sneering expression was unmistakable. Sometimes I saw the same look on my own face in the moments I hated myself the most.

"You will stop this now," he boomed. "You have disgraced our family enough."

I genuinely had no idea what he was on about, and my blank expression served only to enrage him further. "No daughter of mine will make her living as a *dancer* and a *mistress*." He spit the words out like curses.

"The dancer part is true, but I'm afraid I don't know what you're referring to when you say *mistress*," I answered coolly, eyeing him behind me in the mirror.

"Are you telling me the rumors of you and Prince Emmett De Vere are unfounded?"

"I can't be his mistress, he's unmarried."

He didn't think my joke was very funny.

"You bring disgrace on this family."

"You made it clear that I wasn't a member of your family. You wouldn't even pay for Mother's headstone." She wouldn't have one at all if Emmett hadn't paid for it behind my back after listening to me cry about it one night.

"Don't insult me with your insolence."

"I'm the one being insulted."

Just then there was a knock at the door, and a ruddy-faced woman in a high-necked blue gown poked her head in. Behind her skirts peeked two little girls, no older than eight and ten.

A mask fell over my father's face, and he smoothed out his suit jacket. "I thought I told you to wait outside for me, sweet," he said to the woman.

"I tried, but they had other ideas," the woman answered with a smile. The two little girls pushed past her, giggling, and stormed into my dressing room. Their hair, the exact same shade of brown as mine, was tied back in ribbons. They had my eyes too; the resemblance took my breath away. It was like looking at myself as a little girl.

"Can we get her autograph, Papa, please?" they whined, jumping from foot to foot.

Too stunned to speak, I grabbed a fountain pen and scrawled my name on their programs.

"You looked just like a princess up there," the little one whispered to me.

I couldn't answer. My eyes burned with tears, and I was afraid that if I opened my mouth, all that would come out would be a sob.

"We'll meet you in the lobby," the woman said to my father, and she herded the two little girls out behind her.

"Your sisters," he said tightly once they were gone.

"I gathered." My voice cracked. "What does your wife think you're doing back here with me?"

"I don't keep secrets from my wife. She knows who you are, as does half of town, it seems." I was surprised to hear him say it. I'd only been vaguely aware of the rumors. "Your status as a particular favorite of Prince Emmett's has gotten people talking, and because of your clumsy affair, tongues are wagging all over town about your parentage. We lived in peace before your selfish scandal."

"That's not my fault."

"No, but it is your problem."

"What do you expect me to do?"

"You're going to quit the ballet; you're going to stop seeing Prince Emmett, and you're going to enter the season as a respectable debutante and make a suitable match."

The air left my lungs. I couldn't stop dancing. The idea of it felt like dying. "You can't make me do that."

"As it happens, I can. You're looking at the newest patron of the Royal Ballet. As your employer, I'm sorry to inform you that your contract is terminated. My mother will pose as your godmother and sponsor your coming-out in society this spring. I am sorry. It gives me no pleasure to do this."

Tears had begun to fall at this point and I loathed myself for it. I vowed I'd never let him see me weak. I felt ten years old again, wanting to burn his fancy house to the ground. I felt selfish bitterness toward those sweet girls in the hall who had the same face as me, who got to be children in the way I was never allowed.

"You can't make me participate. I'll smash glasses at dinner. I'll be a wallflower at balls."

"That is your choice, but know that if you don't cooperate, you will never see those girls again. Your sisters will want a relationship with you, Faith."

I'd had no family since Mother died.

"I'll consider it," I said.

"I'll be in touch." He strode out of my dressing room, leaving me in pieces in his wake, just as he always did.

I took a carriage directly to Kensington Palace and screamed at the guards until they let me in to see Emmett.

As I told him all that my father had said, he paced on his long legs, making big figure eights, Pig nipping at his heels.

"I'm so sorry, Faith," he said.

I stood and crossed the room to him. "Marry me."

It was a little satisfying to see Emmett shocked. He stopped dead in his tracks and turned to me. "What?"

"Marry me, please, Emmett."

"Why?"

"Because I know you. I like you. Please don't leave me to the horrible men of the ton. I can't bear the thought of being the second wife to some half-alive duke, shuttled off to a country house so my new husband can keep his mistresses in London. Please, Emmett, I can't bear it."

I nearly collapsed in his arms, crying, but kept my dignity.

"I can't."

"Why not?" I snapped.

He looked so full of pity as he replied, "Because we do not love each other."

I wouldn't deny it. I did not love him, and I knew he did not love me. "But we like each other. That's more than most people get."

"Be honest with me, Faith. Do you think you could ever love me?"

There was no sense in lying. We didn't do that to each other. There was so much I admired about Emmett. He was generous and funny and thoughtful. But it had been clear for months that he was never going to truly let me in. I couldn't love someone content to keep me at arm's length like that. We didn't fit together as we should. "I don't think so, no."

He shook his head sadly. "Then I cannot marry you."

He was a romantic in the way only men can afford to be. In that moment, I hated him for it. I picked up a crystal goblet from the table at his bedside and hurled it at him. He ducked, and it shattered against the wall.

I stopped in the doorway. "I'm going to hate you forever for this."

Emmett's eyes welled up with tears, like he had any right to be sad. "I hope that's not true."

I slammed the door without another word, and he didn't chase me. I hated him for that too. Some part of me still does.

He called to see me at my father's home three days later with an unexpected proposal. "Bram is going to take a bride this season. It should be you."

"Me?"

"Bram is kind. He'll be a good husband."

I knew Bram a little from my time with Emmett. He had accompanied us sometimes on walks around the grounds or games of croquet. He was good-natured and easy to be around. He always treated me with respect. I could do much worse than having him as a husband. Even if he didn't choose me to be his bride, my father couldn't say I didn't try at having a proper season. It was my favorite kind of gambit, the kind I won either way.

"With my help, he'll pick you."

We shook on it like we were old pals, and for the first time, I felt hope bloom within me. I wished I could speak through time back into that little attic room and tell my mother her only daughter was going to be a princess.

I met with Emmett for a month leading up to the season and learned all of Bram's likes and dislikes, practiced making conversation and dancing. Emmett had an odd hyperfixation on a maypole, but if there was one thing I was confident about, it was my dancing, so I didn't worry much.

I dressed for the Pact Parade, certain that the winner was going to be me. I wore my confidence like armor, waiting until the last possible second to sign my name, just as Emmett had instructed me. *He'll want to feel as if he's earned you. Bram is noble like that.* Along with Emmett, my grandmother—posing as my godmother—put me through a gauntlet of lessons regarding society manners. I had a new trousseau of dresses and diamonds in my hair.

The two bright spots of my days were Hattie and Bea, my sisters, who had lit up the dark corners of my life. I despised my father with every fiber of my body, but he had made good on his promise of a relationship with my sisters.

I fought as hard as I possibly could during the May Queen competition, but was satisfied with second place. Emmett was adamant that I win, but what did it matter in the end, when I was prepared to shape myself into Bram's perfect girl.

Later that day, when I entered the queen's throne room to make my bargain, I felt very clever indeed.

"I want to know when people are lying to me," I told her. I thought of me as a little girl and the lies my mother told me about my father. I hated dishonesty above all things.

The queen smiled a knowing smile. It looked unnatural on her sharp face. "In return, you may never tell a lie again."

"Deal," I said. I wasn't a hypocrite. It seemed an easy enough bargain, better than giving up a toe and never being able to dance properly again.

"Is that what you're afraid of, dishonesty?" she asked as soon as the deal was done. I thought on her odd question for a moment.

"I'm scared of all sorts of things. Of losing my freedom, of my body failing and having to stop dancing, of loving someone again and losing them like I lost my mother."

"My, you are honest," the queen replied.

I didn't know exactly what form my bargain would take, but I soon found out.

Emmett came to me that night in the garden of my grandmother's house. "It can't be you. I'm sorry. I've changed my mind."

He stood with his hands in his pockets and had the audacity to look sad for me.

A little ping went off in my head. "You're lying."

"I'm sorry." He was gone in the dark before I could argue further. Emmett was always slippery, too hard to pin down, but I think he liked it that way.

We moved into Caledonia Cottage for the remainder of the season, and on the first day, all of Bram's suitors went around the table and shared their bargains. Marion Thorne made up some half-hearted lie about giving up the ability to smell flowers so that she would experience no more headaches. Another little ping went off in my head, and I knew for certain she was lying. *But why?*

Then Emmett started flitting around Ivy Benton, who wasn't nearly as good at sneaking out at night as she thought she was.

If he wanted to ignore me? Fine. Wanting to replace me was unforgivable.

For weeks, it was only Marion who seemed to notice or care. I couldn't lie to her about why I was upset, so I told her the truth.

"He's an idiot," she said.

"You're right." It didn't change anything, but it felt better to no longer be alone.

At first it was small things, the way she laid her hand on my knee or her head on my shoulder. I'd never felt butterflies like that before. I thought everyone else was being dramatic when they'd described it, but with Marion next to me, I suddenly understood.

Marion kissed me for the first time in the garden of Caledonia Cottage under the big weeping willow tree, and it wasn't until her lips touched mine that I felt *it*, that feeling that had always been missing with Emmett.

"I've wanted to do that for so long," she whispered against my mouth, and I didn't need the queen's bargain to know she was telling the truth.

"I wish you would have done it sooner."

From that moment on, we were inseparable.

I was stupid to ask Emmett to kiss me at Count Doncaster's ball. I was so mad for Marion, I thought maybe the pressure of the season had warped my sense of reality and I was imagining the force of my feelings for her. I pulled Emmett into a drawing room and begged him to kiss me.

"Why?" he asked, his eyes soft. He always was exceptionally pretty.

"I need to compare it to something else."

He leaned in slowly, reluctantly, overthinking everything as usual. Emmett and I are good at kissing each other, we've had plenty of practice, but that kiss in the Doncasters' drawing room felt nothing but hollow.

I pulled back, smiling. "I felt nothing."

He grinned. "I should be offended."

"But you're not."

"I'm happy for you, I hope you know that. I'll do all I can for you both."

"What about Ivy?" I asked him. "What will you do?"

"I'm not sure what you're referring to." His voice turned remote.

I walked toward the door. "We don't do that. Don't start lying to me now."

"There's never going to be anything between Ivy Benton and me." And my gift from the queen told me he thought he was telling the truth. I didn't feel jealous. I just felt sad for him.

Later that night, I told Marion about my silly kiss with Emmett and all that it confirmed for me. She trailed her finger over my leg, and I finally worked up the nerve to ask her the question I'd wanted to since the first time I saw her at the Pact Parade.

"Is there a reason you pretended we'd never met?" I asked.

Her finger stopped. She looked up at me, brown eyes wide with shock. "What?"

"That first day of the season, you introduced yourself to me like we'd never met before."

"We hadn't." Marion's brows were furrowed as she searched her memory. "I would have remembered, I'm sure of it."

I knew she wasn't lying; I would have been able to tell if she was. I was hurt that she didn't remember.

It was a few months before my father had arrived in my dressing room and mucked everything up. Marion, her mother, and her sister were in their private balcony box for a performance of *La Sylphide*. Her mother, a patroness of the ballet, brought her daughters backstage after the performance to meet a few of the dancers.

Marion looked so confident, that was the first thing I noticed about her. She held her head like she knew she was the kind of person who mattered. I curtsied as I met her family, and her mother smiled warmly and said, "Oh, no need for all that."

Marion's sister was chatty, but Marion said hardly a word, just looked at me with those clever eyes of hers.

"It was nice meeting you," she said in a voice softer than what I'd expected.

"You as well, Lady Thorne." And then she was gone. I didn't see her again until the Pact Parade, where she introduced herself. It was silly of me to think she'd remember the meeting, no matter how significant it felt to me.

"I would have remembered meeting you," Marion says once more.

"You did, at the ballet with your mother and sister."

"I haven't been to the ballet since I was a child."

"That's not true, you came last fall to *La Sylphide*. I played a witch."

Marion sits down and puts her head in her hands. "What else happened?"

"I made polite conversation with your family while you stood staring at me, completely silent."

Marion groans in embarrassment.

"No, I found it rather charming," I say with a laugh. "I complimented your necklace, which you tried to take off and give to me. I politely declined, but the next day, there it was in my dressing room, wrapped in a bow. I wore it the day of the Pact Parade, but you didn't even remember me, so I got too embarrassed to wear it again. I have it upstairs."

Marion looks up at me, tears welling in her eyes. "I know what she took from me."

I sit down next to her and put my head on her shoulder. "What?"

"Queen Mor, *my bargain*. I traded away my happiest memory in exchange for writing talent. Faith, meeting *you* must have been my happiest memory."

She was telling the truth.

I blink away the memory and come back to the downstairs drawing room of Caledonia Cottage, where Ivy Benton sits next to me, her lips bruised like she's just been kissing.

Ivy is always lying; I'm sure it's Emmett's doing. It's why I had to move out of that room with her and in with Marion. I don't regret that decision at all now, even though Marion drives me mad, staying up all night, scribbling in her endless notebooks.

I feel a little guilty that Ivy thinks I don't like her because of her feelings for Emmett. I actually think she and Emmett would make a good match. How unfortunate that it's impossible for them to be together.

It seems only determined anti-romantic Ivy Benton was strong enough to scale bleeding-heart Emmett's thousand-foot-high walls. I don't even know if she's realized yet just how devoted he is to her. He never looked at me the way he looks at her, not even close.

That was part of Emmett's and my problem. He was never practical enough for me. Marion is all practicality. Shoved under her mattress is a timetable of ships leaving London for ports all around the world. At night, we pore over it and dream about the places we could go together. Next to the timetable are the half-finished manuscripts along with lists of publishers and the price they'll pay per word once they're finished.

It's easy enough to leave England. Queen Mor takes pride in telling her subjects we are not her prisoners. But returning will be difficult. Once we leave, the ports will be shut to us, by any legal means, forever.

The last day before the queen's announcement of the winner feels like the stillness just before a thunderstorm rolls in on the horizon. None of us quite knows what to say to each other. We pack our trunks while Emmy and Olive crack jokes; we're all moving out of this cottage regardless of what tomorrow's results are.

We did the calculations last night, all gathered around the sitting room fireplace. Ivy Benton is winning, barely, with a score of

3.3. Marion and Emmy are tied at 3.6, and Olive and I are tied with 4. The queen never said explicitly that our scores would determine the winner, so it could be anyone's game.

If it's Marion or me, we'll run.

I hope it's Olive, for her and Bram's sake. She's been pacing up and down the halls, ranting that the scores could mean nothing, that it doesn't matter that she's losing.

All day, we wait, yet no footman comes to gather us. No one has the stomach to eat, despite Olive carrying tray after tray of tarts and scones and puddings from the kitchen. Just when we think she's done, she comes out with another.

It isn't until I'm in bed that I'm shaken awake by a footman. "Come with me, miss."

It's the grand finale. I can hear the orchestra reaching its final crescendo. It's nearly time to take my bow. I am nothing if not a seasoned performer.

CHAPTER TWENTY-NINE

It's well past midnight when I'm awoken with a start by a footman. He's shaking my shoulder roughly. For a moment I feel like I'm back in the fever dreams of May, but I blink against the sudden light of his lantern and realize I am awake.

"Come with me, miss," he commands. He gives me no time to dress, so I follow him, barefoot, in my nightdress, across the wooden floors.

The room is dark, with only the bouncing light of his lantern to see by, but it is unmistakable that Olive's bed is empty.

I glance across the hall to Faith and Marion's room. Their beds are empty too, the blankets kicked all over the floor like they were pulled off in a hurry.

"Where are you taking me?" I fight to keep my voice steady.

He doesn't answer.

The dew on the lawn is cold on the soles of my feet. The wind whips my unbound hair around my face, but I have no ribbon to tie it back.

Kensington Palace is dark with sleep, but the footman leads me up the main staircase to the throne room, where Queen Mor is waiting for me. I'm reminded of the Pact Parade, walking up these same stairs with my mother by my side. I was frightened then, too. But I'm so much braver now.

"Lady Ivy." Queen Mor greets me with a serene smile. "I do always look forward to our time together." She's perfectly dressed as always, in an ink-black lace gown, her neck dripping with pearls.

I don't want her to know I am afraid. "As do I, ma'am."

"I wish we were meeting under happier circumstances. I've called you here to deliver the news that you have lost."

"Excuse me—" I sputter.

"You've lost. You have not been selected to be Bram's bride. It's over."

"But I'm winning." I say it like a question. Wasn't I winning? Wasn't that what the points system was for?

"My decision is final."

"Will my family be stripped of their titles and their lands?"

"I have no plans for that, currently. But I always reserve the right to change my mind." It isn't quite a relief, but it's something.

I curtsy once more, too numb to do anything else. "Then I thank you for your time and your hospitality, Your Majesty. Please congratulate the Prince of Wales on his engagement on my behalf."

I exit the throne room like I'm sleepwalking. I don't even think to ask who won. Olive, probably. Who knows. It doesn't matter.

I've failed, and so I know what I have to do next.

The footman escorts me down the stairs to the entrance of the palace. Waiting, with its doors open, is a shiny black carriage. "Your things have been packed for you," he says.

"I'm going to be sick," I reply. The footman opens his mouth and closes it, like royal protocol never gave him a script to reply to something like this.

I clutch my stomach. "Please excuse me." I make a run for the side of the building, like I'm going to hurl in the bushes, but at the last second I sprint around the corner and up the hill that leads to the orangery.

There are footsteps behind me, but I am quick, and it's too dark to see properly. The doors to the orangery close behind me, and I'm embraced by the warm humidity of the fruit trees.

I hurry through the tunnels and burst out through the false panel into Emmett's room out of breath and sweaty. Inside his room it's dark and quiet, with only dying embers in the fire and Pig and Emmett breathing softly in tandem. He sits up, awake the moment I step in.

"Ivy?" he asks groggily, running a hand through his hair, wild with sleep.

"I thought you were gone. I heard you were gone." My throat is thick with tears that I swallow. I didn't think he'd be here. I thought I could sit in front of this fire we once built together and feel him, one last time, before I let it all go. See Pig, maybe, if I was lucky. I just needed a moment to breathe before I did what had to be done next.

Emmett never did make anything easy.

He rubs the sleep from his eyes. His torso is bare, revealing his broken collarbone. "Are you all right?"

"I'm fine," I say, but I don't know if it's a lie or not.

"You look like a ghost," he says.

"Why did you leave?" *Me.* I leave that part off. *Why did you leave me?*

He groans and pushes himself more upright. "Because I don't think I'm strong enough to stick around and watch you win."

"Why'd you come back?"

"Because I wasn't strong enough to stay away."

"I thought you didn't like me," I gasp.

He pulls back enough to look me directly in the eye. "Like you? Ivy Benton, I am obsessed with you. It's going to kill me."

I lower myself to the edge of his bed, too far to be touching but close enough to feel the heat of him.

"You're confusing me for someone with strong resolve," he says.

"Emmett, please." I can't shake the masochistic desire to feel something, even if it's pain.

My breath catches in my throat. I want him to lean in, pull me closer, do anything other than stare at me like he knows he can undo me.

He jerks his hand back as if he's been burned. "I can't touch you."

My face burns red with embarrassment. "Because I'm Bram's? Because we're friends? Because I'm the only one stupid enough to think that night in the coaching inn meant something?"

He shakes his head almost imperceptibly and leans in. "Because if I start touching you, I don't think I'll be able to stop."

His brows furrow as he finally looks down at my gauzy white nightdress.

"They pulled me out of bed in the night," I explain. "I was just with the queen. I've lost."

"What?"

"We have to—" But before I can finish, say *find Bram*, he circles his fingers around my wrist, tugs me toward him, and, in one fluid movement, crushes his lips to mine.

I think of what has come before, not what will come after.

And I kiss him back.

He slips his tongue between the seam of my lips, and I open for him, taking everything he's willing to give. His hands fist at the hair at the nape of my neck, and he pulls like he can't have me close enough.

"I'm not strong enough to be under the same roof as you," Emmett confesses against my mouth. "I am sick with the knowing I cannot have you."

I sigh. "You have me now."

He rolls, caging me in with his arms, and tugs at the ribbons of my nightdress.

He takes both my hands in his and clutches them to his chest, right against his breastbone, where I can feel his heart beating. "We could be together, Ivy."

"That's not the plan," I say weakly. It would be so easy to give in. "I can never marry."

"That doesn't matter to me. We'll run away. I'll tell anyone who will listen that you are mine. I'll shout it from rooftops around the world."

For a moment I picture us on a ship's deck, sea spray in our hair, going somewhere far from England.

"You're a prince."

He runs a hand along the edge of my jawline. "I never asked for this. But I am asking for you."

I take a hard look at his face. There are those eyes, the ones from a fever dream. I don't think I'm ever going to be able to sweat him out. "You don't need to ask. I'm already yours."

He kisses my temple, the corner of my mouth, my aching

collarbones, the side of my rib cage. He rucks up my nightdress, exposing my legs. He kisses the bony joint of my ankle, my knee, the jut of my hip bone. Up and up, higher, to the place where I am aching for him.

"Ivy," he whispers against my skin.

I tug my fingers through his dark hair. "Emmett."

I pull his body closer to mine, needing to find friction, to feel him.

I've never experienced wanting like this. I understand now what true desperation is, what could lead someone to trading away parts of themself. Emmett could ask anything of me right now, and I'd give it without hesitation.

His hands rake, white hot, down the length of my bare spine, each vertebra under the pads of his fingers. He sinks his teeth down hard enough to sting at the soft spot between my neck and shoulder, then soothes the wound with gentle licks from his tongue. His mouth trails up the column of my neck to the shell of my ear.

"Do you want to stop?" he asks against my unbound hair.

"No. I want you."

He pulls back to look at me. We're both breathing heavily, and something wordless passes between us.

"I've never wanted anything more than the way I want you." He sighs.

I roll, now on top of him. I need to look at him like this, eyes blown out with wanting, hair a mess all over the pillow. I lower myself down onto him, sinking until we meet, completely. His eyes close in bliss, and I tip my head back, just letting myself adjust to it. "Ivy," he whispers. I don't even know if he realizes he's talking out loud. I rock against him, agonizingly slow, but it doesn't soothe the aching, it just drives us both deeper into this frenzy.

Emmett pulls my nightdress off in one fluid motion and cups my breasts with his hands, covering them completely. "Ivy, Ivy."

There's just searing need and Emmett everywhere. I drag my hands across his chest, through his hair, taking him, and this throbbing, yearning feeling, again and again. I push up on my knees, and then down until we find a rhythm together. His hands are needy, touching everywhere, and I arch against him. I've never been more exposed, but I feel the safest I have ever felt within the walls of this palace.

He's done this before, even if I haven't, and I have the vague sense that it should bother me. But we've never done this with each other, so it's new all the same. In every gasp and touch, there is discovery.

He looses a breath and maneuvers me under him. He moves against me, in me, our hearts beating wildly in sync. Finally, he shudders, and we both shatter, fully and completely. The feeling consumes me until I am on fire, burning with him.

For a moment, all we can do is look at each other, panting and starstruck.

I love him. I'll tell him later, when I can catch my breath.

He pulls me against his sweat-slicked chest and brushes my hair from my eyes. "Are you all right? I didn't—"

"I'm perfect."

Emmett smiles down at me, heart-stoppingly handsome. "You are."

Emmett holds me for a while, but I don't have long; the footmen will be searching for me and I can't let them find me here.

I look at Emmett and imagine a life in which I could have been his. But that's not the life I've found myself in.

It's time. It has to be time.

I slide out of the warmth of his bed, and I want to steal one of his sweaters, but I can't. Bram can't know I was here. He can never know what happened tonight.

Emmett watches as I walk across the room to gather my nightdress from where it landed on the floor. "Ivy?"

"I can't stay," I whisper back. I pray he just lets me leave. One more look from him and I'll break.

"*Bram.*" He says the word like it hurts him.

"Bram," I say. "I should go to him, now before we're found out." Here it is. Plan B. I must hope he cares about me enough to elope. He told me he'd do anything for me.

Dread and guilt pool in my stomach, and suddenly I feel sick all over. Bram deserves better than this. He's a kind boy, one who trusts me and has treated me with respect at every turn.

"He'll be a good husband," Emmett says flatly.

"I'm not good enough for him."

I expect Emmett to protest, but he replies, "Who is?"

I laugh to keep from crying.

"But you will grow to love Bram, I know you will," Emmett says. "He is patient and kind, and you will love him just like everyone else does. And I swear it, I will not resent you, but I'll say it just this once. I would have loved you. I would have loved you so well."

"I know. I know." He needs to hear it twice.

I pad back over to him and take his warm hand in mine. If everything goes according to plan, this will be the last time I ever touch him.

Emmett looks up at me. "I'll be in hell when I see you on his arm, when I picture you in his bed, but I will watch, and I will burn for the rest of my life if this is the only way I get to have you," he says.

"You'll find someone too." I already hate the faceless girl I picture by his side in a white dress. I hope she'll be beautiful and clever and absolutely nothing like me.

He shakes his head. "I think it was always going to be you for me."

"Don't say that," I murmur. "You never would have seen me. I would have been just another wallflower at a ball."

He wrinkles his nose a little as he shakes his head. "I would have seen you."

My chest hitches. I can't cry. Not yet.

"Do you want me to convince you not to go?" Emmett asks. "Because I will. I will get on my knees."

"No." I reply. "Because it won't change anything." And I know it's not actually what he wants, not deep down.

Emmett kisses me softly, one last time. "He's just down the hall. Third door on the right. Good luck."

He walks me to the door.

"I have to go," I whisper, but he's still holding my hand.

"I know, I know."

His fingers slip from mine, and it's over.

CHAPTER THIRTY

Bram is asleep, breathing softly, tucked in the middle of his feather bed. This is the first time I've ever been in his room, and I take a moment to look around. Unlike Emmett's haphazardly placed books and overcrowded desk, everything in Bram's room has been fastidiously placed: his books, the line of crystals by the window, his rings laid out on the vanity.

I duck my head under the canopy and lay a hand on his shoulder. "Bram." I shake him softly. "Bram."

He wakes with a gasp and blinks a few times. "Ivy? What are you doing here?"

It's not hard to cue the tears; they flow freely down my cheeks the minute I let the dam break. "I just spoke to the queen," I cry. "She told me I've lost."

Bram sits up in anger. "That's not her choice to make."

"They tried to escort me from the palace, but I ran from them," I gasp. "I had to see you."

I'll let him fill in the rest. Bram will want to be the savior here. I can't feed it to him too easily.

"But I want *you*," he says urgently. "I was going to pick you."

It breaks my heart to hear him say it. "What do we do?"

Bram pushes himself out of bed, begins pacing the room. "I can't let her do this. It's my life."

"It's not fair," I say.

He crosses the room and cradles my cheek in his hand. "I'm not letting her choose for me. I already chose for myself. I chose you."

My broken heart gives a little thump. "You said yesterday you'd do anything for me."

I can see the moment the idea comes to him. His gray eyes flash. "We could run away, marry elsewhere. Then she'd be forced to accept you."

I pretend to hesitate. "I'm scared."

"I'm not going to let anything happen to you."

He takes me in his arms and kisses me passionately. I feel the ghost of Emmett all over me, but I go soft and pliant against him. It's the worst thing I've ever done.

He's the first one to pull back. "Go, now, before the sun rises, and pack a bag. I'll come for you at dawn."

"I love you," I say. It's not quite a lie. I want to love him, I really do.

"I love you, too." He can't lie. For the second time tonight, my heart shatters.

In a daze, I walk to Belgrave Square in my nightdress through the sleeping streets of London. I'm paranoid the whole walk, constantly swiveling my head to make sure I'm not being followed.

I'm reminded of the night I went out to look for Lydia so many months ago.

The back door service entrance of my family home is unlocked, as always. It's been months since I've set foot in this house, and while nothing about it has changed, I feel so different from the girl I was when I last stood in this spot.

I race up the steps to my room and throw a valise on my bed to fill with clothes for the journey.

I change into my plainest traveling dress, braid my hair, then fling my wardrobe doors open and toss my few day dresses into the case. At the bottom of the wardrobe is my trusty pair of boots, still mud-caked from the day I won May Queen. Mama made me leave them behind when I moved into Kensington Palace.

I place them by the door, ready to run when it's time.

On my tippy-toes, I reach to the highest shelf and grab my summer straw bonnet. The ribbons are stuck under something, and I pull once, twice, then go toppling backward. All of a sudden, dozens of sheets of paper rain down on me, floating like white snowflakes as they land noiselessly on the floor.

I pick up the closest one and find Bram's face staring back at me.

He's been rendered in waxy pastels, but the likeness is undeniable. The square jaw, sun-streaked hair, laughing gray eyes.

I pick up another one, a charcoal sketch of Bram sitting under a tree.

Another: a pencil sketch of Bram astride a galloping horse.

Another: a study of his hands in agonizing detail.

His profile.

His eyes.

His mouth.

There must be one hundred pictures of him here.

My door swings open, revealing Lydia, her white nightdress made dark blue by the dim moonlight.

I freeze, on my knees, the sketches surrounding me.

Her eyes adjust to the low light, and she gets a look at the riot of papers around me. "Oh no." She falls to her hands and knees in a rush and gathers them against her chest.

"It's no use. I've already seen them." My voice sounds far away. I can hardly hear anything over my heart pounding in my ears.

"It's not what you think," she says softly.

"I have absolutely no idea what to think."

She flops down in the middle of the drawings. Her exhausted hands push through them, like she's a child making a snow angel. "I've been having these dreams ever since I returned."

"Dreams?"

She picks up one of the drawings gingerly, a close-up of Bram's face, and runs her pointer finger along the line of his pointed ear. The paper crinkles under the pressure of her fingertip. "His face is the only thing I remember."

"You said they were dreams. That's not the same thing as a memory." Maybe she truly has lost it—whatever fragile thing was holding her together has finally snapped.

She drops her eyes, too embarrassed to look at me. "I know."

I peer up at my sister in the moonlight, her face so much like mine. "I'm sure they're just dreams," I say. Bram's face is in newspapers and statues and public houses all over this city.

"Why are you home?" she asks, as if the strangeness of my presence here has only just hit her.

"I'm running away with Bram. We're eloping."

"Oh," she says weakly. "Are you happy?"

"I will be," I answer hopefully.

She looks to my open valise and starts helping me pack, throwing in chemises, my worn old cloak, the pearls I wore the day of the Pact Parade.

"Are you safe?" she asks, worried.

"Probably not," I answer honestly. "But this is my only option."

She pulls me into a tight hug.

"I love you," I whisper. "You know that, right?"

"It's just about the only thing I do know."

The first light of dawn has begun to leak through the windows, painting my room a pale shade of pearly gray.

A banging at the front door startles us both. I snatch my valise from the bed and latch it as quickly as I can. I pull on my boots next. "Tell Mama and Papa I'll send word soon. Don't worry, everything will be all right."

I sprint down the stairs and throw open the front doors, expecting to see Bram but instead find a footman in familiar Kensington Palace blue livery.

"Her Majesty requests an audience."

My blood turns cold. We must have been found out. She's going to kill me for this, the same way she killed Greer.

"No." I try to slam the door, but the footman blocks it with the toe of his polished boot.

"Ivy?" Lydia calls from the top of the stairs, but she's not fast enough.

"Lydia!" I scream. "Tell Emmett—"

The footman's arms encircle me like a vise, and he picks me up and carries me to the carriage.

Lydia chases us out the front door, but she's left choking on the dust of the carriage as we pull away.

"Please," I beg the footman all the way to the palace. "I'll do anything." He doesn't even look at me.

It takes two of them to haul me out of the carriage and into the palace. I fight every step of the way. The footmen stay silent and stoic as I dig my nails into the flesh of their forearms. I rake a hand across the cheek of the one to my left, leaving a long, bloody scratch. I kick out the back of his knees next, and he falls to the dirt. If she's going to kill me, I'm not going down without a fight.

But in an endless flood, more come. It takes four of them in the end, one on each arm and leg to carry me up the grand staircase as I flail.

"Bram!" I scream. "Emmett!"

But my calls echo off the glass ceiling. No one is coming for me.

The footmen throw me into the throne room and slam the doors behind me. I land hard on my knees, looking up through tangled hair and frustrated tears.

Golden morning light streams through the high windows, throwing rainbows from the diamonds in the queen's tiara.

Queen Mor's skirts are fanned around her, and she sits on the edge of her throne, leaning forward, like she's been waiting impatiently for me.

She's smiling. Her sharp canines are fully on display. She's got a dimple, like her son. This is the first time she's smiled wide enough for me to see it.

"Lady Ivy Benton!" she exclaims cheerfully. "Congratulations!"

CHAPTER THIRTY-ONE

I push myself up off the ground, my knees bloody with carpet burn. "Excuse me?"

She steps down from her throne and crosses the carpeted floor to wrap me in an awkward hug. It's like she's never hugged anyone before. It's too tight. Too sharp. She smells of lilies that wilted days ago.

She pulls back, both hands on my shoulders, and sighs. "Don't tell Bram, but I always wanted a daughter."

"Forgive me, Your Majesty, I'm confused."

"Bram is going to be thrilled. You always were his favorite."

My heartbeat kicks up, and the floor tips under me. "But I lost."

She shakes her head. "It was my final little taste of fun. You passed with flying colors. You should have seen the others. Olive begged. Emmy just stood there. Faith tried to cry but could barely squeeze out a tear. Marion laughed, which I found most unsettling. What an odd girl she turned out to be." She pauses. "But *you*. You were the picture of dignity. Exactly what a princess should be."

I stand, stock-still, like I'm floating somewhere out of my body. She's speaking so quickly I can barely keep up.

"Bram will propose tonight at the Kendalls' ball. You two will be the talk of the town. We'll have the wedding here, of course, on the solstice. You have a sister, right? We can arrange for her to be a lady-in-waiting if you wish, but I will choose the rest."

"I'm—I won?" I still can't wrap my head around what it is she's saying.

"Keep up, please."

I think of the very first night of the season, when Emmett pulled me into that room at the ball and said *If you let me help you, Ivy Benton, you could be queen.*

"There's only one matter left to settle," she says. "The matter of your bargain."

"I didn't make a bargain, ma'am."

She tuts her tongue. "That's exactly the problem. I've lived a long time, and I try to learn from my mistakes. I married my most recent husband without him having made a bargain. He used that bargain for the benefit of another woman's child and has resented me every day for the rest of our marriage for it. I can't have that happening to Bram. You must make a bargain, and then we can proceed." She looks over me carefully and cocks her head. "I could tame your hair? Make you a croquet prodigy? We can just do something small, get it off the table."

"Oh—" I sputter.

A storm cloud passes over her face, and she levels me at once with a glare so venomous it's as if the light in the room dims.

"Unless you want something else?" Her tone is sickly sweet, like rotted fruit.

"I'm not sure what you mean."

"I will ask you this just once, Lady Ivy, then we put the matter to bed forever."

"All right." My voice shakes.

"Would you rather have Prince Emmett De Vere?"

I freeze, my blood sluicing in my veins. "I'm sorry?"

"I'm not ignorant of what happens within the walls of my palace. I've noticed an . . . affection between the two of you. Would you rather have him? Bram deserves a wife who is devoted to him completely. My son has a big heart. It won't do to have it smashed by the people he loves most."

There's a knock at the side door closest to the throne. Queen Mor and I both pause. Prince Consort Edgar is leaning against the doorframe. He's got a pair of wire spectacles on his nose and a book in his hand. "Just wanted to let you know breakfast has been served, darling. I didn't mean to interrupt." Is it a coincidence that he's back?

"I'll be along shortly," she answers, and I watch Emmett's father walk back through the door and know immediately what I have to do.

"No," I say decisively. I excise my mind from my body. I float somewhere up on the muraled ceiling so I don't feel the cracks in my heart so intense it's like my ribs are breaking.

"Emmett and I are merely friends. He was only helping me get to know Bram."

The queen looks me up and down. I'm not sure she believes me.

"As for the matter of the bargain," I continue. "I need time to consider. May I have an hour?"

"I suppose tea is ready, and this would give me time to drink it."

She nods. "See you in an hour, Lady Ivy."

I read in a book once that if sharks stop moving, they die. I feel like that now, like if I stop walking and consider what I've just done, my heart will cease to beat.

I walk down the stairs, out the door, and into the same carriage that brought me here. "Savile Row," I direct the driver.

The footman helps me down from the carriage, his face still bloody from my scratch, but he betrays no emotion. I instruct the driver to wait. "I won't be long."

The tailor's sharp scissors glide through a row of gray tweed. The shop smells of sewing machine oil and warm wool. He pauses as I walk in. "Lady Ivy, a pleasure. Your order is ready. Would you like to examine it, or should I wrap it up?"

"Wrap it up, please. Thank you."

I'm grateful I had the foresight to commission the coat weeks ago, back on a lazy day between Viscountess Bolingbroke's lessons. At the time, I'd pictured delivering it to Emmett as a joke, something to commemorate the end of the season.

Package in hand, I hop back into the carriage and race back to the palace. An hour isn't long, and I have so much I need to say.

Caledonia Cottage feels like a haunted house without the six of us in it. I walk into the sitting room and can see us, like ghosts, sitting around the fire.

But I am alone now, and I have to be strong.

There's a fountain pen and parchment on a small writing desk by the window. I sit down in the hard wooden chair, dip the metal nib into the dark ink, and drag it across the page.

I can't make anything better. I only hope I can make him understand.

Tears stream down my face and neck and into the collar of my dress as I write, but I don't stop to brush them away. I don't have time.

When I am done, I fold the letter and slip it under the ribbon of the box from the tailor.

With only minutes left to spare, I race back across the main palace, shove the box at a footman, and ask that it be delivered to Emmett. I'm running, a clumsy escape on heavy feet. But it will be a bloodless goodbye.

There was never going to be another end to our story. I can see that now.

I burst back into the throne room, hunched over, my hands on my knees, gasping.

"Well," the queen asks. "What have you decided?"

I brush a sweaty lock of hair off my forehead and take the deepest breath I can muster. "I want you to make me forget Prince Emmett."

PRINCE EMMETT DE VERE

There's a knock at the door, but I don't bother getting out of bed. The golden clock on the mantel says it's past nine, but I haven't moved since Ivy left at dawn.

It's playing in my head on a loop, her pale skin in the dark, how she looked splayed out under me and undone. She let me touch her like I'd been dying to since that night in the coaching inn. Earlier than that, if I'm being honest with myself.

I'd had to keep my hands balled into fists at my sides to keep from devouring her as she whimpered in her sleep and wrapped her arms and legs around me. I thought that was torture, but now I realize I didn't know anything about pain, or how bad it was about to get for me.

If I were a better man, good, like Bram, I'd feel guilt or shame about what we did last night, but I'm not good and I'm not ashamed.

I wish I could relive last night forever, nothing else, just Ivy on an endless loop. There was a man who bargained for something like that a few years ago. He ended up going mad and throwing himself into the Thames.

Bram lets himself in, as he always does. Dread punches me in the stomach at the sight of him. He and Ivy should be on the road by now.

He greets me. "As productive as ever, I see."

"Aren't you supposed to be getting engaged tomorrow?" I ask as casually as I can manage. My voice is hoarse. A discarded ribbon from Ivy's nightdress is beside me. I shove it under the quilt hastily before he sees.

Bram throws opens my curtains, flooding the room with light. I squint my eyes and groan.

"That's what I came here to talk about. I've had quite the morning." He plops himself down at my desk and kicks his boots up all over the papers.

"I hate it when you do that," I say.

"I had a little predawn visit from Ivy Benton."

"Oh?" I feign surprise but want to throw up. Her face flashes through my mind, how she looked on top of me, her porcelain skin in the dark.

I love her. I should have told her that.

Bram smiles a little. "She said my mother told her she'd lost. Classic Mother, always with the power plays."

"What did you say?" I'm desperate for more information. Where is Ivy? Is she safe?

"I asked her to elope with me. Who else was I going to marry? Olive, who was so obsessed with the idea of me she nearly swooned every single time I spoke to her? Marion Thorne, who literally fell asleep the only time I tried to have a full conversation with her? Emmy was suitable, but there's something special about Ivy, even if you don't agree."

"But here you are, not eloped."

"I'm getting to that part. I was packing my things, ready to go, when Mother came to my room, very unlike her, and said, 'It'll be Lady Ivy Benton, is that suitable?' I said yes, of course."

Fear strikes me. "Do you think she knew you were planning on running away?"

Bram shrugs, unbothered. "If she did, she gave no indication. I think she just wanted to play one final game, you know how she gets."

"I do." The damn fae and their love of games. With Bram, it's endless games of billiards. Sometimes he whips himself into a near frenzy over it, and we play until dawn. The queen's tastes lean bloodier.

I should be happy. I'm getting everything I wanted. In a few short weeks, if I'm right, her reign will be over and my kind, reasonable brother will be king.

Bram stands. "Anyway, just thought you'd like to know your favorite brother is engaged. I'll let you sleep. You look like absolute shit. Hungover?"

"Yes." It feels like it. I'm wrecked.

Bram reaches the door, bends down, and tosses a large white box onto my bed. "This was at your door."

"Thanks," I reply, and the door shuts behind him.

I lift the lid and find a black wool coat folded neatly and wrapped in tissue paper. On top, tucked under the ribbon, is a letter with a single crease and my name.

I unfold it and begin to read.

Emmett,

 I love you. No, that's not how I should begin. I'm sorry.
I'm so sorry. I can only hope that one day you'll understand.
If you don't understand, then I can only hope that you hate me.

It would be easier if you hate me. Please hate me.

I was told this morning that I am to marry Bram.

It appears that telling me I had lost was just another of Mor's tricks. He will propose tomorrow and I will say yes.

Please believe that I wanted to flee the throne room screaming. That I wanted to run away with you. I wanted it more than I've ever wanted anything.

But this is bigger than the two of us. If we run, we may be destroying our only chance at unseating Queen Mor. I'm doing this for Greer. For my sister. For Eduart. But mostly I'm doing this for you and your father.

Bram deserves a wife who loves him, but I know I could never love him if he's competing with you. So I finally know what bargain I will make. Once I have written this letter, I am going to ask Queen Mor to remove all memory of you from my head. It's the only chance any of us have for peace. I know you will find happiness with someone who isn't me. I pray I am able to become the wife Bram deserves.

Somewhere, across time and space, there's a version of me and a version of you, wearing matching rings, tangled up in front of a fireplace, together. I have to believe that's true.

In another life, it would have been us, but not in this one.

I can't have you in the way you deserve to be had.

Know how desperately I love you.

Know how sorry I am.

And know that I'm doing the best that I can.

Ivy

p.s. I owed you a coat.

I read the letter twice more, trying to understand. It isn't until I set it down that I realize I've torn the edges, that's how tightly I've been gripping it.

There's nothing but roaring in my head. White-hot fear like a forest fire has been set alight, and there's nothing but the animal instinct to run.

I nearly throw the door off its hinges sprinting out of my room and down the marble staircase. I have to stop her, if I could just explain—

I pause at the second-floor landing. Do I make a break for the throne room or the cottage?

There are voices coming from the main hall, the sound of hooves as a carriage pulls up.

I grip the railing, taking the stairs two at a time.

Ivy and Queen Mor are standing in the middle of the soaring foyer. Ivy's blond hair is in two braids. She's wearing a simple gray dress, and her pale skin is covered with dappled light filtering in through the leaves of the tree growing up through the staircase.

I stand there panting, and they both turn to me.

There's a dazed look in Ivy's soft brown eyes. She sinks her teeth into the skin of her full bottom lip and tilts her head. She's so beautiful, it nearly knocks the wind out of me.

She curtsies to me hurriedly, saying, "Your Highness, it's nice to finally meet." There's something odd about her teeth. I look closer and realize there's blood stuck between the gaps of them. She presses her lips together self-consciously, as if she realizes it at the same moment I do.

She can't meet my eye as she tucks a stray golden curl behind her ear. "Bram speaks highly of you. I was quite hoping we could be friends."

It feels like I've been shot. I look down at my own torso, surprised to find my rib cage intact. Musket balls don't pierce. They blow everything wide open into a bloody mess. That's how this feels.

"Friends?"

Mor's gaze snaps to mine, and she shakes her head slightly. If I didn't know her better, I might think she feels sorry for me.

"Ivy—" I say it under my breath. I can't help myself. Every inch of me is begging to reach out to my girl, take her in my arms, kiss her until she remembers. My guts are splattered all over the frescoes on the wall behind me, and the only one who knows I'm bleeding is Mor.

Ivy's eyes flit to the ground. "If you'll excuse me—" She curtsies again, and the footman takes her hand in his and helps her down the steps and into the carriage. Leaving me standing in the foyer, frozen.

Mor turns to me. "It's for the best," she says.

"What did you take in return?" I ask, thinking of her bloody teeth.

She huffs out a small laugh. "Only a molar. The bargain itself seemed punishment enough. But you'll find another girl of the week and Bram will be happy. It's a win-win situation as far as I'm concerned."

"That's easy for you to say. You always win."

She walks back into the palace, and I follow her up the stairs to our respective quarters. She pauses at the top and shrewdly sizes me up with those uncanny eyes of hers. "I gave her the option to marry you."

The fae can't lie. I used to love that about them, but I hate knowing that she's telling the truth.

Reckless, selfless Ivy. It only makes me love her more.

I don't sleep for the next twenty-four hours.

I spend every waking minute in the library, pulling book after book off the shelf, hoping for some new clue, any message from my father.

It's agonizing, like an infected wound, to know he's under the same roof I am and we cannot speak. What will we do when the bargains are broken? I can only hope my father knows, because I do not.

I've never been this reckless before. I'm usually meticulous to leave no trace, lest the queen get wise to us, but I don't care anymore. The shelves are mostly empty, and I'm standing in a sea of half-open books scattered around the library.

Finally, in a volume of medieval poetry, I find a series of faint pencil lines, each underneath a new letter. *SOON*.

I've only ever known love through codes and things half-said. Ivy says exactly what she's thinking at all times. I wish I could be more like her, instead of constantly chewing at the ropes I've tied myself in.

SOON.

It has to be soon, or I'll have lost her forever, and that's not something I'm strong enough to bear.

I think of my father, somewhere in this same palace, but he feels farther away than ever. I can't help but feel that I'm failing him, the mission, all of England. Ivy was only ever supposed to be a means to an end, not a weakness I couldn't afford. But I know now, the thing about love is that you don't realize you're in it until it's too late.

The next day, Bram bursts into my room as I'm preparing for the ball at the Kendalls, I know I shouldn't go. I should make the same excuses I always do and go drink until I can't remember my own name at some shitty pub in the East End. I dismiss my valet as my brother walks in.

Bram sinks down into the chair across from me, his face tight with paternal worry. "Are you going to tell me why you asked your valet to collect your bank statements?"

"I should fire him for gossiping."

"It's not gossip, it's valid concern."

"You're always encouraging me to be more responsible."

Bram sighs. "Please don't tell me you're planning on gambling it away."

"You have to spend money to make money," I reply with a smile I know will drive him up the wall.

"You're not nearly as funny as you think you are."

"I'm laughing."

Bram passes me the stack of papers from the bank. A quick glance at the statements confirm what I suspected. My stipend from the Crown is basically zero, but I have enough inherited from my mother's side of the family that I could take Ivy and me anywhere in the world and build her the kind of life she deserves, then leave the rest to her family.

I asked for the statements a week ago, but I was too late. Now I think I'll go somewhere alone, somewhere I don't have to see Ivy at Bram's side every day.

"Please don't tell me you're thinking of doing something stupid," Bram grumbles.

"I've never done anything stupid in my whole entire life." I grin, even though it hurts.

Bram pulls a small green leather box out of his jacket pocket and flips it open. Inside is a rose-cut diamond set on a narrow gold band.

My stomach hurts.

"Isn't it beautiful?"

"She's going to love it," I say honestly.

Bram pockets the ring box. "You've been in a foul mood. Is it Faith Fairchild again? She's all yours if you want her. I don't get the appeal. She's so goddamn mean. The one time I tried to kiss her, she bit me, but I know we have different tastes."

I look at him in the mirror and force a smile. It looks unnatural on my face with the dark circles under my eyes and the too-long hair.

"You're still coming tonight, right?" he asks.

If I had any sense of self-preservation, I wouldn't, but I can't make myself stay away. My father used to tell me I was a master at hurting my own feelings. *No one tortures you like you do to yourself, my dear boy,* he'd mutter as he bandaged my skinned knees. I didn't understand what he meant at the time, but I do now. There's never been a wound I won't pick at just to make sure it still bleeds.

"Of course I am. I wouldn't dream of missing my favorite brother's engagement party."

The Kendall estate is covered in candles and fresh roses. We've arrived late enough that it's easy for me to slip through the crowd and find a corner to disappear into.

The band whines to a halt and the crowd parts as Bram strides to the center of the floor, Ivy's hand in his.

She's wearing a pale pink gown, pearls wound into her hair. The firelight catches her, and she looks like something from heaven. But there, right on the edge of her dress where her neck meets her shoulder, is the mottled yellow of a healing bruise. The one I left that night.

I'm never going to touch her again. The realization hits me like a blow.

Bram drops to his knee. He's looking up at her with so much love it radiates through the room. Ivy blushes, smiles, clutches her hands to her chest. They're happy. It should be enough, but I've never been a selfless person. It should be me. That's all my one-track brain can fire off. *That should be me. That should be me. That should be me.*

I can't take it. In the end, I'm not strong enough to look.

I push my way through the crowd as the clapping starts and white rose petals rain down from the rafters. Everyone is too distracted to watch me walk out through a side door into the night. I tilt my face up to the sky and try to catch my breath. It's raining. It's always raining in this goddamn country.

I vomit pure champagne into the Kendalls' rosebushes. It burns like the devil coming up, makes my eyes water, or maybe I was already crying. I can't really tell.

There are footsteps behind me, and I look up to see who is witness to my shame.

It's Faith Fairchild, concern all over her face. I've seen Faith in a dozen different rooms, in the middle of the night and sleeping through midmorning. I've seen her so angry she's thrown a glass at my head. I thought I'd seen her in every situation, but I've never seen her look quite like this.

"Emmett." Her voice is thick with pity. "It was always going to end this way."

But Ivy was already mine inside my head.

"You're getting all wet," I reply. The rain runs down across her face. Her hair is already ruined.

"I don't care about that," she says gently. "I care about you."

She approaches me like I'm a feral animal who might bite her and then lays a gloved hand on my shoulder. "You love her, don't you?"

"It doesn't matter now," I say.

"Of course it matters."

I collapse onto her shoulder, unable to stop the sobs that rack my body. I haven't cried like this since my father gave me up. I hate it. I'd rather be vomiting.

She doesn't rub my back in circles or whisper *hush* into my ear. Instead, she grips me in a vice-tight embrace and holds me until I stop shaking.

We're both soaked to the core now, not that it matters. I'm not going back to the party.

Faith ducks inside for a minute to get Marion, and together, the three of us hop into a carriage back to Kensington Palace.

"Do you want me to list Ivy's worst qualities?" asks Faith. "Would that help? She breathes so loud when she sleeps. It made me want to smother her."

"I don't think you're helping, darling," Marion whispers.

Faith refuses to leave me alone. I give her and Marion my bed and sleep in the armchair by the fire. I tend to it all night, thinking of Ivy with each shower of sparks.

Bram is glowing with happiness the next morning and all through the next week. I should leave. I should beg off and drink myself into a stupor in some lord's hunting lodge, like I have every other time something in my life gets hard. But I just can't bring myself to. *What if she needs me?* That's the thought that goes through my head anytime I get close to calling a carriage and running away.

We are getting fitted for new suits when my brother asks me the question I've been dreading. In the end, the answer comes easy. "Of course I'll be your best man."

CHAPTER THIRTY-TWO

It isn't raining on the day of the wedding, which is a miracle in and of itself.

My mother, Lydia, and I are picked up midmorning by a palace carriage and taken to Caledonia Cottage, where we will dress for the wedding. "Isn't rain supposed to be lucky?" I ask, slumped against the velvet seat.

"How much luckier could you get?" Lydia replies.

I run my tongue over the smooth gap in my gum where my upper left molar used to be. Mother tells me to ignore that too, but I can't stop prodding at it like a worry stone.

I've been sleeping in Lydia's room for the past two weeks. Our parents think it's sweet that we're maximizing our last days together under the same roof, but really, I just like that she's awake in the middle of the night too.

The irony of our situation doesn't escape me. All the time I spent raging at her for the bargain she couldn't remember, and now I've gone and done the same thing.

Lydia didn't gloat about my bargain. She's always been a better person than I am.

She just said, "It looks like we're both exactly the same kind of stupid," which almost makes me laugh.

Today is the summer solstice, the longest day of the year. An auspicious beginning to what will be a long and happy marriage. It's splashed all over the papers, my description on every front page in London. The headlines no longer **THE SIX**, but **THE ONE**.

They've embroidered my face on tea towels, there's no backing out now.

Bram and I have barely seen each other. Every waking moment is filled with dress fittings or appointments about table settings or flowers.

Crowds line the streets all the way from our house to the palace. They shout good wishes and wave handkerchiefs as we pass by.

My mother's elbow jabs me in the ribs. "Wave," she urges.

I lean my head out the window, and the crowd goes absolutely wild. I've never felt more lonely in my life.

When we arrive, Marion, Faith, Olive, and Emmy are there in matching cream silk bridesmaid dresses. I missed them all dearly, even Faith.

Olive tames my curls into ringlets and then pins them into an elaborate updo. She looks concerned the whole time, staring at me like she's biting her tongue about something.

"You bite at your lips when you're nervous," I say as she winds the hair by my ears around the hot tong.

"Why would I be nervous? It's your wedding day." She smiles. I have that odd feeling, the one I still can't shake when I look at all of them. We've been living together all season, but why does it feel like there's something I'm forgetting? Could my bargain have included the other girls? That feels unlikely.

"Is there something you need to tell me?" I twirl my engagement ring nervously. It sits next to the pearl ring Bram gave me the day I first thought I could love him. I haven't taken it off.

"Only that you're the most stunning bride we've ever seen," Marion says.

The queen didn't strip anyone of their titles. It seems she's happy enough to let the threat hang over us, or she's been too preoccupied with wedding planning to remember. Regardless, I'll be a princess soon, and I intend to use my status to protect the other girls the best I can. I'm certain Bram will help me.

The season already feels like a dream, like it happened to someone else. I can barely even remember being at the balls and social events. The only moments that feel truly crystallized are the queen's lessons and the moments with the other girls.

Lydia buttons me into my white wedding gown. It's a gauzy confection, with a wide V-neck that hangs off my shoulders and layers upon layers of fine-tooled lace that falls in ruffles across the bodice and skirt.

It's the most beautiful thing I've ever had on my body, but I glance in the mirror anxiously. I was nervous when the atelier decided on this silhouette. The neckline shows the part of my neck where I had that strange, toothy bruise. It took weeks to heal but finally appears to be gone. It's the oddest thing, I can't remember how I got it.

Once I'm in my dress, a footman comes in with a velvet case of royal jewels. I flip open the case to find a pair of diamond drop earrings and a matching necklace. Bram will place a tiara on my head at the altar, as is tradition.

Attached to the jewelry case is a note in Bram's elegant hand. *I cannot wait to be your husband. —Bram.*

My heart swells.

I don't love Bram. I'm honest enough with myself to acknowledge that. But I *will* love him. In time.

I can picture it so clearly, like love is something I've felt before and need to remember how to do again. It's a ghost I'm chasing around corners, just out of reach.

My mother fastens the final piece of my bridal ensemble, not a veil, but a delicate lace cape, attached at my throat with a ribbon, with a billowing hood over my head. My bouquet is small, a tasteful arrangement of lily of the valley, but I clutch it hard to keep my sweaty hands from shaking.

My mother appears over my shoulder in the mirror and gives me a squeeze. "He's the luckiest man in England," she says.

He's not a man, though, not quite. He's something else. But I don't correct her.

I have the same uncanny feeling I had on the day of the Pact Parade, as if I'm looking at myself through a spyglass from the future. The course has already been set, there's no stopping it now.

Lydia goes to stand with the other bridesmaids, my mother leaves to sit with the crowd, and then it is just my father and me waiting at the side door of the cottage.

Prince Emmett appears in the door, tall and broad-shouldered in his ink-black frock coat. He offers a weak smile. "The processional will begin shortly." He glances down at my father's lapel. "You've forgotten your boutonniere."

My father grasps his chest, then mutters "Oh!" and scurries off to retrieve it from the other room, leaving Prince Emmett and me alone.

He drags his eyes from my hem back up to my face and takes a strange, abbreviated breath. I don't know him well enough to understand the expression on his face, but something about it makes my ribs ache.

"I'm sorry we haven't gotten the chance to get to know each other better," I offer, because it seems the polite thing to say.

"We'll have all the time in the world now that you're to be my sister-in-law."

"True," I reply, though I doubt the prince has any intention of sticking around Kensington Palace, not when he's been absent all season.

"Do you love him?" he asks me.

I blink in shock.

He frowns. "I'm sorry, that was rude of me."

"Have you ever been in love?" I ask in return. I don't know what makes me say it.

He nods slowly, like it pains him. "Just once."

"What did it feel like?"

He thinks for a moment, his eyes boring into mine all the while. "Like getting run over by a carriage."

"Hmm." I look down at my bouquet, unable to stand the force of his eye contact. "I wouldn't know what that feels like."

Emmett huffs out a laugh but doesn't smile. "No, I suppose you wouldn't."

My father bursts back into the room, his boutonniere crooked. Prince Emmett straightens it for him while my father mutters something about forgetting his head if it wasn't attached to his neck.

Hundreds of chairs have been set around the long, rectangular pool in the sunken garden. The aisle has been built on a platform over the water. At the far end is the altar, crawling with a rainbow of flowers.

It's a perfect evening here on the longest day of the year, and the sun makes sure to give us all a show. It flashes golden and pink, setting rainbows off the jewels around the necks and silk gowns of all of London's high society. This is the event of the century, and I am the star.

When the sky turns purple and the music from the full orchestra swells, my father squeezes my hand. "There's still time to run," he jokes. But there isn't. Not really.

I run my tongue over the smooth gap in my gum where my molar used to be, and I step out onto the aisle.

My bridesmaids trail behind me, carrying my long train, as is tradition, but I so wish I could see their faces. One reassuring smile from my sister would help me to be brave.

At the altar, bathed in golden light, is Bram. He's in a green velvet coat, a delicate circlet of gold laid on his hair.

The pointed tips of his ears poke through his unruly waves, and he's never looked less human.

But he's beaming. He's staring at me like he loves me. I am lucky, I keep reminding myself, to have this, have *him*.

Why, then, do my eyes keep landing on his brother?

Prince Emmett stands next to him, his jaw clenched, his hands in fists at his side. His all-black suit makes him look dressed for a funeral. In his eyes is an emotion I can't name. Agony is the closest word I can muster, but that doesn't make any sense.

How can he hate me when he doesn't even know me? The whole thing makes my stomach turn with unease.

But I paste a smile on my face. I'm about to become a princess. There's a man who loves me, who wants to make me happy. It's so much more than I ever thought I'd get. My mother and father and

Lydia are going to be safe, protected by my status, and I will live without fear of destitution. My children and their children will be royalty. I haven't just saved my parents and my sister, I've ensured that our family will be safe for generations. Queen Mor is immortal, and she will remember me as she welcomes my great-grandchildren to court.

We make it to the altar, and the music hums to a close.

Bram lowers the hood of my cape, then captures both my hands in his. He looks down at me with his gray eyes, and I am struck, as I always am, by his profound beauty. "Thank you for this," he says, but I'm not entirely sure what he means.

The priestess says something about love and commitment and duty, but the words are nothing but a dull buzzing in my ears.

I can't stop looking at Emmett. He's looking straight ahead, not at either of us. It's a look I recognize well because it's often on my own face, the look of someone who would rather be anywhere but here.

"The rings, please," the priestess drones.

Emmett doesn't move.

The priestess clears her throat. "The rings?"

"Oh." Emmett jumps and digs into his pocket. He pulls out two circles of Welsh gold and places them in the priestess's palm. His hands are shaking.

The sun sinks low on the horizon, a glorious finale on the longest day of the year. The evening dips into twilight as Bram takes my hand in his.

He places the ring around my finger with gentle care and a look in his eyes so full of joy, I can't help but smile back at him. "All that I am and all that I have is yours," Bram promises.

I slide his on in turn. I've done it. It's done.

Bram's eyes well with tears as he picks up my May Queen tiara from where it rests on a velvet pillow on the altar and lowers it onto my head.

"In the power vested in me by Her Eternal Majesty Queen Moryen, I pronounce you husband and wife," says the priestess.

Bram slips his arm around the small of my back and kisses me. It's much too passionate a kiss for a public ceremony like this, and when he pulls back, he's laughing.

Suddenly there's screaming coming from the crowd. Shouts of panicked confusion. People stand, and chairs are toppled.

It's chaos. My head spins, my stomach lurches, and my mouth fills with something acrid and metallic. I spit a mouthful of blood, and it splatters all over the altar.

I lock eyes with Emmett, and it all comes flooding back. That first night in the carriage, the coaching inn, the secret glances across candlelit ballrooms, his hands on my back, his mouth on my neck. I'm nearly knocked backward by the force of the love I feel for him.

I turn to Bram, panicked, but he's still just standing there, laughing like this is the funniest thing in the world.

In the front row, Queen Mor stands, her chair toppling behind her. "No!" she screams. "Bram, what have you done?"

He shakes his head, like this is all some joke she just doesn't understand. "Seize her."

LYDIA BENTON

I don't know where to look. All around, people are shouting, sobbing, screaming so loud it makes my ears ring. A bolt of lightning strikes across the sky just as Lord Bexham trips into me, his hair suddenly returned, and vomits into the bushes.

Ivy is standing at the altar, collapsed in Emmett's arms. I crane my head, searching for my parents, but turn to find Bram's face inches from mine. He smiles, and it stretches across his face lazily until that single dimple pops out. "Hi, darling. I've missed you."

I try to run, but my heels sink into the grass, and as I stumble, Bram's hand encircles my wrist in his and he yanks me back. "I'm not losing you again."

"Please—" My voice shakes. "I won't tell her."

He drags me behind the row of hedges that circle the sunken garden and wraps his hands around my waist, so tight I can't move. "No, don't say that." He sighs against my hair. "Say you missed me too."

And I hate him for it, but I hate me more. I remember the dreams I've had for the last five months, the ones where I'd wake up, my cheeks wet with tears, feeling as if I was forgetting something desperately important. I missed him even when I didn't know he was the one I was missing.

He kisses me hard enough to knock me back to my senses. I shove him by the shoulders, but he's so much bigger than I am. It only makes him angrier. He grabs me by the hair to kiss me harder, so I kick him in the groin. He stumbles back a few feet, his beautiful face screwed up in fury. "I didn't want it to be like this, Lydia."

"You just married my sister." *Ivy.* Oh no.

For my whole life, before I left the house, my mother would kiss my head and say the same thing: *Look out for your sister.*

I can't fail at the only real job I've ever had.

There's a flash of Ivy's white wedding gown somewhere in the chaos. Emmett is beside her, scanning the crowd, a head above everyone else. I wave my arms above my head to get his attention, but Bram wraps me in a bear hug from behind and pins them to my side.

"We have to go now, my love," he whispers.

"No," I growl, and dig my heels into the soft earth.

"But everyone is so excited to see you."

I struggle against him, cursing the small part of me that's grateful to be in his arms again. "Just let me speak with her first."

His beautiful face crumples. "I thought you loved me."

"I do." That's the worst part.

He looks so sad, the golden circlet on his hair reflecting the final rays of sunshine. "I thought if you loved me, you would obey me."

There's nothing I can say, just pure animal struggle as I elbow him in the ribs.

"You never make things easy." He pulls a sword from the scabbard at his side and brings the bejeweled hilt down hard on my temple.

There's a ringing in my ears and the taste of metal in my mouth. *Ivy.* My arms reach for her, but I'm too far away.

And then I'm gone.

I don't need to open my eyes to know where I am when I awake. It always smelled like crushed rose petals here. It was one of my favorite things about the palace when I first arrived, but now the scent hits the back of my throat, sticky-sweet, and I vomit all over the floor.

My bedroom is covered with a thick layer of dust, like he hasn't let anyone enter since the night I left. I swipe my finger along the bedside table, through the grime that covers all my things, exactly as I left them. The silver comb, a blue hair ribbon, the vase of flowers he enchanted so they would never wilt. Even my painting supplies are still here; my easel sits by the diamond-pane window, a landscape half finished.

There's a bracelet of finger-shaped bruises around my wrist where Bram gripped me at the wedding.

I'm woozy with pain, but force myself up and off the four-poster bed. I've got to get back, to warn her.

The door to the bedroom is locked, so Bram's learned at least one lesson. I pull the handle so hard the door shakes, and from the outside, a lock snicks, then another, then the whole doorframe glows as an enchantment is undone.

Eloree steps inside. My former lady's maid looks the same as she did the day I left, with slightly pink skin, golden hair that reaches to the floor, and a dress crafted from fabric that shimmers like the sunset on a pond.

She bursts into tears at the sight of me. "My lady, I feared I'd never see you again." I calculate quickly in my head. The first time,

I was gone for two weeks in the human world, but it felt like four months here.

"How long have I been gone?"

She pulls me into her arms. "Not long." She counts on her eerily long fingers, a puzzled look on her face. "Two years perhaps?"

"Where is he?" I ask.

"His Majesty is gone, but he asked me to keep you safe." Keep me locked up, she means.

"When will he return?"

"No one can be sure these days."

She carries in a tray from the hallway, laden with waxy technicolor fruits, pastries dripping in half-melted icing, and a tankard of fizzy wine. My mouth waters, but I can't bring myself to touch it. I've hungered for the food from the Otherworld for months, craving something I couldn't name. I'd sneak down to the kitchens in the middle of the night and eat everything in sight, shoveling raw sugar by the handful into my mouth. Nothing would sate me. I know why now.

"Would you like me to stay?" Eloree asks.

"No, I need my rest."

She nods. "I'll come later to dress you for the feast."

The door latches behind her and glows once more. I don't bother trying the lock, but I race to the window and find it stuck too.

I find the heaviest object I can, the fire poker, and swing it again and again against the glass until sweat is running down my back and I'm out of breath.

He's enchanted this too.

I collapse in a heap on the floor and bang my head against the stone wall of the tower, cursing myself.

Faerie tales all have the same lesson, really: don't go searching in the dark. But I'd never listened quite as closely as my sister.

When it came time to make my bargain, I panicked. I saw so many girls my age missing toes or memories, all to ensnare some husband they didn't even like.

It was a foregone conclusion that I was to marry Percival Chapwick, and Mama never let an opportunity pass to remind me of it.

And for a long time it was fine, really it was. But all of a sudden it wasn't just some far-off thing. I was nearly eighteen, and it was going to actually happen. I was going to have to leave the home I'd known all my life, my family, and go live in a house with a boy I barely knew.

He lived just down the road. One month before I was supposed to make my bargain, I climbed the garden trellis into his room. He was surprised to find me crawling through his window, and he tried to kiss me, like that's all it was. I pushed him away, which he took like a gentleman. "I want to talk," I said.

"About what?" He was puzzled.

"Anything."

He couldn't manage it. It was stilted and awkward, and I couldn't bear it more than a few minutes before I climbed out the window again.

When I thought of living a life boarded up in a house with a man I couldn't have a conversation with, I felt like I was going to die.

The day of the Pact Parade, my mouth was saying the words before I even knew what I meant. I begged Queen Mor to let me experience something completely new. The mind-numbing existence of my life was going to crush me.

Queen Mor laughed. She told me that she would give me what I wished, but I would never be able to speak of it. I didn't realize that meant I wouldn't remember it. She tricked me. If I were clever, like Ivy, I would have seen it coming.

The Others have to honor the law but not the spirit of the bargain. It's part of the fun for them. I know that now.

The queen certainly had her fun with me. For two years I bore the shame of having made a bad bargain, one I couldn't remember. I was supposed to be my family's shining hope, our way out of rapidly approaching poverty, but in the end, I went and made the exact same mistakes as my parents. Isn't that always the way?

I had a gut feeling that I shouldn't accept any courtships, that something else was waiting for me. It wasn't until this winter that Queen Mor finally held up her end of the bargain.

I awoke in the middle of the night with the strangest sensation, like there was a ribbon tied around my rib cage and someone was on the other end, tugging. I followed the feeling outside and down the street. My feet carried me like I was in a dream all the way to Kensington Park. There I found a peculiar tree, shimmering like a fallen star. I laid my hands upon it and suddenly I was somewhere else.

It was daytime there, that was the first thing I noticed. The grass was softer and a slightly different shade of green than the grass in England. The trees had leaves that were shaped like stars, the flowers smelled of baking bread, and up on a hill was a castle. It was unlike anything I'd ever seen back home, too tall, too sharp, constructed from something like opal that shimmered in the sunlight. I wandered for a while until two palace guards found me. I was so tired and hungry, I thought I imagined the double rows of sharp teeth in their horses' mouths.

They took me to the castle, where I found a revel raging. There were towers of strange food. The sun was blazing outside, but inside, someone had enchanted the ceiling to look like the inky-black Milky Way.

There were hundreds of Others, twirling in gowns that floated like spider's silk, playing fiddles encrusted with gems, kissing wildly up against the walls of the ballroom.

I nearly hit the marble floor with my knees in gratitude. In that moment, I knew that the queen had finally kept her end of the deal. For the first time since I was a child, I was *excited*. I wished Ivy was there with me. It was everything we'd ever dreamed of.

And there, in the middle of it all, was Bram.

He was seated in a magnificent golden throne on a dais, overseeing the whole party. His black doublet hung half-open, embroidered with stars that matched the ceiling. His crown was made of twisted silver, like the branches of a tree, that matched the single earring trailing down to his shoulder. He had one leg crossed over his knee, and his head was resting in his hand like he was bored. I remember thinking, *How could anyone be bored of this?*

The crowd parted as the guards brought me to him.

He smiled in that way only Bram can smile, the kind that lights up his whole face, and he said, "Please don't be afraid. You are very welcome here."

I should have told him I wanted to go home, that would have been the responsible thing to do, but I wanted to stay. I danced at the revel until my feet bled, leaving the marble floor slippery. I'd stick out my hand, and my cup was filled. When I grew tired of dancing, I collapsed at the banquet table and a plate appeared in front of me, piled with candied fruits and sweets I couldn't begin to describe. It was better than anything I'd ever let myself hope for. I didn't think of home once.

Bram had a room prepared for me in the castle, decorated in my favorite colors. His staff brought me a trousseau of dresses in the court fashion and braided flowers into my hair.

It was a few weeks before the melancholy struck. It began with dreams of my sister. The longer I was in the Otherworld, the hazier my life back in London felt, like it was something that happened to someone else. I should have recognized Bram, I should have mourned my family, but every time the memories felt within reach, they'd float away again, just past my grasp.

As we spent more time together, Bram noticed my vague, unplaceable sadness. At first it was during simple afternoon activities. We rode horses around the palace grounds and picked fruit from the orchards.

Bram had only one rule. After that first night, I was never again allowed to attend his court revels. He insisted they weren't safe for me. But I craved the joy of dancing, and I was lonely. Bram would disappear, sometimes for days at a time, and I thought he was below, merrymaking without me.

"I want you to be happy here. This place can be your home if you let it," he said as he wiped tears from my cheek. Every day, cakes showed up in my room that tasted exactly of Mr. Froburg's birthday cake recipe. The same sterling silver brush set from my room back home appeared on my vanity. He brought me paints and charcoals and pastels. I painted well into the night as music drifted up from the revels below. At dawn, Bram would climb into bed beside me and stroke my hair as I cried.

He didn't love the way I imagined love would be. He held me like he wanted to consume me. At the time, I thought that made it even better.

I wasn't surprised when he asked me to marry him. He slipped a moonstone ring on my third finger one night under the strange double moons of the Otherworld and asked me to be his bride. I threw myself into his arms and kissed him so hard my lips were bruised the next morning. He pulled back, smiling. "You forgot to say yes."

We held banquets and went on picnics, and he even had a chair brought into the throne room for me so I could sit at his side while he did his official work. One day, while we were having lunch in the gardens, he placed a crown of daisies atop my head and told me I was the queen of the Otherworld. I just looked at him, bowled over by his beauty. "Don't we need something more official?"

"I'm the king—what could be more official than that?"

But it wasn't enough for me. I grew ruinously sad and unbearably clingy in the lead-up to our wedding ceremony. I'd curl myself around him in bed and beg him not to leave me. I could feel him growing bored with me, and I didn't know how to fix it. I ordered the court ateliers to make me more interesting dresses, I painted him pictures, planted a rose garden, but nothing held his attention. He'd leave, every night, to revel without me.

The morning of our wedding, Eloree, who was perhaps my only true friend in the Otherworld, dressed me in a gown constructed of dozens of layers of tissue-thin spider's silk. It fell in ruffles and waves, as if I was emerging from seafoam. The veil I wore covered my face, which I was grateful for. Struck by an unshakable feeling of loneliness, I cried all through the long walk down the aisle.

All of Bram's court was in attendance, as well as representatives from the surrounding Seelie territories. The palace dripped in flowers and swelled with music. I walked down the aisle alone, clutching a bouquet of roses that smelled of freshly fallen rain. I wished my sister was holding my train, but I forgot my hollow sadness as soon as Bram turned and smiled at me.

We exchanged our vows, and he placed on my head a heavy golden crown that he said had once belonged to his mother. Did I know his mother? I felt I must have, but the thought flitted away as soon as it came.

I slipped a ring on his finger, and he kissed me, hard, just like the day I'd promised to marry him. When he pulled back, he smiled and said something strange. "I'll be right back."

He sprinted down the petal-carpeted aisle and out the door.

"Bram?" I screamed after him, hiking up my skirts and trying to run. But suddenly I blinked awake and was back in my room.

I rose from my bed, still in my wedding gown, and opened the door. It wasn't locked, and no guard waited for me in the hallway. On bare feet I crept across the cold stone floors, back into the main hall of the castle, where my wedding feast was raging without me.

Bram was in the corner, back from wherever he'd run off to, with a foul look on his face. I'd never seen him look so angry. He was deep in conversation with my least favorite of his advisers, the man with the cruel mouth and curtain of black hair that reached the floor.

"It's exactly the same." Bram was ranting, the rings on each of his ringers clicked as he waved his hands in emphasis. "She's one of her subjects. She's been crowned twice. I don't see what the problem is."

The adviser considered. "It must be on English soil, then."

Bram cursed and threw back the rest of whatever was in his

goblet. He jumped as he finally noticed me at his elbow.

"What are you doing up?" There was a cruel tilt to his voice I didn't like at all.

"It's our wedding feast," I replied, confused.

Bram stuck out his arm, and his glass was filled once more. He drank that as well. "Sure, fine."

He stalked off. I didn't know what else to do but grab a drink. My eyes stung, and I was desperate to have something to do with my hands other than twirl my new wedding band around my finger.

The faerie wine was strong, and I should have known better. I had a glass, maybe two, and came to my senses as I twirled on the dance floor, swept up in a crowd of courtiers.

But this was nothing like the revel I remembered from my first night here. It was rotten, like milk that had gone off. The music was in a strange minor key, the laughing faces of the folk looked suddenly like jackals, and the dance floor was smeared with blood.

I looked for the source, concerned that someone had been injured and needed my help, and that's when I saw them. The first humans I'd seen in the better part of a year. There were a dozen or so of them, all gaunt, wearing rags. Their faces were blank, their eyes glazed over, like they hadn't even realized that they'd danced their feet bloody. They'd been enchanted by faeries, who stood in the corner laughing uproariously at their torture. And there, on his throne, laughing along, was Bram.

I ran out of the room, back to my bedchamber, but I didn't lock the door behind me.

Unable to sleep, I waited until the sun rose. I ripped off my wedding dress, pulled on the dress I hadn't worn since I'd arrived, and left my wedding ring on the vanity. I crept through the castle, whose walls I now knew well, and followed the spiral staircase around and around until I reached the damp darkness of the dungeons.

The humans from the revel were locked up there in tiny stone cells, covered with filth. They were so emaciated they could stick their entire arms through the bars, their dirt-crusted fingernails reaching for me.

They begged me for help in strange accents, some I could hardly understand. "How long have you been here?" I asked. They couldn't even remember. But every single one of them had been born in the 1400s. Can you imagine? In that basement for over four hundred years? "When is it?" they asked. I hadn't the heart to tell them it was now 1848. Or was it? Time there seemed such a slippery thing.

They came from an England where sightings of the folk were common. Parents warned children to stay away from tall strangers in the woods and to never follow music that seemingly came from nowhere. They did not heed the warnings, and they paid the price. Now they were brought up during revels to be used as nothing more substantial than a hit of faerie wine.

They begged me to help free them. I was the first other human they'd seen in four centuries. And what could I do?

The key to their cells was hanging right there on a hook, like it had been hung in their eyeline just to torture them further. I passed it through the bars, but they made such a clatter unlocking it that the guard awoke. He lunged for me, but one of the other humans swung the prison gate hard enough that the guard stumbled backward and I got away.

I ran, as fast as I could, until my legs were burning and I couldn't catch my breath, out of the palace and back to the woods where I'd first arrived. I shoved my hands at every tree until they were bloody and raw, and then finally *something* opened and I was spit back out in the middle of London, my memory wiped clean. I loved him. *I loved him.* But I couldn't stay.

There are two truths I didn't know then that I know now.

The first: there is no greater insult to a faerie than tricking him.

The second: once they love you, they will not let you go.

The fire poker clatters to the floor, and I cross the room to my vanity, not in defeat, but with the knowledge that this will be a different kind of fight. My wedding band lies right where I left it. It glints in the dying daylight, somehow not blanketed in dust like everything else. There's another flash of metal, and I reach up to find a necklace hung atop the pointed peak of the vanity mirror. My breath catches as it falls into my hands, cool against my skin. I hold it up to the light, and a strangled cry leaves my lips. It's a necklace with a golden chain, and a small *I* charm, made of pearls. It's missing one stone, a tiny golden crater, right in the center.

My hands shake as I tuck it down the front of my bodice, where it rests against my heart, then I slip my wedding ring back onto my finger and wait.

CHAPTER THIRTY-THREE

I turn to Emmett, nearly fainting in his arms. When I look back up, Bram is nowhere to be seen.

My mother is sitting in the front row, completely still, staring at her hand, where her pinkie finger, the one that has been absent my whole life, is suddenly back.

I turn to my left, to where my attendants stand, and see Olive staring down at her fingernails. I prod at my teeth with my tongue and find that my molar has returned, which explains the blood in my mouth.

A footman reaches for me, but his hands don't close the distance. They turn to dust, and the footman collapses in a heap, leaving nothing but a crumpled livery on the ground.

Hysterical screams go up as a dozen footmen float away on the wind.

Suddenly, from all sides of the garden, the Queen's Guard pours in, weapons at the ready. I expect them to surround Queen Mor, protecting her, but without warning, they attack.

Queen Mor struggles against them, her magic flares, dropping five to the ground all at once. Emmett's father throws his body over hers. I can't tell if he's trying to take her down or protect her. He lets out a strangled cry and pulls back, his white shirt suddenly crimson with wet blood. It's spreading quickly, and he's growing pale. He looks down to see a knife with a golden hilt, buried in his stomach.

Queen Mor snaps her fingers and two guards turn to dust, but she doesn't see the ones behind her. In their hands are thick chains, and the moment the metal touches her skin, it's as if she deflates, all the magic suddenly snuffed out. She hisses, like the chains are burning her skin, and is quickly taken to the ground. The guards haul her writhing body through the garden and down the path, out of sight.

The crowd is in such chaos, I don't think even half of the guests saw their queen being hauled away.

Emmett rushes to Edgar. "Father!" he cries into Prince Consort Edgar's shoulder. "Father?" Emmett pulls back, his hands dripping with blood.

Edgar wheezes in a wet breath.

"Help!" Emmett screams through the chaos. "Somebody help me!"

Emmett tries to stanch the bleeding with his hands, but it's no use. "No—please." He weeps. "I just got you back."

Edgar reaches up and brushes his son's face. "You've done so well." He takes a final rattling breath, and then he is gone.

There is screaming all around, complete and utter mayhem. "Emmett—" I pull him to his feet. "Please, we have to leave, it isn't safe here."

I look to the altar where Marion and Faith are standing, silent and terror-struck. Olive and Emmy have disappeared into the crowd. "Where is Lydia?" I call. But no one answers. I scan the crowd and spot my parents. "Have you seen Lydia?" I ask.

"We thought she was with you," my father answers.

"Go home," I urge them. "Leave now. Bar the doors and don't open them for anyone but me, Emmett, or Lydia."

My mother kisses both my cheeks. "I don't want to leave you."

"I'll follow just as soon as I find Lydia." A lie.

Emmett is next to me, covered in blood and silent with shock. I tug at his hand.

There will be time to mourn Edgar, to figure out how to fight this, but for the moment we're right back to the night we met. "My sister is missing."

I pick up the skirts of my blood-soaked wedding dress and flee.

I sprint off into the relative seclusion of the trees that surround the orangery, but from beyond the garden I hear the awful metallic banging of steel on steel. Citizens have already arrived at the gates, and there will be more by the minute.

Lydia.

I search my muddled thoughts. The last time I saw her, we were walking down the aisle. Where is Bram? Is he safe? We got what we wanted, but why is this all going so wrong?

The silence of the orangery is unsettling after the screaming from outside. There's nothing but the quiet rustling of leaves, but then, suddenly, I hear a low, familiar voice.

We round the corner and find Bram, the golden circlet on his head, surrounded by the Queen's Guard. He doesn't see us at first, he's too busy barking orders.

"The Tower, make sure there are at least six guards at all times. I can get more iron, if need be, but you should have plenty. Secure the west gate, and make sure—" He pauses as he spots us.

"Oh, Emmett, Ivy, what a lovely surprise." He waves off the Queen's Guard—King's Guard now, I suppose. "Leave us."

"What is happening?" I ask.

"You got what you wanted."

Emmett hesitates in confusion.

Bram just grins. "You think I didn't know about your little plans and schemes? This is what I like about humans. You think you're so clever, it really is a joy to watch."

"You knew?" Emmett asks.

"Oh, I've known for ages. Your father always makes such a racket in that library of his. It was cute, watching you two."

"Why not tell me?"

Bram considers for a moment. "Because I had so many other things to do. It's not easy being both a king and a prince. The multitasking! The lies to keep straight! I didn't see the need to add one more thing to my plate. Not when you were already doing the work for me."

"King?" I ask.

"Keep up." Bram claps his hands together. "The door to the Otherworld—I told you all about it, how my mother enchanted it only to open for me? I never gave up my crown there. I was here to reopen the doors between our worlds for us all."

I'm shaking, horrified and confused. "I thought your father was king."

"That old bore? I killed him like"—he counts on his fingers—"three hundred years ago?"

"I thought you couldn't lie," Emmett says.

Bram just laughs again, that same wondrous laugh I've heard a hundred times, so different now. "That was my mother's idea, probably the best one she's ever had. It was a rumor she spread about our kind ages ago. It's very convenient to have humans think you're always telling the truth."

The room tilts, my knees go weak. Emmett's as pale as a ghost.

I think of the pictures of Bram scattered across my bedroom floor. "Where is my sister?" I ask.

Bram smiles. "Safe. I'm quite fond of her, you know."

I launch myself at him, ready to claw his eyes out of his head, but Emmett holds me back as I kick and scream. "Tell me where she is, you bastard! If you've hurt her, I'll kill you! I'll kill you!"

Bram's laughter booms off of the walls. "She's fine! I swear it." He takes a step back, and his face falls as he looks between Emmett and me, standing together. "There is the matter of the two of you to solve, however."

"I told you I—"

"Don't lie to me!" Bram bellows at Emmett. "I already told you not to lie to me about her."

"It's nothing. I love you," I lie. "I love you, please let's just go inside, all right?" I take a step toward him, but Emmett grabs my sleeve and I hesitate.

"I heard the two of you that night," Bram says.

The blood drains from my face.

Emmett steps in front of me. "It was my fault. Don't blame Ivy."

Bram laughs again. "I thought about killing one of you, but we weren't married then, so I've decided to let it go."

"It was a one-time mistake. I'll be devoted to you, please don't hurt him," I beg.

"Of course not." Bram turns back to his King's Guard, and relief pulses through me. Emmett and I turn to run, but Bram snaps his fingers.

"Not so fast. It won't do to have the queen of England's virtue compromised like this. I can't very well pretend to be unaware of an affair happening under the roof of my own palace. How embarrassing for me. How could we expect anyone to take me seriously? I need to get rid of one of you."

"No!" I shout, but Bram snaps again, and suddenly my voice is gone.

"Let me finish," Bram says coolly. "Ivy is tempting, wives are a high-maintenance business, but they do have their purposes. But you, Emmett, have already done so much of the work for me. With your reputation, no one will question that you've disappeared off to some country house to drink yourself into a stupor." He nods to his guards. "Seize him."

My knees hit the ground as I wail noiselessly. Emmett struggles against the four guards who surround him, locking heavy shackles around his arms and legs.

They drag him nearly out the door when Bram snaps again, and they pause. "I am sorry, Emmett. Call it only child syndrome. I don't like to share."

Emmett digs his heels into the floor, thrashing against the guards. He doesn't look at Bram, but at me. "Be safe. Do whatever he says. I'm sorry. I love you. I love you. I love you." The door slams behind them, leaving Bram and me alone.

He glances at his pocket watch. "I've got a coup to get to, but we'll catch up later, yes?"

He waves a hand, and my speech returns to me. I gasp, choking on tears and words unsaid. He extends a hand and pulls me to my feet. This close, his gray eyes glint strangely, his pupils blown out like he's drunk.

"I am sorry about all that," Bram says vaguely, then plants a kiss on my cheek.

He exits through the tunnels, but I race out the main door, hoping to see where the guards have dragged Emmett, but he's nowhere in sight.

I see Marion, Emmy, Faith, and Olive huddled under an oak tree, looking terrified.

"Ivy!" they call, and I race toward them. Together we go to Caledonia Cottage. We push furniture in front of the doors and latch the windows.

I explain everything to them, the May Queen plot, Emmett and me, Bram's confession, and Emmett's imprisonment.

It makes my head spin to think of Bram here at Kensington Palace, pretending to be a normal nineteen-year-old, then crossing through the portal to rule over a cruel court as an immortal king.

"What do we do now?" Olive asks from where she's huddled, wrapped in a blanket by the fire.

"You stay here, stay safe. But I'm going to find Emmett."

CHAPTER THIRTY-FOUR

From what we can see through the windows, a riot has begun outside the palace gates. Torches are burning, and hundreds are begging for an audience with the queen, shouting over each other, so it's just a roar of outraged voices.

"I'm not letting you go alone," Faith says. Marion lays her hand on Faith's shoulder and nods. "If you're going, we are too."

"I'll have you remember, I absolutely cannot stand to be left out," Emmy says.

Olive sniffs back tears. "Oh, fine. Let's go."

"I can't guarantee your safety," I say, overwhelmed with emotion.

Faith pulls on her cloak. "No time for a speech. We get it. Come on."

We circle along a path through Kensington Park that pops us out on a sleepy, moonlit lane off the high street, far from the riot at the gates.

"He said something about the Tower," I explain. It's what we overheard him talking about when we walked in.

The Tower of London is all the way on the other side of town. It will take us hours to walk there and we don't have the time, so we risk hailing a hackney carriage. Still in my wedding dress, the other girls in their bridesmaid gowns, we don't make an inconspicuous group, but we don't have any other options.

Marion passes a thick stack of bills through the window to the driver. "The Tower, and a little extra if you keep this ride between us."

The driver tips his cap.

The streets of London are quiet tonight, as if everyone who isn't rioting at the gates of the palace have barricaded themselves inside their homes. The carriage is so crowded, Olive has to sit on my lap.

The hackney driver lets us out on the dark cobblestone streets in the shadow of the Tower of London. The smell of the Thames is thick and heady tonight.

Olive takes me by the hand. "Let's go."

At the gates is a yeoman guard with a bayonet in his hand. "No one in or out tonight," he barks without looking at us.

I straighten to my full height and stare him down as best I can from six inches below him. "Do you know who I am?"

The guard's gaze flicks down to me.

"I'm Queen Ivy, wife of King Bram. Please don't waste my time with these theatrics."

The guard pauses, and I sneer. "Are you going to make us wait all night? My husband will be hearing about this."

After a moment the guard reaches for his thick metal keys, unlocks the gates, and waves us inside.

The Tower is dark and quiet. The only sound is that of the waves of the Thames crashing at Traitors' Gate and the chattering of the ravens watching us from the eaves.

It's as if we're being surveilled by ghosts as we creep through the Tower.

We split up into two groups, Marion and Faith search one end, and Olive, Emmy, and I search the other. We meet back in the middle on Tower Green.

He's not being held in the basement cells, nor in the queen's apartments or the towers along the ramparts. There is only one place left to look.

"Emmett?" I whisper. The only answer is a *caw-caw* from a raven perched on the ancient turret.

The steep spiral steps to Wakefield Tower are lit with a single flickering torch.

"That's hopeful," Emmy says.

"Oh yes, I feel full of hope." I try to joke, but the words come out sounding as scared as I feel.

"I'm sorry," I say to Faith as we begin to climb. She pauses on the stairs. "Sorry for not telling you the truth, for not pushing Emmett to be more transparent with you, for seeing you as competition when I should have been supporting you." It's not the right time, but I have to say it.

Faith smiles sadly. "It's all forgiven. Let's go get your boy, yeah?"

There are two guards at the door, but I command them to wait at the bottom of the stairs.

The small chamber at the top of the tower is lit only by a beam of moonlight streaming in from the narrow archer's window.

The bars of the cell look new, as if they were only recently put in, and behind them, sitting perfectly still, isn't Emmett. It's Queen Mor.

She's unsettling in her perfection, looking unmussed, even here. I'm struck by how young she looks, stripped of her finery and jewels. Her long black hair hangs in ribbons over her sharp shoulders, and her hands are covered in dried blood. Edgar's blood.

She sighs as we approach her cell. "Not you all, again."

I sit down on the cold ground, as close to the bars as I can get, and the others lower themselves beside me. "Where is Emmett?"

Something like sadness passes over her face like a breeze. "He took Emmett?"

"He's not here?" I ask.

"I'm the only prisoner here tonight."

My hope deflates. "I know you can lie," I say, but for some reason, I don't think she is.

This gets her attention. "You spoke to Bram, then?"

"I'd like to hear the story from you," I say.

"I thought I was doing what was best," she says. "I didn't know what he'd become. You must understand, he's not all bad."

"Emmett loved him and was betrayed."

Mor looks at me with pity. "That was always Emmett's great flaw. He was so hungry for love, he couldn't see the faults in who was offering it to him. His father was all too willing to let you both risk your life for his zealous cause."

"You knew?" I ask.

"People like his father have existed for as long as I have reigned. Rebellion isn't novel."

"Why did you marry Edgar, then?" I ask.

"Because I didn't realize his true motives until he was already my husband. By then I was quite fond of him. It seemed a great inconvenience to kill him."

"But then you killed him anyway."

She doesn't reply, but for the briefest moment, sorrow breaks through her cool mask of detachment.

"Why didn't you stop us?" I ask.

"You weren't really a threat."

"But we were, weren't we? We worked out that the May Queen trial was the key to violating the terms of your bargain."

The queen laughs at us like we are children. And to her, we are. "You think I would have let that trial happen if there was any risk in it? No. The risk was from my own son. He was still king of the Otherworld, which I didn't know. I thought he was telling the truth when he came to me, distraught, a few years ago, with a story of his father ousting him. I loved him too much to see through his lies. I didn't know that when he married, his bride would be both a princess of England and queen of the Otherworld. It didn't matter what girl he chose. This was always going to be the outcome. I understand now why he was so keen to marry."

Queen of the Otherworld. The words settle over me, and some awful part of me is tempted to laugh. I got what my childhood self always wanted, but now I'd do anything to undo it.

"This was always his plan?" I ask.

Queen Mor settles against the back wall of the cell and extends her legs in front of her. "Before you or your parents or your grandparents remember, the portal between our worlds was open. The folk could pass through as they pleased. And oh, did they please. But they didn't call it England in the court of the Otherworld. They called it *the Hunting Grounds*. My kind are easily bored and have long used humans as our playthings. The games were bloody and the humans were always the losers. It got so bad, the folk whipped up a civil war and sat in the trees to watch the battles for fun. I couldn't dance at revels, where the dance floor was so bloody, I slipped. I couldn't bear to smile from my throne as another courtier brought an enchanted human for my entertainment. It wasn't fun anymore. It was disgusting. My people were half out of their minds at all times, intoxicated on human emotion. It was completely undignified. I announced to my court the portal between our world and the Hunting Grounds was closing.

"But there were many who didn't take kindly to that. My son among them. He was young then, and, together with a group of like-minded courtiers, he staged a coup. It placed my then-husband on the throne, but that was always part of his plan. Bram played a long game. I didn't see it coming. I didn't see tonight coming either. I suppose that is my great flaw. I will always believe the best of him.

"As the band of traitors took the palace that night, I had enough time to run, and I will always believe that was intentional. I ran for the woods. My final act there as queen was warding the portal between our world and yours. I enchanted it so that only members of my family could come through. I always harbored a hope that Bram would come to me and we could be a family again. He's got a good heart under all that ambition.

"When I crossed through the portal for the final time, it was onto King Edward's battlefield. You may fault me for this, but I had grown used to being a queen. I had no desire to be a witch in the woods. I wanted a castle. So I made my first bargain with the humans. I do not regret it.

"When Bram passed through the portal four years ago, he came to me on bended knee. He told me he was sorry for the coup, that he was manipulated by his father, that he regretted it and he missed me. He told me he, too, had been deposed in a coup by a rival family, such things are fairly common in the Otherworld, and he begged me for shelter. It was everything I had dreamed of for four hundred lonely years. I welcomed him with open arms."

"Why lie and say he was so young?" I ask.

"Humans aren't fond of being reminded of their own mortality." Mor goes on: "We thought it best that you see Bram as closer to one of you. It would allow him to integrate himself into London society and life at court without humans fearing him."

My stomach is in knots. "How old is he?"

The queen waves her hand vaguely. "We stop counting after one thousand."

Next to me, Olive winces.

"He said he's still king in the Otherworld. He's been going back and forth," I say.

"I know that now," Queen Mor says. "I loved him too much to be suspicious of him."

"How could he rule there and spend so much time here?"

"Time works differently there," Queen Mor explains. "What is only a few hours here could be days there."

"Now that Bram is king, we could do away with the bargain system," Olive says hopefully. "He could still be a just and fair ruler. We could usher in a new age of democracy and equality, just like you wanted, Ivy."

I wonder if the other girls still believe there's good in him. He was skilled at being exactly the right thing to each of us.

The queen laughs once more. "Your soft heart is going to be the death of you, Olive Lisonbee. Bram isn't here to usher in a new age of anything. He's doing the bidding of his courtiers back home. He's here to reopen the portal. He is singularly focused."

Something that isn't sadness but close to it flickers in her eyes. "Steel yourself for what's to come." She turns to me. "And you,

Ivy Benton. You're stronger than you believe. You were always my favorite."

"We could kill her now, get our revenge," Faith suggests.

"You're going to need me," the queen replies icily.

The five of us stand, now towering over her as she sits in her stone cell. "An apology, then," Marion says. "Say you're sorry for what you did to us."

The queen's steely gaze rakes over us, one by one. "I'm not sorry at all."

"Why not?" Emmy asks.

Queen Mor almost smiles. "Look at how strong I made you."

"But what about Greer?" Olive croaks. "What about what you did to our friend?"

The queen waves her off with her hand. "It's been a long night, and I am tired."

There are heavy footfalls on the stone steps. Emmy races to the door and throws her body weight against it, but the guards are pushing in.

"I have just one more question before we take our leave," I say. "Where was Lydia?"

"You already know the answer to that."

I think of myself, lost and cold and alone, searching for a door to the Otherworld the night I first met Emmett. I was right all along. "Why send her there?"

The queen shuts her eyes, dismissing us. "I was bored."

After an eternity, there is only boredom or the lack of it.

But something about her explanation rings hollow. For the first time tonight, I'm not sure if I believe her.

CHAPTER THIRTY-FIVE

The King's Guard bursts into the room, blades drawn, and escorts all five of us out of the Tower and back to Kensington Palace.

"His Majesty's orders," one of them barks. "You're not to leave Kensington again. Any of you."

"Emmett!" I scream as they drag me out of the Tower. But there is no answer except the sloshing of the river and the cry of a raven lifted on the breeze. Wherever Emmett is, it's not here.

There are more guards at the gates, fending off the mob that has multiplied. The violent sea of people shakes our carriage as we pass through the crowd, their hands leaving desperate, sweaty prints on the glass.

"Please, Your Majesty!" they shout once they spot me inside. "Please!"

Someone throws a rock, and one of the windows shatters, raining glass down on Faith and Olive.

I fear the carriage is going to tip when the gates creak open, just wide enough for us to pass through, and the mob is pushed back.

The guards help us down, and I expect them to lock us away in Caledonia Cottage, but they just disperse, leaving us.

From across the lawn, an explosion sounds. We turn to each other, panicked, and race across the grass to find not a battlefield, but a party raging. Fireworks burst in a rainbow of colors over the palace, leaving a shower of sparks in their wake.

"If you want to run, I suggest you do so tonight," I say to the four girls.

"Are you staying?" Marion asks.

Whatever look crosses my face must be answer enough. If Lydia and Emmett truly are imprisoned in the Otherworld, as I fear, then Bram's good graces are my only tool to get them back.

"Then we are staying," Marion says resolutely.

I push through the crowd to find my parents. I'm passed glasses of champagne and stopped every few feet to be given hearty congratulations. It's an odd sight, the ton without the disguise of their bargains. The men are shorter, the women's faces wider and less refined. Some, it seems, left the ceremony in a panic after the bargains were undone, but most stayed to party, unconcerned.

I find my own parents, completely sloshed, around a bonfire with a group of friends. "Ivy, my finger!" My mother wiggles her pinkie at me with pride. "Have you seen your sister?" she asks.

"Why aren't you gone? I told you to get back to the house."

My mother just laughs. "But we're having such fun!" There's a strangeness to the party, something just off-key. I dump the champagne I've been handed in the grass and it sizzles slightly as it hits the ground.

As dawn rises and the celebration dies down, we have no choice but to retreat to our rooms and wait to see what the day will bring.

The other girls find their parents but return to Caledonia Cottage to sleep, not wanting to risk their safety by disobeying orders.

I allow a footman to bring me to my new chambers, in the same apartments as Bram. They're eerily silent, Bram still missing. It's wishful thinking, but maybe he's decided to return to the Otherworld and leave us all be.

I sneak through the empty halls of the palace to Emmett's empty room, my heart breaking at the sight of it. Pig is buried under his blankets, scared of the noise from the fireworks. He's shaking as I scoop him up in my arms. "Come here, you. We'll wait for your dad together, all right?" I whisper.

I bring Pig back to my room, and he settles into bed beside me, his tiny warm body the only comfort I have.

In the end, my exhaustion wins out and I am soon unconscious. I wake to bright sun streaming through the windows. It's late afternoon.

There's an awful moment of realization when I remember last night's events. I look down to the gold wedding band encircling my third finger and resist the urge to toss it into the fire. Now is the time to be brave.

I peer out the window to find a perfectly calm summer day. The grounds are still and silent. The mob at the gates is gone.

I wrap myself in a dressing gown and pad down the stairs on bare feet.

There is odd music coming from the reception hall, the same fiddle tune from the queen's tea party.

From the top of the stairs, I take in the gilded room. It's filled with dozens and dozens of Others, clad in a pastel rainbow of colors. The women's gowns have bell sleeves so long they graze the floor, and the men are in vibrantly embroidered coats, just the same as Bram's. Some wear scarves of odd objects, forks and fishing nets and flour sacks embroidered with golden thread.

They're laughing and dancing to the reel like this is all one big celebration. I'm astonished by how inhuman they look. Seeing them all together as a group, it is easier to register the overlong limbs, the eerily perfect faces, the pointed ears. I can't believe I ever thought Bram could pass as one of us.

And then I realize. It is done. He's opened the door between our worlds.

There's blood on the floor, like someone has spilled a bucketful, but I can't identify the source.

Bram is standing near the front of the room, a golden goblet in his hand, surrounded by fawning courtiers. He's got a crown of emerald vines on his head and a matching earring dangling from one ear.

He spots me, and a wide smile spreads across his face. He raises his cup to me. "My bride!"

The fae courtiers raise their glasses with sharp, hungry smiles.

Bram bounds up the stairs and takes my arm. "Come, wife. I have so many new friends for you to meet. Let us begin."

ACKNOWLEDGMENTS

I can't tell you how glad I am that you're holding this book in your hands because for a long time, I doubted it would ever exist. *The Rose Bargain* was born from a particularly dark period in my life. In the fall of 2023, I was near catatonic with sadness. In my worst moments, I thought I'd never write again. Thank you to the hands that reached down and pulled me out of that deep, dark hole.

To Hillary Jacobson, who let me rest but never quit. Thank you for your unwavering faith not only in the work I create, but in my ability to create it. We've been partners now for the better part of a decade and I can't imagine working with anyone but you.

To my twin pillars, my editors, Erica Sussman at HarperCollins and Sarah Levison across the pond at Electric Monkey. Your enthusiasm and profound kindness made this book an absolute joy to write, and your brilliant minds made it so much better than I ever could have managed on my own. Erica, who carried this book through an editor change, a new baby, and a promotion, but never once made me feel like I wasn't a priority, I am in awe of you and filled with more gratitude than I'll ever be able to express. Sarah, I hope we have many more champagne lunches on the Thames together. You are an absolute light, and I feel profoundly lucky to be one of your authors.

Thank you to Alice Jerman for understanding and advocating for this book from the beginning.

To Aleena Hasan, whose notes were razor-sharp and made me laugh harder than I've ever laughed while editing a book. To Clare Vaughn, who keeps every plate spinning, I've had so much fun working with you. I don't know when you sleep.

To everyone at HarperCollins for welcoming me warmly and championing this book so passionately. Thank you to Maxine Bartow, Erika West, Gweneth Morton, Audrey Diestelkamp, Molly Fehr, Joel Tippie, Amy Ryan, Anna Ravenelle, Melissa Cicchitelli, and Danielle McClelland.

To the Electric Monkey team, thank you to Lindsey Heaven, Lucy Courtenay and Olivia Adams, Emily Sommerfeld and Sophie Porteous, Hannah Penny, and Ingrid Gilmore and Leah Woods for offering so much encouragement and guidance from across the Atlantic (and so much tea when we've gotten to work together in person). I'm truly sorry for my terrible grasp of British slang.

To the incredible team at CAA, Josie Freeman, Berni Barta, and Sarah Mitchell, and Lauren Denney, who work tirelessly to get this story into the hands of readers across the globe.

To my friends who aren't only kind and beautiful and fun, but also whip-smart. Thank you to Emma Benshoff, Susan Lee, Jenna Voris, Serena Kaylor, Diya Mishra, Celine Reese, Sabrina McClain, Emily Sonneland, Hannah Carter, Mary Dombrowski, Kris Kam, and Jordan Gray for the 3:00 a.m. texts, the levelheaded advice, the cabin weekends, and for lending your gorgeous brains to untangle my plot problems.

To my best friend, Casey McQuiston, who reminded me writing should be fun, for slamming the breaks on all my self-destructive spirals, and for always wanting to order mozzarella sticks for the table. I love you more than I could ever write here.

To Emilie Sowers, only you and I know just how much of you is in every book I write. Thank you for agreeing to be my roommate half a lifetime ago.

To my siblings, Thomas, Hannah, and Leah, whom I would risk getting run over by a carriage in the middle of the night for.

To my parents, who taught me to love books by example and have believed in every last one of my harebrained dreams.

To Charles, I'll never be able to capture the kind of love I have for you in writing, but I'll spend my whole life trying.

And finally, thank you to the readers; being able to write books as my actual, real-life job is the greatest gift of my life. How do I even begin to thank you for that? When I first began writing, I often described it as "shouting into the void." I love you for shouting back.